THE LAST CENTENNIAL

THE LAST

CENTENNIAL

by

Patricia Kilina

The Dial Press

New York 1971

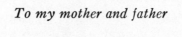

To my mother and father

Afoot

"We've got a little trouble down home," Johnny Chance heard his brother Tom saying from a hundred years away. "Kitie's come back."

Tom Chance was leaning out through the arctic ice sheet of the pickup truck's window, his breath circling on the winter air like a snowy eagle. The truck radio was playing "The Tennessee Waltz." Then the music broke off as the local news broadcaster started talking about Vietnam. The voices sounded like sea birds heard across a bare northern bay.

But Johnny wasn't paying much attention. He was sitting slumped down in his sheepskin jacket, on his least favorite saddle horse, Son of a Bitch. He was pushing his hat back, feeling his braids slide across his collar, so that he could stare up at the sky and admire the way that old bald eagle slid off the blue glacier edge far above them. Johnny was ready to weep as he watched that eagle, his left hand clenching the rein, his right hand playing unthinkingly with the rope coiled by his saddle horn. Icebergs were calving off the blue glacier up there, sliding down into the sea with a roar. That old eagle must have gusted up like a ghost from his nest of sticks, and now he was floating like a breath, waiting to spy some cottontail daring to cross the snow far below. Johnny was afraid of ghosts. Back up there on the hill, Head Chief and John Young Mule were getting ready to die. They were painting their bodies and loading their rifles. Head Chief was putting on an old-time war bonnet that his grandfather had loaned him for the occasion. Down below the hill, on the flat, the soldiers knelt in a skirmish line. The Cheyennes waited too, ready to weep, ready to see their last two heroes die.

"You hear me?" Tom said. "Kitie's come home."

Johnny wasn't paying much attention. He was vaguely aware of the other white waste all around him, the waste he lived in: of little bunches of steers dotted across the snow far away, of the corrals huddled near the cow-camp cabin, and perhaps of a gully with a few fugitive pines hiding in it. He was also vaguely aware of a small feeling toiling across the snowfield of his soul, like a varmint tracking through deep drifts with the shadow of an eagle sliding around it. He didn't have many feelings these days.

"I think I know where that eagle's nest is at," Johnny said softly. "It's up there on Brodie's place, above the old silver mine somewhere."

"Well, you better come down to supper tonight," said Tom. "We all got to figure out what to do about Kitie. Ma Maureen and the girls are for putting the run on her. I think we ought to rehabilitate her. I got this feeling she's fed up with them hippies and all. We've got to make things nice in the family again. And Pa Gene would do two wraps and a hooey in his grave if we threw her out."

"Yeah," said Johnny, his squinted eyes still straining after the eagle. The feeling snarled in him like a kink in the rope, the sudden kink that makes you miss the calf in the arena or even takes a finger off your hand. "Yeah, that little greenhorn whore."

"We goose-egged Kitie before her time was up," said Tom. "I should have taken her in hand when she was in high school wagging her ass all over Cottonwood."

Johnny wasn't paying much attention again, because the eagle was slamming off into the sky like a bullet into the blue-painted breast of a young man. Head Chief and Young Mule were vaulting onto their horses now. Head Chief was twenty-five or so, and the whites had accused him of murdering a settler who caught him butchering a beef off the reservation. Head Chief had killed that beef because the Cheyennes were hungry and the buffalo were gone. Young Mule was only fourteen, and an orphan. His crime was being Head Chief's friend. So the two of them had sworn that they would ride down that hill as suicide fighters, the way the old-time Cheyennes sometimes did. They had often heard the older men tell of the way the suicide fighters rode into the Little Big Horn fight. If they hadn't ridden in and all died fighting, Custer and his men might have got away. Of course, Head Chief and Young Mule probably weren't sure what the old times were like, it being 1890 and both of them being so young. Head Chief had said that he wouldn't let the soldiers hang him in the jail like a dog being strangled for the stewpot, and Young Mule had said that he would die with his friend. None of it made much sense, but they felt it was the right thing to do. When they turned their horses downhill, their hearts must have kinked like a rope as they saw the soldiers' skirmish line far below on the sagebrush flat. But they didn't hesitate —even though it was already 1890, they still had the soul power to do things like that. Beyond the line of blue uniforms, the Northern Cheyennes waited in wagons, their children tied on travois or old horses. They were waiting, waiting, ready to weep.

"One of these days," Johnny said, "I'd like to catch that old eagle."

"Shoot him while you're at it," said Tom. "Gotta get rid of all the varmints around here. I think I got that last old wolf awhile back."

"Don't you touch a feather on that old eagle," said Johnny.

"You'll be the only ex-world champion roper," said Tom, "that can't catch anything but eagles."

Johnny felt that invisible rope kink up about ten times with anger. He sawed Son of a Bitch around and rode away from the pickup. "If you want me down for supper," he snapped back over his shoulder, "you better apologize."

Grinning, Tom stepped on the gas and jounced the truck gently along the frozen rutted road beside Son of a Bitch. "Don't get sore now, Johnny Eagle. I didn't mean no harm. I can't catch eagles, and I was never world champion calf roper either. Turn that horsehide out and get in here, and we'll pick up some nice steaks at the Safeway."

Johnny ignored him, so they rode clear across the pasture that way. Head Chief was galloping down the hill now, shooting as he leaned low into his horse's mane. The kneeling soldiers fired and fired at him as he came ripping across the sagebrush. The bullets jetted up dust everywhere, but still he did not fall. He ran straight through the skirmish line, trampling a couple of soldiers. Then he loosed the reins and gun, and sank from the horse. He fell slowly, war bonnet flapping. Johnny and Tom rode clear to the corrals that way, and Head Chief hit the ground with a puff of dust and lay sprawled, just like in the movies, except that it was 1890 and he was so young.

Without a glance at Tom, Johnny dismounted and savagely began loosening the hind cinch, the one that would prevent his saddle being jerked off if he were still roping in competition. Then he undid the main cinch and pulled the steaming saddle down onto the snow. Tom turned off the truck engine, climbed out, stretched his polar-bear hulk, and stood looking around, his broad pocked face and hard little blue eyes squinting into the snow-bleached sunlight. Young Mule was taking his turn down the hill, shooting too. But the soldiers were warmed up now and they shot his horse out from under him halfway down. So Young Mule crouched in a chokecherry bush and pinged away at them, until the soldiers finally walked up the hill and killed him, the way they might kill a snake with a shovel. The two bodies were laid out side by side, warm and limp, like two eagle chicks whose necks had been wrung right in the nest. The Cheyennes cried over them. For years afterwards they would say that the two boys looked just like they were sleeping.

"Well, how's it go?" asked Tom. "It's been real cold, huh?"

"It goes okay," said Johnny, dragging off the smoking saddle blanket and throwing it over the saddle. He was still snarled up with rage and thinking of those two baby eagles lying there dead, feathers ruffling in the wind, talons curled and limp. They had wanted to die like men and they had done it, because they still knew who they were. They still had the power that you got in dreams. "Okay," said Johnny again. "I'm getting low on salt."

"How you fixed for groceries?"

"Could use a little whiskey." Still not looking at his adopted brother, he led Son of a Bitch toward the horse pasture gate.

Tom fell in behind him. "Sorry, Johnny, they don't sell whiskey at the Safeway." He watched Johnny maneuvering Son of a Bitch through the gate. "You ought to come down to the ranch more often, Johnny. I'm just surrounded by women down there. I have to go out to the barn and talk to the bulls once in a while."

Johnny jerked the sweaty bridle off and watched the steaming little bay Quarter Horse (a nondescript zero of a horse in Johnny's opinion), walk slowly off toward the hayrack, twitching his wet-matted hair loose. "I like it just fine up here. Maybe I'll stay up here the rest of my life."

"Thought you didn't like to be alone places," said Tom, with that gentle lilt in his voice that was blue-uniformed cruelty.

"I'd rather be alone up here than alone down there," said Johnny.

"Heard some interesting news the other day," Tom said as they walked back to the cabin. The two dead boys still lay together, their eyes glazing over. You could plainly see the two little red holes in Head Chief's skull, among the roots of his coarse black hair (the war bonnet had fallen off and lay at his side). The women were keening and crying, and probably a few of them gashed their legs or cut off fingers in mourning for the last Cheyenne warriors to die fighting the U.S. Army. "Jimmy Alderman stopped by, on his way to Texas. We had a great time with him at supper last night. Too bad you weren't there. Jimmy was thinking of driving on up here to see you, but he wasn't sure you were wanting to see anybody. Mighty understanding friend you got there. Anyway, Jimmy says that Sam Burke is thinking about retiring, and maybe thinking about selling Ace of Spades. Whoooee. Every roper this side of hell going to be a-scrambling and a-bidding after that Spades horse."

"You're just full of interesting news," said Johnny, seizing the saddle and blanket up onto his shoulder, going to the cabin and kicking the door open. "Now what would I do with that Spades? Use him for riding ditches?"

"You're afoot, remember?" said Tom, as they went into the cabin.

Johnny kicked the door again so it slammed shut. He hung the saddle on an iron hook near the door, and flung the saddle blanket over a pine bench near the potbellied stove, so it would dry by tomorrow. Tom made sure the door was shut all the way, to keep the little heat the cabin held from rushing out into February. A couple of winters ago they had spent a shocking amount of money making the cabin "nice," as Tom always said. They winterized it, recaulking between the logs and putting on a new insulated roof, so that the place was livable in winter for a single cowboy. That way they could winter a couple hundred head of commercial cattle up there, in case Tom miscalculated the fall cattle market (which he often did).

The cabin had three rooms strung out railroad-style. The first room Johnny had made luxurious in a wild and hairy way. Elk antlers, buffalo skulls, riding gear hung all over the log walls. There were blown-up reproductions of photographs of old-time Indians like Crazy Horse and Geronimo, and of course of Cheyenne chiefs like Lame Deer and Little Wolf. Besides the old stove, bench and woodbox full of wood, there was a big elaborate antique brass bed covered with Hudson Bay blankets and a buffalo robe. An old Navajo sand-painting rug was nailed to the wall behind the bed, like a tapestry, and another rug was nailed over the window so that ghosts couldn't see in. Mud was tracked all over the greyed pine floorboards at the entrance, where a couple pairs of boots toppled against the wall. Bearskins and steer hides covered the rest of the floor.

Tom tossed some new newspapers and magazines—*Life* and the Butte *Montana Standard*—onto the table, beside the old china kerosene lamp and Johnny's books. Johnny saw Tom's eyes squint disapprovingly at the books, which were mostly about the Cheyennes. There was Mari Sandoz' *Cheyenne Autumn*, Grinnell's *The Fighting Cheyennes, The Cheyenne Way,* and *Sweet Medicine.* The most recent one he'd gotten was John Stands in Timber's *Cheyenne Memories.* And tonight there would be the dark book of silence closed tight about the cabin, its pages pressing him flat. There would be the voices moaning and talking around the eaves outside—or would they be little owls calling? And there would be winter moonlight whiter than bone.

Johnny and Tom clomped on into the second room, which was the kitchen. An old iron range rippled out a dull sweet heat. Over one of the lid holes, a big enamel coffee pot stood steaming. On the battered pine table, covered with blue-and-white checked oilcloth, stood an empty plate with bacon grease and egg yolk congealed on it, plus an empty coffee mug and a tin full of sugar cubes. Johnny fished another mug out of the cupboard from among skillets and tin cans, and poured two mugs of coffee. Beyond lay the cabin's third and last room— empty, board floor dusty, corners fuzzed with spider webs.

Tom regarded the thick obsidian brew with some amazement. "How many days you been boiling this stuff?"

"Oh, a few," said Johnny, unzipping his jacket and sitting down on one of two creaky spindle-back chairs. He could feel the kink of anger uncoiling now, like when you let the calf go.

"Just asking," Tom said. "They might want the figure for my obituary."

They sat there sipping the scalding coffee and not talking for a few minutes, listening to the ticking of the coals in the range. Outside there was a whisper of dripping along the eaves, as the Sunday afternoon sunlight melted the snow on the west side of the roof.

"Well, how much did Jimmy think Burke would take for Spades?" Johnny asked.

"Ten thousand, maybe. Burke knows you want Spades. And he wants the horse to go to somebody that'll use him proper. Jimmy says he hasn't taken any offers yet, just telling people he hasn't really made up his mind."

"Well, I haven't made up my mind either," said Johnny. The bodies of Head Chief and Young Mule were floating off, as if they were in a movie and the camera were back-tracking away from them. The body of Morning Star's son had joined them—it was lying across a little creek, long hair floating in the water. The creek and the body floated off together.

"Ma Maureen is going to insist that you go after that horse."

"Ma Maureen still tries to make me eat spinach. Anyway, she is going to have her hands full with Kitie."

"I see you got some more books in there. In school they had to jerk you down to make you read a book."

"Found a new one written by this old Cheyenne name of John Stands in Timber. He was the tribal historian. Some hair-raising stories, with ghosts and fights and all. One story about how the Shoshonis went after a Cheyenne medicine man named Two Childs. Another one about a couple of kids named Head Chief and Young Mule—"

Anger over for the moment, they fell back into the easy unthinking conversation of boyhood, the kind of talk that two boys had to have in a household full of sisters.

"Pa Gene doesn't approve of your reading all that stuff, I know," Tom said sadly. "He thought it was better forgotten about and left behind."

"How do you forget something you never knew?"

"Pa Gene never wanted to know anything about his tribe."

"It's one thing to be one-eighth Assiniboin. It's something else to be a full-blood Cheyenne. It's taken me around twenty-seven years to figure that out." He said "around" because he wasn't sure how old he was.

"I suppose you'll go visit the Tongue River country someday. You'll get to the point where you'll have to know what it looks like, and all."

"No, I don't think so."

"Pa Gene would hoolihan in his grave if you went back there."

"I know, I know. Any other news?"

Tom chuckled, taking off his hat and running his fingers through his wire-brush red-brown hair. "Mrs. Sanders seen me letting Dorothy Fontaine off at her house about seven this morning. I seen the old lady's blind get away from her and roll clean up. Serves her right for being so nosy. Poor Dorothy's reputation ain't going to be worth a three-legged horse. We was down at Gough's Corners for the dance.

Whoooee. The weekly fistfight and all. One of these days, Johnny, you and me got to pick us wives and get married. This bachelor life isn't good for man or beast."

"You marry Dorothy Fontaine," said Johnny, "and I'll marry Sacajawea."

"You ought to ask that Thompson girl out. She's fairly panting."

"I don't want no problems."

"You're just imagining. There ain't much of that kind of feeling in Cottonwood."

"That new woman that owns the Main Street Diner. I stopped in there last week for breakfast on my way up here, and she wouldn't wait on me."

"The hell you say."

"I sat there twenty minutes, and she was washing dishes and all, and there wasn't nobody else in the place. So I asked her, and she hemmed and hawed, and said she wasn't open yet."

"Now, Johnny, you come on down to supper, and we'll see about Kitie."

Johnny closed his eyes. "Just leave me out of all that."

"But, Johnny, Kitie has me scared. I think she's taking drugs."

The truck vibrated madly along the frozen potholed county road. Johnny sat slumped with his boots splayed in the ranch-type midden heap on the truck floor: old stock magazines, halters, an odd spur, a bottle of 6-12 mosquito repellent from last summer, a set of new horseshoes, wirecutters, chunks of dried mud from other boots. Tom drove whistling "The Tennessee Waltz," his hard little blue eyes fixed on the road as if counting the iced-up puddles they shot over, and the fence posts that streamed by on either side. Or maybe he was counting the number of dollars that the Chances were in debt. The truck roared off the edge of the high flat bench country, and sloped crazily down into the valley along Powderhouse Hill. It passed the snow-drifted mound of the old powderhouse, and then it passed Fulton's Greenhouse.

Johnny could see the whole town of Cottonwood from there, as he had thousands of times in his life. Its plan lay exposed in the winter sun as if by archeological excavation. Johnny knew a little about archeology because it was mentioned in those Indian books.

Cottonwood, Montana—population 6973, which was about 1000 less than ten years ago. Main Street cut the town straight in half.

Then its west half was slashed a second time by the Milwaukee and Northern Pacific railroads—a great flash of winter sunlight ran along the rails. At the main railroad crossing, Johnny could see the grey grain elevator poke up as if it hoped to be a monument. Beyond the elevator lay the switching yards and the roundhouse, mostly deserted now that the railroads were cutting down service. Then the western-most quarter of town was cut still a third time by the Cottonwood River, polluted greenish-orange by copper-mine wastes. Along the river banks stood the frame houses and shanties which were "the other side of the tracks." Marilyn, blonde Marilyn, lived in one of those shanties now, and she had gotten fat. Farther west, clear out of town, on a snowy slope above Dog Creek, lay the Hillcrest Cemetery, where Pa Gene was buried. And farther west still was the little hangar and windsock of the Cottonwood airport, where the old local airliners didn't land any longer. The landing strip was drifted over with snow.

South of town, Johnny could see the new sawmill smoldering under a blanket of blue smoke, amid its pyramids of sawdust and its conical slash burners. The smoke drifted sadly over the boggy willow flats, over the peeling billboards advertising motels, over the atrocity of the auto graveyard with its heaps of rusty metal carcasses bleeding into the snow. The Cheyenne bodies must have bled onto the snow that way after Morning Star's band broke out of Fort Robinson to flee north to their home country. The soldiers had dumped the frozen bodies of warriors, women, and children out of the wagons into a trench grave. Johnny's eyes rested on the slash burners, as they always did, because their shape reminded him of the buffalo-hide teepees that had stood there a hundred years ago, when the Cottonwood River was clean and the valley not marked on maps. Of course they hadn't been Cheyenne teepees, but they had belonged to the Metis half-bloods who had been the first age of Cottonwood, and that was close enough.

"Well," said Johnny, "let's have some more CBS news." After a minute he added, "CBS stands for Cottonwood Bull Shit."

"You're sure ringy today, Johnny Eagle," said Tom. "Well, now, let me think. The mayor and the fair board have finally got their script committee together for the centennial. So they're writing the script now, and drinking whiskey. I sure hope they run out of booze before they run out of inspiration. We asked Pint Brodie if we could borrow some of his old buggies and wagons for the parade. He said no, of course."

"That centennial is going to be during the fair, huh?"

"When else? If we have it on the actual date, we won't get as many people into town for it."

"I suppose they'll be after me to play Chief Sitting Bull."

"Hell, no," said Tom as the truck rounded the last curve of Powderhouse Hill onto the valley floor. It shot along the flat stretch of road between the last snowy stubble fields this side of town. "We're going to get us some real Indians."

"What do you mean, *real* Indians?"

Ahead stood the clapboard houses of the little modern development that the Cottonwood people called "Alfalfaville," because it had encroached across the rich alfalfa fields there on the east edge of town. Before it could reach Alfalfaville, though, the truck had to curve up the access road to U.S. Route 10, the four-lane superhighway that had slashed through the valley several years ago. Then the truck had to cross Route 10, and curve down an exit ramp on the other side. The Cottonwood people had a big battle about that highway, because the engineers wanted to run it straight through town. The town had used all their influence with a certain powerful Montana senator in Washington, who got the federal engineers to put a little wiggle in the highway and detour it around the town.

At the foot of the ramp, the truck rattled through an aspen grove and across the new plank bridge over Skillet Creek, which replaced the old bridge washed out by a prehighway spring flood. The creek hadn't been the same since Route 10 came through, and the people in town figured they wouldn't have to put in another bridge for a while. Then the truck stopped rattling as it hit the smooth asphalt of the street through Alfalfaville. Johnny studied the neat snowy lawns, the new little ash and birch trees planted in hopes of prosperity, and the orange-crate houses with their cheap brick chimneys and their self-conscious picture windows. Looking north, Johnny could faintly make out the steam rising from the little hot spring on the other side of Alfalfaville. The permanent camp of Metis half-bloods and French trappers had stood right there. Nobody could find a trace of that camp anymore.

"Well," said Tom, "we want to add a lot of authentic Indian color to the centennial. And we need Indians for the battle scene—you know, for the Skillet Creek fight. So we invited every tribe in Montana to send delegations here for dancing and parading and all. Whoooee. That's ten tribes, fifty or seventy-five from each tribe, that's going to be one hell of a pile of Indians."

"Northern Cheyennes too?" Johnny asked, his heart constricting inside his chest as if a wet strip of rawhide had been twisted around it and then left to dry and shrink in the hot sun.

"Northern Cheyennes too. And the fair board was asking me to donate our south pasture for them to camp in, because that's the only decent place near town to put them."

"Well, there's Mose Hamilton's bull pasture," muttered Johnny, that rawhide shrinking tighter and tighter around his heart.

"Hell, no. Mose's bull pasture is all boggy. His bulls all got hoof rot from standing around in there. No place for tourists to park either. And Skillet Creek is polluted bad with sewage that side of town. Up on our place it's still pretty clean. They got to have water for cooking and all."

"Like hell it's pretty clean, with that Intermountain plant up there on the headwaters."

The truck passed the last Alfalfaville houses, then a dying dairy farm left high and dry by Cottonwood's miniature urban sprawl. Cottonwood bought its milk in boxes at the Safeway now. Next the truck plunged onto wide Grand Avenue, lined with proud, rotten old cottonwood trees. This was Cottonwood's ex-silk-stocking district—its big Victorian brick mansions had dark green pillared porches, gazebos, and flagstoned walks. Some of those houses still belonged to families whose cowmen and sheepmen grandfathers had built Cottonwood, except that now those families ran stores in town. One house, the old Flurie place, had recently been converted into apartments.

"And I suppose," said Johnny, "that if the Cheyennes come, old Alex Feet is going to come with them, and he's going to pester me again about going back to the blanket."

"I don't know if Feet is coming or not. I saw an article about him in the Butte paper the other day. He's getting to be a real big Indian politician. Always going to Washington and wheeling and dealing. Lobbying for Indian claims and Indian civil rights and all. He's on the National Council of American Indians or something like that. Even published a book about the Indian problem. First book on the Indian problem ever written by an Indian, I guess. I suppose he's gotten too big to bother with centennials."

"You sure know everything that's going on. You beat Walter Cronkite to shit and gone," said Johnny.

Tom grinned and shook his head, pleased with himself.

The truck wheeled around a corner onto Silver Street. Here small, peeling, ancient clapboard houses crowded right along the street, flanked by naked lilac bushes. Last summer's dead Virginia creepers clutched their porch screens. This was the Alfalfaville of fifty years ago. Now a lot of immigrant families lived there, including a few Slav and Rumanian DP families from the second world war. Off down Silver Street they caught a glimpse of the red-brick grade school, with the crack down its north wall from an earthquake forty years ago. If it had been a weekday the county students might be just streaming out for recess, playing basketball and pom-pom-pullaway on the cinder playground. But since it was Sunday the kids were scattered all over the county, on ranches or in little rural communities where there was no school. Johnny remembered how Tom used to defend him in those playground fistfights with those little whang-leather ranch kids, till he was big enough to defend himself.

Suddenly the truck came to Main Street. The street was nearly deserted, but a few cars were parked at the new meters, and one over-coated soul was dutifully putting in his parking money, because the police chief exacted on-the-spot five-dollar parking fines even on Sunday. Even the Cottonwood Police Department was facing hard times and tight money, to say nothing of the guards in the state penitentiary on the south edge of town, who grumbled about low pay and prisoners who talked too much about their civil rights. Johnny knew that there were a lot of Indians in the pen, for things like robbing stores on the reservations. Tom stopped the truck for the red light just opposite the Cottonwood Bank and Trust building. The traffic light had gone up five years ago, and right below it there still stood the ornate old iron fountain, now dried up and full of snow and gum wrappers, where travelers and stagecoaches had stopped to water their horses on the way through town.

Tom pointed at the fountain. "For the centennial, everybody is going to have to grow a beard. Then we're going to have water in that thing again, and anybody without a beard is going to get dunked by a special vigilante committee."

Johnny grunted. Since he just naturally didn't have a beard, he could figure on getting dunked.

"Want to go to the movies tonight?" Tom asked, jerking his head at the Orpheum Theater next to the bank. The Orpheum was a sad Grecian thing from the 1920s, its oval windows draped with wreathes, and it looked even sadder now that TV had closed it down on weeknights. James Bond was playing there, in *Goldfinger*. "Maybe Kitie would like to go, and it'd be like when we were kids."

Johnny shook his head, still thinking of how he was going to endure the centennial and seventy-five Northern Cheyennes camping there in town. Maybe he would have to leave Cottonwood during the centennial and go on a pack trip in the mountains.

Tom wheeled the truck out onto Main Street as the light changed and beeped the horn at a shriveled, brown little cowboy in a faded Levi jacket. The cowboy, known to Cottonwood as Skookum Joe, had a hooked nose and wicked little black eyes close together and long white hair sticking out from under his hat. Johnny might have taken Skookum Joe for another Indian, except that he happened to know Skookum was a Greek. Skookum's nationality was all that Cottonwood knew of his past—one winter day he had arrived in Cottonwood by rail, locked in a cement car and half frozen. After he thawed out, he went to work as a ditchdigger and had been in Cottonwood ever since, but without confiding more than his Greekness. Skookum waved back at Tom.

"I had coffee with Skookum at the Keystone this morning," said Tom, "and he told me some mighty interesting things about Pint Brodie. He was out there digging ditches for Brodie last summer. Says the old guy is finally going broke trying to fight the twentieth century. This wild-eyed, no-good Vin is working for him, and Skookum says the two of them just fight all the time. Vin packs a gun, and Skookum says that one of these somedays Vin is going to shoot old Brodie."

Johnny knew just which Vin it was—Marilyn was married to him.

They had to stop at the second red light, the only other one in town, which was just opposite the Corner Bar and the Montana Power Company building. The west side of the street here was all bars— Brown's, the Corner Bar, and several others—and old derelicts in crumpled Stetsons and sheepskin jackets drifted in and out. The number of derelicts had increased since Cottonwood's agricultural economy had started to fail some years ago, and then it had dropped slightly when the sawmill and the Intermountain plant came to town. On the left were Applegates Restaurant, the Toggery Clothing Store, Winnie's Ladies Apparel, the Keystone Fountain and Drugstore, the Rocky Mountain Bakery, and the state-run liquor store with its puritan air and its windows bare of advertising. There were also three boarded-up stores which had gone out of business.

"I wouldn't mind a little whiskey," said Johnny, looking over at Brown's.

Tom grinned and darted those little blue eyes at him. "You can have whiskey when you start roping again. And then you can't have it, because you'll have to stay sober to rope hot lick and get the family out of debt."

"Look who's talking about earning money. You're the one thinking about buying a helicopter to fly around the ranch in."

Tom shrugged. "I was out on the circuit all last year. My luck was running a little thin, that's all. I just ain't as tough a roper as you, am I?"

"You sheep-shit Assiniboin breed," said Johnny, opening the truck door and getting out.

Just as Johnny strode angrily to the curb by the Montana Power building, Tom was wheeling the truck around the corner and screeching the brakes, grinning an invitation to get back in. Johnny knew he was going to get back in, and he did. He jerked open the door, made an angry spring back onto the dusty seat among the rodeo magazines, halters, and 6-12 bottles, and slammed the door shut as hard as he was able.

"You were the big money-winner," said Tom, still grinning, as he backed out onto Main Street again, and swung around and headed straight on. "Thirty-three thousand one year, wasn't it? You don't need to get mad about my mentioning that. And I'll overlook the sheep shit. Sheepmen all going broke anyway."

They passed the old Rainbow Hotel, with its dark doorway and its little neon sign. Its dingy windows framed a forgotten lobby where rubber plants shriveled in corners; the spittoons were never polished anymore, and a few old men sat dying in worn leather chairs by the windows, staring out at the side street. They may have been staring across the street at the little brick building that everybody knew as Kate's. Kate had been hit as hard as anybody by the Cottonwood recession, when the railroads and the sheep ranches dried up in the 1950s. Now that the sawmill and Intermountain had moved in, she was doing better again, though she only had three girls. Kate once had a breed girl there (at least the girl swore she was one-eighth Flathead), and Johnny had felt able to go there. Johnny didn't dare patronize the all-white girls because he wasn't sure what the town's attitude would be. But the breed girl had discontinued service along about the same time as the Milwaukee did, so now Johnny couldn't go to Kate's anymore, and he had to make do by himself. Past Kate's, Johnny caught a glimpse of the mournful maroon railroad station and heard the distant blast of a diesel train. That must be the 4:20 Northern Pacific coming in, the only train that stopped in Cottonwood now.

"How many steaks you think we'll need?" said Tom. "Kitie looks gant as a she-wolf. She'll probably eat two." Suddenly Tom started chuckling, as he turned the truck in before the Safeway super-market at the north edge of Cottonwood, opposite the Silver State Motel and the Texaco gas station.

"What's so funny?" Johnny asked as they got out of the truck.

Their boot heels crunched across the arctic ice, and their breath steamed back over their shoulders as if across a thousand miles of ice pack as they pushed into the supermarket. Inside, it was warm and the music system was playing Mantovani. Tom grabbed an empty cart, still chuckling. Suddenly he said, "Oh my god, here comes Mrs. Paul." He averted his eyes from a stout lady approaching, and made his escape down the soup and canned goods aisle. Johnny followed him with a shrug. "Let's try to stay away from her," said Tom. "I ran into her in the Keystone this morning. She already knows Kitie's back, mostly because Kitie has this motorcycle and she gunned it up and down Main Street a few times before she came on out to the ranch. Mrs. Paul was asking all kinds of nosy questions."

They trundled the cart up to the meat counter, and Tom started chuckling. "Yeah, you should see that Kitie. Wildest looking critter I ever laid eyes on. You have done lost your world title as the Chance family savage, Johnny Eagle."

"Why?"

Tom winked at the butcher in his bloodstained apron and said, "Have you got eight nice New York cuts for a couple of hungry cow-boys? About so thick?" making two inches in the air with thumb and forefinger. Neither of them mentioned the irony of ranchers' buying inflated supermarket beef when they were in debt for growing the steers that the beef came from and could only hope for a 2 per cent net annual profit. No telling how much longer Cottonwood's ranches would be able to hold on.

"Going to eat them all yourselves?" the butcher winked back, hauling a hunk of beef out of the cooler.

Tom turned back to Johnny and lowered his voice. "Yeah, it's beyond belief. Ma Maureen nearly fell over dead when she saw Kitie come in the door. Whoooee. Kitie looks just like those niggers we used to see in the safari movies. She's wearing a gold ring in her nose."

With the steaks wrapped and tied in wax paper, Johnny and Tom successfully avoided Mrs. Paul a second time and got into the truck. They drove on out of town, past the fairgrounds. The grandstand ran right along the old highway here, and last year's faded fair legend still ran along it in big red-and-white letters: "Cottonwood County Fair, Rodeo and Horse Races, August 23, 24, & 25." Next June or so, the fair board would have it repainted with the new dates and would probably add the words "Cottonwood Centennial" somewhere.

Beyond the fairgrounds, they passed the old gravel pit, now filled in with snow. The dead stalks of last summer's mulleins stuck up from its slopes. Then they passed the entrance to Vern Stuart's big ranch, with its sign saying "Registered Quarter Horses." Vern Stuart was about the only Cottonwood rancher who wasn't in debt.

"Well," said Tom, "if you don't get Spades, you can always settle for one of Vern's colts by Bobcat."

"I wouldn't even have Bobcat himself."

"He's a mighty fine using horse."

"He's a good cutting horse, but I've seen him rope, and he ain't my kind of a rope horse."

"It's Spades or bust, huh?"

The truck passed another abandoned dairy farm, then five or six billboards, then the last remaining sign of a row of Burma Shave signs, which read "car in ditch." Finally the truck turned west off the old highway onto a dirt road, past a sign that said "Chance Ranch." The road ran between two rows of young cottonwood trees—Pa Gene had planted those trees, laying two little pipelines along there to keep them watered. The road wound on past a maze of feedlots crowded with fat steers to the magnificent white barns that Pa Gene had built with rodeo winnings and bank loans, after he'd had all the old buildings bulldozed down. On a gentle slope above the barns stood the rambling white clapboard house—very modern, with its huge picture windows, green tile roof, broad brick chimney, and brick patio—that Pa Gene had built with more winnings and bank loans. Ma Maureen spent a lot of money keeping the house painted and perfect. In summer she planted great beds of geraniums from Fulton's Greenhouse along the patio. Adjoining the house was the ranch office in its own neat white building. It had desks, fluorescent lighting, bulletin boards with maps showing water rights, men coming and going, even a shortwave radio for constant contact with the hay ranch and cow camp. The entire ranch had an air of desperate prosperity on credit.

"It's bust," Johnny said.

The family were all eating silently and tensely at the big plank redwood table in the ranch kitchen glittering with appliances. The huge aluminum skillets where Ma Maureen had fried the steaks still smoked a little, set aside on the electric stove. Head Chief and Young Mule were dead now, and their bodies lay cold and rigid in that timber-and-rock-heaped grave off in the Tongue River hills.

Tom was sitting at the head of the table, as befitted his attempt to make the family nice now that Pa Gene was dead. Ma Maureen sat at the other end, and they were handing around the platters of steaks, baked potatoes, and hot biscuits to the four girls and Johnny. And there were dishes of home-canned string beans and thick purple choke-cherry preserves, Ma Maureen was proud of her commissary; she still held out against Birdseye frozen foods and spent every summer and fall with the kitchen turned into a steaming maelstrom of boiling kettles and cheesecloth strainers. The trouble was that Ma Maureen's way of economizing wound up costing her more than supermarket beans and jam.

Johnny took plenty of the chokecherry, for he'd read that the Cheyennes loved chokecherries, and he sat there eating without a word, busy with his nighttime thoughts. Now and then he moved a vague glance at Kitie, who sat cautiously out of Ma Maureen's slapping reach, just as she had all her life, because she got herself slapped more than the other children. And nobody said a word. Johnny guessed that they were all scared, even Ma Maureen, because Tom had said he would take off his cowhide belt and whip anybody who lit into Kitie right away.

Kitie was wearing this shirt that looked as if it had been hand-dyed in splotches of red, blue, and green. Her faded bell-bottom jeans had gotten the same treatment, only with chlorox. Cinched around her gaunt waist was a six-inch-wide black belt with chains wrapped around it. In the fluorescent kitchen light, her long hair—the same red-brown, wavy, woolly hair that all Gene's children had (save Pat, the throw-back, who was horsehair brunette)—spread out shaggily, voluptuously, over her shoulders. Kitie kept trying to push the hair behind her ears, but it stubbornly sprang free again, and the ends of it kept brushing her steak, getting white with cooled fat. Around her neck was a whole fistful of necklaces. Some were strings of purple and red seeds, others were the tourist-type Indian bead jobs that Johnny happened to know were now made in Hong Kong. Kitie sawed at her steak with shaky deliberation, reached out for her fourth biscuit already, spread it thickly with Ma Maureen's fresh sweet home-churned butter.

The ring in her nose wasn't as big as Tom had led him to believe. It looked just like a regular gold earring and hung through a tiny hole in the side of her left nostril, glinting as she chewed. Johnny remembered a juicy Kitie whose oval face was gently freckled like a meadowlark egg—now she had a lean, prowling varmint air. She looked rubbed to the bone by high-speed headwinds and hysterias that he couldn't know about. Her face had changed too—her flattened nose, pouting mouth, and bristly copper eyelashes were blunter and more primeval now. Her hazel eyes stayed fixed on her plate with manic concentration. Her nose kept running, and she kept sniffling and wiping it on her color-splotched sleeve. Johnny thought of the motorcycle he'd seen parked in the ranch garage, with a glittery helmet and a pair of goggles hung from one handlebar, and her sleeping bag still strapped to the back. He wondered what drugs she had been using.

"Johnny," said Ma Maureen sharply, "you're eating too much jam. Take some more beans."

Johnny ignored her and took more chokecherry. Just to make her mad, he even spread some chokecherry on his steak. After all, the Cheyennes had used to mix chokecherry with buffalo meat to make pemmican. Ma Maureen shrugged and sighed.

They ate everything on the table, without saying any more than "Pass the salt" or "Any more biscuits?" The other girls all looked scrubbed, innocent, and priggish in their stovepipe jeans, boots, and checked wool shirts. Ma Maureen wouldn't let them wear the psyche-delic-type Western clothes always featured now in the pages of *Hoofs and Horns,* even though the girls cried that rodeo queens wore those fringed sarapes and bell-bottom frontier pantsuits. Fern, the wistful youngest at seventeen, wore her hair in a wavy bob. Thicker, earthier Ruby, who was twenty-three, wore pigtails. Pat, the oldest girl at twenty-five, had her black hair cut almost as short as a boy's and always went around with her jaw stuck out like a barracuda's. None of them had made up their minds to marry yet, because they were too engrossed and comfortable, and perhaps too cowed by Pa Gene's ghost, to leave home. Only Kitie had dared to flout the law that women were hard-muscled helpmeets.

Even Ma Maureen wore jeans, though she was bursting out of them these days. She didn't cut such a pretty figure on a horse any more. In her day, as Pa Gene's bride, she had been acclaimed the world's champion lady saddle-bronc rider (she had made exhibition rides with her stirrups tied down, as modesty and sanity demanded). But these days she was acclaimed for her children, cow herd, and commissary, in that order, and her rodeo activities consisted of publicity and committee work. Even Ma Maureen had her greying brick-red hair braided in pigtails, and went boldly without makeup like her daughters, and sometimes wept like an adolescent when she received Holy Communion at Sunday mass. And even Ma Maureen kept her ferocious glass-green eyes on her plate as she scraped a last knifeful of extravagant chokecherry onto the last biscuit (so as not to waste either), because Tom had told her to keep quiet, and Tom was Pa Gene's son.

Suddenly Kitie put her coffee cup on the saucer with a clack. She sat bolt upright and announced in a high, unreal voice: "I got screwed in San Francisco, busted in Chicago, stoned in New York, and tear-gassed in Washington. Anything else you want to know?"

"I knew it!" shouted Ma Maureen, forgetting Tom's warning. "You've come home here just to make trouble. We were getting along just fine without you. You better leave tomorrow, do you hear?" Meanwhile, the Cheyennes straggled mournfully back down out of the hills, leaving Head Chief and Young Mule buried there among those dry, pine-covered little hills where a scream would go unheard. Perhaps some of the Indians slashed themselves or cut off fingers in their grief.

"Now, Ma Maureen, you pipe down," said Tom. "The girl has come home here because she needs us."

"I can't hold up my head in Cottonwood with this loose girl in my house," Ma Maureen kept shouting. She tried to pry her handkerchief out of her tight pants pocket.

"Like, I'm in the very best Western tradition," said Kitie. "I mean, the West was won by dropouts, freaks, and creeps."

Suddenly Ma Maureen forgot her handkerchief and leaned toward Kitie, into slapping distance. "If you've been living poor like those hippies, where did you get money for that flashy motorcycle, huh? You been working in some place like Kate's?"

Kitie leaned right back toward Maureen. "I cannot tell a lie. I got the bread dealing heroin in New York."

"What?" shouted Ma Maureen. She had read about the evils of

heroin in *The Reader's Digest*. Pat stood up and announced that she wasn't going to listen to all this nonsense. The other girls cringed dutifully, eyes on their plates.

"Pipe down, all of you," roared Tom, bringing his huge fist down on the table so that all the coffee cups had tidal waves. "What would Pa Gene say?"

At mention of Gene, everyone went silent and ate the last of what was on his plate. Ma Maureen started to sob. "I'm sure glad Gene isn't alive to see this," she said. Head Chief and Young Mule were dead now, and the worms and little insects were discovering their fresh bodies there under the mound of rocks and timber. They were black and melting now, seething with maggots. And the tribe would mark with rocks the path that the two of them had taken as they made their great charge down the hill, because the people didn't want to forget. Johnny didn't know what had happened to the body of Morning Star's son, except that the soldiers took its fine beaded moccasins for souvenirs. And he didn't want to think about what had happened to Two Childs' body.

"In New York, even the top call girls only get a hundred dollars a throw," Kitie explained patiently. "The chicks who give up pussy on the streets downtown get a lot less than that. Sometimes just a meal or a place to crash."

Ma Maureen made a strangled Irish sound, looking at Tom. "I never thought I'd hear such language at my own supper table, in my own kitchen."

"How much did you make selling dope?" Pat asked sarcastically. "Sounds like you really looked the moneymaking scene over before you picked a career."

Kitie shrugged pleasantly, wiping her nose again and spearing her last piece of steak. "Oh, I made seventy-five dollars or more a day, selling five-dollar cuts around the East Village. I had a big clientele, because I was fucking honest and never burned nobody."

"Don't use such language," said Maureen, "and don't talk with your mouth full, and don't wipe your nose on your sleeve."

"Some dealers will sell you five dollars' worth of talcum powder," Kitie went on with her mouth full, "and not enough shit in it to get a cockroach off."

The family sat with shoulders hunched, taking this information in. Slowly coming out of his fantasy world, Johnny noticed that Fern and Ruby were fascinated in spite of themselves.

"Well," said Tom heavily, "Pa Gene was always an optimist. He'd say, 'Kitie, whatever you're going to be, be a good one.' "

"Are you, uh, taking heroin?" Fern asked Kitie.

"Baby, are you kidding? I'm not that dumb," said Kitie. "I was shooting speed. Speed is bad enough, but heroin is worse. You have an awful crash after a rush on speed, and lots of the kids would shoot smack afterward to help them get down. But I never used smack. It's real bad shit, everybody knows that."

"I take it," said Pat, who had been class valedictorian of the family, "that shit is synonymous with dope."

"That's right, baby," said Kitie coolly. "Both four-letter words."

"Well," said Ma Maureen, running her thickened, freckled fingers back through her hair that was steamy from the stove, "I hope you don't intend to go into business selling dope to the school kids in Cottonwood, or you'll end up in the pen."

"I'd like to remind everybody of something," said Tom. They all looked at him. "Remember how we used to catch Kitie making up stories about all kinds of things? There's a pretty fair chance that she's making up this selling heroin stuff too, just to pull our legs." They all nodded, considering this. "For instance," Tom went on, "I just figured out that we got letters from Kitie postmarked Berkeley about the time of the Chicago thing." They all nodded again. Kitie shrugged.

"I know a few kids in the high school who smoke marijuana," said Fern.

"Pot is for babies," snorted Kitie.

Maureen turned crazed eyes at Fern. "There's really marijuana in town?"

Fern dropped her eyes. "Not much, I guess. I just heard a couple of the kids bragging about it." Nothing was left under the timbers and rocks now but two slender skeletons. The rain sluiced and the frost heaved. The rocks washed away and the timbers settled or rolled aside, until finally the skeletons could be seen.

"Well, I haven't come home to pervert Cottonwood," said Kitie wearily. She leaned back in her chair and closed her eyes. "I've kicked all that shit. Like, speed and all of it."

"Wasn't it hard?" Fern asked, hanging on Kitie's every word. "I mean, you hear about addicts climbing the walls when they withdraw—"

"Listen, baby, don't believe everything you read in the fucking media about heads. Speed isn't that hard to kick. And I didn't bring any home with me. So there. Isn't there any more coffee? I'm dropping off."

Tom got up and brought the pyrex pot from the stove to pour her some coffee. "How far did you come today, Kitie?" he asked gently.

Kitie stretched shakily. Johnny could see that she was sensing more support from the male side of the family. "From Bismarck, South Dakota. That bike really covers country, man," she grinned. "Like, you should kick all that horseback shit and start riding bikes to herd cows with."

The other girls went into their after-supper maneuver, as well trained and coordinated as in their rodeo acts. They cleared away plates, scraped them into the garbage can, stacked them in the dishwasher, put away leftovers. Maureen went into the pantry and came out carrying a three-layer fudge cake on a fine modern china platter. She stood there holding it, her face trying to piece itself back together into everyday cheerfulness. Then she came slowly to the table carrying the cake with a ritual melancholy. Johnny felt pity prick his heart like a spur—hers was the effort of a modern American rural woman who believes that she can stir the world back together with her electric mixer. Ma Maureen was almost all modern, an enemy of germs and superstitions who was always saying wistfully that there ought to be vaccinations for the evils of the soul. She was a throwback only in her fondness for spanking children—she had always made Johnny sleep without a night-light and spanked him when he screamed about the dark. But still the nighttime thoughts went sliding through Johnny's head like a terrible filmstrip: now and then, as World War I and the Depression came and went, an old Indian or two would make the lonely walk up into the hills to look at the heap of bleached timbers. Among them lay a few white splintered leg bones, a pelvis, and two skulls. You could still tell which skull was Head Chief's because it had two bullet holes close together in it. Ma Maureen set the chocolate cake on the table, looked at Kitie, and said crisply, "If I'd known you were coming, I wouldn't have baked a cake."

"Hey," said Kitie, looking at Johnny, "poke that wooden Indian. He hasn't said a fucking word all evening, not even when I used such foul language."

Johnny looked up from his coffee cup. "Howdy," he said. Snow was falling, whiter than bones. It perched white on the timbers like arctic eagles. Then gentle spring rains sluiced off the snow, and the dark gaze of Young Mule's and Head Chief's skulls looked once more at the world—or, to be more precise, at any summer grass that might grow up in front of them. Johnny looked back down at the chunk of cake that Ma Maureen was putting on his plate.

"You lay off Johnny now," Tom told Kitie. "He has got problems of his own."

"What's the matter with him? Hey, wooden Indian, I'm here. Yoo-hoo." She waved across the table at him with mock irony. "It's me, Kitie." A tooth, then another tooth, loosened from Young Mule's upper jaw and fell with a tickle of sound among the rocks.

"Leave him alone," said Tom angrily. "A lot of water's gone over the dam while you were away. Pa Gene died. You didn't even know he was killed. We tried to locate you for the funeral. And Johnny wasn't so good either. He lost old Rattler and he's afoot now. He hasn't rodeoed for a while."

"I didn't come down here to have my problems discussed," said Johnny.

When they'd finished the cake, Johnny and Tom took second cups of coffee into the living room. Tom turned on the color TV so that he could listen to Walter Cronkite. Ma Maureen and the girls cleaned up the kitchen, ignoring Kitie, so she came slowly into the living room too and curled up in one end of the newly upholstered sofa. She sat looking around at the new drapes across the picture window, at the modern armchairs in brown cowhide, at the sooty granite fireplace heaped with white ashes, at the beige wall-to-wall carpeting, at the shelf of rodeo trophies, and the shiny bar where Pa Gene had cheerfully served whiskey to all his rodeo cronies (their annual whiskey bill alone was almost worth a bank loan). Kitie looked as if she were trying to readjust these spots in her memory.

"I remember you two," she said bitterly, playing with her necklaces. "Don't think I've forgotten. You were always so busy and so self-righteous. And those shitty sisters of mine haven't mellowed with age either. I remember how they always locked me in the saddle room so I couldn't tag after them. Like, I used to sit in there and cry for hours, until Pa Gene heard me and let me out."

"Let's let bygones be bygones," said Tom. "Pa Gene is gone, and we have to keep things nice. You're welcome to stay, if you make yourself useful and don't cause no trouble."

"Oh, I'll cause trouble all right. I can see that, man," said Kitie.

Johnny sat sipping coffee as the frost cracked slowly away at the bones, breaking the necklaces of vertebrae, cracking the pelvis like a piece of fine white china.

"Well, why did you come here, then?" Tom wanted to know.

"Like, I don't know yet. I've been through the whole crock of shit, and I still don't know. And, for your information, neither does anybody else—except for a few narrow-minded chauvinists here and there. I dropped out of Berkeley, you know. I was doing the hippy thing on the Haight, the flower child thing, and it was beautiful when I pioneered it. Like when Pa Gene made me the kite when I was little. The best and only thing Pa Gene ever did for me. Remember that outasight kite he made? Gee, wow, seven feet long, with lots of layers of brown paper to make it strong, and a mile-long tail of torn-up sheets. Man, what a powerful kite. And when he took it out in March and flew it in the upper field, I just screamed with joy."

"Why else do you think we called you Kitie?" Johnny felt moved to ask.

"Ugh, wooden Indian speak," said Kitie.

"Aw, shut up," said Johnny, and went back to thinking about bones.

"I flew plenty of kites down there on the Haight. And I did the Buddhist thing too, and said my Hare Krishna and my Om like a good girl. But then, you know, the tourists and the plastic monsters and the media moved in and spoiled it all. And Buddhism, well, it's all right for Hindus and Vietnamese, but, like, it doesn't work for Anglos. It's phoney. So then I went into politics, and I campaigned for McCarthy and cried over RFK and was in Chicago and got my head busted by the pigs and all. But, you know, I couldn't figure out what some of those kids were after. For instance, I belonged to SDS, see, and we went back to Chicago to have our own convention, and it was a beautiful moment to show that we had more dignity and unity than anybody else. But instead of keeping their shit together, everybody split up in their own little factions, the Weathermen and all the rest, and they were all screaming and quarreling. And, well, I could see that there was never going to be any revolution. Besides, there's nothing for chicks to do in the movement. Those cats wanted me around to type manifestos and make coffee and hand out pussy, but that's all, man. I left politics."

"So you're a Commie?" asked Tom in that lilting tone of voice that Johnny knew meant Tom didn't believe a word of the foregoing narrative.

"I was, but I kicked that too. If you really want to know, I even burned my copy of Chairman Mao."

"So then what did you do?" Johnny asked, feeling vaguely touched by this odyssey and drawn halfway out of his fantasies again.

"So then I thought maybe I needed to straighten out my own head, instead of America's head. So I went to New York and made the drug scene, and when I wasn't getting ripped and making money, I marched in moratoriums. Seven or eight of us had this crummy pad —apartment to you—on the Lower East Side, plus a guard dog to keep the real addicts out. You know, the junkies. They steal everything. All the kids there are from bourgeois families like this one, and they're all trying to un-bourgeois themselves and don't care if they die trying. But after awhile I could see that my head wasn't getting any more together. So I decided to go West."

"So now what?"

Kitie's nervous little-girl voice was a curious accompaniment to Walter Cronkite's. "I wish I knew, man. I'm sick of hearing about Vietnam, and I can see that all my efforts haven't changed a fucking thing. I'd go out against pollution, except that I can see that Nixon and his capitalist stooges are trying to use the environment thing as a smokescreen, see, to divert the peace movement into it. And, man, nobody's going to use me as a smokescreen. I thought about joining a commune, but it's too late for that. All the communes are fed up with freaks coming in to crash, and they've gotten more exclusive than the jet set. So I thought maybe I'd go homestead somewhere."

"Homestead?" Tom was incredulous, and slapped his thigh. "You don't mean it!"

"I'm not jiving you. If I could find somebody to do it with me, and if I could find a piece of land somewhere . . . in Alaska, or even around here."

Tom leaned back in his leather chair, bellowing with laughter. Even Johnny found himself grinning. "Kitie," said Tom, "you're sitting on a homestead right now. A ten-thousand-acre one, with five thousand head of cows and some of the best damn horses around. And you just couldn't wait to leave it."

"I want to homestead *by* myself and *for* myself," Kitie said angrily, "not for you cowboy capitalist creeps."

Tom dug out his wadded-up handerchief and wiped the tears out of his eyes. "Haven't laughed so hard since the time we wired that firecracker into Pint Brodie's starter and he lost all his antifreeze."

"Did you try Woodstock?" Johnny asked.

"Woodstock was a trip and a half," said Kitie, sniffling. "But it'll never happen again, no matter how hard they try."

Ma Maureen came in, hands still damp, and sat down, her eyes pouring their green poison on Kitie. "The girls and I have talked it over," she said. "You can stay if you follow certain rules."

"Yes, Ma Maureen. What rules?" Kitie asked in a singsong voice.

"You pitch in and work. You wear Christian clothes, not them pagan rags. You stay off dope. If I catch you with any marijuana from those school kids, out you go. No filthy language. And no running around with men in town. As long as you're under this roof, you're not going to behave like one of Kate's employees."

"What does Uncle Tom say about the rules?"

"They're mighty good ones," said Tom. "I vote yes."

"And what does the wooden Indian say?"

Johnny catapaulted himself out of his chair. In Head Chief's skull, the little bridge of bone between the two bullet holes fell out. He grabbed Kitie up out of the corner of the sofa by one shoulder. His hand transmitted to his brain the information that there was no bra strap, therefore no bra. "You lay off that wooden Indian stuff," he said. "You're only seven-eighths less Indian than I am."

Kitie smiled slowly, as if coming back from a long distance away. "Oh wow, a tough cat. Well, I'm a tough chick." She stuck out her tongue.

So Johnny gave her a couple of sharp little cracks back and forth with the flat of his hand, and shoved her back into the sofa corner. The girls all cheered, "Hurray!" They had spent their lives being marshaled by Pat, who often used a quirt on them. Even Tom and Ma Maureen whooped applause. Then Johnny bent over her and grabbed the little gold ring. He let his eyes telegraph to hers the information that he might jerk it loose.

"Johnny, please." She raised her hands involuntarily, and all the color slid down out of her face. "Please don't."

He twisted the ring a little. "How'd they make the hole? Novocaine?"

"No, an icecube. Please let go, Johnny." Down the neck of her shirt, he saw one of her breasts, girlish and softly freckled, with the dark nipple looking swollen, as if someone had abused it. He felt the feeling coming on that meant nothing but loneliness and misery.

So he let her go, turned on his bootheel, strode into the front hall, and yanked his sheepskin jacket from among the other jackets hanging there.

"Johnny." Tom got up and followed him to the door. "Where you off to?"

"I'm taking the other pickup and going back to cow camp for some peace and quiet. And keep that juvenile delinquent away from me."

Shrugging into the jacket, he seized his gloves and burst away from them, into the freezing night. Tom had the decency not to follow him. He headed blindly for the garage.

The hard snow groaned under his boots. Above him the sky boiled with stars that were really bonfires of ghostly camps. A meteor fell, smoking whitely. Over the hills and buttes to the north, a feeble red aurora borealis played its terrible red searchlights back and forth, perhaps trying to pick out one of those camps that had floated off into the night sky. And they came migrating across the snow and ice, wearing their little trail across the tundra. In his mind they were always coming, just arriving, and it was all before them still, all the suffering and destruction. They were gentle people, dark people, who hadn't seen horses yet. They urged on the big shaggy dogs that dragged their bundle-loaded travois, their breath smoking whitely like slow-motion meteors on the night air. He could hear their voices far off across the ice fields. Every winter he could feel them arriving like that.

But if anyone asked him what they said, he would have to say, "It's nothing. Just something hurting in my bones. Just something hurting in my bleached bones." And when he got to cow camp, he would have to sleep with the light on, as he always did, because he was still afraid of the dark.

"I was born on the Tongue River reservation, but I don't remember it."

Johnny talked slow and haltingly, looking away now and then, as if he were being interviewed by a reporter from *Life* magazine. And there would be photographs of that face with which he was too familiar—that too-handsome black face of his, with its gun-metal gleam on forehead and nose, and its deepset brown Asiatic eyes looking anxiously out over his cheekbones, out of the shadow cast by his hat brim, as if he were still squinting across some treeless steppe. He was aware that his shoulders hunched forward defensively against the long black braids, which were coarse and shiny as horsehair, plaited neatly and fastened with rubberbands. He was aware that his hair had a few auburn streaks in it—the books said Morning Star's son had hair like that.

"The Tongue River. That's where they keep the Northern Cheyennes, over near Ashland, Birney, Lame Deer, around there. There's the Northern Cheyennes and the Southern Cheyennes, you know. The Northerners call themselve the Suhtai, or Buffalo People. I read somewhere that the government tried to put both tribes together on one reservation down in Oklahoma. But the Northern Cheyennes got homesick for the high country up north. A lot of them died of malaria in the damp and the heat down there. So they just up and left. The government tried to stop them, but the Suhtai just traveled and fought and starved till they got back to the Tongue River country. The government tried to make them go south again, and a lot of the people committed suicide. There was one old woman dying, and her last words were something about how nice the wind sounded in the pine trees along the Tongue River. That land was always theirs, all that sagebrush prairie and pine hills, and it still is. The government had to give up and let them stay there. They still have half a million acres along the Tongue River."

The reporter would be taking notes as Johnny went on. "My parents left the reservation when I was a little boy. They went away looking for work, because they were afraid they'd starve if they stayed. I mean my real parents, my Indian parents. It must take a lot to make a Cheyenne leave the Tongue River."

Johnny was alone, of course. He was leaning on the horse-pasture gate, watching Son of a Bitch rolling in the snow, wiggling and grunting with all four hoofs in the air. The hot, salty saddle would be lying beached on its side in the snow, as if forever, and the sweaty bridle hung forgotten over Johnny's arm as he was being interviewed.

"My father was named Fred Eagle. Eagle—that's a good one. The eagle was a big thing to the Cheyennes. I read all about that. The eagle belonged to the Thunder, who belonged to God. They used to build special traps to catch eagles, and wore their tailfeathers to show what big men they were. And they used whistles made of eagle wingbones in the Sun Dance. And my mother was named Maggie Eagle, of course.

"I guess Fred was always drunk and all. They lived in this old log hut on the reservation, and in the summer they moved into a canvas tent. There was no work, and my mother was always coughing like a piece of her tail was going to come up, and there was no doctor. So one day they just up and left, without asking permission of the government people in the reservation. They thought they'd go for just a little while. But afterwards, they were afraid to go back. They thought the government might punish them.

"So they turned up on my dad's ranch here, looking for work. My adopted dad, that is. They tell me I was about four years old, clutching my mother's hand, with nothing on but a dirty undershirt and snot running down to my chin. And they stood there in the afternoon sunshine outside the bunkhouse, very polite and quiet, and my father, my real father, was clutching his dusty straw hat in his skinny black hands, and my mother's faded gingham dress was blowing in the wind, above her moccasins full of holes. And Fred asked in real bad English if there was any work. That's how Pa Gene told me it was. He said he would never forget it.

"Maybe Fred and Maggie had heard tell somewhere that Pa Gene was one-fourth Indian himself. Or so he said. He always said his grandfather married an Assiniboin woman. The records around here mention her too. There's a lot of people brag about being one-quarter Indian, but they usually lay claim to be Cherokee. Sheer envy, I guess, the way they never envied the black man. But I guess Pa Gene wasn't lying. He sure looked part Indian, with his wiry black hair and his high cheekbones. Well, so Gene looked at the three of us standing there. My father was smiling shy, like, and he had these huge yellow crooked teeth and gentle bloodshot eyes and shaking hands and a rough face that looked like the white man's disc harrow had farmed it over good. My mother was only about twenty, but she already had grey hair. And Pa Gene decided that maybe he needed another hired man around the barns, and he told them to stay.

"I don't remember anything about the reservation, you understand. I don't remember anything except something that scares me. Something that I heard people talk about when I was little, or something that maybe I saw. Something about the dark, or something moving in the willows, or something lying out in the open still alive. Bones scattered along a hillside, or buried under a sandstone ledge. Maybe that's why I never went back. Fred and Maggie never went back either. They got real homesick and cried a lot, but they was always

afraid that the government people would come find them and take
away the money that Fred made. Fred always hid when he saw somebody strange at the ranch. Of course, he didn't dare go into Cottonwood to buy whiskey, but he drank most anything around the ranch.
For instance, he stole vanilla from the cookhouse and drank that. It
nearly killed Pa Gene to look at them. I guess it hit him then what it
meant to be an Indian. He tried to help them, but they were a hundred
years past helping.

"One morning they found Fred lying dead in the barnyard. He
had drunk up a whole bottle of wood alcohol. My mother didn't say
much for a day or so, and then she hung herself with an old bridle
rein from a rafter in the saddle-horse barn. Glad it wasn't me that
found her hanging there. My father, Pa Gene, that is, took them back
to the Tongue River country to be buried, and that was when he decided to adopt me. I had caught TB from Maggie, and he wanted to
get me into the hospital at Galen. I had kin back on the reservation,
of course, and I guess they wanted me back, but the government people took me away from my kin and fixed it up for Pa Gene to raise
me as a white man."

"So you've never been back?" the reporter might insist.

"No."

"You're a traitor to your race," the reporter might say. In real
life, of course, reporters didn't say things like that when they were
interviewing.

"That's what you think," Johnny answered.

And he talked on, haltingly slow, clutching the sweaty bridle.
"So the Chances brought me up. I was supposed to be one of six white
children. They had the blood of an Assiniboin great-grandmother running somewhere there, but they were white, all right. But you know
what happens when you put one odd-colored horse into a bunch of
solid-color horses. Even the animals are like that. Tom, of course,
was real pleased to have an all-Indian brother, and he went around
school bragging and he beat up any kids that teased me. That old
envy again. But I think Ma Maureen was afraid of me even then.

"So I went to grade school and high school here in Cottonwood,
and on the rare occasions when I stuck my nose in a book, I read about
how the Indians were varmints that scalped those poor settlers, and
how they were dirty savages. And I learned to cheer at the movies
when the U.S. cavalry came charging up. That's what happens to you.
There's no point in going back to something like the Tongue River,

is there? Pa Gene even told me that I have land there, land that was Fred's, unless the government men have leased it or sold it away from me. Well, I don't need that land. I can live without it. The Tongue River is a bad dream.

"Pa Gene didn't see any point in being Indian either. He always told me that I shouldn't be ashamed of it—he wasn't ashamed. But he said I should try to be white inside, because that was all there was left to be. And the kids in town called me Tonto and Chief Sitting Bull. If I looked twice at a girl, they called her my squaw. If I got a haircut, they called it scalping. I learned pretty quick that I had to play their game my way. I had to make them like me, but not get caught at it. You don't dare get caught. If you do, it's worse than not waking up.

"No, I didn't grow my braids in high school. I was too timid about things like that then. I grew them later, when I started rodeoing."

And the reporter would be taking it all down on his tape recorder, for transcribing later. Now and then the reporter would ask a question that would keep Johnny talking.

"In high school I played basketball and went out for track. I was the shortest forward on the team, but I was the best shot too, so they started liking me. Cottonwood was a B team. Once in a while, when we played other B teams, we'd run into Indian players. Like, for instance, Wolf Point always had a couple Indians on their team, and so did St. Ignatius. They played dirty too. I remember one of them that wore long braids, and he used those damn braids to quirt us other players right across the eyes. Half the time the referees never called it a foul either. I never talked to those Indian kids, so they never talked to me. That was the closest I got to my own kind in those days. No, I never played football—too light for that. But I placed second in the hundred-yard dash at State my senior year. Somewheres I read about an Indian named Deerfoot who was a great distance runner, a hundred years ago. But the coach told me distance running was dangerous for kids. Anyway, I guess I succeeded in making the kids like me, because my junior year they elected me to the student council, and my senior year I was class vice-president and also top athlete.

"But you know, there was this girl in my class that I was crazy about. I'd never cared for a girl before that, and I guess I haven't since then either. This was Marilyn Rainville. She was a town girl, blonde and real beautiful. My senior year I asked her to the Prom.

And there was this big fuss about it, and her parents made her say no, after she'd already said yes. Guess they thought I would scalp her. She's married to this crazy little Slav now, and has three little blonde brats, and she got real fat. I look the other way when I run into her in town. After that, I used to have about one crush a year on some white girl, but I didn't dare date anybody.

"Pa Gene had us pointed toward rodeo. At home basketball and track could be talked about for five minutes, but the rest of the day it was rodeo. Rodeo people always coming and going and calling up. Pa Gene was real popular, in a way I could never quite figure out so I could do the same, and he had friends everywhere. Tom and I were already competing in junior and high-school rodeos by the time we were freshmen, and we had to be as tough ropers as Pa Gene. The girls, of course, had to make do with barrel racing and trick riding. Pa Gene would never let either of them rope—said it was the best way in the world to lose a finger. Even during school we used to manage to get out on the circuit. And because Pa Gene was such a great man, he knew how to make you love the thing he wanted you to do. So I was a good boy, and the only thing I ever wanted to do—aside from sleep with Marilyn Rainville—was rope.

"Tom and I are real different ropers, though. Tom is so big and strong that he don't need no brain. One time Jimmy Alderman got mad at Tom and called him the cowboy King Kong. Tom does everything with muscle, so he can get away with being a little sloppy sometimes. He even has a muscle for a soul. And he doesn't fuss about his horses the way I do. Matter of fact, Tom doesn't really savvy horses much. He is really a better dogger than he is roper. I was always too light for dogging. I was a pretty fair bronc rider, but my heart wasn't in it.

"Me, I'm what they call a brain roper, a scientific roper. To rope good, I have to make up for my lack of size and strength and use my natural speed and agility. Pa Gene taught me how to study and study, to work out the littlest things. For instance, he gave me the idea to bail out on the right side instead of the left. It saves you a second or two, because you don't have to duck under the rope on your way to the calf, and then flank the calf down. I'm not big and beefy enough to flank a calf fast. My way, I come up to the calf on the other side and just leg him down. Pa Gene told me that some Indian ropers he'd seen had the habit of falling off on the right. I guess that's why I latched onto the idea. But it does save time too.

"I had to be a pretty roper too. It got attention from the crowds.

First I got up gumption to grow braids. Then I started wearing real colorful clothes. Pa Gene didn't object, but Ma Maureen just had a fit. And I had this picturesque horse too, old Rattler. Me and Rattler looked real wild when we broke out of the box.

"You see, I had got kind of crazy about having just the right horse. To do my kind of roping, you can't rope off any old skag. When I was in high school, I had two good using horses that I had broke myself, but neither was what you'd call great. Then one winter Pa Gene was off on the circuit and he came home with this big, rough-looking Appaloosa colt that he'd bought from some Indian roper. He'd been down at this jackpot roping in Oklahoma and seen the colt and thought he had the makings of a real great rope horse. That colt was the hairiest, orneriest thing you ever saw, with a china eye and a ratty little tail. He was spotted all over, what they call a "leopard phase" Appaloosa. We named him Rattler because of his snakey head. When he was grown he weighed about twelve hundred pounds. He wasn't a pretty, Hollywood kind of horse, but he sure could catch the crowd's eye.

"As long as he lived, there wasn't any horse like Rattler. Every roper in the country wanted to buy a seat on him. He could rate a calf like an IBM computer. When he stopped, he sat down and stuck his hind legs in the ground clear to Red China. He broke my rope lots of times. He threw some of the best ropers in the business that way. Like, once he threw Jimmy Alderman down at Phoenix. Jimmy got back on to try with his second loop, because he'd missed the calf. And old Rattler was mad because Jimmy had missed, and he started in switching that ratty tail of his, just like a cat. When Jimmy threw that second loop, Rattler dumped him again, harder. Jimmy used to say Rattler had disc brakes like a racing car. I had to keep boots on him fore and hind to keep him from skinning himself all up.

"With a horse like that working for you, you can do anything. You understand that. Without a good using horse, a roper is all afoot —body and soul. And if he has a good horse and loses him, he might as well go drown hisself in the creek. There's only one horse in the country now that can come up to Rattler, and that's Ace of Spades.

"You know about Ace of Spades. No? Well, Spades belongs to Sam Burke. Burke is from Flagstaff, Arizona. A real tough roper, but getting old. I hear rumors that Sam is retiring and that he might sell Spades. He knows I've had my eye on that horse ever since I lost Rattler. After Rattler died, I bought a seat on Spades and rode him the rest of the season. He was a great using horse, everything I could ask, except that he didn't have Rattler's killing stop. He's a buckskin Quarter-Horse gelding, eight years old, with black points and a black dorsal stripe, weighs about eleven hundred. A young horse, that a fellow could grow old gracefully with. The boys like to kid me, saying I like circus horses, but that Spades is another crowd-getter. He has a beautiful head and foxy little black ears, and his coat is real golden color. If I were an Indian out stealing horses in the old days, and I crawled into some Crow or Shoshoni camp, I'd find that Spades horse picketed right in front of some chief's teepee, with medicine tied on his neck. He'd be a great buffalo or war horse. I read somewhere that the first horses the Cheyennes got hold of were buckskins and roans.

"But the horse-stealing days are over, for sure. I've got a few thousand cached away in a bank that Tom don't know about. I guess it would be enough for a down payment on Spades, and Burke would let me pay the rest out of winnings. But I haven't even called Burke up to ask if he's really selling the horse. Only one thing holding me back, and I don't even know what it is.

"Jimmy Alderman tried to help me figure out what the problem was. But we both knew I had to find it out for myself. I was close to Jimmy in a way I never was with Pa Gene or Tom, though of course I would have rode through fire for the two of them. (At least, I *suppose* I would have.) When I first started rodeoing, it was a lonely business. Even having Pa Gene as my father didn't help. The other guys respected my roping, all right, but they just never came around. A few even picked on me, because I like to wear colorful clothes. The clothes companies give us stuff to wear, you know, for promotion. So these guys called me Pocahontas. Wasn't much point fighting with them, because they could all whip me. I thought sometimes about learning karate, so I could kill some of them with my bare hands.

"Well anyway, one day in Phoenix, Jimmy Alderman stepped in. Somebody said Pocahontas, and Jimmy beat the stuffing out of him. Jimmy just loves to fight. He was born with a black eye. If he ever had to choose between roping and fighting, he'd sell his rope horse. After Phoenix, Jimmy had a free seat on my Rattler any time. He wasn't well mounted then, so he was real pleased. The next season the two of us won nearly $50,000 roping off Rattler. Sam Burke started coming around too, and next thing I knew, all the boys were being friendly. I just knew better than to run around with white girls in front of them.

"Jimmy's a real good friend. I can tell him how I feel, and he just says, 'Yeah.' He doesn't have a drop of Indian blood either. We ran after women together and everything. These days he's letting me figure things out, and I haven't seen him much. But he knows I'm here, and I know he's there."

"If Burke let you use Spades," the reporter would ask, "why did you keep doing so badly during that time?"

"Because a roper like me has to have his own horse."

"So it started when Rattler died."

"Yeah. Rattler stepped on a nail. I soaked the hoof in turpentine and got the best vet around. But blood poisoning set in. He died down in his stall, with his ugly head on my knees. I cried like a woman. Might as well be honest about it. A man shouldn't cry even over his best rope horse.

"But it wasn't just being afoot. It was something on the inside of me that went bad then. Part of it was the pressure—trying to stay on top, feeling the other ropers always out to get me, playing at being a popular, white-skinned Indian. I got so I spent a lot of time looking in the mirror. There was times I was turned down at hotels and restaurants, and I got in a few fights—Jimmy Alderman taught me how to fight. There was this feeling of being mad that started to eat up my belt buckle. And no matter how much money I won, the family and the ranch always ate it up. Tom was always making things nice, and Ma Maureen was forcing the girls to go to college, the way she couldn't make me and Tom do. Tom talks awful big, but he never made much money, except one year when he had a hot streak dogging. Alex Feet was after me then too. I started feeling guilty about things I couldn't put a name to, things that weren't even my fault. And I started feeling afraid of things I didn't know about and couldn't even see.

"But there's more to it, even. I started reading books about the Cheyennes round about that time. You see, it was the only way I could find out anything about them without actually listening to Feet and going back to the Tongue River. And, well, it was real nice to find out that my tribe was so interesting and famous and all, and that they was one of the few tribes in the country that managed to hold onto a lot of their old ways and their language. But some of the things I read really disturbed me. They'd stick in my mind like I was dreaming with my eyes open. For instance, there was Morning Star's son. They don't even know his name. Morning Star was leading one of the Cheyenne bands that fled back north from Oklahoma. Well, after one of those running fights they had with the U.S. Army, the soldiers found one of his sons lying dead in a creek. He was good-looking, the book said, with long, yellow-streaked hair, and looked like he was asleep. My hair is like that, with those streaks. I could feel myself lying there in the water, my nose and my mouth full of water and me not able to move. Those soldiers were bending over to yank off those beautiful beaded moccasins that the book said I was wearing. My moccasins are probably in somebody's Indian collection somewhere in the country. That's how I felt about things I read. The same for the story about Head Chief and Young Mule. And the one about Two Childs, the medicine man—that was the worst one of all. To go back into that world was like waking up in the night and no light to turn on. And, you know, I must have learned to be afraid of the dark after my parents died, because back in that log hut on the Tongue River, there wasn't no light at night.

"Then Pa Gene was killed last year." As he said that, Johnny's eyes shifted from the reporter to Kitie, who had ambled up just then and was listening.

"That was in Pendleton, right?" The reporter's voice would be gentler, very respectful and discreet.

"Why don't you take the reporter to see Daddy's grave?" Kitie spoke up.

So the dusty pickup was standing there, like something in a dream with the eyes open, and the three of them got in and drove out to the Hillcrest Cemetery. The reporter jounced uncomfortably on the muddy seat, with his city shoes perched on the pile of old stock magazines, halters, horseshoes, and such. At the cemetery it was July. The place was a mirage of green lawn scorched blue-green, and of cottonwood trees rustling drily like straw amid a shimmering desert of overgrazed sheep pasture. Johnny, Kitie, and the reporter got slowly out of the pickup and walked slowly, wading dreamlike, along the gravel paths.

Among the tombstones sprinklers whirled merrily, carefully spinning out the crystal drops sucked from a special pipeline that went down to the main Cottonwood ditch. In Cottonwood, one thing was surer than death and taxes, and that was irrigation. The big trees sighed everywhere in the hot wind, benignly shading alike the sleek new tombstones and the crumbling brick monuments of the earliest French settlers. On the scorched limey hillsides bordering the cemetery, clouds of wild white gypsophilia rested like a mist without moisture.

The three of them stood looking at the Chance plot, shaded by several big blue spruces. The three older granite tombstones were already a little weathered, especially the one under which lay Gene Chance's grandfather, William Gordon Chance, who had come to Cottonwood as a buffalo hunter, stayed to ranch, and was killed in the Cottonwood County range war over water rights. The other two stones stood over Gene's parents. Missing was the tombstone of Gene's grandmother, the mysterious Assiniboin who had gone back to her people, leaving her children behind. The newest grave was a modest little granite plaque level with the grass, and the letters chiseled on it read "Eugene Chance 1916–1968." On the corners of the plot stood four brick jars with sun-blasted geraniums and blue lobelia trailing down the sides, which Ma Maureen had bought at Fulton's Greenhouse. Imagining it all, Johnny felt a spooky closeness of Pa Gene's ghost.

"How did Daddy die?" Kitie asked, hands stuck in pockets. (Actually, Johnny debated with himself whether Kitie or the reporter should ask this question, and finally decided it was most fitting that Kitie ask it.)

"Well, it happened when we were at Pendleton that year," Johnny said. "Pa Gene was roping in the final go-round. The calf cut over in front and upset his horse. He was riding that big sorrel named Sundown. Guess you don't remember Sundown. Anyway, Sundown went head over and hoolihaned right on Gene and crushed his chest. We were all there and saw it happen. Only time in my life that I ever heard Ma Maureen scream. Tom and I rode with him in the ambulance. He never did regain consciousness. He died that night in the hospital. For a while after, we just didn't know what hit us. Tom is riding Sundown now. Anyway, pretty soon I realized that, now that Pa Gene was dead, he could see my thoughts, and that he hated all the things I was thinking about."

Kitie stood gravely looking down at her father's grave, the hot wind fanning out her mane of wavy hair. After a minute she moved herself slowly off to the scorched hillside beyond, her chlorine-dyed bell-bottoms flapping solemnly around her ankles. Johnny and the reporter followed her with their eyes. Bending here and there, she gathered a big fistful of the white gypsophilia. The reporter seemed overwhelmed by that cemetery, more desolate than if it had contained ten thousand badmen hung with their boots on. Then Kitie ambled slowly back and bent to lay the gypsophilia on Gene's gravestone. It already looked wilted, and the wind rolled the bunch of it to the edge of the stone.

"Groove, Daddy," she said to the gravestone.

"My great-grandparents were buried under a pile of rocks some-where," said Johnny. "Or stuck in under a sandstone ledge."

"I'd like you to fuck me on Daddy's grave," said Kitie. "Let's come up here some night and fuck." The reporter wrote Kitie's words down on his little notepad with his ballpoint pen.

"Nothing left now," said Johnny, "but a few beads and bits of leather."

"Let's get out of here," said Kitie. "Too much green revolution around here. I can smell all these nice wet mossy bones."

"And you're the one who wants to farm," Johnny said. The three of them walked back to the truck, which still stood baking in the sun back down the road, little heat waves dancing over its roof.

"You say you went to pieces that year," said the reporter as they drove out of the cemetery, "but you actually placed second in the world finals."

"Well, I did pretty good up through Denver. If a cowboy takes top money in Denver, it's pretty hard to catch up with him before the end of that year. But the next year was hell. I started drinking some, and Tom was always after me, saying what would Pa Gene say, and so on. In the fall I got busted up—bronc broke my leg against the gate. That was the first time I ever got hurt bad, and I didn't like it much. To tell you the truth, I think one of the reasons I rope is that I'm scared of getting busted up riding broncs and bulls. Well, anyway, when I got out of the hospital, I was going to quit rodeo and go to Vietnam."

"Vietnam!" Kitie shot up straight as a geyser on the dirty truck seat. "Like, you were going to *enlist?*"

"I had this crazy idea, Kitie. I was going to count coups on the Viet Cong and take scalps. I read how a lot of Indians left the reser-vations during World War II and went off to the Pacific to kill Japs. For instance, the Northern Cheyennes would go off alone in the pine hills and do the sun dance, the old way. They'd have their medicine dream and get their power. Then they'd go join the Marines. But the army doctors took one look at my busted leg and gave me a 4-F. I tried three times. Finally Tom came and found me, and made me come home."

"You did the sun dance?" the reporter asked. He was having a hard time taking notes in the jouncing truck. "What's that?"

"No, I never did it. I figured I'd get around to it if they let me join the army. No point in doing it if I couldn't get to Vietnam."

"But what is it, man?" Kitie insisted.

"Well, the white people think of it as a torture ceremony, but there's more to it than that. All the Plains tribes had a sun dance of some kind. The Northern Cheyennes had theirs in early summer, when the grass was green and the buffalo were fat. The chiefs would go out and cut down a young cottonwood tree. Then they'd set the tree up as a centerpole and build a special lodge of green saplings around it. The pole had a crotch left at the top to build an eagle nest in—they called that the Thunder's nest. Now, when the dance got started, the most important people were the Sacred Woman and the head priest. There was all kinds of painting up and pipe smoking and singing and dancing for four days. They had a green altar with a painted buffalo skull. The Sacred Woman was supposed to be the buffalo, and she and the head priest, uh, they made love. That was part of the ceremony. It kept the grass green and the buffalo fat and the tribe healthy for the coming year."

"Groovy," said Kitie. "Better than the Kama Sutra. But where does the torture come in?"

"Well, men who wanted to make special offerings of their own would go off alone during the dance. They'd starve themselves a little bit first. Then one night they'd skewer their selves onto rawhide ropes and tie the ropes to a tree. Then they'd dance for hours, all night long, jerking at the ropes. In the morning they'd come down and put the bloody ropes on the altar. Or if you didn't feel like doing that, you could cut hunks of skin off your arms and legs and offer those. Either way, you proved that you had power."

"Euuch," said Kitie. "Bet they don't do it anymore."

"They sure do. The government tried hard to stop the sun dance, back in the twenties. There was this big fuss when the missionaries found out about the Sacred Woman business. But the Cheyennes are real stubborn. They still have a sun dance most every year, and once in a while somebody sets in and cuts himself up. And I guess the Sacred Woman and the priest go off somewhere where the missionaries can't find them, and—"

"—ball," Kitie finished for him as he hesitated.

"Yeah." Johnny giggled a little. "Imagine doing that in St. Mary's Catholic Church in town."

"But you didn't do the sun dance. Scared, huh?" asked Kitie.

"It sounds to me," said the reporter, "like you have read a lot of books on anthropology."

Johnny looked gravely at the reporter. "According to the books, the Indians don't think much of anthropologists."

Johnny sighed and got down from the corral fence. Son of a Bitch, his hide twitching off snow and dirt, was moving across the pasture to join the other horses by a willow clump along the creek. Johnny heaved the sweaty saddle to his shoulder and, carrying the bridle over his arm, trudged back along the path toward the cabin. At the cabin, he remembered that he wasn't sure he'd shut a gate down below, between the upper and lower pastures. So he let the saddle fall with a crump on the snow by the cabin door and trudged down the path to the corrals. Sure enough, the gate was unchained. He snapped the chain shut, and stood leaning against the gate for a moment, looking down across the benchlands toward Cottonwood in the evening distance. Something tightened in him like a cinch.

The lights already winked down in town, through the blue smog from the sawmill. The lights, of course, were really campfires, and the blue haze was rising from a thousand white lodges pitched there along the Cottonwood River. You could sight a big camp miles away by the haze it made. Something pried in him, like a bit prying apart a horse's jaws. He had seen photographs of camps like that, taken in the old days. The horse herd drifted along the river banks, but the best horses were tethered in front of the lodges, half safe from thieves and within easy reach. One of them would be a buckskin with black legs and medicine tied to a string around his neck. And in the lodge near where that horse was tied, a young blonde woman without a face sat on the tanned robes, wearing an elkskin dress hung with rows of elk teeth.

Johnny looked up and saw the old eagle drifting high above, or thought that he saw it. Dreamily he undid the copper buttons of his Levis and brought out from between his shirttails the dark penis that was scarcely his own. The young woman gently called him by his name, and he could not answer. Embracing the gate pole with his left arm, he made love to himself with his right hand. The gate shuddered rhythmically, and the vibrations went humming out along the barbed wire fence on both sides until they died in the arctic distance. The gate chain clanked and clanked. That young woman was under him, with her elkskin dress pushed up and all her elk teeth clacking tenderly, and her legs and arms were doubled all around him. Something moved in the willows. An owl called. A shadow drifted across the rocky hillside. Someone was moaning just beyond the top of the hill, there where the waving grass and the blue sky kept trying to commit genocide on each other. John Stands in Timber drew up his horse, shivering a little, as he heard a clear woman's voice singing a war song from the old days, off beyond the old Indian graves. Johnny gnawed the pole, getting a mouthful of tasteless rain-softened splinters, and his hat fell off as the gate gave a final drumming jerk. The singing voice was nearer, like a pair of burning eyes just beyond a nearby clump of willows. Then it was farther away, a small owl sifting off like dark flour through the pines into the night.

Slowly the barbed wire fence stopped vibrating. Johnny leaned against the gate, going limp and looking down at the thick, milky stuff dripping slowly from the poles down into the hoof-trampled snow. In half an hour it would be frozen, a North Pole in miniature. He put the penis back in as if he were putting a wrench back in a toolbox. It was not his at all, that was for sure. Slowly he looked up at the sky, now that deep crystal blue of Montana winter evenings, and wondered if the old eagle had flown off. If it were summer, that old eagle would be headed to its wild nest of sticks on a cliff edge somewhere, where its mate guarded the eggs with angry yellow eyes and opened beak.

Johnny and Tom were feeding the steers late that afternoon. Tom had come up to talk about Kitie and had fallen in to help Johnny with the rest of his chores. The little team pulled the sleigh-wagon slowly across the hard snow on red runners. Their reins were wrapped around a post sticking up at the wagon's head and their nostrils smoked in the twilight blue like hot springs in an empty, snow-drifted Yellowstone. Johnny and Tom were busy up on the wagon, cutting open bales of hay and pushing them off the wagon onto the snow. The steers came to meet them, crunching ankle-deep in the wind-sculptured snow. Back from the sleigh-wagon wound a string of shaggy brown backs as more steers jostled and ate, scuffing the hay across the snow.

"Whoooee. That Kitie has got Cottonwood all in an uproar," said Tom, bending over and cutting bale twine with his jackknife.

"What's she up to now?"

"She's obeying Ma Maureen's rules, all right, but it still leaves her room to swing a whole dozen cats in. For instance, Ma Maureen forgot to say Kitie couldn't ride her motorcycle. So Kitie has been gunning her motorcycle up and down Main Street. Finally the police chief gave her a speeding ticket. Ma Maureen had a fit."

Johnny grunted, pushing another bale off onto the snow, where it broke open into sections under the hungry pink muzzles and tongues of a dozen steers. "You suppose Ma Maureen is going to report Kitie for selling dope back in New York?"

"She's just faking about that," said Tom. "You know how Kitie used to lie all the time about everything, to impress people. She said something to me the other day about how she worked in some duds shop, down there in what's its place, the East Village. And she said she made some other money doing naked modeling, too."

"You mean nude modeling," said Johnny.

"Oh, I forgot," said Tom. "You're the other sophisticate in the family."

"Supposing she's lying about the modeling too?" said Johnny. "Maybe she made all that money selling secrets to the Russians."

"Whoooee. If she did, they was fabricated secrets," said Tom.

They kept working, in a kind of rhythm that they had learned down the years. The horses, too, kept walking all by themselves. They knew the route, and they circled slowly out over the field, their necks bent in a businesslike, virtuous way, both pulling their weight equally. "What really has Ma Maureen worried," Tom went on, "is that Fern is real impressed with Kitie."

"Fern is impressed by just about most anything."

"Damn right," said Tom, "and she's at the age where she doesn't know any better. Ma Maureen just wishes that Kitie would up and go. But it looks like she's going to stay on home awhile. The other day I caught Kitie and Fern talking. Kitie was telling Fern about how the cops beat her up in Chicago, and Fern was just sitting there with her eyes getting magnified. Maybe we have to get Kitie out of the house for a while till she simmers down some."

"Where you plan to put her?" Johnny asked with sober irony. "In the pen? Maybe send her to Warm Springs?"

"For instance. Last Sunday we was all getting ready to go in to town to mass. Ma Maureen had to go and tell Kitie that she'd better get ready to go to mass too. And Kitie said no, thanks, she'd stay home and mass-turbate."

Johnny burst out laughing. He had to sit down on a bale and laugh.

"It ain't all that funny," growled Tom, still bending and cutting. "Whooee. Lot of hay we're throwing around here."

"What's the cow market doing?"

"If it don't go up pretty soon, we're going to have the use of these steers and that's all. The old banker is getting mighty restless."

"I don't know why you had to go and buy out the Haley Ranch. That's all we needed was a million-dollar mortgage."

"Well, it seemed like the proper thing to do at the time," said Tom. "We couldn't let Intermountain buy it up, could we? Land is going to go up around here. Someday we'll sell the place at a profit. Anyway, if you were doing your part, things would be a whole lot easier."

"I'm doing my part. I'm sitting up here feeding these steers that you bought when the market was high."

"One of these somedays, Johnny Eagle," said Tom softly, turning around and facing Johnny, "I am going to run a pitchfork straight through you."

"Not if you want to pay off that debt, you won't," said Johnny, not even looking at Tom, and pushing another bale off.

Tom was silent for a moment. Johnny guessed that he was controlling himself. Finally Tom said, "Pa Gene would have known just what to do."

"Yeah, he was a pretty good manager," said Johnny. "Now he's just growing six feet of irrigated pasture."

"Well, there's one way you can help out extra, if you're not going to rodeo."

"What's that?"

"Take Kitie off our necks and keep her up here."

"Here at cow camp? You mean, *stay* with me up here?" He remembered seeing her breasts down the neck of her shirt.

"Maybe you can even get some work out of her. There's an extra room in the cabin—we could fix it all up for her."

"No, thanks. I want my peace and quiet."

"I mean it, Johnny. You've got to take her on. Things are going on something terrible down there. Pat, for instance, just hates Kitie. Pat calls her a Commie whore, and Kitie calls Pat a smart-ass fascist. The other night the two of them got in a fistfight in the living room. I always thought Pat was mighty tough, but Kitie just beat the living shit out of her, and they were a-slashing and a-scratching and a-pulling each other's hair. Bet it took half a dozen of them big Chicago cops to get Kitie to jail. And Ruby was cheering for Pat, and Fern was cheering for Kitie, so the two of *them* started into fighting. And Ma Maureen was screaming and crying. It was beyond belief."

"If Kitie comes up here, she'll be picking on me instead. Nothing doing."

"Well, I asked her, and she said she'd come up, long as you didn't pull her nose ring no more."

"I said nothing doing." Johnny bent to shove off another bale. Suddenly he felt the steel tines of Tom's pitchfork pressed against his ribs. His heart gave a great leap and started stampeding like a spooked horse. "Now, Tom," he said shakily, "if this wagon gives a jerk, it'll be you they'll haul off to the pen, not Kitie."

"Now you listen to me," said Tom in a white, wind-sculptured little voice. "I'm head of this family, and Pa Gene is watching me to see what I do. I'll bet Pa Gene is about to puke on his harp seeing what you turned into." He kept the pitchfork pressed to Johnny's side, pinning him against the wagon's headboard where the reins were tied. Johnny stayed frozen in that bent-over position, his eyes half shut, like a cottontail freezing as the shadow of an eagle sailed over it. His braids brushed the bales, picking up dried green bits of thistle. The sudden sweat on his body almost glowed there under his clothes, like alarm-clock numerals in the dark. He was reminded again how afraid he was.

"I'm bringing Kitie up here tomorrow," said Tom. "You push her around all you want. But I'm not hearing any more lip from you. Savvy? I've got half a notion to go buy that Spades horse, and just put him in the corral here for you to stare at."

"If you buy that horse without my sayso, I'll leave town," said Johnny shakily.

Tom took the pitchfork away from his side, and Johnny straightened up. They went on forking hay to the steers without a word. The team kept walking slowly, almost in lockstep, their harness jingling gently in the icy blue air. Evening was coming on—already the valley brimmed with arctic shadows, and the lights were coming on in town like washes of phosphorescence on the waves all across a northern bay.

"It's the least you can do for your little sister," said Tom.

"She ain't my sister," said Johnny, again not looking at Tom. He kept cutting bales and forking them off the sleigh with the same steadfastness as the horses—that equine virtue that hid so much hysteria and stampedes.

He sensed that Tom straightened up, towering like a dinosaur standing up on its hind legs. Tom struck his pitchfork into a bale and leaned on it for a moment. "One of these somedays," said Tom softly, "I guess we're going to come around to that, aren't we?"

"I guess so," said Johnny. His heart was still clanging on his ribs like a hammer on a white-hot sparking horseshoe, but he dared to say the words. It was the only fair way to warn Tom, and the only safe way. He realized then that he had begun to say the words when he hid away that last winnings as a down payment for Spades. He had told Tom that the money was stolen from his hotel.

The sleigh-wagon was empty now, scuffs of timothy seed and crushed thistle scattered across its old board bed. Johnny threw down his pitchfork, unwrapped the reins from around the post, and whistled at the team. The horses switched their tails and broke into a smart trot across the crusted snow, circling back toward the cow camp. Tom leaned against the headboard, shook a cigarette out of his pack, and lit it. Now and then Johnny felt Tom glance at him. That gaze felt like the polar night coming on, with aurora borealis stalking across the ice fields like glowing monsters.

It occurred to him that Kitie might keep away those monsters when they came to stalk around the cow-camp cabin.

A couple of days later, at noon, he heard Kitie's motorcycle far off as he stood at the cow-camp range, frying some corned beef hash. It sounded like she was just coming up the little rise where Skillet Creek cut down through the hills to the valley floor. Any minute now she'd hit the ninety-degree curve where the unpaved county road went around the corner of a quarter section over there. He stood waiting, the skillet in his hand. Finally he heard the screech of tires and the gunning of the motor as she skidded around that curve. He couldn't help himself and grinned.

Going to the window and squinting through the dusty old panes, he could make out a dark speck far off on the road. The speck swelled into a full-size motorcycle driven by a full-size demon of a girl in a red windbreaker and a sparkling helmet. He watched her brake wildly at the gate, skidding some more on the ice. She climbed off to unchain the gate, then rode the bike through, neglecting to rechain the gate, and came blatting, idling, and bumping along the frozen ruts of the pasture road to the cabin. Now Johnny could see off along the road another speck swelling into a blue pickup truck—that must be Tom, coming with her things.

He went to the door and stood there with thumbs hooked in his Levi pockets, his breath blowing white on the air. She shut off the engine, propped the bike by the well pump, and came slowly toward him, pulling off her black shiny goggles, then her mica helmet. She tried to smooth back her hair, which was windblown into a nightmare snarl. Her eyes were red and swollen, and tears had smeared dust down on her cheeks.

"What's the trouble?" he said. "Tom whip you?"

"I had a bad night, man," she said. "I had an afterflash. That happens sometimes when you've been shooting speed. I had this idea that I was going to walk to Washington to confer with President Nixon once and for all about the state of the world. I knew he'd listen to me. But Fern told me I went for a walk in the barnyard last night without no clothes on."

"Well, if you're going to stay up here with the cattle, the first thing you learn is that you don't ever leave a gate open."

She looked at him open mouthed, as if she had just blown in from another planet and was trying to understand his earth language.

"Go back and shut the gate," he said, looking as ferocious as he could, though all the while he wanted to double up and laugh.

"Jive-ass redskin," she said. She trudged back along the road to the gate and shut it, then trudged back again. She wasn't wearing gloves, and her hands were white and shrunken with cold. She shuffled into the cabin, looked around vaguely, then sat down on Johnny's bed and sniffled, wiping her nose on her finger. She looked so helpless and sick that he felt his feelings struggling to go toward her, like a calf straining toward freedom at the end of the rope. He went back into the kitchen, poured a mug of black coffee, and gave it to her.

"Thanks," she said hoarsely.

"Thanks, jive-ass redskin?"

"No. Just thanks." She gave him a wispy little smile.

The blue pickup pulled to a stop outside, and Tom got out. "Jive-ass redskin," Kitie said to Johnny, "Tom would've closed the gate."

Tom came in. "Well, here is the Mayflower Movers with Miss Katherine Chance's possessions, such as they are. Miss Chance didn't like the chintz stuff Ma Maureen was all set to give her, so she drove her bike clear over to Missoula yesterday and did some shopping in them boo-tiques where the university kids buy their junk. Kitie, you must have quite a bit of money left. Can we borrow some, if the old banker starts getting tough?"

"You make me exactly half sick," said Kitie, sipping her coffee.

"Now, honest, Kitie, what were you *really* working at in New York?"

"I told you, man," said Kitie. "I was in the chorus of this rock musical. It was a big hit and we made a lot of profits, only the police closed it for obscenity."

"Liar," said Tom. "All right, Johnny, let's unload this stuff."

Johnny and Tom carried in the old brass bed, one like Johnny's that had been in storage down at the ranch. Then they lugged in the mattress, pillows, and blankets while Kitie swept the dust off the floor in her new room. Tom rigged up a bar for her to hang her clothes on—they were mostly shirts and pants. Kitie made up the bed and covered it with a piece of what she said was a hand-blocked Indian print, which had elephants and dancing ladies all over it. She hung another such print over her window, then tacked a lot of posters all over the log walls. The posters had pictures of Che Guevara, Black Panthers, signs of the zodiac, and other things that Johnny recognized as being out of Tom's ken. Tom and Johnny threw down on the floor a few more bearskins and buffalo hides from the big trunkful of old stuff down at the ranch.

When they'd finished, Kitie stood with hands on hips and said, "Well, it's more bourgeois and elegant than what we had in New York."

"I'd better put up a door there," said Tom, "so you can close it."

"Oh, I've got these," Kitie said. She fished dozens of long strings of beads out of a sack and started tacking them up across the doorway.

"Looks like the leading prostitute in the Casbah lives here," said Tom, scowling. "I'll get a door one of these days, and you take them beady things down."

Johnny listened to them as he squatted down before the potbellied stove there in her room, rattling it around and making sure it would work before he built a fire in it. He kept having this urge to laugh.

When Tom had gone, Johnny went back to his hash, which was sitting covered on the back of the range. He fried some eggs, set out plates and mugs, and he and Kitie sat down and ate dinner. "This is the last meal I cook," he said. "From now on, you cook."

"Okay," she said pleasantly, scooping at her plate, a dribble of egg yolk in the corner of her mouth. Johnny had an urge to lean over to her and lick it away, but he didn't. "You'll be sorry—like, all I can cook is toast and jelly. That was what we lived on in the East Village. Speed freaks believe in a good breakfast, with a lot of sweets. The rest of the time they're too spaced out to know what they're eating, if anything."

"You can make dandy toast by laying the bread on top of a hot lid," said Johnny. "Tom brings up bread once a week."

"I'll make bread myself," said Kitie grandly, "so we don't have to eat that store shit with chemicals in it."

"What Tom brings is homemade. Ma Maureen makes it."

"In an experiment," Kitie went on as if she hadn't heard, "they fed these rats with store-shit bread for three months, and they died of malnutrition."

"It's just like when we were little," said Johnny. "Nobody listening."

Kitie giggled. Since she'd eaten, her face had colored up a little and she looked almost healthy. She had her bushy hair tied back by an old scarf. "I came home thinking that I could escape from everything that's tearing the country up. I started being sorry that I'd left Cottonwood and thinking that it might be a nice place after all. You know, a clean little backwater where none of the problems had gotten to yet. But Cottonwood has everything that New York has. It's got smog and traffic problems and people arguing about Vietnam and backed-up sewage and urban blight and the right percentage of pigs and heads. Like, I wish Ma Maureen knew how many kids in town are smoking grass. Cottonwood is the end of the line, baby. It's the jumping-off place into zero. No matter where you're coming from, there's nowhere you can get to from here."

"You really tried everything, huh?"

"Everything but one," she said dreamily, sniffling and finally licking away that dribble of egg yolk. "I never joined the struggle for Indian civil rights."

"You mean there is one?"

"Dumb redskin. I saw your books in there. You're reading up on Indian history? Pa Gene wouldn't like that, would he? Well, like, it's *now* that you ought to be reading up on. You haven't read Stan Steiner's *New Indians*, have you? Or *We Talk, You Listen* by Vine Deloria. He's this groovy Sioux. But I'm going to stay out of all that."

"Why?"

"Well, I was into black civil rights. I demonstrated and marched and knocked my ass out of joint for them, see, but they didn't want any help from honky liberals. The Indians are the same. They've got this red power thing going. So I'm not going to waste my time on that. But you ought to get into it. They'd accept you, if you ever got over being such a whitenose."

"A what?"

"Whitenose. That's what the Indians call an Indian who goes white. Same as when the black folks say Uncle Tom."

"I've got enough problems of my own without getting wound up in Indian politics."

"Pa Gene didn't do right to raise us that way."

"Yes, he did," said Johnny, getting panicky and eager to end the conversation.

"Then cut off your braids."

Johnny hunched his shoulders at this truth. "My braids are just for show business," he lied.

"No, I'm kidding," she said. "Don't cut them off. They look real kinky. If you walked through the East Village with your hair loose, you'd get joyfully raped."

"Mighty hard to rape a wooden Indian," said Johnny, as he got up and threw the eggshells and empty corned beef tin into the garbage sack. He wondered if she knew he had peeked at her breasts, and if maybe she didn't mind.

"Did women run after you much?"

"I'll say. Especially after I was on that TV show back there. I was invited to a few society shindigs too."

"No shortage of pussy?"

Johnny actually felt himself blushing. Pa Gene had raised him and Tom very strictly in the matter of discussing things like this with women. "Not much. But it kind of made me sick. They were after my black hide and my world title, not my poor lonesome heart. To them I was like some kind of wild animal in a cage—you know, like the mountain lion in that free zoo on the road to Butte. I got mad and treated a couple of them pretty rough. And you know something? They *liked* that."

"Bored with white women, Johnny?"

"I'll say." He kept wondering at the avidity of her questioning. He was about to add that his great dream was to sleep with a full-blood Indian girl, but he didn't.

"Ever been in love?"

"No. I guess not. Unless you count all the blonde girls that I had crushes on in high school."

"I was in love a few times. But I'm kicking that love shit for a while too. Like, I'm on vacation from it. It's worse than speed. But just for a while, though. Love is when you don't know what else to do."

An earthquake bang snapped Johnny out of his sleep. He sat up, sure he was half insane, suddenly drenched with sweat and trembling. First he had to remember who he was. Then he saw the rectangle of the open cabin door, with grey light glowing in it like radium. The door kept bumping gently against the log wall as great gusts of chinook wind, snow-melting wind, came washing into the cabin. He had lain there sleeping and all the time the door had been open.

Fright slashed across him. He groped shakily for the pistol that hung in its holster from the brass bedpost by his head. Had he heard footsteps crunching on the snow while he was asleep, or had he only dreamed it? A prowler or an escaped convict must have jimmied the door open and was somewhere in the cabin. Without making a sound, shaking so hard that he was afraid he'd jerk off a shot involuntarily, he drew the pistol from the holster and slipped out from under the blankets and buffalo robe.

Standing there in his long johns, he looked around in the dark, then fumblingly lit the kerosene lamp by his bed. Peering into the kitchen, he nearly fired at a long black shadow there, then realized that it was thrown against the wall by the moonlight shining through the little window. Maybe the prowler was in with Kitie. Maybe he had knifed her and raped her while Johnny slept. Johnny parted the strings of beads and peered into Kitie's room. There, the same moonlight shone murkily through the dusty window onto her bed, where the blankets hung half down on the floor. The bed was empty. He was alone.

He stood with his mind gone blank for a moment. Then, cold as water pouring up from some dark subterranean spring, thoughts came to him again. Why had she gone out, leaving the door open like that? He padded back into his own room and, in the soothing yellow light of the kerosene lamp, he looked at the alarm clock. It was 2:30 in the morning. Maybe she was having insomnia and wanted to take a walk. Finally he decided that he'd better go out and look for her. If something happened to her out there, he would never hear the end of it from Tom. And Pa Gene's ghost would really set in on him then.

So he grabbed his Levis off the chair and pulled them on, then jerked his boots onto his bare feet without socks, and seized his sheepskin jacket. He ran out of the cabin without even bothering to tie back his loose hair, slipping the pistol into the jacket pocket.

The warm chinook wind came across those flats as if rolling up out of some abyss at the edge of the world. It moaned and whispered around the corrals, slammed against the cabin. Then it tore loose and slipped on, free again, like some tremendous mute monster. It resounded with distances, with migrations, with echoes of people talking far off, with skulls bleaching on the prairies. A ghastly moonlight bathed the great flats. The dots of cattle far off seemed remote and cruel—the cattle would not help him if anything went wrong tonight.

Johnny walked slowly, his hair blowing around him. He cast around near the cabin, trying to find her tracks in the wet snow. The chinook had already bared patches of dead grass and half-thawed earth. He had to keep pushing his hair out of his eyes and mouth with both hands. Finally he found her tracks—they led straight away across the open flats, due east. She was walking fast, and she was barefoot.

He broke into a trot and lined out along those tracks. Supposing she stepped in a patch of prickly pear with bare feet? And what was she doing without shoes anyway? Then it occurred to him that she must be having one of those afterflashes she talked about. She was starting out to see President Nixon again. At least he didn't see any other tracks following hers.

He trotted for nearly half an hour, panting heavily, sometimes walking to catch his breath. But he didn't stop, because he was really getting worried. In the moonlight her tracks kept going straight, printed dark into the slushy snow. Suddenly her stride lengthened— she apparently had started running herself. Was it from exhilaration or terror? He cast around for more tracks, but saw nothing, so kept trotting faster.

The wind cried "aaaaaaaaaaaaaahhhhhhhh" across the flat and "sssssssssshhhhh" up the gullies. At times he was sure he heard footsteps, or sagebrush crackling under the weight of a foot, and he stopped, hackles bristling, eyes straining. He thought he heard a crunch of feet on snow, thin, terrible feet stealing down from the arctic, an aurora borealis stalking the world, and a scream lost on the ice fields—a scream that no one had uttered and no one had heard. He wanted to shout her name, but he was afraid of attracting something's attention.

Then he was sure he heard something again. It came from over a little rise, in a little coulee beyond. He stood listening, suddenly shaking all over again, grasping the pistol in one pocket and the jackknife in the other. Slowly he followed her tracks up over the little rise. What he heard was a singing, crooning sound. At that moment he remembered every one of the Indian ghost stories he had ever read, especially of how Stands in Timber told of hearing the woman singing near the old graves on the reservation.

He came to the top of the rise and saw a thin, pale human figure. It was standing bent over some distance away, long hair blowing wide and pale in the moonlight like a negative image of his own hair. It looked very much like Kitie. He walked closer, and realized with a landslide of horror inside him, as if his whole stomach were sliding downhill, that she was naked there in the snow.

He walked up close. She had her back to him, still bent over, holding herself with her arms, her thighs pressed together. "Kitie," he said. She did not turn. He could see that she was shivering violently, her buttocks squeezed together—even in the moonlight he could make out the gooseflesh all over her skin. "Kitie," he said again, now about fifteen or twenty feet away. "It's me."

She turned, the wind blowing away from her face, as if she had heard him for the first time. As she held her chill-cramped arms across her breasts, she stared and stared at him with her black glittering eyes.

"Mr. President," she said.

"Kitie, for chrissake," he said and strode up to her.

She stumbled back from him a few steps, one hand flying to her mouth, and uttered a thin icy scream. As he tried to grab her, she screamed again, and still again, until he wondered what she saw. It occurred to him that maybe she was seeing what he always turned his eyes from. She stumbled again and fell backwards. As he bent over her, she screamed a fourth time. He fell on his knees beside her and tried to seize her arms. She gurgled and snarled, flailing at him with fists and feet.

He flared into anger then. It was an anger for battle blood, for striking sharp things into the chests of too-real enemies. He grabbed one of her wrists and hit her flat across the cheek, then hit her again. Her head snapped this way, then that. Her hair flared out on the night like a flash of light, her cheek going pale as phosphorescence with the imprint of his hand. He hit her still again and again, until her eyes rolled shut and her mouth went limp. A roar of hoofs cascaded through his head, light and shadows of legs and bellies flashing over him, like movies and history books all blurred together. Shots and dust lit the night more brightly than an oil refinery fire. Bodies thudded into the sagebrush, horses crashed down screaming. Runaway wagons bounced and blazed, trailing black smoke, then rolled off cut banks to smash on the sandbars below. Kneeling behind bushes and breastworks, Indians fired, then reloaded their rickety old rifles and fired again. Arrows quivered in blue-shirted backs. Black hands seized hair, circled the scalp with a knife point, then ripped the scalp away, leaving the top of the head looking like a peeled ripe tomato. He was riding, careening, firing again and again across his buckskin horse's neck. He rode straight in among the enemy, and his power was so great that bullets whined straight through him without touching hair or bone of him. He counted coups everywhere, insolently striking live enemies with his bare hand. And if they cornered him somewhere, he would not accept mercy from them. He would sign to them to come in and kill him if they could, the way Two Childs had done.

Kitie kneeled bent over in the snow, sobbing slowly, A string of saliva hung from her open mouth. He took off his belt and tied her arms behind her back, then jerked her to her feet. "Get on back now," he snapped. She staggered and moaned, her hair damp and curling with snow. "Get on. You're a prisoner."

He marched her back to cow camp. The wind blew their hair wildly. He marched her, hard, cold, and spent with virtue. The women prisoners wept as the warriors unfeelingly prodded them along. Their blonde braids or coifs were falling loose, and their gingham and lace dresses were ripped and smudged with soot. Wailing towheaded children clutched their mothers. The warriors did not even discuss what they would do with the prisoners. If they pleased, they might offer the women on the prairie, for the military societies to have a good time with. Or the women would make good slaves, to help their Indian wives pack water, tan hides, and cook. The children would be raised as Cheyennes, just as captured children of other tribes were raised as Cheyennes, for that was the way they did things: the right way, the Cheyenne way. When the girl-child captives grew up, they could even marry warriors—at least, that was the way things sometimes turned out.

When Johnny shoved her in the cabin door, he was already feeling sorry for her. Poor prisoner—her husband or father or brothers were lying back there among the charred wagons and the dead horses bristling with arrows. And to think that the Indians didn't even count white scalps! Her dead husband's scalp wasn't worth enough to offer at the Sacred Lodge where the Cheyennes kept their buffalo medicine. He would show her that the Indians knew how to show pity, that they didn't make war against women and children (as long as they didn't think too long about things like the Sand Creek massacre, when the soldiers roared with laughter as they knocked over fleeing Indian children with single shots, like rabbits, and cut off the women's private parts to adorn their hats and saddles). He would show her! After all, he could afford to be generous. He had done so many great things that he could walk up to any Cheyenne girl he pleased and talk to her even when her mother was around, and the mother would have to feel herself honored. He had done so many great things that the whole camp went silent when his name was mentioned.

"Get to bed," Johnny snapped, and shoved her through the kitchen into her bedroom. If she caught pneumonia, Tom would really sic Pa Gene's ghost on him. He pushed her into bed with her arms still trussed, then got the kerosene lamp and set it by her bed. She was lying doubled up, shaking and sobbing with cold, nothing visible but the mass of coppery hair and one mottled shoulder in the lamp's golden light. He wished that he had some whiskey to get down her, but of course Tom didn't allow him to have whiskey up there. So he stoked up the dying fire in the kitchen range and put a fresh pot of coffee on to boil.

Then he went back to her, flung his sheepskin jacket over a chair, and sat on the edge of her bed in just his Levis, naked to the waist. Reaching under the quilt, he undid the belt from her arms. "If you're not good, I'll hit you some more," he said softly. "You can't escape. The camp is guarded, and your folks are all dead."

She turned her face to him, blinking, a strand of wavy hair caught between her lips. "Please listen, Mr. President," she said.

He pulled her feet out from under the blankets and tried to chafe warmth into them—they were bone white and snow cold. He stroked her slender pale legs, which lay heavy as mastodon bones in his hands. All the time his penis was hurting inside his Levis. After a while he was shaking as much as she was, only not from cold. When the coffee boiled, he fumblingly tried to force some between her lips, and a few drops spilled onto her mottled breasts with their tight purple nipples. He brushed the drops away, then touched her breasts. After all, he had done a lot of fine things, and she was his prisoner. Nobody was going to ask him what he did with her. She was outside the Suhtai law, outside the blood and gentleness that he could call his own if he ever decided to.

So he pulled off his Levis and boots and slid in with her naked, trying with sudden desperation to warm her with his own body. If he couldn't warm her, she would die. He would have to cover her body with rocks and travel on. Someday his migrations would bring him back to that spot. He would find the rocks scattered and her skull bleaching among them. Sadly he would turn over the skull with his foot and remember what a fine-looking prisoner she had been.

"Kitie, you have to get warm," he kept whispering. He held her half-frozen hands in his armpits and drew her chill-cramped feet between his thighs, the two hottest parts of him. She kept talking about presenting her list of nonnegotiable demands to the president. He learned how this stranger from another country felt to his hands. Her tight nipples softened against his own fire-scorched breast. He rubbed her all over, trying to squeeze his heat into her, willing that his own blood might freeze to red crystals so that hers could thaw hot. She kept muttering, embracing him awkwardly, saying, "Oh, yes, Mr. President." Her frozen thighs opened like a lead through northern ice in warm weather. Even her lips down there felt stiff as he drove up into her frosted entrails the sun-heated blade of his secret war.

"You don't dare run off again, or I'll have to kill you," he whispered barely aloud as he looked down into her face. The old brass bed jerked and clanked under them. In the lamp light, her tangled hair, wiry as copper filament, spread across the pillow. She looked up at him steadily, and her pupils gaped dark as the shafts of abandoned mines. Her lips were suffused with pink again, and a little parted. He didn't kiss them, though. He guessed that Indians kissed, but he didn't feel like kissing a prisoner.

The morning light drifted in through the dusty, rain-spattered old glass. The light almost had a sound to it, like a moan coming from over the top of some hill—the moan of someone lying wounded and abandoned there. Rainbow whorl imperfections from the old glass reflected across their naked bodies as they lay there among the twisted army blankets. The buffalo robe hung halfway down to the floor. Kitie idly traced the whorls on Johnny's torso. It occurred to him that his body was dark, old and polished like a dead tree where the cattle always rubbed.

"I made it with a lot of black cats," Kitie said, "but you're the first red cat I ever made it with."

"I bet red cats were mighty scarce in San Francisco, Chicago, New York, and Washington," said Johnny. He found that his ears were straining to hear Tom's truck coming, though the clock said 7 A.M. and Tom would still be busy with chores down at the ranch. Tom never came up to camp this early. He imagined how Tom would open the cabin door and surprise the two of them like that.

"Do chicks run after you?"

"Not around here much. They did some when I was competing. Even then I had to be careful. Like, the other fellows didn't need to get the idea that I was too successful with their women. Even Tom got jealous sometimes. Only guy that never got jealous was Jimmy Alderman. We used to have a great old time."

"You made it with a lot of white chicks?"

"Never did keep track. They'd come sniffing around, you know. Less trouble that way. I didn't have to go out looking."

"You like making it with white chicks?" Kitie persisted.

Johnny snorted. "My dream is making it with a full-blood girl."

"But you never get around to it," said Kitie. Johnny stirred restlessly and didn't answer. "It's what I told you. You've been brainwashed, like those black dudes who don't know nothing but white girls. They've had our great American ideal of Miss America blonde boobs wired into their brains." Johnny shrugged. "If you were a man, you'd kick me out of this bed and go back to the Tongue River and screw somebody."

"You talk too damn much," said Johnny, turning over. Kitie changed position too, to stay lying against him. Their hair—his dark and stiff as horsehair, hers soft and coppery as metal silk—was tangled between them.

"Actually, I'm kicking this sex shit," said Kitie. "I was this huge computer, see. They wired me up to India and Sweden and Woodstock, and they fed all this data about sex into me. They were trying to find out something. But they fed in so much data that I blew my fuse, and they lost all their fucking data. They'll never get it back, either."

"So you're going to computerize Cottonwood."

"Like, they thought that if only they could be naked, they'd be free. But to be really naked, you have to be free already."

"I guess we better rise and shine," said Johnny, "before Tom comes around."

"And you," said Kitie in her singsong voice, "are wired into the computer's ass. You're the original cybernetic wooden Indian."

Sitting up on the edge of the bed, Johnny leaned back a little and grabbed her nose ring. They looked at each other for a minute, and Kitie got a little pale. Johnny let go the nose ring.

"I'm not in love with you anyhow," she said.

"I don't want no loving," said Johnny, getting up, his bare feet flinching from the cold boards. He quickly pulled on his long underwear, then jerked open the grilled door of the stove and thrust some kindling onto the last sad pink coals. "I just want a nice quiet piece once a week. If you want more than that, then you'd better move back down to the ranch."

She sat there, knees drawn up to her breasts, and traced the whorls in the old pioneer glass of the windowpanes. "You'll get what you give," she said softly.

"I give what I feel like giving," he snapped, straightening up with a piece of kindling in his hand, feeling like hitting her with it. He took what she said to be a comment on his lovemaking abilities. He guessed that he made love the way he dug postholes.

Kitie moved her shoulders softly and tiredly, in a movement that wasn't quite a shrug. "Okay. I'll be your old lady," she said.

Johnny could feel Tom's and Ma Maureen's anger as the Chances drove the great herd of steers along the county road toward Cottonwood. A light March snow was stinging down over the brown backs. The distant mountains were blotted out, and the nearer buttes loomed spookily through the falling snow. The snow came dragging like travois, along its deep-worn trail. The gentle people crossed the desert, filtered through the jungle, gazed on the Andes. Pyramids, snarling with stone animal faces, heaved up above the treetops, then crumbled under green vines. Pueblos rose on the mesas like desert reefs raised by human polyps, yet already they were empty, strewn with shards of painted pottery, and the winds sang over them. Already, on the northern plains, the scant traces of nomad life—charred traces of camp-

fires, circles of teepee stones, buffalo falls, eagle pits, tumbled breastworks where battles had been fought, burials under sandstone ledges—
were blown over by dust. Johnny saw all these things in his mind as he
absentmindedly watched Tom and Ma Maureen galloping ahead in
order to reach Route 10 before the cattle did, so that they could
point the herd across into town and keep them from scattering along
the highway.

Johnny and the four girls brought up the drag, whistling the herd
along, squinting into the snow, flicking at backs with their rope ends
or quirts. The steers were hard to drive because they didn't know the
way. They had been driven up to cow camp for the first time in their
lives last summer, and now they were leaving it, headed for the
shipping trucks, then a megalopolis of feedlots somewhere in the Mid-
west, and finally massacre on the concrete floor of some slaughterhouse. The steers eddied every which way, their breath rolling up like
steam from a valley of hot springs. They bawled, foamy muzzles
thrust up at the hissing sky, as if in protest at being made so functional. They made Johnny think whole newsreels of thoughts about
the Cherokees being herded to Oklahoma and the Apaches being
loaded into boxcars for shipping to Florida and the Northern Cheyennes being pushed and prodded toward the open-air slaughterhouse
of the damp south country, where malaria stunned them like so many
beeves.

He flicked his rope end savagely at the steers' tails, knowing that,
sooner or later that day, Tom and Ma Maureen were going to start
lecturing him about buying Spades and hitting the circuit again. Tom
was selling the steers in desperation, for just a small profit. The
market had rallied a little, but now it was peaking off again. Hay was
scarce—it had been a dry year everywhere in the state, crops had
been short, hay was expensive and their own stored hay was running
out. If they expected to hold back enough hay to finish wintering
their cow herd and their horses, they had to sell. The banker had
put his solemn imprimatur on the sale, but the banker was a Butte
man and knew even less about the holy mysteries of the cow market
than Tom did. Tom and Ma Maureen had been angry about it for
days now, and the fact that the steers were staging what Kitie called
a "bawl-in" was making them even angrier. Tom was still a saber-
toothed brute and hadn't evolved yet into the uses of patience. Ma
Maureen had evolved somewhat beyond such uses.

Johnny saw Kitie inexpertly pushing the drag steers too hard, and he snapped, "Don't push them." But he let his eye insinuate a grim wink.

"Plastic wooden Indian," Kitie snapped back, playing the scene to perfection. They kept up their quarreling in public as a cover. Every day now Johnny's fear of Tom's stumbling upon their sleeping together was rammed deeper into his flesh, like a splintered plank as a bronc broke you through the arena fence. Johnny worried about Tom's discovering their secret even more than he worried about returning to the arena, or about ghosts.

Kitie looked dude pretty on Son of a Bitch, wearing her New York-bought leather jacket with the longest, most impractical fringe Johnny had ever seen or imagined. Her bell-bottoms hung over riding boots borrowed from Fern. Son of a Bitch plodded along, being his mediocre, pedigreed AQHBA self, and Kitie wallowed gracefully in the saddle like a tourist riding down into Grand Canyon.

"Kitie, you say such awful things to Johnny," said Fern with awe, turning her horse over toward them. Ruby ignored them uncertainly. Pat was over on the far side of the drag, whooping and whistling with professional straightfacedness. It was the first time the whole family had been together since Kitie had been banished to cow camp.

"Fern!" shouted Pat. "Mind your p's and q's there, or they'll scatter back up the road!" Meekly Fern obeyed and turned away.

Kitie kept inadvertently crowding the drag steers, until finally Pat came trotting over, glowering under her snow-dusted hat brim, dark lower lip stuck out, gloved hand gripping her quirt. "Quit pushing them, you hippy chippy."

Kitie reined Son of a Bitch around to face Pat with queenly cheerfulness. "Quit living, you plastic shit."

In an instant Johnny realized that Kitie had made a big mistake to turn her horse around, and he felt in his marrow what Pat was going to do even before she did it. Grinning with all her big even white teeth, Pat brought her quirt cracking down across Son of a Bitch's snowy rump. The horse's muscles jerked with fright, then catapulted him away up the road. Jolted half out of the saddle, Kitie screamed a kite-nosediving-into-a-pasture scream, dropped one rein, and grabbed the saddle horn.

Johnny jerked his horse around to gallop after her. But then he saw that Son of a Bitch, always lazy, was already slowing down because he was heading away from the home ranch. Kitie was hauling herself back into the saddle. She grabbed the rein she'd dropped and came circling back.

From ahead, Johnny heard a furious shouting through the bawls of the cattle. Tom and Ma Maureen were sitting their horses at the edge of the highway, looking back and waving their arms. Apparently they'd seen the Kitie-Pat incident, and they'd scold even more later on.

Then Tom rode out across the new four-lane highway. The cleated shoes of his horse—Pa Gene's great sorrel roping horse, Sundown—rang noisily on the concrete. Taking off his hat, Tom planted Sundown right in the middle of the southbound lane and began waving his hat slowly back and forth to stop the approaching cars and trucks. Snow sifted down, ignored, into his hair. On the other side of the crossing, Ma Maureen halted her bay mare and started flagging her hat at northbound cars.

This was a ritual that they repeated two or three times a year, every time they drove cattle between the home ranch and cow camp. When Route 10 had come slashing up through the valley, it had ended four generations of unobstructed Chance cattle driving. It also cut off old Pinter Brodie, who had his own cow camp up there. Other ranchers up and down the valley found their activities similarly disrupted. So they all had a confrontation with the highway people and demanded a total of six cattle passes. The highway people compromised by building three, none of them located where the Chances and Brodie had to cross. So both outfits, two or three times a year, grimly took revenge on the U.S. interstate defense-highway system by driving their big herds right up across the expressway, taking their time and stopping as much traffic as they could.

Kitie came trotting up, boucing hopelessly in the saddle. She glared at Pat. "If I was a juice head," she said, "I'd float your black little heart in my martini instead of an olive."

"I prefer whiskey myself," said Pat, "so I'll use your little heart for an icecube."

Johnny smiled to himself a little—he knew that Ma Maureen and Tom didn't allow Pat to drink anything stronger than soda pop.

"Tom will use you both for target practice," said Ruby, "if you don't quit fighting."

The steers streamed up the expressway ramp with a rolling clatter of hoofs on asphalt. Tom and Ma Maureen were still waving their hats, and a couple dozen cars were already backed up on either side. (It was funnier in summer, when the tourists came through. Sometimes the tourists got out and took snapshots of what they thought was the real West.) A Volkswagen with a California license blew its horn impatiently, and the driver leaned out and shouted something at Tom. But Tom simply swung Sundown around so that the horse's big blonde butt faced square into the driver's face. The steers poured across the highway. Ma Maureen headed off a few steers that started up the northbound lane toward Helena. Her bay mare skidded on the snowy asphalt with a shriek of metal shoes, then hauled herself together, eyes rolling wildly.

Still the cattle poured and flowed across, a dizzying mass of legs and hoofs, a boiling of brown backs. Their innocent, stupefied eyes rolled under their curly white brows. They piled against each other, muzzles heaping up, like pack ice. The ice was going out, groaning and cracking, breaking up into great grinding floes. Polar bears stalked along the floes with sinister white grace. Wide leads of black water opened up. The gentle people with their pack dogs and their travois had gone safely over. They were safe on the other side, Asia behind them, America before, with ten thousand miles of open tundra, plain, and desert before them. They felt safe, not knowing what awaited them. Spring blew in the air, even there in the Arctic. It would be hundreds of years yet before they saw their first buffalo or their first horse.

The Volkswagen driver kept honking and cursing at Tom. "Hey," he shouted, "who do you think you are? Hey! Hey!" Finally he stepped on the gas and started inching the car forward toward Sundown's legs. Sundown felt the car coming, and he tensed up and started jigging around.

"Well," said Pat to Kitie, "now that the steers are sold, I guess we'll be having the pleasure of your company at home again."

"You're weird," Kitie told her. "You're a sadist dyke in a six-gun hat."

"What's a dyke?" asked Fern.

"You dummy," said Ruby, "that's what the Dutch boy put his finger in." At this Kitie gave a yelp of laughter.

"Shut up now and get to work," Johnny told them all. "If these steers stampede and run off a pound each, we'll have to hock Ma Maureen's dishwasher."

The Volkswagen's bumper touched Sundown's hind legs, and the horse shuddered. Johnny could tell by the humping of Tom's shoulders that Tom was furious now. "Hey! Hey!" the driver kept shouting, grinning fiendishly as he leaned out the window.

"What's happening up there?" said Kitie.

"Oh," said Johnny, "Tom's having a little trouble being a traffic cop." He wondered if Sundown would kick the headlights out. "That's a mighty little car to be taking on that great big steer-jerking son of a bitch."

They watched Tom, raging, spur Sundown forward a few paces and take a fresh stand. He apparently was afraid that the car would hurt his horse's legs. But the Volkswagen driver crept insolently forward till his bumper again nosed against Sundown's hocks. Car and horse were near the cattle now, who scattered away from them. Johnny could see that if the arrogant little VW tried to drive through the herd, the steers would scatter all over the county. He started stiffening with anger himself. If the herd hadn't blocked his way, he would have ridden up there to help Tom somehow.

Then he saw Tom move with the sudden speed of those huge meat-eating lizards who once stalked around on their hind legs. Tom took down his rope, shook out a quick loop, and spurred Sundown ahead again a few steps, but at an angle. Then he leaned back and neatly dropped the loop around the Volkswagen's bumper. Before the driver could even shout one last "Hey!" Tom rode Sundown hard off to the right and jerked the little car around so that it was perched on the shoulder, facing down the embankment into a deep ditch full of snow and dead thistles. All the drivers of the backed-up cars and trucks were leaning out their windows, mouths open.

The VW driver opened the door and got out, shouting a variety of U.S. choice obscenities. His wife had her hands over her eyes, and two children cowered in the back seat among comic books and boxes of Kleenex. Tom just sat there grinning evilly on Sundown, who was busy keeping the slack rope tight, the way he would in the arena.

"If you don't talk nice to me," Tom said to the VW driver in his quietest, most lilting voice, "I'll just drag this little tuna-fish can of yours over to the town dump."

"You motherfucking drugstore cowboy," shouted the driver, "you're obstructing a public highway. You're infringing my civil rights to travel."

Still the cattle kept streaming across the highway, a frantic backdrop to the antic tableau of Tom and the Volkswagen. Kitie bent over her saddle horn, laughing so hard that tears melted the snow stuck to her eyelashes. Pat, Johnny, and Ruby all had the proper little smiles.

Tom hit Sundown with the spurs again and jerked the Volkswagen farther around, so that it faced back in the direction it had come from. "As one motherfucker to another," he called back over his shoulder, "I invite you to exercise your civil rights to the fullest extent and go back to California."

"I'm driving straight into this town and have you arrested," howled the driver.

"You do that," said Tom. "You'll get arrested for molesting my livestock."

The herd was nearly across the highway now. The drag was coming up the ramp, Johnny and the girls fanning out down the embankments to keep the steers in a bunch. Johnny wondered how Tom was going to get his good broken-in manila rope off that bumper without giving up the advantage of being safe on the horse. Then he saw Tom climb coolly down off Sundown and walk toward the little car with that rolling gorilla gait of his. Sundown stood braced, holding the rope as tight as if it were a big Mexican steer he had down there. The driver stood hunched and furious beside the car's open door. His wife was pleading, "Joe, please don't fight. Please don't."

As Tom's hulk approached, his shadow falling across the car's hood like some movie monster's, the driver hesitated, his eyes telegraphing a flurry of punches that his mind held back. Then as Tom, grinning cheerfully, bent to loosen the rope from the bumper, the driver's shoulders slumped. Tom turned his back scornfully on the man as he walked back to Sundown, coiling the rope.

The last of the steers clattered across the highway. Pat galloped off to head back ten or fifteen head that had plunged off the townside embankment beyond Tom. Johnny, Kitie, and Fern came clattering by on the tail of the last steers. The driver of the Volkswagen looked hopelessly at this arrogant display of regionalism. For a moment, it occurred to Johnny that they must all look wild and incomprehensible as they loomed up out of the snow and crossed that familiar highway like phantoms out of the past, their hat brims pulled low, collars turned up, their horses' manes windblown and tattered looking.

"Hollywood cowboys," shouted the driver after them, and raised his middle finger.

They glanced scornfully at him, Kitie raising her finger in return, and rattled on by. Tom stepped up on Sundown and rode off too. Ma Maureen clamped her hat back on her snow-whitened bun and vacated her position on the highway. The long lines of cars and trucks moved again, some gasping their engines to life. As the Chances followed the drag down the exit ramp toward Alfalfaville, Johnny glanced back and saw that the VW driver was having to wait until all the southbound traffic passed before he could turn his car around. Johnny was interested to observe himself feeling pity for this victim of Tom's.

As they maneuvered the herd along a street that skirted Alfalfaville and led toward the fairgrounds, Johnny rode along swatting steer tails with his rope end and wondering about what Tom had done. Was it a real act, unthinking and primitive as the sun dance? Or was it some centennial celebration that was playing itself out, with brass bands and clouds of dust, in the arena of his adopted brother's mind? He wondered what people were like when they were alone, with no need to parade. He had no idea if he was like other people, because he knew that he went on parading when he was alone, even when he was asleep, above all when he slept with Kitie. "Cut that prisoner crap and kiss me," she would always cry. They quarreled about kissing all the time—every night she tried to trick him into normalcy, or at least into some new movie. Shaking into sullenness, he would avoid her for two or three days. But when the shortage pained him, he would rage at her, slap her around, make menacing grabs at her nose ring, tie her to the clinking brass bed, and put on his own centennial pageant of what he wistfully wished was rape. Their blood was already mixed in her. Her head wrenched and flailed under his, that coarse coppery hair stuck to her fiery cheeks, those hazel eyes rolling unseeingly. Her eyes had green irises sifted through with dark flakes, as if with chips from an obsidian arrowhead thrown away somewhere when half-finished. Kitie Chance, great-granddaughter of a squaw man.

Their conversations echoed in his mind like ghost footfalls in an empty cabin. "Kitie, don't forget to take your pill." "Don't worry, I never forget it. Do you think I want to have a baby by a wooden Indian?" "Where do you get the pills? At the drugstore in town, they'd know. . . ." "Listen, baby, I brought a year's supply of pills back from New York. And if you aren't good, I'll stop taking them, and when I get pregnant you'll have to marry me." "If you do that, I'll extricate that nose ring of yours." "There's no reason why we couldn't get married." "How? You're my sister."

A few steers broke away from the herd and stampeded across one of the largest lawns in Alfalfaville, through a karaghana hedge, and finally through a clothesline of frozen sheets and towels. Tom spurred

Sundown along the driveway leading past the house, and across the backyard. The housewife leaned out the window and wailed a lament for her laundry and hedge, her hair done up in puritanical pincurls with an old red scarf tied around her head. Churning around in the back yard, Sundown finally flushed the steers out from back of the garage. Leaving a trail of spattered smoking manure, the steers charged back through the laundry and the hedge a second time, finally into the street again, where they plunged into the herd.

They went on fighting the steers past the fairgrounds, out onto the old highway. "Actually, we did her a favor," said Tom. "The cleats on Sundown's shoes aerated her lawn for her, and those steers put down some good organic fertilizer."

"Maybe we'd make more money in the nursery business," said Ma Maureen bitterly.

"You're talking like a bunch of Chinese warlords," said Kitie.

"You shut up," Pat told Kitie. "Who asked you?"

"If Johnny was roping now, he could have roped those steers out of there," said Tom.

"If Johnny had Ace of Spades," said Ma Maureen, "we wouldn't have to sell these steers at all. We could wait till the market went up."

"If I ever buy Spades," Johnny snapped, "it'll be to get away from your nagging."

"Nagging?" cried Ma Maureen, riding alongside Johnny. Her lined, florid face was still handsome under her hat brim. Her broad back and buttocks, looking broader still in a red-and-black-checked wool jacket, moved with heavy grace as her horse walked along. She looked like Calamity Jane painted by Rubens. "It's for your own good, child. You're no good like this. You really want to rodeo again, only you don't know it."

"I know what I want," he said.

"A mother knows what her children want."

"You're not my mother," said Johnny, glaring straight ahead at the manure-plastered rumps of the steers.

"Well!" said Ma Maureen. She did her one-minute pageant of playing the offended, sacrificing pioneer woman with rifle at her shoulder, standing at the door of her sod house.

"Johnny, you shut up now," said Tom. "You're being disrespect-ful."

Johnny jerked his horse away to head off a couple of steers who detoured off among the empty, snow-drifted racehorse barns.

Finally they strung the herd along one side of the old two-lane highway, now little traveled save by vehicles coming in from ranches or communities up on the northwest corner of the valley. The road was all potholed now, and the center stripe almost washed off, as the state highway department didn't look after it any more. A car with a Butte license passed them slowly, the family staring out at them with grave curiosity. Johnny wondered again how they all looked to outsiders: the Chances, one of the best-known rodeo dynasties in the country, with their busyness, their quarrels, and their cheerful cruelties, all as stylized and flowery as the handstamping on a good saddle. He wished that he could fade himself through a photograph of the Chance family, so that he could be somebody looking at them.

He wished that he could be in some huge crowded grandstand, to watch the Chances perform one by one, in some terrible floodlit arena at night, with the dust hanging golden in the floodlights and the threat of dew already dampening the programs and the chute gates. He would have liked to sit up there in the stands and watch a younger, slimmer Ma Maureen ride a bronc (her stirrups tied down, of course). He would watch Tom rope a calf or two, and hope that he would know nothing at all about roping, so that he could judge Tom as pure spectacle. Pa Gene would rope a calf too, because Pa Gene would be uncomfortably undead. Pat would gallop her horse around the barrels in the girls' barrel race. Between events somewhere, Fern and Ruby would put on their trick-riding act. Fern would race her white horse along before the smoky, applauding crowd, light and poised on the saddle in a Roman stand, her hands held out to the people in a sweet gesture assuring them they didn't need to tell her who she was. Kitie would be perched on the arena fence in her chloroxed bell-bottoms, mocking them and envying them.

Maybe, Johnny thought, if he tried hard enough, he could see himself roping a calf off Rattler in a great cloud of golden dust. Maybe if he could see them all, including himself, as a stranger would, he would be able to know them. Perhaps when the Cottonwood centennial finally came round this summer, he would finally know them once and for all.

One June afternoon Johnny and Kitie were riding around counting the cattle. Tom had moved one of the big cow herds up there from the Haley Ranch, where they had wintered on the hay pastures. So

Johnny had to keep the cows and calves counted carefully and check the water.

As they rode, the cool wind thrummed his hat brim, and he could smell the wild roses in bloom. The cottonwoods were in full fresh leaf, their long catkins loosing the cotton that blew off like a gentle snow squall, drifting in the grass. The cows' white briskets were tinted healthy gold from the carotene in the new grass. In the old days, it would have been buffalo looking fat, not whiteface cows, and it would have been time for the Suhtai to think of having a sun dance. Nowadays, he had read, they celebrated it on the Fourth of July, with an American flag flying near the medicine lodge. As he looked around at the green hills (by July they would be burnt tan), he felt two feelings at once: a senseless happiness and an even more senseless nostalgia for things he couldn't remember.

They rode blissfully down into the moist bottom of Skillet Creek. As they rounded a graceful little grove of aspen, Kitie gave a shriek and stopped her horse. They were standing at the edge of a whole meadow of shooting stars in bloom. The delicate cyclamen blooms bobbed and waved on their long wiry stems as gusts of wind played through them.

"Oh wow," said Kitie, "there's a million of them. What are they?" She got down off her horse.

"Shooting stars," said Johnny, dismounting too.

Kitie kneeled and put her face down into them. "Let's not pick any," she said. "Let's not damage the environment. Wow, wow, there are flowers everywhere. What are those blue things?"

They walked slowly, arms around each other, leading the horses. Johnny was wishing that she was the Buffalo Woman and imagined for a moment that he was in love with her. Kitie was pointing at a patch of blue flowers in starlike sprays that blew gently in the fluttering shadows of the aspens.

"That's camas," said Johnny. "The Indians used to dig the roots and eat them. They had to be careful about cooking them, though—the stuff's poisonous."

They let the horses graze and sat down in the grass. "I don't think I'd better go to Alaska," Kitie said. "I think I'd better stay here. I mean, let's get married, Johnny. We'll have the last flower wedding, and we'll start a commune at cow camp, and we'll rebuild the country from the ground up. Maybe the only really effective revo-

lution is to ignore all that shit out there." She pulled off her shirt and
bent over, bathing her breasts among the shooting stars.

"I doubt Cottonwood would appreciate the idea of a flower wedding," said Johnny dryly. "I can just see it all written up on the
society page of the *Post*. They'd even let the prisoners out of the pen
to help lynch us."

"Johnny, sometimes I don't think you love me at all." Kitie sat
pouting, her jeans already unbuttoned down to the crotch, and the
wispy shadow of her hair playing over her shoulders and breasts as
the wind tossed her mane about.

"Who said anything about love?" said Johnny. "I sure didn't.
You're a big girl now anyway. Time to quit playing with dolls." His
mind was moving off into the sun dance—he could smell sagebrush
incense, hear the shrill blowing of the whistles made from eagle wing-
bones and the dancing moccasins tramping on the dust.

"But I'm in love with you, and you never even kiss me. Like, I
got so bored with the Kama Sutra, and I never thought I'd die for a
kiss." She lay looking up at him, her hair blowing out among the
shooting stars. The flowers pressed out, crushed, around her head like
a halo. She raised her hips a little to let him pull off her jeans.

"We've got to be real careful," said Johnny, as he unbuttoned
his own jeans. He looked around, but couldn't see a sign of a human
being anywhere. Sometimes old Pinter Brodie cut down through there,
riding home from his own cow camp. "I've got this feeling somebody
is watching us through a pair of high-powered binoculars, and he's
writing everything we do in a little black tally book." He bent over
her, pulled a single shooting star and teased her nipples with it.

"Now you've gone and wrecked the environment," she said.

"Think of all the flowers you're lying on and mashing," he said.

She giggled, pulled another shooting star and started tickling his
penis with it. He wondered what she would look like if she were all
painted for the sun dance. He had seen photographs taken during the
modern sun dance—those Northern Cheyennes really covered that poor
Buffalo Woman with paint. It would be sticky business making love
to her. For the first time, with all that cottonwood freshness around
and the eagle whistles shrilling in his ears, he was able to put his face
down to Kitie's face and sift over it with his lips, like an archeologist
sifting for beads and bits of leather under some sandstone ledge somewhere. Finally he kissed her on the mouth—her nose ring kept getting
in the way, and of course he could taste the paint on her face. Kitie

said "Mmm," and kissed him back. Her mouth tasted of sagebrush and as he penetrated her, a shrilling sound seemed to come from their very bodies, as if their bones were hollowed eagle wing-bones in the mouths of the painted dancers. For a moment he wanted to curse Kitie for being so real, but he kept kissing her the whole time, with that tenderness of spicy new cottonwood leaves and chokecherry in bloom.

Afterwards, as they drowsily pulled on their clothes, Kitie said, "Johnny, I really want to marry you. Like, I have this feeling that I'd like to have a baby and plant a garden somewhere."

He shook his head with slow, newly budded out happiness. "We haven't got much longer. One of these days I'm going to have to make up my mind about rodeoing again. Anyway, it's against the law, marrying you."

"And you kissed me so nicely, you red-ass creep." She sat up, buttoning her shirt, smiling vaguely at the shooting stars that still swayed around them. A few crushed and faded blooms were stuck in her hair. "And I'd probably be a lousy mother and a lousy gardener, the way I was a lousy politician and a lousy head."

They caught their horses and rode on. Every once in a while Johnny felt obliged to reach over and stroke her arm. He wondered what had come over him. "It must be the way the grass looks," he thought.

As they rode along a slope below a lunar-looking hogsback, Johnny noticed a large bird sitting in the browse some distance away, near a patch of dog rose in bloom. "Looks like an eagle," he told Kitie, "but it's too small." He had already turned his head away and was riding on, when some impulse made him look back. The bird opened its wings and was flapping as if unable to leave the ground. It was an eagle—a young one, not quite full-grown.

Feeling a gust of excitement across his skin, like the wind blasting little ripples across a creek, Johnny turned his horse in that direction, wondering how close he would be able to get, wondering if the eagle were sick or injured. Kitie followed, asking, "What is it?"

When they rode up to about a hundred feet off, the eagle leaped and flapped madly again. Now Johnny could see that the eagle was all right—it just had a huge fat woodchuck there on the ground and was trying to fly off with it, but the chuck was too heavy. The chuck's velvet-brown fur had the same live burnish as the dog-rose wood, and had come into purple bloom with blood. The eagle stood on the chuck with its talons sunk in the wet fur.

"Euuuch," said Kitie. "The poor woodchuck."

"He must have been real dumb," said Johnny. "Anyway, it's an honor to be et by eagles. You stay here now. I want to see how close up I can get."

"I want to see too."

"You stay here or I'll liberate your nose ring."

Johnny urged Son of a Bitch gently forward. The horse's bulging eyes were fixed on the eagle, and his ears strained forward. The eagle flapped again, his wings beating the air like copter blades and actually stirring the new grass all around, like the wash from a copter taking off. He lifted the woodchuck a few inches off the ground, then had to drop back. Now Johnny could see that the chuck was still alive—its paws moved feebly, its eyes glittered, and its mouth opened, displaying the bloody teeth.

As Johnny came to within fifty feet, the eagle just crouched down there on its prey, taking the defensive. It spread its wings slightly, letting them droop over the ground, and its stuck its neck way out, opening its cruel yellow beak and glaring at Johnny. Son of a Bitch gave a long rattling snort and stopped dead. Johnny felt the horse trembling, but he spurred him still closer. That thrill of awe and reverence hummed all through him now, like the electricity through the high-tension power line that ran along the hills below. He wondered if the old Indian eagle catchers had felt like that. His thoughts cascaded back into the past again, and he was a Suhtai eagle catcher crouching in the pit where generations of Cheyennes had crouched, waiting under the foliage-camouflaged sticks for the eagle to stoop and take the bait.

He rode up to within twenty-five feet and sat there marveling at the young bird's tenacity. The eagle just crouched there unmoving, beak opened wide. All he needed was a bunch of arrows in one yellow fist to look just like the American emblem. Johnny thought to himself that maybe the poor eagle couldn't get off the ground because he was so full of DDT.

"You're not much, are you?" he said softly to the eagle. "Just a snot-nosed orphan, aren't you?"

Then it occurred to Johnny that, if he could catch the bird, it might be young enough to tame. If not, he could just keep the bird around to look at, in a big cage or something. He found that he had no desire to kill the bird to please Tom, and he certainly had no need to spoil its adolescent magnificence by robbing it of its tailfeathers.

But if he could rope the bird, he might be able to capture it unhurt. All he had to do was stay out of reach of those talons.

So, without thinking things through any further, he reached for the rope hanging by his pommel—that rope that he hadn't touched since he stopped competing a year ago. He unbuckled the strap that carried it, quickly hefted it, and built a small, professional loop. It would have to be a slightly wider loop than usual, to make sure that it fell cleanly over those opened, drooping wings.

Then he gathered Son of a Bitch up, swung the loop a few times (he was so out of practice that it felt strange), and then threw it. For a moment, as the loop snaked out through the air, he was afraid that he would miss. But the honda struck the eagle square on the shoulder, flipping the loop neatly over one wing and under the other. He quickly jerked the slack to tighten the loop firmly around the bird's body and dallied the other end of the rope around the saddle horn.

The eagle gave a scream like a woman. It loosed the dying wood-chuck and beat into the air to fly off. But of course it hit the end of the rope and bounced. At that, screaming even louder, it wheeled back. The next thing Johnny knew, the eagle was on top of him and he was wishing he had never been born to dream of eagles.

He had only a split second to duck in the saddle, one arm shielding his eyes from those sacred talons. He dropped the rope and felt Son of a Bitch jerk under him like a freight train being humped. Then the horse wheeled and bolted off with classic Quarter-Horse speed. John tried to haul Son of a Bitch to a stop, but then he had to drop the reins and defend himself with both arms, because the eagle was pounding him and beating him with wings and talons and beak. Then the eagle flew off, only to hit the end of the rope again and attack them again as they careened along.

Next Johnny lost his hat and tried to shield the back of his neck with one arm. The flailing wings dizzied him. He felt the talons tearing his shirt, raking his shoulder blades and ribs. Son of a Bitch gave a terrified blat, dumped his head between his knees, and, good Quarter Horse though he was, started bucking like a mustang colt. Johnny grabbed the saddle horn, because he didn't want to fall and get hung up in the rope and maybe get dragged and mutilated. Then he had to let go the horn, because the eagle was beating him up a third time. He could smell the ripe carrion odor of the bird, glimpse its bloody claws. Son of a Bitch was doing a veteran bronc's type of bucking—first he lined out, throwing his hind heels high. Then, driven steadily crazier by the eagle, he went to spinning and hitting on all fours, coughing up a gutty blat at every jump. Blindly Johnny fumbled to loose his dally from the horn, but he felt himself coming loose. The sweet June sunlight shone between his pants and the saddle. He felt himself lose one stirrup, then the other. After all, his heart had never been in stomping broncs.

His last thought, as he was jolted off into air, was to fall on the left side instead of the right, where the coils of rope were trailing. Then he slammed into the dust as hard as he ever had in the arena and rolled.

He sat up dizzily, gasping for breath. He was sitting in a huge patch of bitterroots in bloom, the pink, rose, and white petals fluttering in the wind. Many of the bitterroots were crushed by S.O.B.'s hoofs. Nothing was left of Johnny's shirt but the collar and cuffs and the strip of buttons down the front—the rest was bloody ribbons. Dazedly he noted rose-red beads of blood growing on his chest, the way the bitterroot buds must have looked when they pushed up through the earth. Son of a Bitch and the eagle were still performing their act some ways off. Again and again the eagle would try to flee, then ricochet back and work the horse over again. Watching it, Johnny burst into hysterical laughter, still sitting there in the bitterroots. An emotion was pushing up in him that was stronger than any he'd felt for a long time. It burst his veins like the red bittersweet sap that made cottonwood buds sticky to the touch. It roared in his ears like a dry creek bed suddenly bank-full with melting snow.

Finally Son of a Bitch bucked himself out and just galloped away. The eagle had to go with him, alternately flying, dragging, screaming, and flapping. They disappeared over the next rise beyond the hogsback.

Kitie trotted up and jumped off her horse. "Are you all right?" She was so pale that her freckles stood out like Rattler's leopard spots.

Johnny got shakily up and staggered this way and that, laughing so hard that he could hardly stand up. "Kitie, did you see it?" He whooped with laughter, snow-tears melting down his cheeks. There were hot trickles going down his back too, and he knew they weren't tears. He rested his head on Kitie's shoulder for a moment, but couldn't stop laughing. "Did you see what I did?" He felt sick with joy at his own chinook, his own June. It occurred to him that, because of the joy, he wasn't noticing the pain much.

After a few minutes he quieted down and stood smiling at the sagebrush growing up the steep slope of the hogsback. "Tom will give me hell now," he said. "I suppose that horse is spoiled for good." But he wasn't able to worry about Tom—he felt too clean and good, too worthwhile and weighted with purpose. Green leaves were budding straight out of his fingers and toes. The prickly pear of his heart was busy pushing out one frail waxy yellow bloom. He was ripe for cutting, like a young cottonwood sapling awaiting the axes of the Suhtai chiefs.

"That eagle," said Kitie, "was fucking solid."

"I like you," he told her, kissing her again and stroking her arm, agitated like aspen leaves with an immemorial fiery pain. A foreign tenderness flapped inside of him, trying to fly out through his eyes, his hands, his mouth.

Kitie frowned, turning her face away from him. "Like, it was okay before. But now I know you're freaking out."

He turned away, his feelings not all hurt by this remark, and hunted for his hat. It was lying in the browse some distance away. As he shakily picked it up, he noticed something else. On the hoof-trampled dust, a fallen eagle feather was lying. Scarcely daring to breathe, he picked it up. It was a young, sleek feather. He held it gingerly, as if it had power to harm him. He stood very straight and his heart felt pressed down among all those rose thorns, those prickly-pear spines, by some tremendous hoof. Supposing that poor little eagle was hurt now, a wing or a leg broken as it dragged behind his horse? Supposing it was dead, its noble ribs crushed by a kick—that good little eagle who had repaid his stupidity by leaving him this priceless feather.

"Johnny, we'd better get you to the doctor." Kitie pulled his arm.

Clutching the feather, he painfully mounted behind Kitie and they rode back to cow camp. His hurts swelled and throbbed. He had a few thoughts about blood poisoning—eagle talons were unsanitary, Ma Maureen would say.

They found Son of a Bitch waiting, sweaty and wild eyed, in front of the cow-camp barn. He had a few deep talon scratches on his neck and shoulders. The dusty rope trailed empty from the saddle horn. Johnny breathed a sigh of relief that was as long as the wind. He hoped that the little eagle had flown back and gotten his wood-chuck before he flew back up toward the old silver mine. They un-saddled Son of a Bitch and dusted some sulfa powder on his injuries.

Then they rode Kitie's bike down to Cottonwood. In the brick medical center on Main Street, in the little office smelling of alcohol,

Dr. Erickson cleaned and painted Johnny's wounds and confirmed his fears on the septic nature of eagle claws. Johnny kept tight hold of the eagle feather and grinned at Kitie. Then the two of them rode the bike on home.

At the dinner table that night, Ma Maureen, Tom, and the girls screamed eaglelike with laughter when Johnny told the story on himself. Tom's displeasure at any damage done to the horse was overridden by hilarity at the cause of that damage. "Poor old Son of a Bitch," said Tom, "he'll go to bucking every time he sees a chicken now."

"We'll sell him to Jim Shoulders for rodeo using," said Johnny. "If he bucks like he did today, he'll be worth ten times what he is now "

"Well, how did it feel to rope again?" said Ma Maureen. "And, Johnny, take that ugly feather out of your braid. Don't eagles have lice?" She made a grab for the feather.

"It felt pretty good," said Johnny, ducking her grab. He knew where his emotion was leading him, and he didn't hang back. "I haven't forgotten how either. But I'm going to need a better using horse than that old S.O.B., though, if I'm going to make a professional eagle roper."

"It's gonna make it mighty tough on the other fellows," said Tom, "if we're going to add eagle roping as a new event. They'll have to wear bulletproof shirts, and helmets with bars over the face part, like them football players wear on TV."

"Do you think the conservationists would let Jim Shoulders buy up fifty or sixty eagles for his stock string? Think of the trouble he's going to have shipping them dang eagles around the suicide circuit." Ma Maureen fell in with the gag, saying this with a perfectly straight face, but still trying to grab at Johnny's feather. The girls kept giggling and falling against each other.

"I'll put on an exhibition eagle roping at the Cottonwood rodeo," said Johnny. "Tom, you're organizing the rodeo, so you gotta get the eagles. But I'll have to get me a better using horse and start practicing. Guess I'd better call up Sam Burke and talk turkey. I mean, talk eagle."

Their laughter died off a little as they watched him get up and hobble painfully to the phone on the wall. Johnny guessed that they thought he was going to play-act the whole thing—pretend he was calling Burke with the hook held down. He lifted the phone and dialed the Cottonwood operator.

"Operator," he said, "I want to make a person-to-person call to Mr. Sam Burke in Flagstaff, Arizona." They were all suddenly silent, staring at him. "This is Johnny Chance at 475-2993. Yeah, I'll wait."

Suddenly Ma Maureen got up from the table, came up and put her arm around him. He hugged her back without looking at her. After all, she was his mother. Tom got up too, his face flushed red with excitement. The girls sat with their eyes on him, their ice cream melting in pools on their plates.

Then Sam Burke's deep voice sounded in the phone, from far off down there in the canyon country. "Howdy, friend Johnny. Where you been keeping yourself?"

"Been keeping myself to myself, mostly," said Johnny. "How are things down there?"

"Oh . . . we had a long hard winter. I sorta retired, you know. Running my ranch full-time now. And losing money full-time. Once in a while I go to a rodeo, but I promised my old lady I wouldn't enter no more."

They talked for some minutes about rodeo, the economy, politics, Vietnam, and the general state of the world, while all the time Johnny knew that Sam knew he was calling up about Ace of Spades. His stomach kinked itself up as he wondered if, when he got around to mentioning it, Burke would say he'd already sold the horse, or that Spades had gone bad in the legs or was dead.

Finally Johnny said, "Say, Sam, I keep hearing that you got a pretty good rope horse for sale."

"You mean Spades? Shucks, he ain't no good. Just an old pet. My kids keep trying to take him away from me." As he listened to this, Johnny got faint from fright. He and Sam had never been friends, as he had with Jimmy Alderman, but he knew that the old Arizona roper admired him from a distance, without a word or a gesture. Burke was fond of saying that if General Custer had been a roper, Johnny would have massacred him all over again. But Burke was sounding like he wouldn't sell the horse out of sentimentality.

"Well," said Johnny shakily, "as you know, I've been hurting for a horse ever since old Rattler died. I was wondering if you'd consider selling that old pet. We was wondering if I could come down there and talk about it."

"Why, Johnny," said that voice from the strange and distant canyon country, "I been expecting you to call for six months now. That horse has been eating me out of house and home. I've got half a notion to bill you for all the hay and horse cookies he's gone through."

The Chevrolet truck and the aluminum horse trailer, dusty from two weeks' travel across the United States, pulled up in front of the Chance house. As Tom braked, Johnny could feel the horse in back shift his weight skillfully. He, Tom, and Kitie got stiffly out of the truck. They had phoned Ma Maureen from their last gasoline stop to alert her. She must have seen them coming up the lane, because she came running out the front door, needles and thread pinned to the bosom of her gingham apron.

"Looks like she's still sewing them centennial costumes for the girls," said Tom.

"She borrowed more books from the library than I ever did," Johnny added bitterly, "looking for old pictures to copy them costumes from."

"Hope she doesn't finish the one she's not making for me," said Kitie, stretching.

Ruby came running out after Ma Maureen, wearing a half-sewn-together pioneer-type dress with lace pinned experimentally on the bosom. Over in the practice arena, Fern was galloping back and forth on her albino gelding, wearing the purple lamé outfit that Ma Maureen always said was too good to practice in. She was practicing a Roman stand, her slender, glittering body standing straight on the saddle, her dark bob lifting silkily, as the albino rattled along with his tail plumed up. When Fern saw the trailer, she dropped down into the saddle and wheeled her trick horse over toward the gate.

Ma Maureen was hugging Tom and tweaking the beard he was growing for the centennial. Then she hugged Johnny. She didn't hug Kitie. "How was the trip? What took you so long coming back?"

Tom laughed and jerked his thumb at Johnny. "He made me drive thirty miles an hour all the way from Flagstaff. He was just scared to death that something was going to happen to that new toy horse of his."

Johnny kept quiet as he unlatched the tailgate of the trailer. He could have commented further on the trip. Kitie had vacillated between staying home with the women, fighting with them, and feeling sexual frustrations, or going with the men, fighting with Tom, and feeling sexual frustrations. She and Johnny had had to keep their hands off each other and stage false-front quarrels for Tom's benefit all the way to Flagstaff and back. Tom helped Johnny lower the tail-gate carefully to the ground. Inside the trailer's gloom there gleamed the dusky-gold rump and ebony hocks of the famous horse. The short black tail whisked busily at the flies, and the horse tramped around impatiently, shaking the trailer, wanting to get out.

"So, boy," Johnny said, slipping in beside Spades, stroking his neck and then untying his halter rope. Gently he backed Spades down the ramp into the July sunshine and walked him clear of the truck, just in case Spades might spook at something and bark his shins.

The women all stood at attention, their faces full of admiration. Pat and two of the hired men came up just as Fern arrived and jumped off her albino.

"Well, he sure is a picture," said Ma Maureen. "I expected a soft horse with a hay belly."

"Burke was using him out in the open," said Tom. "He's hard as a woman's heart and ready to go."

Spades stood firm and square on his neat slate hoofs and his shining black legs. His chest and gaskins were as powerfully muscled as a boxer's. His mane and forelock blew gently as he looked this way and that, his little jet ears nearly touching at the tips as they strained toward every new sound. Then he swung his head around to lip Johnny's sleeve and left a wet place. He was all controlled benevolence and peaceful power. At the touch of the horse's muzzle, Johnny felt the voluptuous warmth that he had felt many times now since he wrote out the check days ago and gave it to Burke. (He'd written the check on the family account too, not on his hidden money, which Tom still didn't know about.) The eagle feather fluttered where he had tied it in Spades's mane.

Ma Maureen spotted the feather and frowned with full Irish intolerance. "Johnny, why is that dirty old feather hanging there? Eagles have lice. It spoils his looks." She moved to jerk the feather off.

Johnny put up his hand to guard the feather. Hoping to divert her attention, he said, "Burke was right about Spades being an old pet. He let him wander loose around the ranch. The kids would just shinny up on him and ride around with the halter on. Maybe I'm get-ting old, but for instance you don't have to fight this horse into the trailer, the way you had to do with Rattler. It's kind of nice."

"Well, have you roped off him yet?" Ma Maureen asked, never one to delay pressuring for too long. "Does he feel as good as you remembered?"

"Hell, we roped calves for a whole day down there," said Tom, "before we sat down and talked money."

"It was awkward, like, getting off him on the left," said Johnny. "I'll have to retrain him for the right before I rope off him any more."

"Procrastinator," said Ma Maureen.

"He doesn't have Rattler's terrific power," said Johnny, starting to panic the way he always did when she pressured him. "But he's got a good square sliding stop, all right—he softens those calves up good. And he's got a faster start than Rattler, I think. He has a funny way of squatting right down in the box and bracing his butt against the boards. And then he just jumps right out of there."

A car pulled up and a tall man with a baggy suit and a grey crewcut got out, carrying a flash camera. It was the photographer from the Cottonwood *Post*.

"I called the *Post* this morning," said Ma Maureen. "No harm in there being a little extra rodeo news in the paper. We gotta start getting people stirred up."

The man with the camera came up, shook hands with Tom and Johnny. "So this is the famous Ace of Spades," he said, looking the horse over with a city man's nervous eye.

"Yup," said Johnny.

The photographer was snapping pictures from this angle and that. Spades stood there bored, moving one ear at the flashbulbs like a Hollywood veteran. "Can I ask how much you paid for him?"

"Ten thousand," said Tom. Ma Maureen rolled her eyes and winced, a gesture that the *Post* man missed, one that summed up several family conferences, plus a conference with the banker. They had managed to persuade the banker about the existential eccentricities of ropers like Johnny.

"I suppose Burke was fond of the horse," said the *Post* man, who seemed to have a talent for asking all the wrong questions.

"Course he was," said Tom. "Spades was like a member of the wedding."

"Then why would he sell him?"

"Well," said Johnny, wishing he were back up at cow camp and just riding Spades around to count cows, "a horse like this belongs to everybody, in a way. Guys that are hard up for a horse can buy shares in him and ride him. If a guy is a friend, he has a seat on your horse for free. Now if Spades had been old, Burke would have kept him for riding off into the sunset with. But Spades is young, so Burke figured a young roper ought to have him. And he knows he can ride this horse any time he gets in the mood to enter a rodeo, without paying me a cent of his winnings."

"I think that's real nice," said the *Post* man. "Well, as long as I'm here, I might as well amplify my story and do a picture feature. It looks like the Chances are getting ready for the rodeo and the centennial. Anything else I can snap?" He turned to Fern. "Young lady, how about doing a few more stunts?"

"Sure," said Fern, always delighted to show off. They all trooped toward the practice arena. Ruby went to change her clothes and saddle her own trick horse. Johnny pulled his saddle out of the back of the truck—he wanted to exercise Spades, who had been standing in the trailer since morning. In the practice arena, Fern and Ruby galloped back and forth while the photographer hung on the fence, flashing pictures happily. Ruby, who was less daring, did her fender drag, hanging from the side of the saddle. But Fern rattled past at full gallop, doing her Cossack death drag, hanging upside down by one leg hooked through the strap, the other glittering leg thrust ballerinalike into the air. Her mica-bright body floated like a scarf at the horse's flank, her head inches from the pumping legs. Pat and Johnny saddled up their horses, and Pat obliged the *Post* man by doing a few turns around the cloverleaf barrels. But Johnny didn't do anything—he just rode blissfully around, feeling how responsive and silken the horse was.

"Pat," shouted the *Post* man from the fence, "are we going to see another installment of the Pat Chance-Beth Stuart rivalry this year?"

"You bet," said Pat. "This year I'm going to lick her." They all grinned at each other. Beth Stuart had beaten Pat every time they met, including at the Cottonwood rodeo. Pat hated Beth Stuart with a fury bordering on the comic, while Beth appeared oblivious to Pat.

"She wins all the time," said Pat, "because her daddy bought her a racehorse, and she doesn't have anything else to do but practice."

They all booed her. Pat shrugged and did another turn around the barrels. Ma Maureen smiled it off and told the *Post* man not to quote Pat.

"Johnny, I'll run in some calves," said Tom, "and you can rope a few."

"Nope," said Johnny. "I just want to loosen him up."

They all looked at each other. "It's good publicity," said Tom.

"I don't want to get off him on the left no more," said Johnny. "Tomorrow I start converting him for a righthand bailout."

"Are you definitely planning a comeback?" asked the *Post* man.

"I didn't buy this expensive horse just to bring in the milk cows," snapped Johnny.

"Well," said the *Post* man, becoming aware of the crossfire of family emotions in the air, "do you plan to compete at the Cottonwood rodeo?"

"He'd better," said Tom. "He'll be one of our major drawing cards. That's why I'd like to see a picture of him roping in the paper."

Johnny stopped Spades right in front of them all. "Look," he said, beginning to feel that alone-in-the-dark feeling of all the months when he'd tried to go on roping without Rattler. "I haven't touched a rope for a year. I've got a lot of practicing to do. When I'm good and ready, maybe I'll go up to the jackpot roping at Ellis for a Saturday or two. And then we'll see. And if you don't like it, maybe I'll start playing polo."

"No, you don't," said Tom. "This here is a roping pony. And if you don't like it, then the banker will take him back."

The *Post* man made a wild-eyed effort to get himself out of the invisible crossfire. He turned to Kitie, who was hunkering beside him on top of the fence, in her chlorox-riddled bell-bottoms and her see-through flowered shirt (on the trip, she had made a major concession regarding this shirt, because she was wearing a bra under it). "We haven't heard from you yet, Miss . . . ah . . ."

"I'm Kitie," said Kitie.

The *Post* man had obviously heard tell of Kitie in town, but had never seen her before. "Oh, you're Kitie. You home from college for the summer?"

Johnny listened to them talking with a certain apprehension, and he sensed that the rest of the family felt the same way.

"That's right," said Kitie sweetly. "I'm in my junior year at an experimental school in New York. It's called the New York City College of Life."

Johnny noticed Ma Maureen biting her lower lip and looking at Tom.

"That sounds real interesting," said the *Post* man, taking notes. "What are you majoring in?" He kept looking at the ring in her nose.

"There isn't any major," said Kitie. "You take courses over a broad spectrum. The whole purpose is to release individual creativity —you know, let it hang out. For instance, I was doing social work among teenage drug addicts. Did you know that New York has no center for the treatment of these young addicts? It's a crime. Society has to remedy this crime." Kitie brandished her fist. "And I was into an art thing, fabric design, and so on . . . ."

Johnny saw Ma Maureen quietly stealing away. Tom's shoulders slumped.

"And what's your rodeo specialty, Kitie?" The *Post* man obviously wanted to ask if everybody in New York City wore gold rings in their noses, but he didn't dare. "Anything you care to demonstrate for my good old camera here? I'll bet you're an expert trick roper."

Johnny realized that his throat had gotten dry. He turned Spades away, sure that Kitie was going to say in her high bluebell voice, "No, I fuck in a hundred and five different positions."

"Well," said Kitie, "I'm not a very good rider, see. I don't dig horses much. So I took up cross-country motorcycle racing. Wanna see my bike?"

For a couple of weeks, Johnny did nothing but train Spades for a righthand bailout. He trucked the horse up to cow camp and had a nervous moment or two when he turned Spades out with the other saddle horses. They came up, eyes hard and bright, and went through that curious equine ritual of standing forehead to forehead with Spades, sniffing and staring, then suddenly squealing like mustangs and striking at each other with their front feet. Johnny hung by the fence, afraid that one of them would injure Spades, but the ritual ended without damages. For a few days the other horses ignored Spades, and with a pang Johnny watched the buckskin grazing alone. But after that Spades edged his way into the bunch and was accepted. In fact, he struck up a friendship with the unworthy Son of a Bitch, who still had the eagle-roping scabs peeling off his neck.

Johnny and Kitie resumed their cow-camp idyll, but both of them felt that it was coming to an end. Every morning when Johnny woke up, the first thing he did after he got dressed was to look into the horse pasture, to make sure Spades hadn't been shot or stolen during the night. At Johnny's whistle, Spades would raise his head, utter a low whicker that made his nostrils and chest pulsate, and walk quickly over to the gate. Johnny would halter him and say, "Why, you old pet," and Spades would sniff around his pockets for the horse cookies that Burke had told him Spades liked.

Just the mere possession of this horse was a gloating joy. As he ran his hand along Spades's neck, he thought that people must have learned to loom satin from feeling such hair. He never got tired of looking at Spades's head, to savor the alertness of those ears that were sharp and fine as Indian arrowheads, or to consider the expression of noble intelligence in Spades's wide-set eyes. When he rode Spades around to look at the cows, the horse responded with a psychic willingness that showed his trust in humans and in circumstance had never been betrayed.

"It's a funny thing, when you think about the Indian ideas on animals," Johnny told Kitie. "Men could get power from animals, but it didn't work the other way round. The animals were higher, and controlled things."

"Maybe it was better that way," said Kitie. "Look what this country got when it started thinking that men were better than animals."

"Speechmaking Kitie. All you need is a podium and a brass band."

"The trouble is," said Kitie, "that we, like, can't get back to that nice primitive thing. We're stuck with all our problems and our wishful thinking."

"Then why do you keep nagging me to go back to my tribe?"

"I don't mean you should live in the past." She turned on him almost angrily. "The Indians have problems *now*. This heavy power trip of yours is irresponsible and childish."

Kitie was ignoring the fact that when Johnny started practicing roping in a couple of weeks, he would have to move back down to the ranch, where he could be handy to the practice arena and the little bunch of brahma calves Tom kept for practice. She insisted she was going to have a garden, and spaded up a patch in back of the cabin, tossing aside all the big rocks. The next day her muscles were so sore that she could hardly creep out of Johnny's bed. She had bought a lot of seeds off the Burpee stand in the Safeway supermarket. Johnny discovered that she was as ignorant about gardening as about horses— he even had to show her how to stake a string across the patch to get straight rows, and to soak certain seeds overnight to make them germinate faster.

"Throw them corn seeds out," he said. "Growing season is too short for corn here. You can't eat sweet peas, you know. And you'll have to have a trellis for them."

"I know, man," she said patiently. "I like the way they smell, and Fern says they're easy to grow."

So Johnny helped her rig up a chicken-wire trellis on the cabin's south side. It took her a whole day to get the seeds in the ground, bending, grunting, and sweating. Then Johnny told her she'd have to fence the garden or the cows would devastate it. He got the posthole digger and dug her four holes, then left her to tamp in four cedar posts and staple chicken wire to them. Finally, as several days went by without rain, he had to remind her that the seeds wouldn't germinate if she didn't keep the soil moist. So she was out at the well half the day, pumping and filling the water can.

"Like, it's a lot of work, isn't it?" she said.

"You're the one wants to homestead," he said. "Supposing you really had to weave your own cloth and make soap and all? People got old fast in those days. The Indians thought it was better to die young in battle than die old in bed. I guess they were right."

"Speechmaking Johnny," she gibed. "Podium and brass band."

One morning he was rescuing the coffee from the range where she'd left it to boil too long, when he heard her give a Kitie-watching-kites scream outside. He looked out the window.

"My radishes are coming up," she said. The screams were repeated on succeeding mornings as the lettuce, string beans, and sweet peas came up. Then, one morning, he heard another kind of scream, as tragic as that of some pioneer female finding her husband scalped down by the corral. He went out and found Kitie sobbing against the chicken-wire fence. All the little green shoots in the garden were nipped off. Johnny saw tracks where a deer had leaped the fence and walked along assassinating the newborn lettuce.

Johnny tried to comfort her. "Get some more radish and lettuce seeds. They grow fast."

"I can't do anything," she sobbed.

"You fuck awful good."

She stamped off. "Sometimes," she flung over her shoulder, "you're enough to make a militant femininist out of me."

She nagged him more and more about getting married and having a baby, until, frantic from this pressure added to that from the rest of the family, he started avoiding her at night. His desire for her was no longer green, but curing yellow in the July sun, like the grass on the hills around them. Finally Spades was trained for righthand bailouts, and Johnny had to actually start practicing. He suggested that both he and Kitie move back down to the home ranch, but she cried and stormed, insisting that Ma Maureen and the girls would drive her crazy. So Johnny had to compromise—he kept Spades down home.

Every afternoon, after he'd finished his cow-camp chores, he drove down to Cottonwood, got in a couple of hours in the arena, then went back up to cow camp to spend the night, ostensibly to protect Kitie from escaped convicts.

He practiced only because the family drove him to it, reminding him of the million-dollar debt and of the ten-thousand-dollar loan for Spades. Tom was elsewhere all the time, either busy with the centennial planning or off somewhere on the circuit. Ma Maureen was busy with rodeo publicity and the hay-baling operation, while the girls kept books, did housekeeping, and carried on their own rodeo activities. Pat won $2580 in seven straight barrel races, and Fern and Ruby were contracted more often now for their trick-riding act.

But as Johnny roped calves all alone in the practice arena, in the shade of the cottonwood trees, with the dust of Spade's skidding stop drifting away from him again and again, he realized something. Despite the purchase of this good horse, the best using horse in the U.S., he was still afoot.

So it was late on that long-feared afternoon that Johnny rode alone up across the upper pasture. It was the right time of day to be going off to do it, but he felt himself flutter with apprehension like aspen leaves in a breeze. Not only would he try to do it, but he'd be out there alone all night.

It wasn't going to be easy. First of all, he hadn't been able to find all the proper equipment. He had no idea which kind of sagebrush was the sacred kind, though he figured it must be the fragrant silver sage. He didn't have any eagle-bone whistle either, or a sweat lodge for purification. But he did have a twenty-foot-long strip of leather for making new bridle reins that had been lying around the cabin and one of the buffalo skulls off the cabin wall. He also had two choke-cherry skewers that he'd whittled himself—he had driven over to Ma Maureen's favorite chokecherry thicket to get the wood. That book *Sweet Medicine* gave you some instructions on how to do it—Tall Bull, for instance, had done it in 1947.

Second of all, you had to have help while doing it, and Kitie had refused to come with him. She had told him he was some new kind of freak. He would have to manage everything alone. Third, he would need a lone cottonwood high on a hill somewhere there on their summer range. But he couldn't think where such a tree was, though he knew of plenty of cottonwoods down in the creek bottoms. Finally, he would have to pray to Maheo, the Cheyenne almighty. Yet he had never been very good at praying to the white man's almighty, and he figured he wouldn't have improved at praying just from the mere act of switching over.

He should have fasted and prayed beforehand. Then an animal would have come to him in the dream and given him power to face the ordeal. It probably would have been an eagle, or maybe a horse. But he didn't know if he even had the proper Indian ideas about animals, in order to have the right kind of dream. His ideas about animals, and about the whole impending business, were probably full-blood white ideas.

So he rode aimlessly for a while over the upper pasture, thinking about those two skewers in the saddle bag and the jackknife in his pocket that he had honed extra sharp on the pumice stone last night. Down in the valley, he could see flashes of evening sunlight off the windshields of cars speeding along route 10. A jet plane flew over high up, rumbling softly. He craned his neck, looking for the plane, until he got a cramp in one shoulder. Finally for one moment, the sun reflected off the plane at just the right angle and he saw a single flash of light up there, as if the plane had exploded. He thought that maybe he ought to pray to the cars or to that plane—those were the totem animals of the white man.

He drew rein near the telephone line that crossed the pasture. His eyes followed the solitary file of telephone poles across the hills. The pale-green glass insulators glinted red in the setting sun. He rode up closer and sat there on Spades, listening hypnotized by the hum of the wires. The poles looked like trees that had died there where they stood, and the telephone company crews had simply cut off the branches before they strung the wires.

Then it occured to him that a telephone pole would be the perfect kind of tree. Judging by what he had read, Maheo was broadminded and would understand. He still hesitated for a while, sitting there look-ing at the nearest pole, shivering a little as if feeling himself too close to some terrible contained force. Then he decided that he might as well get going.

So he climbed off Spades and fished his equipment out of the saddlebag. Spades stood grazing where Johnny left him. Hoping that he wouldn't get electrocuted, Johnny walked shakily toward the tele-phone pole, telling himself that wood and leather were poor conductors of electricity, and that the evening sky was clear, with no thunderstorms around to make one think twice about going near a phone line.

He took a long look around, making sure that nobody was in sight anywhere on the hills. Then he tied the leather strip around the pole and split the ends to tie with. He put the buffalo skull at the foot of the pole, then pulled up a lot of silversage and made the half-circle path that the book said you were supposed to walk back and forth on.

Then he was able to busy himself a few more minutes by undressing. He took off his hat, shirt, boots, and Levis, and stood there in his cotton briefs, feeling the setting sun hot on his skin. The smell of torn sage was as sharp as alcohol on a cut. Nothing saw him but the emptiness of the hills, with their antelope trails and their fugitive pines hiding in the gullies.

Finally he picked up the jackknife. He was so frightened that he had to urinate against a nearby clump of ordinary sagebrush, and that saved him for another minute. Then he looked around for Spades—the horse was grazing nearby, oblivious, his powerful hindquarters bulging with muscles as he made step after slow step, snatching at grass. Johnny turned his eyes back to the telephone pole and looked pleadingly at the top of it. The wires sang, and the glass insulators held some kind of secret. Voices streamed along the wires, voices in dreams that talked, laughed, discussed—voices of ghosts on the lonely slope of the cemetery, Pa Gene's voice, voices of ghosts around the cabin, voices in the thickets and around the old Indian graves up in the hills of the Tongue River country, the voices of women singing old war songs.

Johnny opened the jackknife. He had sterilized it by holding the blade in a match flame. At least in the old days, you didn't have to make the incisions yourself. The medicine man did that for you, and all you had to do was smile.

So there he stood with the knife, and nothing else to busy himself with. He looked down at his chest—the dark skin looked so smooth, good, and innocent that it seemed a shame to spoil it. He raised the knife and shakily pressed the point into the skin above and to the inside of the right nipple. A shiny bead of blood welled there, winking in the red evening light. The sight of it simply amazed him. He realized that his mouth and knees were trembling uncontrollably. He would have to do it quickly, or he might be standing there all day tomorrow too, and likely would get sunstroke.

So he mustered the little courage he had, and sliced the knife point downward about three inches. He was amazed even more to see his skin part neatly, like the velvet curtain opening in the Orpheum

Theater down in town. He watched with fascination, as if it were some-body else's skin. For a moment the incision was empty, pink and white. Then blood filled it, welled up into a row of beads, and started dripping down his ribs, finally splashing hotly on his cotton briefs.

"Oh, my god," he moaned to himself, not praying, just exclaim-ing. Now too frightened to stop, he made another quick cut an inch from that, and then two more on the other breast. That was where the books said they had to be made, and the Catlin prints showed them there too. The whole front of his body was dripping with blood now, like the cabin eaves in winter when the snow melted on a sunny afternoon. The blood glittered in the dying light, and lost its shine only when it coagulated. Nearly weeping with fear and pain, he man-aged to get the knife blade under the two strips of skin and lift them loose.

"Oh, god," he kept moaning. "Jesus god." The knife slid from his fingers. His knees were shaking so much that he had to kneel down to stay steady—not to pray at all. Then he slid a chokecherry skewer under each strip of skin and tied them hard in place with the split ends of the leather strip. It occurred to him that he hadn't sterilized the leather—he would probably die of some unnamed infection. When he'd finished, his fingers were sticky with blood.

Then he managed to get to his feet, weaving as if he were drunk. The pole towered over him, singing its electric song. The dark cliff of the sky leaned out over him—it was going to fall on him with a great roar. Maybe he was already dizzy from blood loss. Now he was sup-posed to dance at the end of the leather strips, walking back and forth along the half-circle of sage and jerking his tied flesh against the chokecherry skewers. But he didn't know how to dance Indian-style, just Western-style rock. So he just started walking back and forth. He felt really silly then, silly and sick. Supposing somebody came along now—some kid on his way home from poaching up in the national forest, or Pinter Brodie, who always cut across everybody's land because he didn't believe in fences.

He jerked gently, and the tearing pain nearly doubled him up. Very shortly he would exhaust what little self-control he had. Now and then he jerked again, very gently. If he was going to tear himself loose in proper Suhtai style, he would have to jerk harder than that. He could visualize his flesh tearing, strings of it breaking apart. The blood kept trickling down the front of his body—his briefs were soaked in front and his knees felt wet.

He would stand and think about it for five minutes or so, then jerk again, and not accomplish anything. His braids kept falling forward and getting wet with blood, and he kept shoving them back over his shoulders. The night came stalking like something mutilated, like armies of severed arms and legs. In the sky above, nighthawks were busy catching insects, and their wings sobbed like warriors' widows weeping and cutting off fingers. "Kwi-kwi-kwi-kwi-kwi-kwi———kwi ———kwi," mourned the wings. After Johnny had fooled around for about an hour, with longer and longer waits between jerks, he decided that he didn't have the courage or power to finish it properly, and that he might as well give up. He could try again some time in the future, when perhaps he would have more guts. After all, in the old days, not every Indian succeeded the first time and, while the tribe made him live in disgrace for a while, they were always happy to give him a second chance.

So he tried to untie the skewers from his flesh. But, after fumbling blindly, madly with the knots for a few minutes, scarcely able to see in the dark, he realized that they were so tight, so slippery and swollen with blood, that he couldn't untie them. Then the thought came that he could cut himself loose with the knife without hurting himself too much, but when he looked for the knife, he couldn't see it in the dark. He walked back and forth across the sagebrush several times before he could make out the knife in the grass—it lay a good ten feet back, near his clothes. Shakily he lay down on the ground and tried to reach it with his foot, but he couldn't. He hunted for a stick or something else to pull it toward him with, but of course there were no sticks lying around there—the nearest trees were in a gully about a mile away. The leather strip was all in one piece, tied around the pole, and it was too sturdy for him to break with his bare hands.

Then was when he panicked. If he couldn't get loose, then he was trapped there, for the ghosts to get, until Kitie came looking for him tomorrow or went down to Cottonwood to tell the family that he was missing. Then they would search the hills and find him tied up to the pole like that, and he would never hear the end of it. He tried a couple more times to jerk loose, but he couldn't, and the blood only ran more freely. It he lost too much blood, he might die.

Nearly in tears, he looked around to where Spades was grazing. Then he wondered if Spades' saddle pockets had any other implement, like wire cutters, that he might use to cut himself loose. In a low shaking voice he called the horse. "Hey, Spades." He heard his own voice in the dark, strangely familiar, like a warm pool of kerosene-lamp light in the cabin. With his trembling lips he managed to make the whistle that brought the horse up to the pasture gate every morning.

Spades raised his head, jaws grinding busily, eyes shining virtuously in the starlight. With maddening casualness he swung around and ambled toward Johnny, being careful not to step on his dragging reins. But when he smelled the blood, he stopped short, shot his ears forward and blasted a long, hollow snort.

"Come here, you Spades." Johnny held out an imploring hand, standing at the very limit of the leather. Spades backed away a few steps, still snorting. Johnny called his using horse every bad name he could think of. But Spades turned and went off, presenting his magnificent rump again for Johnny's inspection, pulling grass about thirty feet away. Shaking and sobbing, Johnny pulled some grass and attracted the horse's attention again, holding out the grass. Spades gave the grass a bored look and would not move his shiny black legs a step closer.

The stars slid down on Johnny with a roar, like a glacier of fire calving off into the sea of his flesh. Flaming whales breached among the glowing ice floes. Johnny lay down, trying to hide in the dry grass, his mouth seared with the aurora borealis of thirst. Now and then he picked at the knots again, but the wounds kept bleeding and soon the moisture had swelled the knots even more tightly. He kept thinking about how he could free himself with one good jerk. He could see himself doing it, over and over, like the instant replay in the TV ballgames. Over and over he could hear footsteps coming toward him. He was sure he heard someone singing the old strongheart songs off beyond forgotten stony graves, and told himself that whoever the singer was, he was wasting his breath on Johnny Eagle Chance. Something terrible lay in the grass some distance away, its breath bubbling and hissing. The dark glacier of the night ground him to a fine dust of terror.

Then, about midnight, as he lay there in a daze, he realized that he could hear Spades's grass pulling coming closer and closer. He could hear the horse's hoofs strike ground as Spades kicked at flies. By then he was shivering with cold as a night breeze stirred the dry grass. He lay very quietly, wondering if the horse would come close enough so that he could grab the reins. He felt less alone now. Pretty soon Spade's dark muzzle came into view, the black lips snatching hungrily at grass, the jaw muscles rippling as he chewed, ground-up grass slobbered over the bit. The horse's bulk towered up into the stars. But the reins dragged just out of reach.

Then Spades made another step or two, bringing the reins just a little closer. Johnny didn't want to call the horse again, maybe reminding Spades of the blood. If he moved quickly, he might be able to grab the reins before Spades could pull away. ·

So he lunged up out of the grass and grabbed like a madman. His blood-blackened fingers closed around the reins. Spades plunged away sideways, frightened out of his wits by the sudden movement. Johnny held onto the reins, shouting, "Stand!" Suddenly he felt himself jerked off through the grass after the horse. A searing pain in his chest made him howl like a run-over dog and drop the reins.

He sat up, moaning, grimacing. The leather and the two skewers lay loose in the grass, and the torn skin dangled free on his chest.

He felt no release, no victory. He hadn't done it himself—it had been an accident, just as much as if Spades had stepped on his toe. And he had spent the night foaming at the mouth with terror.

Stooped with pain, he walked over to his clothes and managed to get them on. His shirt front soaked through with blood right away. It took him a while to catch Spades, but finally he got downwind from the horse and maneuvered up to him. As he flexed his muscles while mounting, his chest stung. He remembered reading about how happy Whistling Elk had been when he had done it. He wondered how it was possible to be so happy.

When he dragged himself back to the cabin, Kitie told him all over again that he was a freak. Next morning early he had to ride her motorcycle alone down to Cottonwood. Dr. Erickson sewed him up a second time. "Been roping eagles again?" the doctor wanted to know. Johnny knew from the expression in Erickson's eyes that he suspected the cuts were self-inflicted, but he didn't ask, and Johnny didn't volunteer an explanation.

When Tom got back from the circuit and heard there'd be a doctor bill, he was furious. It was just another unnecessary expense by an able-bodied roper who wasn't earning a cent. Johnny found himself the subject of more family clashes than ever. They all had different reasons for criticizing what he'd done. Kitie kept saying, "Like, you make me exactly all the way sick."

But Ma Maureen was the angriest of all. She took Johnny aside, as if he were still that small boy with snot running down his chin, and gave him a long lecture. "You want to go to Heaven?" she cried. "You want to see God?"

She crowded him so hard that he had to pretend he'd reached the desired hardness and serenity while tied to that telephone pole. "Yeah, you call him God," he said. "The Cheyennes think he's Maheo." They were both talking at once.

"That's all heathen superstition," she shouted. "All the heathens and pagans and savages have to leave their superstitions and just come to Jesus and Mary. Look at me—I'm a purebred Irish, but I don't believe in the little people. There's a lot of Irish as don't know any better than the Cheyennes, and they talk about their banshees. You're headed straight for the fires of Hell."

"What makes you so sure that Jesus and Mary aren't just plain superstition? The Cheyennes have got a story about a virgin and child—"

"That's heresy," she shouted. "Heretics, Johnny, they sizzle in Hell like a standing rib roast."

"Me, I'm getting out of Hell."

"After all I've suffered for you and put up with for you."

"You're just plain intolerant. Even a savage is more tolerant than you."

"Why, Johnny, we couldn't be civilized without a little intolerance."

"You're so intolerant that—," Johnny rummaged in his memory for a case history. He was shaking with anger, and the blood rushed, throbbing, to his hurts. "That when I was little and afraid of the dark, you made me sleep without a light."

Then there came the August morning when he stood outside the cow-camp cabin and, straining his eyes, looked toward the valley. He thought he saw a lot of white things strung out along Skillet Creek, in the Chance south pasture. There hadn't been any white things there yesterday. A pale drift of smoke overhung the pasture. He felt his stomach plunge like a bronc and goose pimples budding everywhere on his skin. Going into the cabin, he seized his binoculars out of the case that hung from a nail by the bed.

"What is it?" asked Kitie, pulling on her bell-bottom jeans. She was nude to the waist, and her breasts jerked softly as she moved, with the nipples looking like dark, swollen peony buds.

He went back outdoors with the binoculars (he had looked through them so many times to watch the eagles). Standing by the cabin corner, he adjusted the lens until the green, red, and brown blurs crystallized into Cottonwood. He could see the cars driving along the streets. He swept his field of vision north, searching until he focused on the pasture. The Indian teepees were going up along the creek, in the shade of the cottonwood trees. They looked so familiar, so expected, that he actually remembered them with a rasp of nostalgia. He shuddered with excitement. A couple dozen lodges already stood completed, the weathered canvas covers draped neatly over the frameworks of pine poles. Men and women were raising more poles into other frameworks. Horses were tramping down out of decrepit trailers. Dogs and dark-haired children scurried. A few cooking fires already burned, sending up their tender blue columns of smoke. More trucks and cars were pulling in to the campground.

Kitie came wandering out of the cabin, still shirtless, her navel moving gently above the waistband of her jeans. "The eagles again?"

"No. Look." He gave her the binoculars. "That big pasture just east of the fairgrounds."

"I don't see anything." She peered, squinted, moved the binoculars around. "Oh, there. Wow. Gee, wow. Indians."

"Yeah. Flatheads, Crows, Blackfeet, Crees. And Northern Cheyennes. I'll bet old Alex Feet is down there somewhere."

"Who's he? I mean, I thought you didn't know any Indians."

"I managed to steer clear of them most of the time. He was one got in my way. He's not the chief, but he's, like, the head tribal leader or something. He came to see me once or twice when I was rodeoing. I had gone and admitted to some gunsel reporter that I was Cheyenne, because everybody knew I was adopted, and they were curious what tribe I was from. Feet must have read it somewhere. So he tried to talk me into getting involved with the Cheyennes. I told him nothing doing. So then he scolded me and told me the people were bad off and needed money and leadership and all. That they needed Indians like me who knew how to move in the whitenose world."

"And, like, you told him to split?"

Johnny took the binoculars and looked at the camp again. He was sure that he wouldn't get any closer to that camp than the magnification inside those binoculars. But it didn't do him any harm to look from up there. After a while he started spying on Cottonwood again. He realized that he could see Main Street clearly. He saw a couple of girls in long, old-fashioned dresses with bustles parade across the side street by the Cottonwood Bank & Trust, holding ruffled parasols over their heads. The centennial promotors had tried to persuade the Cottonwoodians to live in 1890s dress for three days. Then a group of men strode past in the other direction, wearing fringed buckskin shirts, beads, heavy boots, and slouch hats, and walking with exaggerated swagger. The men turned to raise their hats at the two bustled girls, a mute, distant theatrical gesture, and one slapped another on the back. Johnny burst out laughing and pushed the glasses into Kitie's hands again.

"Look again," he said. "They're already playing pioneers down there."

Kitie looked, started laughing too. "Christ, an old surrey with the fringe on the top, and a pinto horse pulling it."

"That must be Bob Anderson's surrey. He had it in a shed somewhere."

They took turns looking, poking each other and laughing with harsh delight. "There goes an old beer wagon, by god," said Johnny. "Wonder where they scared up those six matched Belgians? Yeow, I can see the brasses on the harness sparkle from here. The wagon says 'Brown's Bar' on the side, I think. . . ."

"And there goes a fat old lady, it looks like Mrs. Paul too. Her dress looks like a real antique. Bet she dug it out of a trunk. A real big trunk." They giggled, Johnny's arm around Kitie, sides pressing together. "Couple of guys just came out of the Corner Bar and they're having a real nice fistfight right on the street. Here comes the police chief. . . ."

They were so absorbed in their amusements that they didn't notice anything until a voice said behind them, "What's going on here?" It was Tom's voice.

They both jerked as if shot, then turned around. Tom stood there, thumbs hooked in his belt. Johnny felt all his blood falling within him, falling as if from a great height, as if he were a waterfall. Even the scabs on his chest plunged dizzily down into some canyon. Tom's face was pale and his eyes squinted smaller than ever with puzzlement and rage.

"What's going on here?" he repeated looking at shirtless Kitie.

Johnny could only stand mute, clutching the binoculars. Kitie tried to brazen it out, as if she had a heavy sweater on. "We were watching the goings-on down in town," she said cheerfully.

"Get in there and put your shirt on," Tom said in a voice as hard and brutal as a spiked horseshoe.

"What's the fuss about?" said Kitie. She sauntered past Tom as slowly as she dared, into the cabin.

Tom glared at Johnny. "You encourage her to run around without no clothes?"

Johnny tried to be casual too, but he had never been as tough a liar as roper. "You're up here early."

"You wasn't expecting me, huh? I wanted to finish work early today, because I got rodeo business to do." Tom turned away with his slow hulking walk, like an elephant walking on its hind legs, and went into the cabin. Johnny stood there motionless in the sunlight. He realized that he was shaking violently, and he wondered why. After all, he'd always known that he and Kitie were going to get found out. In a place like Cottonwood, the only safe secrets were in the cemetery or the smoldering town dump.

Then, through the open cabin window, he heard Tom roar, "Your bed is made and his is all messed up."

"I made the bed already." Kitie's voice quavered just a little.

"You're a liar. There's dust on that spread. You haven't slept there for weeks."

Johnny heard scuffling, then a cracking sound. Kitie shrieked, "Oh, Tom, don't. Oh, Tom, no. No, Tom. Please." There was another crack, then another, and another. Tom was probably hitting her with his heavy cowhide belt. Johnny's knees eroded to white powder under a great glacier of fear, and he couldn't move himself to go in there and defend her. "Please, Tom," Kitie kept sobbing and shrieking. There were bumps and crashes of furniture, and more solemn cracks. Finally the noises stopped. Kitie was still sobbing, though—it sounded like she was lying on the floor. He felt the breeze play with the loose hair at the ends of his braids.

Then Tom stomped slowly out of the cabin again, buckling his belt back on. It occurred to Johnny that he hadn't even thought of running, which he could have done while Tom was busy beating Kitie. Then he noticed that Tom's face looked rosy and relaxed, and he wondered if Tom had blasted all his rage out now, so he just stood there.

"That's the cure for what ails America," said Tom cheerfully. "A few more kids need to get beat up a few more times." He came slowly up to Johnny. That was when Johnny realized that he should have run after all. "So that's why you stayed on up here, huh? It's enough to make a dog puke."

"You made me let her stay here."

"And when I think what Pa Gene went through for you." Tom was still smiling, as if he'd just come out of church, and then, before Johnny could duck, Tom swung one of his gorilla arms. Johnny's jaw took the fist like a car being tailgated. He staggered backwards, dropping the binoculars. Jimmy Alderman had taught him to fight, but there was no point in fighting Tom—he stood five nine and weighed 145, while Tom stood six three and weighed 225. When Johnny got up, Tom punched him in the stomach, and, as he doubled over, uppercut him in the jaw. Johnny went sprawling on his back in the grass.

Tom stood over him. Johnny rolled over, curling up on his side, expecting Tom to stomp him or kick him in the groin. But Tom just let him lie there. "You son of a redskin bitch," said Tom. "If I hurt you too much, you won't be roping day after tomorrow. And that's what I want you to do, is rope. So I can rope better, and show everybody what a tinfoil champ you are."

Dazed, Johnny was trying to draw breath. Blood ran into his mouth from a split lip. "Who says I'm going to rope?"

"I do," said Tom. "Because if you don't, the banker is going to foreclose on that expensive horse of yours." Tom shambled back toward the cabin like a Frankenstein in a straw Stetson, silhouetted against the blue sky. "Kitie!" he barked. "Come out here. We're going."

Sitting weakly up, Johnny saw Kitie come stumbling out of the cabin, bent over, buttoning on one of her tie-dyed shirts. She was holding a rag to her nose, and the rag was soaked with blood. Tom must have hit her in the nose. Without a word she walked off along the grassy ruts of the pasture road, to where the pickup was parked.

When the truck had driven off, all Johnny could see, as he stood up slowly, was the grey dust drifting gently away from the road, through the barbed wire fence, to settle in the grass. When he went into the cabin, somewhat bent over himself, he saw something glint on the board floor. He picked it up. It was Kitie's nose ring, the film of blood on it already drying to a brown crust.

The next couple of days were a bad time for Johnny, as Cottonwood shifted into fair time and frontier spirit. Banners and bunting went up along Main Street. At the north and south town lines, big cloth signs stretched across the highway proclaiming "Welcome to Cottonwood Rodeo, Fair, and Centennial Celebration." At the fairgrounds, the pageant actors went through their dress rehearsal, with much flurry of costumes, buckboards, and stages rattling around, teams getting mixed up, and the director shouting directions through a bullhorn. The town men were grooming their beards and mustaches proudly, and women put finishing touches on their old-time dresses.

But out on the Chance ranch, there was anything but celebration. Ma Maureen had a fit and told Kitie that, since she was no better than an animal, she would have to be locked up in the house at night. For some strange reason, Kitie let herself be locked up. Johnny moved down from cow camp permanently, but Ma Maureen told him he was another animal and would have to sleep outdoors. So Johnny had to get a cot and move into the saddle-horse barn with Spades. The other girls all knew about it too, because they had heard Ma Maureen yelling. Pat and Ruby were shudderingly disgusted, and wouldn't speak to Kitie or Johnny.

Of course, nothing could prevent Kitie from seeing Johnny during the daytime, as Ma Maureen let her out then. Apparently Ma Maureen believed that evil things were done only at night. So Johnny and Kitie managed to make love a couple of times in the saddle-horse barn, when nobody was around. Kitie kept nagging feverishly about getting married, but Johnny felt too sorry for her to get upset about it, so he even kissed her. Afterward Kitie would lie looking up at Johnny with a fanaticism made comical by the bandage on her nose, and she would say, "Baby, if it weren't for you, I'd split the world in two getting out of here."

Johnny knew that Cottonwood was getting discontented with Kitie—Fern had told him so. A few women had already said bad things to Kitie on the street. Many families had warned their children away from her. The police chief was watching to catch her with marijuana. Johnny wondered if the gossip included his and Kitie's cow-camp romance as well. But he felt himself curiously distant from Kitie now.

Perhaps this was because all night, every night, Johnny could hear drumming and singing drifting across the south pasture from the Indian camp. Wondering if Alex Feet and the Cheyennes were there got to be like a rheumatic ache in his once-broken leg. And Kitie kept nagging him, "You have to go over there. I mean, quit copping out. Don't be a dead-think honky all your life."

During the day, if Tom or Ma Maureen weren't around, Fern sometimes sneaked into the barn to talk to Johnny and Kitie. Kitie had some joints that she said she bought from some Mexican jockey named Speedy Gonzalez over at the fairgrounds. All three of them sat in a self-pitying little huddle on bales of hay and smoked the grass, analyzing family life in detail and with much high-class oratory. Johnny hoped that the grass would give him that nice drowsy feeling he'd read about, that would help him forget about Alex Feet and Tom's showing him up in the calf roping. But instead the grass made him think about how Feet and Tom were after him. He had a feeling of journeying alone and in a great hurry, with only one skinny horse and a couple of strips of jerked meat, across an endless plain. He was going in the opposite direction of the Cheyennes who had broken out of the Oklahoma reservation—he was trying to get away from the Tongue River instead of home to it.

"Yeah, man," said Kitie, "sometimes that stuff makes you paranoid." So Johnny switched back to Marlboros.

One afternoon Tom caught Fern and Kitie in the barn there and took off his cowhide belt and whipped both girls back to the house. But Fern, instead of apologizing and cowering as she usually did, just wept sullenly and said, "Pa Gene wouldn't have whipped us." Tom hit her a couple more licks for that. After that, Ma Maureen kept Fern locked up too.

When Fern wasn't around, Kitie told Johnny, "Fern is going to follow me out of here. She won't have the same style as me, though. Her idea of revolution is sleeping with Jimmy Alderman. So christ knows what'll happen to her out there in the motherfucking world. She doesn't know how to take care of herself the way old Kitie does. Fern's a born groupie."

The last evening before the fair, as Johnny, Kitie, and Fern sat on a bale of hay in the barn, they could hear the singing start up over in the Indian camp again. Tom was in town at the rodeo offce, and Ma Maureen was looking after some last-minute publicity on local TV. But they'd be back soon, and Kitie and Fern would have to go in. Johnny got up off the bale and prowled around the barn awhile, listening to the drumming, wondering what the Indians were doing over there. The song was a monotonous "hai-yah, hai-yah," in minor key, with an accompaniment that sounded like hundreds of sticks clacking in unison. He thought of all the African safari films he'd seen, where bwana sits by the fire, skin prickling with fear as he listens to the Watusi drums throbbing off across the veld.

Finally he said softly, almost as if to himself, "Well, I guess I go, don't I?"

"I want to go with you," said Kitie.

"And me," said Fern.

"No, I want to go alone," said Johnny, already opening the door of the saddle cupboard. "And Tom will whip the both of you."

"Please, baby, I want to go with you," said Kitie.

"Not this time, for christ's sake. Next time, maybe, if there is one."

Kitie shrugged morosely. Both girls sat watching as he dragged out his gear and saddled Spades. He made sure the eagle feather was in its place in Spades's mane. Then he ruffled the girls' hair and said, "Sleep tight."

Kitie shook her head away from his hand angrily, and she and Fern went toward the house. Johnny led Spades out, shut the barn door, and mounted. He realized that he was trembling lightly. He rode softly across the barnyard into the deepening twilight.

In a few more minutes he was away from the ranch buildings and out in the big south field. Nothing but a mile of rolling country now separated him from whatever destiny, if any, awaited.

It was a windless, moonless night, with the stars smudged a little by the blue smog from the sawmill. Nighthawks dipped after insects high above, their vibrating wings sounding the "kwi-kwi-kwi-kwi-kwi-kwi———kwi" that manifest destiny had not yet gotten around to silencing. Ahead, all along the dark mass of cottonwoods fringing the creek, Johnny could see the hundred lodges thrown into red relief by the campfires. Headlights of cars and trucks swung and glared along the lodges, adding their own technological glare.

As Johnny rode closer, he passed Indian horses grazing loose. They were mostly big, rangy, rough-looking coldbloods—even in the dark he could make out the many brands blotching their hides. He remembered the old turn-of-the-century photographs of great camps sprawled across rivers and the horses roaming loose on the flats. He was riding into that photograph, yet it receded from him into a ghostly blue distance.

As he topped the last rise, one last little band of horses trotted out of his way, their unshod hoofs clacking on rocks. He stopped Spades, looking down at the camp. It occurred to him that he would have to ask around to find where the Cheyennes were located. The old timidity pressed against his heart, making it smoke and melt the way a hot horseshoe melts hoof. He sat there awhile, his heart rolling in his breast like the white-ringed eye of a frightened horse. If he didn't go down there tonight, he would wind up walking around on the deserted campground a week from now, looking at the trash and the trampled grass and kicking in the cold ashes of the campfires.

He suddenly became aware that he could hear a child crying down the slope. It was a hoarse, terrified wailing that scarcely paused for breath. He focused his attention on the noise, and finally made out a small, pale figure. He urged Spades down the slope to see what was happening and found a small naked Indian boy wandering around alone. The boy was about two years old, with an uncut shock of black hair. His ribs and belly stuck out grotesquely with malnutrition, and his little penis waggled as he stumbled over the rocks in his bare feet. Johnny got down off of Spades and intercepted the boy, who kept howling uncomprehendingly as Johnny squatted before him and gripped his shoulders gently. He smelled like those caged varmints in the free zoo on the road to Butte, and liquid snot had run down from his nose into his mouth, hanging in strings off his chin. Johnny felt a little sick to his stomach as he took out his bandana handkerchief and managed to wipe off the snot. He had to throw away the handkerchief. The child's thin little arms burned his hands.

"Hey, don't cry," he said, feeling awkward.

The boy, of course, went on bawling. As he paused between one go-round of howls and the next, he opened his slanted little eyes briefly. That was when Johnny could see, even in the dark, that the eyes were milky white. The child was blind from trachoma.

Johhny bowed his head and couldn't look at the boy for a minute. Then he picked the boy up, deciding that he could risk a louse or two. He felt the child's hand brush, then seize hold of, one of his braids. Leading Spades, he walked slowly toward the camp, intending to ask at every teepee until he located the child's mother. The child went on yowling dismally in his ear, drowning out the singing-and-clicking celebration nearby.

Then he saw a young woman weaving toward him, drunk. She had a messy black bob, ragged jeans and denim jacket, and thick lips smeared with lipstick. She was trying to focus her eyes on the child and was saying something in Indian. When she got close, Johnny could smell the cheap wine. He saw that one of her eyes was white, like the child's. She reached out, staggered, and nearly fell against Johnny, who flinched back from her.

"This your kid?" he asked.

"Yah, me," she said, taking the boy away from him. She cuffed the child a few times, and he stopped crying right away. She pointed at the boy's eyes. "No see," she said. She rolled her eyes at Johnny coquettishly, and he realized she had taken him for an inhabitant of the camp and that she thought him good-looking.

"Where are the Northern Cheyennes?" he asked, edging away with Spades.

"Cheyenne?" she repeated, blinking and still trying to focus her eyes. She thought a minute. "Hem Cheyenne," she said, pointing vaguely in a way that suggested he go to the downstream end of the camp.

He got away from her as fast as he could, and walked along the edge of the camp. He felt its enigmatic, cruel life teeming everywhere among the cottonwoods—bleak, yet as busy as a prairie-dog colony. Crewcut boys in striped T-shirts scuffled among the teepees, which he could see now were made of weathered canvas, not buffalo skins. Some were regular camping tents. Rusty, battered trucks, and horse trailers stood everywhere. Gum wrappers, cigarette butts, and empty Gallo wine bottles already littered the ground. He saw two boys beating a mongrel dog with sticks—the dog was lame, and it yipped as it tried to keep ahead of the blows. Cheap enamel cooking pots sat steaming over fires. A boy and girl clad in faded Levis passed Johnny, arms around each other—they slid a glance at him and giggled (he wondered why). Then a tall, blotchy-faced youth passed, still wearing a dance costume—satin shirt, beaded vest, breech clout, feather roach on his head, strings of bells wound around his legs that spilled trails of voluptuous sound with every stride. The youth glanced at Johnny indifferently and went on, whistling, "Hey, Jude." The singing and clicking faded behind Johnny—he still didn't know what they were doing back there. He passed a huddle of old men gossiping by a teepee, rolling cigarettes with papers and sacks of Bull Durham, waving gnarled hands. Some of them had wispy grey braids. Johnny was aware that they stopped talking to stare at his horse.

Finally only a few lodges remained, tucked away in a bend of the creek. There a young man in the eternal Levis was unhaltering four or five horses, letting them go. He was quirt lean, pine straight, hat brim pulled insolently low, with neat braids even longer than Johnny's, their tassels trembling at thigh level. As he turned the last horse loose, Johnny stopped nearby and, afraid that his voice would crack like a teenager's from nervousness, said, "Say, are the Cheyennes around here somewhere?"

"If it's Northern Cheyennes you're looking for," said the young man in good English, one hand in his pocket now, hunching, hefting the halters, speaking past his cigarette and squinting in its smoke.

"I'm looking for Alex Feet."

The youth was looking him up and down with crafty insouciance now. "He's my dad."

Johnny was unable to meet those investigating eyes any longer. He looked down, turned away, pretended to check his cinches. "Tell Alex somebody he was looking for is here." After a moment he dared to look back again. The youth was still looking at him, but thoughtfully now.

"Okay," said the youth. "Come on."

Then walked without speaking toward the very last lodge, that stood near the creek by a dense clutch of willows. The grass was barely trampled here, and the rubbish kept picked up. The youth called out in what Johnny supposed was the Suhtai language. After a minute or so, a great barrel-chested Indian that Johnny recognized stepped out the flap door of the teepee and stood up. His close-cut hair was gunmetal grey, though Johnny knew him to be in his late fifties. He smiled slowly with thin, dry, fine-cut lips and came walking over to Johnny with a rolling walk like a bear's walk. He was wearing a wrinkled, old-fashioned, zooty striped suit with wide lapels and scuffed brown cowboy boots. His red wool tie had a silver clasp with a pendant spur. Alex Feet looked like a big old simpleminded cowman who would think nothing of crunching around all day over rough country in bad weather on a raw hard-mouthed horse hunting for one lost cow. He didn't look much like a writer, politician, and speechmaker. Johnny felt Alex Feet's shrewd little black eyes taking in the telltale details—the eagle feather tied in Spades's mane and his swollen lip where Tom had punched him.

"Johnny," said Alex softly. Johnny felt his own smaller, leaner hand swallowed by Alex's black calloused paw. Johnny was sure that Alex guessed everything, and he wanted to cringe with embarrassment. He waited for some too-frank words from Alex that would give him an excuse to climb on Spades and ride off.

But all Alex said was, "Tie up your horse and come in, Johnny."

Johnny tied Spades to the willows. He felt Alex's eyes flicking appreciatively over the buckskin horse, and heard him say something to his son, who muttered a reply and hunkered down with his back against the willows—Johnny guessed he'd told the boy to watch Spades. Then he found himself ducking in front of Alex through the teepee door.

Inside, an old woman with a broad shiny face and her hair knotted on the back of her head was fussing with a big chipped enamel coffee pot. The smoke from the fire spiraled up gently through the sooty smokehole. Near her, amid a disarray of blankets, saddles, and battered metal trunks, sat a sullen-looking, crosseyed teenage girl with glasses. She had lengthened her bristly braids in the old way by tying twists of beaver pelt to them. She was wearing a red flannel shirt and eating potato chips noisily.

"That's my wife, Belle," said Alex, "and my daughter, Dora. That was Billy out there. We started out with five, but lost three when they were little."

Johnny nodded as politely as he could and sat down on the blankets crosslegged, trying not to stare at everything. To fill time, he offered Alex a cigarette, and they smoked a little while the old woman fixed them two steaming plastic mugs of black coffee.

After a few minutes, though, Johnny felt obliged to say something, so he said, "The reason I came over is, I wanted to find out what all that damn singing is for."

"Oh, that," said Alex, chuckling. "That's the Indians having fun at their favorite sucker game. It's a guessing game called Hand, with bets thrown in. They land in Cottonwood with one paper dollar held together with scotch tape in their jeans, and they just can't wait to lose that dollar playing Hand. The tribes have been getting together to skin each other at Hand for hundreds of years. Men used to gamble away teepees and horses, even wives. Now it's just a worn-out paper dollar, and an inflated one at that. If you want, we'll sneak over and watch them play after a while. Don't get carried away, though. You might lose that nice little buckskin to some wino Cree."

"Did you about give up on me?" Johnny found himself saying stupidly.

Alex chuckled softly again, his whole muscular bulk flexing with the contained laugh. "Well . . . friend of mine saw you roping at jackpots. Said you were riding this Cheyenne-looking little buckskin with eagle medicine tied on its neck. I figured you were getting warm."

Johnny found himself chuckling too. The coffee smelled of camp smoke and dust. He supposed that Belle carried the water in from the creek, and was glad all of a sudden that Tom had located the camp upstream from Cottonwood sewage. Belle kept smiling toothlessly at him. He was also aware of Dora's hostile stare.

"I didn't do so good in them jackpots," he said.

"You're moving again, though. I got worried when I didn't see you moving around, there, for a while."

"I had a bad year."

"We've had a pretty good year. Well, not all that good. But the ice is beginning to go out. After a hundred years, it's going out. Sometimes I didn't think I'd live to see the day."

"I hear you travel a lot now."

Alex sipped his coffee, looking at the fire. "Well, the book is selling good. I get asked all over. You know, TV talk shows, book lunches, and cocktail parties in New York. I wear my dirty old boots, and I just twang those society masochists like a guitar string. Traveled more miles by plane in one year than the whole tribe ever traveled by horse, car, or foot in history. But we got a lot of work to do yet. We're beginning to get the publicity that we needed so bad—we can thank the black folks for starting that. But now that whitey is realizing there's also something called the Indian problem, the next thing will be to do something about the problem. And that won't be easy."

"What all has got to be done?" Johnny asked, relieved that Alex was diverting the conversation away from the subject of Johnny Eagle Chance.

"All we want," said Alex, "is for the government to stop running our lives for us. All we want is to be left alone, so we can solve our problems."

"Sounds pretty simple."

"It ain't, though, Johnny. The white man just can't leave people with problems alone. He can't solve his own problems either, but he has this itch to be always do-gooding. For instance, he oughta send his Peace Corps into the middle-class suburbs there in the East. Boy, I seen some things there that really need rectifying. So the Indian people are going to have to show their teeth, so they can be independent. Trouble is, we don't have the economic power that the blacks have, to put any bite in our teeth." Alex fished in a battered brown suitcase plastered with airline stickers, and brought out a new book. "Here,

Johnny, compliments of the author." He pulled a ballpoint pen out of his shirt pocket and autographed the flyleaf, then gave the book to Johnny. "Don't read it, Johnny. Just keep it around. It's a real bitter book. Not much in it that you don't already know."

Johnny inspected the cover. It showed the famous nickel-head Indian to which an artist had added some gritted white teeth, comic-book style. The title was *Biting the Dust*. Suddenly he felt a push of feeling for Alex, because of the way Alex was talking around things, the way grass grows up around stones, instead of coming to the point and asking questions or making comments. They sat there and drank another mug of coffee, while Dora kept munching potato chips in the background. Johnny just kept Alex talking and watched him perform. He liked, for instance, the way Alex's big-knuckled dark hands with their scratched silver rings moved expressively in the air.

After a while Alex said, "Why don't we take a little walk through the camp? I gotta talk to a few guys. I won't introduce you, if you want, and you can just stop, look, and listen."

As they stooped out the teepee, Johnny looked anxiously for Spades. But the horse was there, half asleep, one hind foot cocked, Billy still sitting by him.

"We've got a little trouble with your centennial committee," said Alex, as they walked slowly among the teepees to where the singing was still going on.

"The hell you say," said Johnny, knowing this meant Tom.

"Yeah. Seems the Indians got the idea that the centennial people were going to feed them. And seems the centennial people had no such intentions. I don't know whether it's a misunderstanding or just plain meanness. But I do know that a lot of Indians spent their last dollar on gas to get here. Some of them are pretty sore. A lot of them are talking about turning right around and going home, but they haven't got a cent."

Johnny felt his cheeks burning. "My brother Tom is head of the centennial committee."

"I know," said Alex softly.

"I'm plenty sore at Tom myself right now," said Johnny, "but I don't think he did it on purpose. I remember him talking last winter about where to put the camp. The town wanted him to put it some-where else, but he wouldn't, because he said the water was bad there."

"Well, I don't know," said Alex. "We went uptown to the rodeo office and tried to talk to him today. He looked real distressed and all, but he said that he just didn't have the money, and that we'd have to make out on our own."

"Did you threaten to pull out right then and there?"

"I never threaten anything without thinking it through first," said Alex. "If I had the money, I'd pay everybody's way home myself. But all the money from the book is plowed into other things. Well, anyway . . . a few of us are going to have a little meeting tonight and try to plan some strategy. We have the upper hand, of course, because we can spoil their centennial for them. No Indians, no pageant performance. But we'd have to do it without too much bad publicity for ourselves."

They came up to the big crowd and edged their way to where the singing and clacking was coming from. Alex didn't say anything, just let him look. The players were divided into two sides. Each side sat crosslegged along a pole laid on the ground. They beat sticks on the pole to keep time, and all sang that monotonous, nasal "hai-yah, hai-yah" melody over and over. One side had five willow stakes jabbed into the ground before it, and the other side had only three stakes. On the five-stake side, a leather-faced woman with buckteeth had a pair of worn little bones, one marked. She bent and swayed, as if possession of the bones made her drunk, and behind her back she passed the bones back and forth from one hand to the other, faster than a blur. Suddenly she yipped and shot out both arms, the bones clenched in her fists. The crowd of Indians buzzed with suspense.

On the other side, a wrinkled old man grunted and struck his left arm with his right hand. The buck-toothed woman laughed and threw the bones on the ground .The guess was wrong—the marked bone had been in the right hand. Yelps of delight and groans of disappointment drifted up from the crowd as a sixth willow stake was tossed over. The buck-toothed woman stabbed the stake into the ground with the other five. Then she grabbed up the bones again. Her teammates sang on, and she swayed and played with the bones.

Alex whispered in Johnny's ear, "That Assiniboin woman is real good. If she went down to Las Vegas, she'd put the Mafia out of business." Johnny stood with his eyes fixed on those polished bones, beginning to get the spooky feeling that the Indians were playing his own midnight dreams back and forth.

But Alex drew him gently away from the game, and they walked on. Alex's mind was already back to the food problem. "The ironic thing is, we donated some buffalo for a barbecue for the whole town.

The Crows did that. The buffalo were culls from their herd down there. The Crows always were brownnosing up to the whites. That'll teach them. Now they're sore and talking about reclaiming those carcasses to feed the camp with. This came up at another little meeting we had last night. And somebody piped up—I think it was John Bear Necklace, he's a Blackfoot—and asked, 'Do the Crows want to be Indian givers?' That got a big laugh."

"I'd talk to Tom," said Johnny sadly, "but he wouldn't listen to me."

"Nobody's going to twist your arm to get involved," said Alex. "They've all writ you off as a whitenoser and an Uncle Tomahawks anyway."

So Johnny leaned, unnoticed, against the back of a truck and smoked a cigarette while a group of tribal leaders met in front of one lodge. The Indians discussed and argued, sometimes in broken English, sometimes in their own languages. When Alex talked, Johnny expected that they would all show him some respect, but instead they gave a lot of argument. One tall young Crow named James Little Elk kept shaking his fist and saying that the young radicals were all ready to loot stores if food money wasn't forthcoming. Alex kept reminding him that Cottonwood had a crack riot squad used to put down prisoner rebellions in the pen, and that the Indians would get busted extra good. One thing seemed sure: the Indians were stuck there in Cottonwood, because a lot of them didn't have money to leave. Yet the only effective thing would be to threaten to leave all together. After an hour of oratory, the meeting broke up with nothing settled.

Alex rejoined Johnny and they walked back toward the Cheyenne lodges. Alex looked depressed. "We have to avoid violence," he said. "We're not going to make the mistakes that the black people make. Everybody loses when there's violence."

"Supposing somebody donated the money to feed the camp. Would they take it?" Johnny asked.

"Sure they'd take it," answered Alex with sad sarcasm. "The government has trained us to live on welfare. Back in the old days, too, Indians beggared themselves giving things away. The Cheyennes still tell about one of the chiefs who got off his horse, just like that, and gave it to some poor Arapahoe who was afoot. But who's going to donate money?"

"Me," said Johnny.

They had reached Alex's lodge again. Alex swung around and

looked at him hard for a moment or two, while the "hai-yah, hai-yah" of the stick game droned on nearby. Alex looked down as if he didn't know what to say and drew something with his boot toe in the dust. Then he looked up again. "You're welcome to spend the night," he said softly. "Belle can find an extra blanket somewheres. And we'll talk about it."

That night Johnny slept fitfully in the Feet teepee, curled up on Spades's saddle blanket with a human blanket thrown over him. The ground was hard, he shivered with cold, and his mind stampeded with thoughts. All around him the Feet family snored and breathed softly. The stick game went on long past midnight, until Johnny figured that every dollar bill in the camp must have changed hands at least three times. In a nearby teepee, some transistor radio wailed out Western music from the Butte station. Finally, along about the time the last coals sighed out in the fire and the sky paled, the camp quieted down. Johnny kept thinking about the first go-round of roping he'd face in a few hours, and found that he was curiously unhappy about being there in the Indian camp. When the Feets started getting up around seven o'clock, he was very stiff and upset.

He and Alex went down to the creek to check on Spades and wash their faces. While Johnny, Billy, and Dora sat combing their braids, Belle brought a bucket of water and boiled coffee and made fry bread. She fried the dough in a big skillet of hot grease, and they all broke it hot, sitting around.

"Once you've eaten Indian fry bread," said Alex teasingly, "you won't be able to leave."

Belle touched Johnny's arm with her gnarled mahogany hand. "You knowing where is nice place picking chokecherry? You telling me, I make nice chokecherry for fry bread."

Johnny's mind was half on calf roping, but he was able to make a small smile at Belle. "Sure," he said. "I'll take you where my white mother picks chokecherry, over across the river."

"His white mother!" Dora laughed savagely, speaking her first words in English.

"You shut up now," Alex told her. "I saw you eating all them potato chips last night."

So later that morning, Johnny and Alex climbed into Alex's pickup truck and they drove into town to have their confrontation with Tom. They parked right in front of the bunting-draped city hall, and went into the building and up to the second-floor where the rodeo office was.

The rodeo office was crowded with cowboys and girl barrel racers who'd just gotten into town the night before or that morning. Everybody was busy filling out entry blanks and paying their entry fees to Tom. When the rodeo people saw Johnny, there was a lot of "Howdy, Johnny," and quiet handshaking and backslapping. He could tell that word had gotten around that he would try to make a comeback at the Cottonwood rodeo.

Jimmy Alderman came in about then. He was a stocky, red-faced, six-foot Oklahoman who always dressed in impeccable conservative rodeo wear, even a tie. His face lit up when he saw Johnny. "Howdy, friend," he said, shaking Johnny's hand. Johnny was glad to see Jimmy, but realized guiltily that he hadn't thought much of Jimmy for months now. Jimmy's eyes slid to Alex, who was standing there looking so obviously like a full-blood Indian, and then back to Johnny. His eyes didn't even question Johnny—they merely said that they understood. That was the good thing about Jimmy Alderman.

"So how's that little Arizona pony been working out?" said Jimmy.

"Oh, pretty good," said Johnny, "You'll see him make a run this afternoon."

"Well, fellas," Jimmy announced to all in the office, "guess I'll be moving along."

"Gee, stick around a little," said another contestant. "The fun ain't started yet."

Jimmy indicated Johnny and said, "Ain't any use *any* ropers staying here in Cottonwood if this feller enters." Johnny glanced at Alex, wishing he could be so sure.

When Tom saw Johnny his face broke into its most fiendishly cheerful grin. "Howdy there," he echoed the others and whipped out an entry blank. "You all ready to place second?"

"You sheep-shit Assiniboin breed," said Johnny softly, taking the blank and slapping his hundred-dollar entry fee down on the table. A couple of the nearby contestants, among them Jimmy Alderman, caught his words. Their faces went straight and they pretended they didn't hear. Alex stood back, listening. "If I place second," said Johnny, "you're gonna place third."

"Why, Johnny, you sound real determined." Tom took the money.

"And I got something else to tell you," said Johnny. "It's about feeding the Indians."

Tom looked at Alex, then back at Johnny. "We had a big discussion about this yesterday. I'm mighty sorry about the misunderstanding, but I never said we were going to feed all those people. We just don't have the money."

"And I'll show you again," said Alex, "your letters to the tribal councils, in which you implied that food was included in the deal."

"Implication is something else," said Tom.

"How would you like to have your centennial spoiled?" said Johnny. "Supposing somebody up and gave those Indians money to get home? Supposing they all left today?"

Tom stood with lips pressed into a straight line, eyes on Johnny's entry blank. Finally he said, "Who's going to do that?"

"Me."

Tom laughed his mastodon laugh. "You don't have any money."

"You bet I do. I've got some up in a bank in Butte, that I was keeping to replace Rattler with, but it was never enough. It isn't enough to feed the camp either, but it's enough to move it out of here. All I have to do is drive to Butte and withdraw it, and by centennial time tonight this camp will be gone."

All the contestants were listening now, shifting uneasily in their boots. The rodeo office had gotten quiet—a typewriter was clacking somewhere, and there was that musty odor of filing cabinets in a small-town office.

Tom bent over and leaned his knuckles on the table, thinking. Finally he said softly, "Well, Johnny, like I said, we just don't have the money. I spent the last nickel of our centennial funds on fireworks to make things nice. If I have to pay a week's grocery bill for five-hundred Indians, it's going to have to come out of my winnings here. Which means that you might as well tear this up, Johnny." He handed back the entry blank. "Because you haven't got a chance."

"Well, I'm going to compete," said Johnny, getting angry now, "so you just hang onto this piece of paper." He was about to add that, in case he beat Tom and took the winnings himself, he would be magnanimous and pay the grocery bill for Tom. But he decided that would be a risky boast, so he kept his mouth shut. He, Jimmy, and Alex stalked out of the rodeo office together, and the murmuring contestants let them pass through, trying to figure out what it was all about.

When the three of them reached the street, Alex started chuckling. "You'll make an Indian," he said, "the way you were running down the poor Assiniboins."

When word rippled through the Indian camp that whitenoser Johnny Chance had out-politicked the centennial committee, Johnny felt uncomfortable as the Indians' attention focused on him. He didn't want to be looked at so hard. Some of the tribal leaders showed quiet appreciation. Others stayed aloof, their squinted black eyes questioning. But Johnny did feel good when, around eleven o'clock, he saw a couple of delivery trucks come into the camp from the Safeway, loaded with coffee, flour, beef, and other staples that Tom had picked out at Alex's advice. The Indian women flocked up and carried their groceries away. Soon beef was boiling on campfires all through the camp.

Around noon, the townspeople and tourists started to trickle into the camp to see the dancing, their shoes white with the pasture dust. A couple of old Indians rolled out the big drum, sat down by it, and hit the first thumps with their padded sticks. The dancers, who had been milling around in their finery and smoking cigarettes, ground their butts out under moccasined feet and fell into a slow, weaving circle around the drummers. The old men sat beating and chanting monotonously in high falsetto voices, as the dancers made sharp slashes of sound with the sleigh bells wound around their legs. One short, wiry, handsome dancer in a red satin shirt and a full eagle-feather headdress excelled at graceful weaving. Now and then he danced in place, turning in a full circle, showing himself off from every angle, like a male bird doing a mating dance.

"That's a Blackfoot name of Carl Reibuhr," said Alex. "He's a real fancy dancer. Wins prizes at the intertribal get-togethers."

"What kind of dance is that? War dance?"

Alex snorted. "It's a show-biz dance. We plains Indians have just about lost all our real dances. The real dances weren't for show, you know. They were all religious. So when the tribes started getting together for affairs like this, they had trouble with the real dances, because of the taboos. Somehow everybody picked up this one dance from the Omahas that didn't give anybody any trouble. I think the old-time Indians would die laughing if they could see this dance."

They went back to Alex's teepee. Johnny was getting more and more nervous about roping, which he would be doing in a couple of hours, and Alex tried to distract him. Stepping around the fire to the other side of the teepee, he pawed among the bedrolls, then came back carrying a small metal trunk. He put it down with a grunt, the ash from his dangling cigarette falling off onto the scuffed lid. He kneeled and searched in his pockets, finally fished up a keyring with dozens of battered rusty keys on it, and started thumbing through them. "A lot of these keys," he said, "I don't even know what they're for anymore. I've had some of them for twenty years. One was to lock up the Sacred Hat with, but she's with somebody else now."

"What's the Sacred Hat?" Johnny asked. He already knew what Ishiwun, the Sacred Hat, was, but he wanted to hear Alex tell about it.

Alex finally found the key he wanted and started fumbling with the padlock on the little trunk. "Oh, she's an old headdress with horns, made from a buffalo cow. Nobody know how old. She's the thing that gives the tribe their power. The old keeper of the hat died, and they couldn't find anybody to take his place. I had her for a while, but I wasn't a good keeper because I had to travel all the time. The keeper is supposed to live with the hat in a special teepee and pray all the time, to keep her from being polluted and losing her power. I kept her locked up, and Belle watched her while I was gone. But the hat, you know, she didn't like that. She got mad and started bumping around, making noises. Belle got so scared sometimes that she would hardly go near the hat. Finally we had a big tribal meeting about it and twisted Frank Walking Bull's arm to be keeper. He's old and doesn't travel, and he's ideal. So he's got the hat now, and she's real peaceful."

Johnny felt his scalp prickling with awe. "So the hat really has power," he said. He watched Alex's fingers, which seemed to be trembling with some emotion, still fumbling with the padlock.

"Well, the old people believe she does. Belle sure believes it. She heard the noises," said Alex, finally jimmying the padlock open. "Some of the young people believe too. My kids believe in the hat. But some of the kids don't give a damn. It's the same with the sun dance. We still have them, but the old men who knew some of the parts of it are dead now. I suppose the day will come . . . ."

"Do you believe in power?"

Alex slowly raised the trunk lid. His gaze suddenly shifted from its contents up to Johnny's face, pouring over him like a black light. "Power," said Alex, "isn't in things."

These words made Johnny want to shout out loud with desperation. "But do you have power, Alex?"

Alex's eyes didn't shift, and Johnny had to look down. "I have power," said Alex.

"How did you get it? Did you fast and see things and all?"

"I got it from eating Wheaties." Alex lifted an eagle-feather bonnet out of the trunk. It was a real one, richly hung with animal tails,

and its browband worked with dyed porcupine quills in that design
Johnny knew was taken from Ishiwun's browband. Alex tenderly laid
the bonnet on the plaid blanket. Johnny dared to reach and touch the
feathers.

"Took a few years to collect those," said Alex. "All my white
rancher friends, every time they'd shoot an eagle, they'd save me the
feathers. Couldn't let them poor eagles go to waste. Belle did the work.
She was trying to revive the real handicrafts, and she figured out how
to prepare the quills the old way, soaking them and chewing them and
dying them with plant dyes. We used quills before beads came in with
the white traders."

Alex was pulling out other things too: fringed hide shirts and
leggings, moccasins, breechclouts, and a magnificent, stained, antique-
looking breastplate of elk shin-bones. Johnny touched the breastplate.
"This looks old," he said.

"It is," said Alex. "A private collector gave it to me. We're sure
it's Cheyenne. I've compared it with Cheyennes wearing them in old
photographs. Somebody wore it in plenty of battles. The rest of the
stuff is new. Belle made it all, chewed the elkskin and everything."
He pointed at a woman's dress that still lay in the bottom of the
trunk, its breast hung with rows and rows of elk teeth. "That's Dora's.
It was a job collecting those teeth too. I went down to the elk shoot
at Jackson Hole and got a lot of them."

Johnny fingered the elkskin clothes. They felt strange, alive and
spooky under his hand, almost as if they could start making noises
like Ishiwun. "Some of these are yours?"

"Yeah, I wear them for ceremonials and show business. Try them
on."

"Me?"

"Try them on."

Johnny sat still for a moment, his inside constricting with a
curious mixture of fear and excitement. Then he stood up and quickly
shucked his clothes. Standing there naked, feeling a little shy, he could
feel the fire's heat on the backs of his thighs. Alex handed him a
breechclout and he pulled it up around his waist.

Alex chuckled. "Belle made me that years ago, when I was more
skinnier. Billy wears it now," he said as Johnny bent and pulled on
the moccasins.

Alex got up, holding the precious old breastplate, and apparently
was about to slip it over Johnny's head when his eyes fixed on Johnny's

chest. Johnny suddenly realized that he'd noticed the scars there, and that he'd realize what they meant. Heat rushing into his cheeks, he turned away. Alex's big hand closed on his arm as if he were a child, forcing him to turn back. Johnny stood rigid, waiting for comments from Alex. But Alex, his mouth now a grim line, just slipped the breastplate over his head and adjusted it gently. The darkened old bones, shiny with use, felt cool against his skin.

"I never did that," said Alex softly, bending to pick up the eagle bonnet. "Most of the men in my generation did, though. In those days the government wouldn't let us have the sun dance at all, even without the torture. So the men would go up in the hills alone and do it. But I never did. John Stands in Timber didn't either. We were about the only ones. I guess we just didn't feel the need. Matter of fact, I didn't do much of anything Indian until I realized I had no business going to the white man's church. So I pulled out and started going to the Native American Church there on the reservation. Peyote made me puke at first, and to be real honest with you, I didn't see all kinds of things, the way the others were always saying they did. But I felt better about it."

"The sun dance didn't work for me," said Johnny.

Alex lifted the eagle bonnet onto Johnny's head. A cold shudder shattered Johnny, as he thought how that bonnet might have been pulled off the rotted, insect-riddled skull of Head Chief. He could feel the rottenness against his own skull and could smell the odor of old bones that clung to the feathers. It had a smell like a place where soup had dried up.

"It doesn't work for everybody," said Alex. "Even in the old days, it didn't always work." He stepped back, smiled a little. "Too bad your dad can't see you."

"Did you know him?"

"We were about the same age. He didn't last long at the reservation school. I think the only English word he ever learned was 'goddamn.' I remember when he got married. He was so poor he only had one old horse to give for your mother. He was a good man, but simple as a child, and couldn't think straight about much of anything. And of course I remember when they brought the two of them back to bury them."

"Where?" Johnny felt his chest shake under the elk shin-bones and realized with some astonishment that he was going to cry.

"Up in the hills somewhere."

Johnny stood clenching and unclenching his fists, trying to will back into his eyes the two small tears that had started to migrate down his cheeks.

"I'll loan you the clothes," said Alex, "if you'd like to ride in the Indian scenes in the pageant. Be a great joke. Nobody in town would recognize you."

Johnny suddenly felt that he had to get those things off his body. They all had an earth and stone smell. He pulled off the eagle bonnet. "It's playing at being Indian," he said. "It's playing in a movie."

For the first time a glint of hurt showed in Alex's eyes. "It may look that way. But what else are we supposed to do? Play at being white men?" He made a small furious gesture. "Even the white men play at being white men. The whole town of Cottonwood, for instance."

Johnny turned away and had to bend over, wanting to weep so badly that his chest hurt. He wanted to say how sorry he was for having said such an unkind thing, but an inertia as heavy as a sandstone ledge lay on him. He was buried in a hollow under that ledge, his body thrust in there after a battle. Finally he said, "They're beautiful clothes, Alex."

Alex sighed heavily and took the eagle bonnet from Johnny's hands. "We have to reach back over a hundred years and pick up the loose ends," said Alex. "The loose ends where things were cut off." Johnny took off the breastplate, breechclout and moccasins, and, while Alex folded the things back in the trunk, he pulled his own clothes back on.

"It's hardest to help your kids pick up the loose ends," Alex went on. "The kids really suffer. I tried to put into the book how much they suffer. Especially in school, the BIA schools and the public schools, where the white teachers tell them that their people were dirty savages." Alex sat down crosslegged, staring into the fire. "The kids come out of school hating themselves. And a lot of them don't come out of school at all. They kill themselves there. We've got the highest suicide rate in the country. You wouldn't believe it—ten-year-old children hanging themselves in the showers. We had three suicides on the reservation last year. Our Billy got real wild for a while, drinking and all, but I've got him mostly straightened out now. Billy has got a levelheaded insolence that saved him. He's going to study law at the University of New Mexico this fall—got one of those Indian scholarships they give down there. But we had a real time with Dora. She tried to kill herself twice. Finally we took her out of school." Alex chuckled bitterly. "Good thing I was earning a little money by then, because if we'd been on welfare, the BIA would have cut off our welfare if we kept her out of school."

"But that's not legal!" said Johnny.

"The BIA can do anything they please with the Indians. You see, the law of this here United States democracy don't apply in practice to the Indians. Dora can sing nice, and we got her interested in learning the old Cheyenne songs now. But she's full of hatred. I get pretty bitter sometimes, but I know hatred doesn't work. Dora doesn't know that yet. She just hates white people. She won't dance when they're around, won't ride in parades or anything. She's a real fire-eating radical. If we ever have any Red Panthers, she'll be our Angela Davis. She was even giving me a bad time about letting you stay here, saying you were the worst whitenoser in the country. . . ."

Johnny sat crushed with sadness, still with that smell of rain-soaked bones in his nostrils. He was amazed that Alex would tell him all these private family things, and felt he had to reciprocate.

"Yeah," he said, "we've got one like that in our family too. My sister Kitie."

A couple of hours later, before a packed grandstand, with all those Indians watching and his own family watching too, he roped in the first go-round of the calf roping. Even with Spades working hard for him, he was pretty bad—his time was 19.4 seconds. Tom roped a calf in fourteen flat, and went on to do very well in both the steer-wrestling and bull-riding events. The Indians applauded Johnny with certain warmth, but he just wanted to crawl away from Cottonwood and go die somewhere.

And Kitie said, half in tears, "Johnny, baby, I miss you. Can't I come over to the camp and see you?"

And he snapped at her, "Look, just leave me alone for a couple more days."

That night it thunderstormed and rained, and Alex invited in some other Cheyennes to a big feed. They all sat around together, dishing Belle's fried beef and bread onto plates. The rain nearly put out the fire, but everybody seemed cheerful—Johnny could see that the Indians loved the excitement and socializing of the camps and would have been disappointed to pick up and go home. He felt a new kind of emptiness—he couldn't fantasize anymore, because he had walked into his fantasy. He would have liked to talk with the Cheyenne men so that he didn't have to think about those 19.4 seconds. But none of them knew much English. So Billy sat by Johnny, translating the jokes and trying to teach him a few words of Cheyenne, and he felt left out. Alex was a grand-style host, making everybody laugh all the time. Outside, the stick game started up as if it weren't raining at all.

When everyone had eaten and quieted down, Alex spoke softly to Dora.

"He's asking her to sing," whispered Billy.

"Will she do it?" Johnny whispered back.

"She ain't very modest," said Billy wryly.

Dora shifted her position a little and everyone got very quiet. As the rain pattered on the canvas, she sang in a low, hoarse, sure voice that was as flat as the plains, as cutting as the sky edge. She sang without moving a muscle, her face immobile, yet almost ecstatic, her eyes fixed on some invisible object in front of her. At that moment she acquired a certain homely dignity. She was less an uncombed juvenile delinquent with suicidal tendencies, and more a medicine woman with a terrible dark power gotten from some animal whose name nobody knew. Johnny wondered if the voice that John Stands in Timber had heard singing off beyond the old graves had sounded like that. He decided that he approved of this harsh, unembellished way of singing, with no Mantovani violins. Looking around at the Indians' faces, he saw that they were all listening with the same ecstatic concentration, their eyes fixed on her.

"Is this the real thing?" he whispered to Billy.

"Yeah," said Billy. "Not for tourists."

Dora sang for half an hour, one song after another, and everyone in the teepee stayed quiet the whole time. Finally Billy put his mouth close to Johnny's ear and said, "There was this anthropologist heard about Dora and he came up to Birney with his tape recorder. And she wouldn't sing for him."

When the Indians left and the Feet went to sleep, Johnny lay awake on Spades's saddle blanket, thinking about ugly Dora. A curious tenderness and peace made him nearly forget about that afternoon. Across the teepee, he could just barely make out her sleeping form beyond Belle's, rolled up in a blanket with her teeth clenched like some wild animal.

The next morning the weather cleared, and Johnny kept his promise to Belle about the chokecherries. Just about the time he and the
Feet were getting into Alex's truck with pails, Kitie and Fern came
wandering through the camp. All the Indians stared at Kitie's clothes.
Johnny gave Kitie an angry look, but Alex invited the two girls to
come along chokecherry picking.

As they drove through town with the young people riding, windblown, in the back of the truck, Johnny saw at once that Alex had
made a big mistake. Dora and Kitie hated each other immediately.
In fact, Dora hated Kitie so much that she again broke her rule about
never speaking English.

As they crossed the little concrete bridge over the Cottonwood
River, Dora said, her crossed eyes glaring through her thick glasses,
"I guess you must be one of those hippies who want to be Indians.
We've had a lot of them coming around."

"Oh, wow," said Kitie, giggling. "Oh, gee. I'm one-eighth Indian,
so I don't need to go on any heavy Indian trips."

They drove out across the drenched, shorn hayfields. There, on
the edge of a great cattail swamp bordering the river, a thicket of
chokecherry grew. The leaves were already yellowing, and the dark-
red clusters of berries hung thick and heavy among them. Johnny
knew that farther east on the plains, where it was hotter, the chokecherry season was over by now. As the truck pulled up, a lot of black-
birds flew up and whirred off—they had been feasting there. They all
got out of the truck.

Alex stretched in the hot sun. "This is nice," he said.

They all started picking cherries—even Alex helped. Dora kept
on complaining—in English—about how their lives were suddenly
overrun with Uncle Tomahawks and whitenosers. She muttered on and
on, picking furiously, filling her pail faster than anyone. Johnny kept
watching her as she moved, dark fingers flying, hair full of wet yellow
leaves, as she pushed away deeper into the brush. She was earthy,
angry, sure of herself, radiating that awful power. Fern didn't say
anything, keeping close to Kitie. Kitie whistled cheerfully. Billy kept
looking keenly from Kitie to Fern, as if trying to decide which of
them was most attractive. Belle looked very happy, the sun filtering
through the leaves onto her wrinkled old face. "Indians all the time
picking berries in the old days," she said.

"And him," said Dora, looking at Johnny significantly. "What
does he want from us? He must want something."

"Maybe he's as much Cheyenne as you," Alex said pleasantly, reaching for a high branch hung with many berries.

"Are you kidding?" said Dora.

Alex said something to her in Suhtai then. She stopped picking and turned to stare at Johnny, the bucket hanging forgotten from her hand. Belle and Billy stared too. Johnny stood wondering what Alex could have said to produce this reaction. Then he realized Alex had told them about the sun dance. He flushed so hot that he was sure he'd turned the same color as the chokecherries he held in his hand. He dropped them in his bucket, then turned away and pushed off through the brush in another direction, getting wetter, nearly losing his hat, and picked berries by himself.

Pretty soon he saw Dora picking her way toward him. She didn't even glance at him, but she was working her way toward him sooner or later. When she was six feet away, she put down her bucket. They were screened from the others by a maze of branches and dripping, yellow, sunlit leaves. A spicy late-summer smell rose up around them. Dora looked straight into his sideways-flitting eyes and said in that hard, hoarse voice, "Show me."

"Alex saw it. Don't you believe him?"

"Show me."

So he unbuttoned his shirt and showed her the scars. She came closer and inspected them with myopic intensity. He thought sorrowfully of the difference between the courageous man she thought him to be and the coward he really was. He wanted to tell her how it really happened, but he couldn't. He reflected that this was extra cowardice.

"That's good," she said. She touched one of the scars with her red-stained fingers. He felt himself vibrate, as if the power in her could flow into him like electric current. He raised his own moist, purpled fingers and closed them gently around her hand. Her gaze faltered, and after a moment she pulled her hand away with shy surliness and turned away to pick up her pail.

That afternoon, in the second go-round of the calf roping, he did even worse than yesterday. His time was 20.3 and Tom's time was 13.5. With cold will, Tom was leading all contestants in the bull riding and steer wrestling as well. And Kitie said to Johnny, "You creep, I saw you holding hands with that dumb Dora in the brush." And he snarled at her, "I never told you I loved you. So if you don't like it, why don't you just leave?"

Then it seemed to Johnny that, from where he was, inside the photograph, the photograph was real and flowing. And out there beyond, it was Cottonwood that was now frozen into a cheerful documentary, a phantasmagoria of things across the wide Missouri. It was a moment that would never come again. One hundred years ago, Cottonwood was a few smokey teepees pitched near a hot spring and a Metis half-blood idly panning for gold along some gravel bar. One hundred years from now, Cottonwood would be a five-thousand-acre asphalt parking lot in a suburb of Los Angeles or Chicago, depending on which megalopolis sprawled in that direction first. It was a moment that would never come again, as Cottonwood acted out its own centennial pageant.

Johnny knew that the townspeople, too, were searching for a lost self along some gravel bar, or in some mysterious, untrodden cottonwood grove with the sunlight filtering in. Or among the thickets of yellow roses gone wild in the ghost towns and among the old silver mines. Or beyond the toppling hollyhocks that still came up faithfully by some fallen-in cabin. Or on every abandoned ranch and wheat farm that the bankers had foreclosed on. Or surely in the glint that flashed along the railroad tracks, where the Milwaukee Olympian Hiawatha ran no more. The people of Cottonwood, too, had been sacrificed, and he was willing to allow them that. They, too, had been betrayed by manifest destiny.

He did not even go see the pageant that Saturday night. Instead he sat there with Belle and Dora in the Indian camp, panicked by the thought that tomorrow was Sunday, the last day of the rodeo, and the only day he had left to redeem himself as a roper with all those red soul brothers looking on. That evening he walked around in the half-deserted camp, and looked across the old highway at the fairgrounds ablaze with floodlights. He knew that there was a capacity crowd because the parking field was jammed with cars and clouds of cigarette smoke drifted up from the grandstand into the lights. A lot of Indians, including Alex and Billy, had dressed up and taken their horses over there to be ready to perform. Now and then he could catch a word from among the echoes of the announcer's voice as it ricocheted around the fairgrounds, and the word told him exactly where the pageant performers were in the script. The tunes that the band played told him the same.

The first scene was the camp of Metis and Frenchmen, with the half-blood coming in with the nugget he had found. There followed

a mob scene representing the gold rush, with prospectors and honky-
tonk ladies parading across the arena—Johnny could faintly hear the
band playing "Oh, Susannah." Scene 2 was the arrival of the cattle
business, with a herd of Mexican steers (Tom had borrowed them
from the rodeo contractor) being galloped across the arena. From
where he was in the camp, all Johnny could see was a great cloud of
golden dust billowing up into the floodlights, and he heard the band
playing, "Goodbye, Old Paint."

Then the Indians took over, for Scene 3. Hundreds of mounted
Indians, painted and bristling with feathers, swept down on the U.S.
Army supply train just as they had during the Skillet Creek fight. By
now the air above the fairgrounds was a mushroom cloud of dust.
Johnny wondered how much ironic relish Alex and the rest must feel
as they celebrated a victory which had gotten them nowhere. The
fairgrounds resounded with fake gunfire and Johnny could visualize
the rodeo arena littered with "dead" troopers and Indians as the tribes
decimated the supply train. The band played "Garry Owen."

Scene 5 was the Cottonwood County range war, as William
Chance joined forces with Fitz Brodie against some ranchers up the
valley over the Skillet Creek water rights. A bullet that Johnny could
not see cut down the great-grandfather that was not his, and William
Gordon Chance fell from his saddle dead onto the arena dust. The
band played "O Bury Me Not."

Scene 6 continued the blood-letting, as the local stockmen vigi-
lantes hunted down Henry Tuner and his gang of cattle rustlers. They
hung them right in the arena, on faked gallows on which Tom and the
local carpenters had expended a lot of ingenuity—a real old-time neck-
tie party calculated to chill the spectators and make them glad that
they lived in the humane twentieth century. The band played Chopin's
"Funeral March" (not a Western tune, but one that everybody recognized) as the bodies were toted out of the arena.

Scene 7 was more lighthearted, as the centennial cast reenacted
the great match race between Marcus Daley's famous Thoroughbred
Tammany and Fitz Brodie's half-Thoroughbred, half-mustang Reveille.
As the bettors surged and shouted and ladies drove up in carriages,
the two local horses paraded to the old-fashioned tape (which had
been resurrected from some shed there on the fairgrounds) with borrowed jockeys in old-fashioned silks on their backs. The band, of
course, played "Camptown Racetrack" as Reveille whirled across the

finish line a head in front of Tammany, and several local fortunes changed hands as the bets were paid off.

"Those were some doings, in those days," Johnny thought, as he walked around the camp with Dora, kicking at rocks.

Then the railroads came, with an amazing iron horse that the local blacksmiths had worked for months to create, its big black stack belching fire as it chugged across the arena. The packed stands oh'd and ah'd, then broke into applause. (Music: "Casey Jones.") And the sheepherders and honyokers came, to the tune of "My Little Old Sod Shanty." Then there was a Gay Nineties extravaganza, with a mass of ladies and gentlemen waltzing all over the dusty arena and the band playing "Blue Danube."

Finally Johnny stood there listening to the grand finale. He knew that the script called for the entire cast to parade through the arena, bowing and waving at the crowd, as the band played "Home on the Range." The grandstands applauded wildly as the announcer read the last lines of the script, describing how Cottonwood had lived through great days, and if everybody had faith in the future, they could create a new heroic era. Then the sky above the fairgrounds lit up with sky rockets and aerial bombs, and the echoes went rolling off across the valley —those fireworks that had left Tome unable to pay for Indian groceries.

As the grandstands emptied and people started driving cars out of the parking field, the Indians came riding back into camp, turned out their horses and took off their war bonnets. Johnny sat with Belle and Dora outside the teepee looking sadly at the smoke and dust still hanging in the floodlights' glare. The script hadn't mentioned anything about the 1929 market crash or the Depression or two world wars, because nobody in town was ready to feel that kind of nostalgia yet.

Johnny pondered how the script had twisted things or glossed them over. How the land, yanked from buffalo worship into Protestant hymn singing and Catholic candle lighting, had taken its revenge. How the town mourned the dwindling of its few gaunt customs—Grange suppers, the word-of-honor deal, the right to carry firearms, roping calves at branding time, cooking for the threshing crews, lambing, the little grocery store—the same way the Cheyennes mourned their sun dance. He pondered how Cottonwood would dry up like a tumbleweed someday and be blown off by some big wind and fetch up against some barbed wire fence of doomsday, because the same forces that made it grow were now gnawing its roots away.

It was a moment that would never come again. Tomorrow, in the spicy dusty noon hour, in the field near the fairgrounds, the sweet charred odor of the buffalo carcasses would drift away from the barbecue pits. A long line of buckskinned men and parasoled, bustled women would file past the laden picnic tables, and white-hatted chefs would deftly carve. The people would load their paper plates with smoking slices of fine-grained, grass-fattened buffalo meat, potato salad, baked beans, cold slaw, hot rolls, slabs of butter, and apple pie baked by the church ladies. Everyone would sit on the dusty grass, in the shade of the cottonwood trees, and eat their fill of buffalo meat with ketchup, while across the road in the camp, the Indians were busy frying corn-fed beef.

So Johnny decided he would go into town and get drunk. Maybe all he needed was a good cleansing spree. He'd been a good boy for too long, up there at cow camp, with just one woman and no whiskey at all. Besides, he hadn't seen much of Jimmy Alderman.

When he got to town, he found hundreds of people self-consciously doing square dances along Main Street. A handful of rodeo contestants were joining in. A caller piped through a bullhorn, "Aaaaaaall promenade home!" Men's boots stomped the asphalt and women's flounced skirts swept it—echoes of all-night dances of a hundred years ago. Johnny stopped to see if Jimmy Alderman was there dancing, but he didn't see him, so he went on up Main Street, looking into each bar.

As he passed the Elks Club, he heard the eerie wail of an electric guitar and saw the Cottonwood kids spilling in and out, so he peered in. The Elks had sponsored a dance for the kids, to try and keep them out of trouble, and had engaged an Indian country-rock band who called themselves the Super Chiefs. Johnny smiled as he saw the musicians over the sea of young heads—four wild-looking, long-haired Indian boys in satin shirts and bell-bottom jeans like Kitie's. They were writhing and leaping with their guitars, amid the microphones, amplifiers, electric organ, and the tangled cords on the stage floor. Johnny thought he glimpsed Kitie's mass of coppery-red hair in the crowd, and he didn't feel the slightest nostalgia for her. If she was there, it meant she had revolted against Ma Maureen's curfew law.

Farther up the street, Johnny glimpsed Jimmy Alderman in Brown's, so he went in. Most of the other rodeo contestants were

lined up at the bar, numbing the day's bruises. The bar was crowded
with shot glasses, puddled with whiskey. A few men were dancing with
girls near the jukebox, all of whose scratched records seemed to play
"The Tennessee Waltz." Johnny strode through them feeling raunchy
and wild.

"Howdy, Johnny," the contestants all said, and in a moment he
found himself drawn up to the bar beside Jimmy. Mary, the barmaid,
pushed a brimming shot glass toward him. Johnny poured the whiskey
down his throat, thinking that when all was said and done, it was
more effective than marijuana.

"Tomorrow," said Jimmy, "I'm going to wish I was one of them
fellers that goes to bed early." He looked thoughtful and glassy-eyed.

"Tomorrow, I just don't know what I'm going to wish," said
Johnny.

They stood hunched there, as they had in many bars in many
cities and towns across the United States, with the whoops, jokes, and
dancing jostling them. Johnny finished his second whiskey and it
went down like skin peeling off. Mary came to pour a third, but
Jimmy reached out, fumblingly put his hand over Johnny's glass, and
shook his head slowly for a long time. Mary went away. So, feeling
that familiar glacier of meekness grind him to dust, Johnny let him
have his way. Anyway, his head already felt like a train speeding past
—that diesel train that didn't stop at the Cottonwood station any
more.

"I can't rope and I can't get drunk," said Johnny. "Maybe I
better quit rodeo and go to Hollywood."

"It's Fern," said Jimmy. "I know your ma thinks I'm too wild
for her, but I just can't get her out of my mind. Hope you don't mind
my saying so."

"Hell, I don't mind. She ain't my sister anyway. Why don't you
marry her? She's needing to settle down."

"A flat broke, patched-up drunk like me." Jimmy grinned drunkenly—both of them knew he would be fresh as milk by grand entry
time tomorrow afternoon.

"I'll take that $2500 I was gonna give the Indians and give it to
you two for a wedding present." Johnny suddenly found himself talking louder and getting angry. The way was just as hard for Fern,
Jimmy, and Kitie as it was for himself, Dora, Alex, and all those
Indians camped out there. "That's what happens. You get intolerant

and ask for too much, and you end up with nothing. There was a time when they knew how to make good out of all the bad things, instead of throwing the bad things out with the garbage."

"What bad things is that?" said Jimmy, who didn't cover his own glass as Mary poured him another.

"Fucking, and killing, and seeing things in the dark."

Johnny looked over his shoulder to see if there was some blonde Marilyn around that he could dance with, if nobody else in the bar objected, but he didn't see one that he liked. Then he felt like picking a fight with somebody, even Jimmy, even though he knew he'd be kicked around and get his face spoiled. But everyone was cheerfully paying no attention to him. At that moment, the white man's useful degradations lay even farther away, even more snow-desolate, than the sun dance of a century ago.

So the next thing he knew, he was walking with Jimmy along the dark highway out of town, back toward the Indian camp. He was only a little dizzy and not at all cleansed. He was busy telling Jimmy that he wouldn't object if Jimmy slept with Fern right now, and Jimmy was too cheerfully drunk to understand the significance of this. After all, he owed Jimmy Alderman a lot. A long time ago, Jimmy Alderman had put the finishing social touches on a very tough young Indian roper.

The next morning was Sunday morning, the last day of the Cottonwood centennial and rodeo. Johnny sat crushed with depression on his blanket in the Feet teepee, struggling to comb his hair without the luxury of the mirror that he'd always enjoyed at home. At moments he was beginning to miss the big white ranch house with geraniums planted around it and Ma Maureen. Belle was boiling coffee, Billy was out catching horses, and Alex had gone off to talk Indian politics with somebody. Johnny kept working away with the comb, sure that he was making more snarls instead of less.

Dora got down on her knees in front of Johnny and said, "Give me that comb. In the old days, the women combed the men's hair."

Meekly Johnny let her do it, looking down, enjoying the touch of her fingers against his head as she expertly parted and smoothed his hair, then started braiding.

"Not all time," said Belle, cackling cheerfully. "Just sometimes, if wife very good or husband very lazy." She took the bucket and went out for water.

When they were alone, Johnny put both hands up to Dora's face and held it. She pulled back, nearly knocking off her glasses, but he held her. Her fingers tightened in his hair, and she dropped the comb. Her eyes got even more crossed, and then she closed them. All the time Johnny was studying her round dark face with its large-pored skin and feeling her coarse hair. He wondered why he felt this way about this ugly teenage girl, the first Cheyenne girl he had ever laid eyes on. In fact, he asked himself why none of the females in the camp looked pretty to him. Alex had pointed out a Sioux girl who had been Miss Indian America two years ago, and Johnny had privately sworn that the girl was homely. He figured that Kitie was right about Anglo-Saxon tits being wired into his brain. But he had to touch Dora, and he knew that she wanted him to touch her. For a minute their faces were close together—say, about twelve inches. Then he heard Belle's footsteps coming back, and he let her go.

Kitie stood there holding her motorcycle, wearing her red windbreaker, her mica helmet, and her goggles. Her sleeping bag and other things were packed on the bike. Her bush of red-brown hair stuck out from under the helmet, her face was blank, and above her bandaged nose her eyes were like two slots in a vending machine. Johnny stood there feeling upset and helpless. Fern stood there too, cheeks tie-dyed with tears, wearing her black silk Gay Nineties dress with muttonleg sleeves and rhinestone buttons that Ma Maureen had made her. Beyond them, on the edge of the campgrounds, hundreds of Indians were gathering for the noon-hour centennial parade through town. Feathered and beaded, they galloped their horses up and down with exuberant yells, boiling up dust everywhere.

"Well, I'm going," said Kitie.

"Bye, Kitie," said Fern. The two sisters touched hands.

"I'm sorry," said Johnny. He really was, too.

"No, you're not," said Kitie, her voice dammed up with tears. "I got you to come to the camp. But you like that shitty Dora, and you're not sorry."

"Where you figuring on going?"

"I don't know," said Kitie. "I might go to South America and join the guerrillas. I might go back to New York and start a bomb factory. I'll blow up Dow Chemical and General Motors and the White House."

"Kitie, write me a letter, won't you?" Johnny felt sick with guilt,

hearing the thousands of hoofs rattling over the ground off over there.
And he told himself that this was all he needed to make sure he'd fail
spectacularly in the calf roping a couple of hours from now.

Straddling the motorcycle, she furiously kicked it into life. "No,
I won't write you a letter," she shouted over the engine. "I'll send you
a bomb in the mail." The motorcycle vibrated with maniac exu-
berance, the exhaust kicking up its own echo of the horses' dust.
Suddenly Kitie bent over the handlebars, weeping. Her lips moved,
and she seemed to be saying, "Johnny, Johnny, Johnny," over and
over again, but the howl of the motor drowned her voice. Johnny
moved toward her to grab her by the shoulders, shake her, comfort
her. But she saw him coming. She twisted the throttle, lifted up her
feet, and the motorcycle shot away from him.

He stood watching her streak along the dusty track to the pasture
gate, scaring a few Indian horses. She turned sharply onto the old
highway, her windbreaker ballooning out bravely. The whining, pop-
ping howl of the engine soared in pitch. Then she disappeared behind
the cottonwood trees and the first houses at the city limit. Johnny
figured she would make one last grand sweep down Main Street on
her way out of town. He thought of her garden drying up at cow
camp. Long after the sound of the bike had died away, he still
imagined that he could hear it, though there was nothing around but
the shouts of the riders and the drumming of their mounts.

Fern stood sobbing softly, chin sunk on her lace bosom, her bob
and her long stiff skirt flaring in the wind. Johnny took a couple of
slow, sorrowful crunching steps toward her and touched her shoulder.
She swayed against him, clutching his shirt. Her hair blew against his
mouth. Under the Cheyenne law, brothers and sisters had little to do
with each other. Johnny dared to let her lean against him, hoping that
this, maybe, would free him, if nothing else would.

"You'll get along all right," he said.

"No, I won't."

"Yes, you will. Jimmy Alderman will see to it that you do."

As the murmur of the packed grandstands flowed down into the
dusty arena, Johnny rode Spades around in slow circles, hefting his
loop nervously, his pigging string clenched in his teeth.

He felt himself to be a desperate and empty silhouette against
that film setting of crowd, arena, contestants, pickup men on stocky

little horses, the broncs and bulls in the corrals, the dusty afternoon sunlight. In fact, he imagined himself to be a hole in the shape of a horse and rider. He would be the next roper out of the box, and still his soul staggered and floundered, like a hog-tied calf trying to get up.

He had gone through all the ritual prerodeo gestures that usually calmed his nervousness, but this time none of them had helped. First, he had dressed the way his public had learned to expect: in the wildest of the clothes that the manufacturers had sent him. He wondered for the first time if he dressed that way just because he thought he should, or because there was something in Indian genes that gravitated toward pretty clothes. He had on a pale lavender silk shirt, a cream-colored, high-quality felt hat. An Indian-print silk scarf which Kitie had given him was floating at his neck—it had fat lavender Oriental horses printed on it. The chaps he'd worn for bronc riding were brown with baroque lavender appliques, and he'd left the bottom buckle undone for extra flapping drama as he spurred the bronc. His soft cream-colored boots were richly stitched. Then, as the rodeo got underway, he had checked all his equipment over and over again with neurotic delicacy, though he didn't change anything for fear of bad luck. Theoretically, he had practiced enough all summer to get his edge back—but he knew it wasn't going to be enough.

Out of the corner of his eye, he could see the Indians crowded along the arena fences, squatting on top or peering through the heavy planks: silent, avid men, women, and children, most of them in Levis with hats pulled low, some of them in dance feathers. He could feel their warmth and support. And he knew that wasn't going to be enough either.

Behind him, he heard the bang and the rap of hoofs, as the chute gate popped open and Tom's Sundown jumped out after the calf. He closed his eyes, hearing the rising shriek of the crowd. He could imagine how Tom's loop sailed out, how the calf jerked around at the end of it. Tom would be down and running now, flanking the calf down with a swift brutal jerk, bending, tying madly, flinging his arms up to hooey. The grandstand noise died off.

"Ladies and gentlemen," said the announcer, his voice ricocheting around the fairgrounds, "thirteen flat for Tom Chance. Thirteen flat. Mighty nice time." There was a polite patter of applause.

Johnny imagined the calf being untied, Tom walking back to Sundown and mounting, and the calf galloping across the ring to the holding pen. Tom was probably feeling pretty smug with that thirteen seconds. The other contestants would have to hurry to beat it, or Tom would take the purse.

"Next contestant, ladies and gents, is Johnny Chance." The announcer's voice echoed everywhere, from grandstand to race barns to billboards and back.

The applause sprang up like new spring grass. The Indians were clapping madly along the fence. The Cottonwoodians were clapping too—less madly, perhaps, but after all he was theirs, even if he was a redskin varmint. He was the only world-champion rodeo cowboy that they could brag about. He listened to the applause and wanted to slide down somewhere between his horse and his horse's shadow, and just disappear.

"Johnny Chance," repeated the announcer, sounding as if he would shave ten seconds off Johnny's time just to be Christian. "Give him a big hand, ladies and gents. He's been out of competition for a year, and he's making a comeback. Let's encourage this boy to do his very best. Maybe we'll get to see that supersonic hot lick of his."

Without looking up to acknowledge the applause, Johnny rode into the box, holding the loop ready in his right. The applause choked off into a ringing silence. After all, he was the old enemy, so they weren't sure whether they wanted to see him wild, gorgeous, pitiless, and free before their eyes, or sprawled harmless in the dust with his horse galloping off riderless. Johnny saw the junior brahma calf's tawny back there in the chute to his right. Spades turned around without the rein even touching his neck—his ears were cocked back, and he was listening for confident vibrations from his rider. Johnny felt Spades squat down, bracing his butt against the heavy planks at the back of the box. The horse seemed to vibrate with controlled excitement.

"Sweet medicine horse," Johnny wanted to say, "go rope the calf your own self, and leave me here to die."

The chute door popped the calf out. Without the faintest signal from Johnny, Spades jumped into a gallop with perfect timing, his chest not quite brushing the tape as it snapped back in front of him. Automatically Johnny swung his loop, feeling Spades changing leads to rate the calf's dodging and shifting as it ran across the arena. Feeling that he moved with ghastly slowness, like a dead man, Johnny hurled the loop. It hit the calf's head all right, but when Johnny pitched his slack, it popped off again.

"Shit," Johnny said to himself, scarcely hearing the groan of disappointment that welled up from the crowd. Fumbling and losing precious seconds, he finally snatched out the second loop. The calf galloped to the fence on the other side. As it doubled back, Spades doubled, too, nimble as a cat. In another second, he was pounding along behind the calf at just the perfect distance and angle for a throw. Johnny hurled the second loop, and he knew it was going to miss. It did, tumbling off the calf's head into the dust, then trailing after Spades.

"Shit," Johnny repeated. He rode slowly back across the arena as the hazers drove the calf to the pens. He didn't even lift his head to look at the Indians along the fence, not even at Alex Feet who was standing there somewhere.

The announcer was outdoing himself in Christianity. "Give him a big hand anyway, ladies and gentlemen. These are the heartbreaks of the game. These things happen to the best of them. We're going to wish Johnny better luck next time out." The crowd dutifully applauded.

Johnny left the arena and dismounted, coiling up his dusty rope. He was aware of a few sympathetic people grouping around, and he tightened his lips, ignoring them. Out of the corner of his eye, he saw a familiar pair of scuffed brown boots and knew that Alex Feet had come up. He also knew that Alex was too smart to say anything to him right then.

Tom walked over to Johnny, grinning cheerfully. "That was a beautiful performance, Johnny boy. Whoooee." Jimmy Alderman had come up too, and Johnny saw Jimmy almost open his mouth to tell Tom to shut up. Then he sensed that Jimmy thought better of meddling in family business. Johnny looked hard at Tom for a moment, then went on coiling his rope.

Then, to his amazement, Tom took Spades by the reins and started to lead him off. For a moment, Johnny simply stared. Then, with one swift convulsive move, he leaped and grabbed Tom's sleeve, managing to haul that human bulldozer to a stop. Spades jerked his head up, his black ears swiveling wildly. "Where you going with my horse?" Johnny said, his voice shaking.

"Your horse?" said Tom, affecting pleasant surprise.

"God damn you, give me those reins."

"Why, Johnny, this is the banker's horse," said Tom. Johnny tried to jerk the reins loose, but Tom simply shoved him aside with a gentle twitch of muscle. Spades stood there with head strained high, dark eyes white-ringed and rolling, sensing this crossfire of emotion around him.

Johnny stood turned to glacier. If he hit Tom, Tom would hit him back, and then would proceed to smash him like a beer bottle on a rock, the way he had done up at cow camp. All the Indians would see it. As he stood in that moment of hesitation, Tom grinned again, pulled his sleeve from Johnny's fingers, and walked off. The confused but obedient Spades fell in behind Tom. Johnny watched the horse's black-speckled golden rump swaying off in the afternoon sunlight, the short black tail held out nervously.

Choked with fury, as if a rope had jerked tight around his own throat, Johnny turned to face Alex and Jimmy. Alex's eyes were narrowed and dark with angry sorrow. Then, suddenly, the big Cheyenne swung around and ran off, with the loping clumsy gait that any old man would have in cowboy boots. He ran toward the chutes with such an air of purpose, dodging in and out among knots of Indians, contestants, and tied horses, that Johnny and Jimmy Alderman had to follow him slowly. Alex ran up the little wooden stairway to the announcer's booth above the chutes. The last roper was just going into the box, the last roper of the last go-round of the Cottonwood centennial and rodeo. Looking up, Johnny saw Alex talking fast with the announcer.

Dora, Belle, and a few other Cheyennes came over to Johnny. "What he up to?" Belle asked. "Never see him run so fast, except from bear one time."

"I don't know," said Johnny.

The last roper tied up for a time of 17.2 seconds. Tom had won the calf roping. He would be able to pay the Indian grocery bill. There were a few moments of silence as the announcer conferred with Alex and the judges, and the crowd murmured restively. Then the announcer said, in that tone of voice reserved for special occasions, "Folks, we've got something cooking here. Something not on the program. Something you're really going to enjoy too. I'm now going to hand the mike to one of our Indian guests who've come to Cottonwood to help make our centennial a success. Namely, Alex Feet, one of the tribal leaders of the Northern Cheyennes, from over at Lame Deer, Montana. . . ."

The mike plunked as it changed hands, amid a ripple of polite applause that died out right away. Alex stood there with the mike at his mouth, looking big and powerful, his barrel chest pushing his tie out between the lapels of his old-fashioned suit, the way he must look at Senate investigations and intertribal congresses. And then Alex's voice, as dark and opal-smooth as an old tree-trunk where generations of buffalo had scratched, filled the fairgrounds.

"Ladies and gentlemen," said Alex, "it took some doing to get all these Indians to Cottonwood. We traveled a long ways, from every part of the state, and we spent lots of money for gas, and all . . . and one of the reasons all us Indians came here was to see a little fancy roping by another Indian name of Johnny Chance."

He paused gravely. The stands were silent. Then, as the delicacy of this little joke sank in, people started giggling. A soft ripple of laughing swept the fairgrounds. The Indians were slapping their knees and poking one another.

"And now," said Alex, "we've got to turn around and go home again . . . and spend all that money for gas all over again. . . ." The laughing got louder. "And for the next few days every Indian in Montana is going to be cussing in gas stations, just because Johnny had a little hard luck. . . ." Listening to this, Johnny was still so angry that he was about to go beat Alex up for making fun of his hard luck in public.

"Folks, just think," Alex went on, "about all those poor Texaco and Gulf and Esso guys being cussed out all over the place by all these Blackfeet and Sioux and Crees. We just gotta prevent it. So I'm going to make a little proposition." The laughter died right off. "This was the last go-round of the rodeo, so Johnny has missed his chance at both the purse and the day money. But I'd like to propose that we give Johnny an extra, free go-round. The show ain't running late, so we got plenty of time. Johnny's plenty mad now, and I'll bet that he won't miss no more calves. Can we get, say, fifteen calves to the box over there? Johnny, are you down there? What do you say, Johnny?"

The crowd was applauding happily. Johnny just stood there, not knowing what to think. The men in the corrals were already hazing a bunch of calves into the chute that led to the box.

"And, Johnny, tell you what. We Indians love to gamble. If I was going to make you a fancy wager, I'd put up, say, a hundred dollars for every calf you rope in fifteen seconds or under. But I gotta save some money for gasoline. . . ." The crowd started laughing again. "What with inflation and all, they're going to raise the price of gas twice before I can get home to Lame Deer. . . ." The crowd was swaying, choking with laughter. "So, Johnny, I'll put up one dollar for every calf in fifteen or less. Where's your horse, Johnny? I saw some-body leading Johnny's horse off to the barns. . . ."

Alex said an aside to the announcer, who spoke into the mike himself. "Will whoever went off with Johnny's horse bring him back here?" The voice went rolling around the fairgrounds like the crack of doom—Tom could have heard it if he were already halfway back to the ranch.

Suddenly Johnny felt some midnight bubble of laughter burst in his throat. If he'd been alone, like when he roped the eagle, he could have let go and laughed like a crazy man. As it was, he had to keep a pretty straight face. In about one minute, Tom came galloping up on Spades, his face grey as dust. Without a word, he got off, shoved the reins angrily at Johnny and stalked away.

With a fierce, voluptuous joy, Johnny ran his hand down Spades's neck, checked the mane to make sure Tom hadn't jerked the eagle feather out and thrown it down somewhere among the greasy ham-burger papers and cigarette butts. The feather was there. He climbed on and rode into the arena, Jimmy Alderman swinging the gate open before him. Something burned bright under his breastbone, throwing the whole arena into strange light, giving every man and horse and other object in it a terrible shadow. Pa Gene's ghost was going to watch him now. The applause swelled toward him again, like cumulus clouds bringing an afternoon thunderstorm.

He shook out his loop and rode into the box. Far from being in a happy daze, he was hard, cold, and lucid. As Spades braced himself against the planks, he felt that the horse sensed the change in him, that Spades too was ready to be pitiless and full of immortal skill.

The calf popped out. Spades ran it down, and he roped it, fell off, and tied it. "Twelve point five seconds," cried the announcer. The crowd heaved itself up into a joyous roar.

Something hurt under Johnny's breastbone, as if it were going to break open from some budding pressure beneath. He roped a second calf, then a third and a fourth, depriving Alex of a dollar each time. The grandstand was a tunnel of noise. The cowboys hung intent from the fences and the bucking chutes. They clustered, stiff and ecstatic, in front of the chutes. Again and again Spades made perfect runs, sweeping Johnny up to the calf in scant seconds, sitting and skidding to a stop in a bomb burst of dust, holding the rope right while Johnny ran and tied. And Pa Gene was watching his son roping tough, roping hot lick. Spades's dust drifted off again and again, faster and faster, as if tossed up by bullets striking the dirt in a film being speeded up. Wild, furious, ecstatic, Johnny sailed off the horse to land running, his braids flying. He was aware that he lost his hat, that on the eleventh run he tied up in 9.8 seconds to break his own world record of three years ago, that he was Head Chief, Young Mule, and Morning Star's son all at once. The grandstand slid down over him with a roar of applause, like a many-colored glacier breaking loose from the blue glacier of the sky. The Indians were waving and clapping wildly along the fence. He kept roping—twelve, thirteen.

"Johnny," said Alex, stepping to the mike as Johnny took the rope off number thirteen. The crowd hushed quickly to hear Alex speak. "Johnny," said Alex again, faking sadness and pausing dramatically. The crowd rustled with titters, sensing what Alex was going to say. Johnny grinned dizzily, thinking what a hell of a vice-president Alex would make, for all that speechmaking on TV.

"Johnny," Alex went on in a grave note of accusation, "can I borrow some of them dollars back to get home with?" The crowd laughed.

"Just two more calves, folks," said the announcer. "They got some brahmer bulls waiting down there in the chutes for the bull-riding event, and Johnny is waving such a magic loop today that if we let him have any more than fifteen calves, them bulls might die of old age before Johnny ties one in over fifteen. Folks, you realize that we're watching some rodeo history here this afternoon. . . ." His thick cornball voice rolled across the arena into the grandstands like blown dust. "This is going to be one of them things that rodeo people reminisce about, years from now. And you'll be one up if you can say, 'I was in Cottonwood that day that Johnny Chance roped fifteen under fifteen. . . .' "

Johnny made his run on the fourteenth, working with sweet ease now. As he bailed out, he felt a numb blow on his left hand. Probably he had struck it against the saddle horn. He paid no attention, ran down the rope to the bug-eyed calf, legged it down, and wrapped it up fast. He felt a wetness on his hands as he worked and he thought, "Lord, is it raining again?" He straightened up to hooey, signing to the judge that he'd tied. Something was stinging his left hand. Just at that moment he sensed a commotion around the chutes. Men were running toward him.

He looked down at his hand. The little finger was gone.

"Time on this one—13.9," said the announcer.

The men reached him, Jimmy Alderman first. "Johnny, your hand," Jimmy said.

"Yeah," he said stupidly, not feeling any pain yet.

"Oh, oh, folks," said the announcer, his voice suddenly tight, "we've had an accident down there."

Jimmy Alderman whipped out a clean handkerchief and sopped the blood now running steadily from the stump. The finger had been jerked cleanly off by the rope as it snapped taut against the saddle horn. "It's okay now," said Johnny, still with the same unperturbed stupidity. He bent, fumbling, to pick up his rope and start coiling it.

The men tugged at him. Indians were starting to run out to him. "Come on," they said, "the ambulance." Everybody was talking at once. "The finger. Where is it?" "Find the finger." "Maybe the doctor can sew it back on." "Yeah, them doctors can do amazing things." Cowboys were walking around everywhere looking down at the trampled dirt. "Must be here somewhere. Here's where old Spades sat down."

But Johnny felt an uncontrollable motion toward the last calf waiting in the chute, as if he were moving at eighty miles an hour and couldn't brake himself. He stepped up on Spades, who stood waiting. Jimmy Alderman seized Spades's reins and said, "Johnny, get over there to the ambulance."

"For christ's sake," said Johnny, "I'll get me a new finger at the five and ten."

He rode past Jimmy toward the box. He vaguely realized that he was raging mad again, but it was more than excitement now and had nothing to do with Tom. Pa Gene's ghost was there, sitting on the fence and watching him. Pa Gene's ghost understood and forgave. At that moment a memory poured out of some black hole in his mind. He remembered Two Childs the medicine man, surrounded by Shoshonis, wounded and afoot. The Shoshonis signed to him that they thought he was brave, that they wanted to spare him. But Two Childs signed to them to come in and kill him. They wounded him again and again, but he kept getting up, pulling Shoshonis off their horses and killing them. Finally the Shoshonis were so frightened of his power that they fell on him all at once. They cut off his head and both his arms and legs, and threw the members as far off across the prairie as they could. Then they galloped off leaving the bleeding trunk lying there in the trampled grass. When Plenty Crows, the only other Cheyenne left alive in that fight, crept out of his hiding place under a nearby sandstone ledge, he found the torso lying there like that. It was still alive. The chest was moving up and down, and bright red blood was bubbling and whistling at the severed neck. Johnny realized then that he had not learned that story first from Stands in Timber's book, but that he remembered it, that he had heard it told somewhere back in the black hole of his childhood, somewhere back in that Tongue River country that he didn't remember.

A shimmering hush fell on the rodeo grounds as he rode into the box. The men moved toward the chutes, leaving the arena clear. "We found the finger," Jimmy Alderman shouted.

The tape snapped for the last time as the fifteenth calf leaped out. Johnny galloped and swung and leaped down, ran and tied, fumbling a little because the seared-off place on his hand was throbbing with pain now.

"Fourteen flat!" cried the announcer. The crowd came to its feet, a flurry of waving programs and flapping hands. Johnny felt his rage collapsing now. The hard edge of things was blurring. He felt drained, sick, peaceful, and inclined to think somewhat about his finger. He picked up his rope and walked slowly back to Spades, as the applause beat down on him pitilessly like sunlight on a mutilated body abandoned on the plain. He figured that he could manage being Two Childs too.

The men were running up to him again, Alex Feet among them. Jimmy Alderman showed him the finger. It was a limp, brown, fine-boned finger, mashed off at the end and very dusty. He took it curiously, not even sure it was his.

"For god's sake, Johnny," said Alex, "I'm real sorry."

"You owe me fifteen dollars," said Johnny. He handed the finger to Alex and added, "A little sun-dance offering."

"This feller," said Jimmy Alderman, "he'd do anything for money."

Both he and Alex grabbed Johnny by the arms like a child and hustled him through the gate. People poured around him everywhere and faces spilled over him: Dora's face, pained and open-mouthed, Ma Maureen's face, pale and expressionless with shock. Fern, wearing her gold-lamé trick costume, hugged him and he hugged her dazedly back. Ma Maureen was trying to spur her horse through the crowd toward him. Yes, he figured that the family would want him to move back into the house now that he was roping good. He knew what he would

do with that $2500 in the bank in Butte now—he would use it to start
buying Spades back from the banker, since he didn't need it for
Indian groceries any more.

He grabbed Dora's and Belle's arms as the ambulance pulled
slowly up, its siren yowling mournfully. "Take my horse back to the
camp," he said to them. "Don't let anybody near my horse."

The attendants slapped a gauze against the hand to stanch the
bleeding, then shoved Johnny into the back of the ambulance. Gene
Chance lay there on a stretcher, crushed and dying, covered with a
sheet. Alex leaped in too, saying, "I'm going with you." The ambulance
was surrounded by a mob of Indians, a northern sea of dark faces
shining with summer sweat and tundra flowers in bloom. The patchy
skin of the half-bloods, the red lipstick on the women's thick lips, the
gunmetal gleam on cheekbones and foreheads, the coarse black and
brown hair, the dark Asiatic eyes—all claimed him now. Gene Chance
was dying, going away into gentleness, into a blue distance, into a
brightness of eagles, where all time and all horror was seen and for-
given.

The ambulance started moving slowly through the crowd, the
siren moaning. Faces slid past the windows. A few Indians ran alongside the ambulance, looking in. He looked back out at them, meeting
their eyes.

At that moment, the sting in his hand shifted upward to his
eyes. Two seared places there in his eyes were going to drop red tears.
He wished that he could tell them that a lot of ropers lost fingers, but
that a good using horse was worth more than a whole hand. He wished
he could tell them that right now he liked old Alex Feet so much that
he would give Alex his one good horse to be able to marry his ugly
crosseyed daughter. He wished he could tell them—but pretty soon
they'd hear the news anyway—that when the Cottonwood centennial
was over and the camp was struck, he would be going over to the
Tongue River country to visit for a little while.

"Just to see it, Johnny," Pa Gene would have told him. "That's a
mighty nice country over there. The wind makes a good sound in the
pines, over there in those hills, on the Tongue River."

Speedy Gonzalez Was the Fastest Mouse in Mexico

The cottonwood trees were burning. As if in a cold morning fire, they were turning yellow with a ghastly crackling sound.

Shivering because she'd forgotten her jacket and because she'd made up her mind about things, Beth Stuart rode her little bay stallion at a walk along the gravel road toward the fairgrounds. Every year about this time, her mother said between teeth clenched cracking tight, "I thought I told you never to go around those trashy racetrack people again." Along the road, early frost turned the grass to sparkling skeletons, and clumps of prickly pear bore their sun-seared pink fruit. It was August 26, the last day of the Cottonwood County Fair, rodeo, and centennial, and Speedy Gonzalez still hadn't come yet.

Beth was riding away from her father's horse ranch. Back there, the aluminum roofs of the new barns steamed gently. The crisp pine corrals were only a little weather-grayed yet. The big white brick house with its portico, its shingled office building, its barnyard ringed with sheds—all were sheltered in a crowd of big-cottonwood trees. One would have thought it was a peaceful place. But dread had come to the cottonwoods—they already sifted their first yellow ashes down into the sun-scorched grass. "Those trashy racetrack people. And that good-for-nothing jockey, that Gonzalez." Every year about this time, her father told her mother to leave the girl alone, and the cottonwoods waited patiently for the annual atrocity. Their skeletons were left lying on the blue plain of the sky, their yellow ashes in drifts.

"Walk, you Flash," Beth said to the little Quarter-Horse stallion, brushing him with her spurs, making him move a little faster. Like some stallions, Flash was lazy, but if you brushed him a little, just right, he would run through the sun. "Walk out, you Flash of horse, you morning horse. We're going to see Speedy." The stallion swiveled his ears back to listen to her voice and walked harder.

Beth came to the fork in the road. The right fork ran west, looking like a dusty ribbon lost from some turn-of-the-century gown, toward the old asphalt highway and Cottonwood. The town was just any Montana town, with its air of desperation at not having been there long enough, at not having made up its mind about things. This year Cottonwood was trying to cure its desperation by celebrating its centennial and by counting its years of history like so many silver dollars. Beth had seen towns all over Montana, all over the West, as she traveled with her father to rodeos and horse shows, and she had learned that they were all alike, all hurting with wind and distance. She thought of the cathedral towers of Europe drifting down their gold leaf, and she knew for the first time just how new and desolate Cottonwood was.

The left fork ran east, winding up into bare hills clawed by ravines. The hills were smoked over with silver sage that hinted at horses' skulls lost in the grass. Beth didn't draw rein, but she looked over her shoulder at the hills as she rode on past the fork, straight ahead toward the fairgrounds. Remembering, she became aware of the familiar pain in her body, like dry thistle leaves pressed to her flesh. It was just a year ago that Speedy had said to her, "Today we'll work the horses out crosscountry, like we used to do down on the Santa Cruz." And so he and Beth had ridden up there on the hills, where they flattened into a sweep of open bench country. The wind had made booming noises, like dry waves, across the grass, and a thunderstorm had muttered off in the southwest.

"We'll show Speedy," she said to Flash. "We'll show him that I almost lost my horse ears. And my long wavy tail. That I'm not a horse any longer, like the Godolphin Arabian in the old prints."

Flash did not reply, of course, just kept walking hard. His ears swung to the wind of her talk like the old windsock at the Cottonwood airport, beside the abandoned landing strip where weeds now grew in the cracks in the concrete.

She sat Flash as she should, as she had for many miles and many days. The rein hand rested beside the saddle horn, the right fist was squared on her hip casually, the way her father always rode. She was expert enough that *Hoofs and Horns* had asked her to write a series of articles on how to train a barrel horse and ride to win in girls' barrel racing. She had put on her blue shirt with the pearl snap buttons, because she had recently discovered that her eyes were gray and that blue opened them inwards, like distance before running horses. After the year at college and the summer in Europe, she still wore her curly hair short (it was pale blonde, like a good, new manila rope, but she had washed it just that morning, combed it carefully dry, and clamped her Stetson on it at the proper angle as a rodeo professional would. A little light makeup, pale lipstick, sun-bleached Levis, stirrup-scarred Justin black boots, and little aluminum spurs completed her toilette.

She had the idea that even with the blue shirt on, she was still plain as a granary, with a gap between her two front teeth like a gate left open. Her mother had run up big dentist bills trying to fix those front teeth. But she knew that Speedy didn't care how plain she was. "Beth, leave here with me and the horses tomorrow morning," he had said last year.

"Hey, Flash," she said to the stallion, "I'm half horse and half alligator, with a little touch of Elizabeth Taylor."

As she thought of Speedy, her stomach was falling, the way she always felt a cottonwood tree was falling when she looked at it against a sky full of moving clouds.

At the fork, she ran into Pinter Brodie and Brodie's cowboy, Vin. They came riding along the right fork from the old highway. Brodie was a crazy old white-haired cowman from up the valley. The two men had an air of going off to work cattle—their horses swung along briskly. Beth frowned a little—she had always had a funny feeling about Brodie. He was the only person in Cottonwood who could see her horse ears. She was sure he could see them.

"Howdy," they said as they fell in with her.

"Howdy," Beth answered. The three of them rode in silence for a little way.

"Mighty early in the morning for a little girl to be outdoors," said Pinter Brodie.

Beth tried not to blush, but she blushed anyway. "I'm going to the fairgrounds to practice my horse around the barrels," she said. It was only half a lie.

Brodie chuckled a little and indicated his own elderly black saddle horse. "I hear tell your little horse is playing this horse's great-grandsire in the centennial pageant."

"Yeah," said Beth. "They asked me to do it because they needed somebody that could ride jockey style." She kept blushing, feeling Brodie's eyes on what was left of her horse ears.

Brodie kept chuckling, as if he thought her riding Flash in the pageant was funny. He made her so uncomfortable that she was relieved when they left her at the edge of the fairgrounds. Maybe Pinter Brodie had horse ears himself.

She rode along the cottonwood-shaded lane that led to the race-track. The cottonwoods rattled softly, their September death rattle coming up out of their barky throats. A few leaves already dripped like yellow blood. She rode through chasms of sun and shadow, throwing her head back and looking fixedly at the tops of the cottonwoods as they passed over her. They fell slowly against the turning sky, like cathedral towers. She was falling down the sky, as if down a blue cliff, into a silent sea. Cathedrals slid slowly down the cliff, as if some bulldozer was shoving mountains of yellow leaves over the edge. Shadows of horses haunted the cottonwoods, disappearing behind this trunk or that, tails swishing flies under the cool boughs, shoulders and flanks shuddering flamelike under flybites.

Finally Beth saw the white board fence of the track ahead. A soft flurry of running hoofs reached her ears—horses would already be working out on the strip. She pulled up beside the gate to the track, and her stomach toppled without a sound, like towers against the sky, as she thought of what would happen with Speedy sometime in the next few days. She was sure it would happen, because, even though he was already a few days late, she was sure he would come.

She sat there looking over the gate at the little half-mile track. A few horses were cantering gently, exercise boys standing in the stirrups. "Look at that sad little track," she told Flash. "Not like Belmont or Saratoga, or when we drug Flo and David to the races at Ascot." She had lived in color photographs of Hialeah and Tanforan, tracks with elegant clubhouses and an impossibly green infield that might have had flamingos wandering loose in it. "You turn a herd of flamingos out here, and they'd starve," she told Flash.

She decided that the Cottonwood track definitely looked littler than ever. Its stretch didn't curve away into infinite distance anymore. In its weedy sun-baked infield, tumbleweeds blew south when the wind shifted north. The white paint was flaking off the rickety cedar-pole rail. There was a weather-beaten arena, plus corrals and chutes for handling rodeo stock, for what the local fair board chose to call the Cottonwood World Championship Rodeo. Finally, there was a grand-stand built in 1890 and never painted since. Beyond the track, in the shade of the cottonwood trees, stood the livestock exhibition buildings and the rows of rain-darkened, unpainted barns where the gyps stabled their racehorses. "Bullrings" the gyps called these little tracks, maybe because of the way the horses had to go skidding and scrabbling around the turns. Beyond the track, she could see the big field belonging to the Chance ranch, where a lot of Indians were camping, as part of the centennial.

Somewhere over there among the barns, Walt Fromann might be giving Speedy a leg up on California Count right now, and leading the horse toward the gap onto the track. Walt and Speedy usually arrived three days before the fair started to make sure they got good stalls. Speedy was always muttering about how rundown those barns were, and how the loose shingles let rain drip in on the horses. This year they were late coming—Beth had already looked for them five mornings now. They might have had a breakdown on the road somewhere. Maybe they arrived in the middle of last night, just in time to enter their best horse in the Cottonwood Derby that day.

Beth bent from the saddle to unchain the gate, pulled it a few feet open, and spurred Flash through onto the track. Then she dragged the gate shut, carefully rechained it, and sat up, drawing a deep breath. For a moment she regretted not having put her little flat saddle on Flash, so that she could gallop for real with Speedy. But she wanted to work Flash out around the barrels in the arena later, so she told herself she'd done the right thing to throw her regular Balanced Ride on him. Now, since Flash was already loosened up, she touched him into the same gentle exercise canter that the Thoroughbreds were doing. She held Flash to the outside of the strip, leaving the pole clear so that any faster-moving horse could breeze by. She would just ease around the track and see if one of those exercise boys was Speedy. "H'lo, Beth," he would say, and their horses would fall in side by side. "How's it go?" as if it had been a day, and not a year, since he mournfully told her good-bye standing by the cab of Walt's horse van.

As she cantered along, she kept sweeping her eyes over the track. The place really looked dreary this year, in fact. Couldn't the fair board afford just one coat of whitewash? She'd have to talk to Tom Chance, the board chairman, about that. She'd appeal to Tom's pride —he was a good rodeo organizer and promoter, being a contestant himself, and he knew what people liked to see. He had made Cottonwood's fair one of the few popular money-making fairs left in the state. The trouble was that Tom didn't really care about Thoroughbreds—he just tolerated them as something that happened between rodeo events, something that people would buy seats in order to bet on.

Half a dozen years ago, when she first started to hang around the fairgrounds to rodeo and help her father show in the Quarter-Horse classes, the track's infield had been all green grass, and its rail was straight and freshly whitewashed. And the burnished young Thoroughbreds that flitted along the pole were sound and in bloom. Actually, the track had seen even more glorious days, but those had ended before her memory came into being. Beth wasn't much interested in Cottonwood history, but she had heard tell that it once was the scene of the most prestigious and exciting race meets in Montana. Wealthy cowmen and mine owners had gotten together there to race the Thoroughbreds that they'd taken up as a hobby. There, for instance, thousands of gold dollars had changed hands as a local horse named Reveille, owned by Pinter's grandfather Fitz Brodie, had beaten Marcus Daley's famous Tammany by a nose. Then the rich stockmen and copper kings had turned to wino gyps, and the gold dollars to silver and finally to paper. The Cottonwood race meet, too, was part of that painful centennial. Every year she had seen the grandstand shed more of its paint, like some kind of cottonwood losing its white leaves. The famous horses got skinnier and older, and their clarion names became names like Go-Go Girl and Detergent. Or had she only imagined those horses? In the sky over the track, the Eiffel Tower, the watchtowers of Bologna and the Gothic spire of Toledo cathedral all fell slowly in the silence, collapsing with an unheard roar onto the rain-darkened shingle roofs of the race stables. Looking at the tower of Toledo cathedral, she had thought only of cottonwood trees and of Speedy, and she had wondered why, along in February, he had stopped writing to her at school.

As Flash galloped past the rodeo arena, Beth looked at the three red-and-white barrels set out in a big triangle. Later on she'd come back and work Flash out around the barrels. Speedy and Walt would hang over the arena fence, watching her, and Walt would time her with his stopwatch. Of course, she didn't care for barrel racing as much as she once had, but she'd entered this year out of habit. She had entered every year since her father gave her Flash for Christmas five years ago. ("My daughter ride a gentleman horse? It's positively indecent," her mother had said.) Her father knew she wanted a stallion, and he knew too her ache for racehorses. But, being a Quarter-Horse man, he was damned if he would buy her one of those bony bangtails, he told her. So he scoured the West to find a young Quarter Horse that had raced successfully and would make a good barrel horse. He had seen Flash down in Phoenix, found him sound as a stone and gentle as dew, and paid $6000 for him. Beth had since trained and sold several barrel horses for high profits, but she would never part with Flash, even if he was a little lazy. Last year she had won the Cottonwood barrel-racing event, as well as others at rodeos around the circuit, and everybody knew that if she could take the time away from helping her father ranch, she would maybe be world champion. Last year, when she won by a full second, Speedy had smiled (one of those scant times when he did smile) and said, "Too bad you won't ever make a jockey."

As Flash cantered happily along into the first turn, Beth felt rather than heard that another horse was running up on them. She glanced around and saw a blaze-faced sorrel breezing down the home stretch past the arena. He was running red like the edge of day crossing the earth, running silent like light and leaving the sound of his hoofbeats behind. The rider was crouched in his mane. Her heart flared up—from a distance that sorrel looked like California Count, Walt's groceries horse and Speedy's favorite. Speedy sometimes said, brushing the Count's glittering hide, "The day this horse goes, I go too."

With a rush of sound catching up, the sorrel swept by Beth. His hoofs rapped on the freshly harrowed strip, and every leap ripped a snorting pant from his nostrils. But Beth's heart settled like dust. It was not the California Count, just a rundown, scabby old stallion who looked lame on the near front leg. And the jockey was not Speedy but a little old man, sun-shriveled as a prune.

Beth rode completely around the track, getting a good look at all the horses on the strip. Any strange horse might be from Walt's string, because he kept buying new ones and putting old ones up for claiming—all but the Count. But none of the riders was Speedy. So she left the track and rode on down the little dirt road until the rows of barns opened up before her. Her eyes strained to see Walt's big green horse van parked somewhere in the shade.

The race barns squatted under the cottonwood trees. They had crooked stall doors, rusted hinges, and shingles curling from the roof beams. Their plank walls were rotting away where they touched the earth. Some do-gooder ought to throw away a few thousand dollars fixing those barns up, she thought. Here and there, from around corners, mysterious horses neighed or slid away into doorways of silence. Next to an empty horse trailer nearby, a man in a shiny, baggy old black suit squatted on his heels, heating a rusty kettle of water over a wood fire. On the trampled, manure-strewn ground beside him lay a wad of soiled gallop bandages.

In the tow ring, horses circled like a tired merry-go-round, their bony backs draped with old blankets or rugs. Walt's horses, at least, wore the bright-colored coolers that a Thoroughbred deserved. A pony boy slouched on a wall-eyed pinto gelding as he led two blanketed horses, and his reddened eyes went half-shut as he sang, "Down in the valley, the valley so low." A black gelding and a gray mare trotted side by side past Beth, holding out their thin tails. They were led by a sleepy boy who stumbled between them, tugging at their lead shanks. The sight of the boy pushed a prickle of pain against Beth's heart, like a dry thistle stuck in her flesh. Last year Speedy had been so tired all the time, and preoccupied with his hurting back. Her fingernails dug into her palms as she looked at the two horses' ankles, swollen, horny, and pitted with scars of the firing needle. Speedy would run his hand lovingly down the Count's legs, crooning, "Ay, caray, cool as iron, twice as hard."

She rode around, looking for Walt's truck. Dogs yelped. People mucked stalls, cleaned tack, carried water, looked for lost hoof picks or currycombs. Romping dirty children screamed and scuffled. Indians from the camp loitered around, their eyes on the horses. Feed tubs rattled. Everywhere wood fires sent their blue autumn smoke into the air, and the whiff of it made her think of last year, made her feel as if the thistle leaf was wrapping itself around her whole body. Here and there people said, "H'lo, Beth," and she said, "Hiya," absently. She knew many of them, and later on she'd talk with them a little, listening to them tell how O'Leary's Fantan won the county derby in such and such town, listening to them discuss old Indian remedies for curing fistulas. "You skin the hair back off the first joint of the tail. Then you cut off the joint and let it bleed good. . . ."

All around her, the track lived its little once-a-year life. The pony boy broke off his song and called to the man in the black suit, "Hey, Jim, whatcha call that horse?"

And Jim, bending over his steaming pail, twisting water from the wet bandages, straightened and shouted back, "Robbie, this is Go-None. And they sure had second sight when they named him." Laughter drifted like smoke from the people on the tow ring, and Jim bent again, feeling Go-None's knobby ankles. Walt had horses whose pedigrees sometimes carried names like Noor or other illustrious California studs. And there was always California Count, who was by Fleetwood, who was by Count Fleet, who was by Man O'War.

Beth pulled Flash aside to let a feed truck jounce past. The truck's rusted door was painted with the legend "Jennings Feed Company Also Chicken Feed and Molasses." The truck stopped at each owner's stalls, and the driver yelled out the window. "Bob, you want two?" "Yah, two straw," came the muffled reply from inside a stall. "Okay, come take 'em away." So Bob came slogging out of the stall, seized a bale hook, and dragged two bales of straw down off the truck.

"Say," the pony boy hollered to no one in particular, "did anyone watch that Minstrel's Jinx run in Great Falls? Never seen that dog run so fast as that day." No one answered or commented. Beth kept looking in stall after stall, and it was beginning to seem that she had only imagined Speedy. The pony boy stretched in the saddle. His T-shirt was filthy and his hair full of straw. "They say his jockey got hit in the face with some dirt. By the time he got the dirt outta his eyes and hit the Jinx one or two, it was too late, they say." No one said anything. The pony boy started to sing again.

On the other side of the tow ring, a crazy-eyed brown mare danced around as a clubfooted man tried to hold her. He stumped and leaped on his clubfoot, jerking at the chain lead until Beth thought the mare's nose would snap off. "You think you're pretty hot," the man shouted at the mare. "I'll show you a condition book and you won't look so good."

Beth rode mournfully around a little while longer, seeing a few more familiar faces. "Hiya, Beth," "Hiya." Old Mrs. Perez, who had a thumb bit off by a horse. Gimpy Sullivan, who was usually drunk and who had an old horse that liked rum almost as much as he did. Why did they stick with it, she wondered. (She was aware that a year ago, or two or three, she would not have wondered at all.) Why did they stick with the cheap race meets and county fairs and little rodeos all over the West? All she knew of their life was what she had seen here, and what Speedy and Walt had told her. They had a dry wind blowing in their heads, a wanderlust of highways, horse barns, and the little tracks steaming in the dawn light. By tomorrow they'd be on their way again. They packed in their tack trunks generations of unpaid feed bills and all the arts of winding rundown bandages and easing bowed tendons. She had drunk their coffee, walked their horses on the tow ring, swapped jokes with them. But she had never seen their midnight poker games in their trailer houses, because she always had to be home by dark. Nor had she slept in the horse vans where they spread their sleeping bags on the hoof-scarred wooden floor. Nor did she know the 4 A.M. cafes along the highways, with soggy hot cakes and greasy fried eggs. She knew enough about the horse business to know how hard it was, now that horses were no longer a way of life but a madness.

Beth looked up. A faint roar came down from the sky, like an invisible tower collapsing, like the invisible cottonwood tree falling over at last. It was a jet plane. She saw its white contrail cutting the sky neatly in half, like a fine saw cutting into a blue brain. Walt's truck was nowhere in sight.

She wondered if Walt had bought a new truck, or if he and Speedy would arrive later this morning. They had to come this morning. She hadn't looked in all the barns yet.

So she got off Flash and tied him under a cottonwood tree. Then she started walking up and down all the shed rows, peering in all the stalls, looking for California Count.

Her mother was angry that her only daughter should be at the fairgrounds, or even on a horse at all. Ever since Beth was a little girl, her mother had tried hard to keep her in dresses—first little ruffled pinafores, later velvet dresses with lace collars and black patent-leather shoes. But Beth always escaped to the horse barns and got manure all over the shiny shoes. She tore the dresses crawling through barbed wire fences.

Because there were fields afire with dew in the dawn light, and if Beth looked long enough into a drop of dew, she fell right into it, into a bottomless canyon shot through with rainbows. There were patches of wild iris in the boggy places in the meadows, and if Beth looked at the blue flowers long enough, they opened their mouths with yellow teeth and swallowed her down. There were wild phlox and bitterroots blowing gently on the dry hills in June—Beth ran after them, and they took flight like pink sparrows. She tore up whole handfuls of them, but they escaped her by wilting immediately. She brought them home to her mother, and her mother threw them out. Beth learned not to bring home any flowers.

There were also creeks that turned to light and flitted off too, right over the cottonwood trees that grew along them. There were stones that looked her right in the eye. Or was she the patch of iris, the creek, the stones? Or was she all of them together? Everything was too much for her, as if she were more than just herself. She blew away like dew on a hot wind. Her flesh tore like a thousand bitterroot stems. Everything hurt her, yet she would never have said, "Stop."

Best of all, there were brood mares grazing in the fields. They towered over Beth like cottonwood trees. Their legs were like tree trunks, and their manes hung thick and green like branches. Their bellies covered the whole sky—it was like the clouds had suddenly laced themselves with big veins and started breathing. The mares put their noses down to Beth and blew her away like dandelion fluff. Even the furry foals were taller than Beth—they had legs longer than evening shadows and eyes like living opal. The foals sniffed Beth, but they couldn't blow her away—she sniffed them back, and it was a contest to see who could blow who away. The foals had noses like brown moss. Finally they all blew away together in the morning sunlight, like dandelion fluff, like milkweed down, like the cotton from the cottonwood trees in June, drifting away to whiten the meadows.

When she got home, she found that the foals had nibbled and torn her lace collars. Her mother's hands fluttered into the air like startled magpies. She had a dim memory of her mother's lamenting about some future event called a debut and crying, "But she's turning out to be a tomboy!"

Her mother, Florence Stuart, was a tiny, slender woman from a family back East whose importance she had tried to impress upon the Cottonwood people. Beth's father called her Flo. Beth always tried to figure out why her father and mother had ever gotten married anyhow, because her mother was always saying things to her father in a voice as small and sharp as a horseshoe nail; afterwards her father would just shrug cheerfully and leave the house. Her mother still made frequent trips to New York to buy clothes and see old friends, and her bridge club and church friends in town looked open-mouthed at her hats, suits, and shoes made by people named Mainbocher and Delman. There weren't any clothes like that in the window of Winnie's Ladies Apparel on Main Street. Flo went to the Episcopal church in town and managed to make even the oldest, bleached-bone pioneer Catholics and Baptists, like the Chances, feel uncomfortable. Flo introduced them to something called collecting Colonial antiques, when they'd just realized that late-Victorian furniture wasn't new anymore. The most carefree ranch wives, with their Levi jackets and their sun-scorched grins, always made themselves defiantly boisterous around Flo, who never had a hair blown out of place even in March, and who wore a dress even to tend her roses. She created a grand-style life in the big brick house Vern had inherited. When horse buyers came, she always had little candlelight dinners, during which nobody could see what they were eating. At least, that was the way the Cottonwood people saw Flo. Beth sensed that while they did not find her awesome enough to be tragic, they found her too frightening to be ridiculous.

Her father, Vernon Stuart, was little too—little, punchy, and slow talking, the way a Quarter Horse would be if a Quarter Horse could talk. Vern had a drawl inherited from his Southern grandfather, who had fled after the Civil War and come up to Montana and started this ranch. When you came to think of it, their small size was all her parents had in common. Vern was always cheerful, no matter what kinds of horseshoe-nail things Flo said to him (such as that she thought she'd married a millionaire). Vern had narrowed gray eyes that flashed with a new idea sometimes, the way a barn window does when the rising sun hits it. He had done a little rodeoing when he was young and had been smart enough to invest in good Quarter Horse bloodlines before they became fashionable. In his spare time he did a little amateur painting of Western scenes. He had won blue ribbons at the fair with his paintings—the Cottonwood people all commented on how real they looked. All the bars in town had at least one of Vern's paintings on the wall. Vern's ambition was to paint careening horses and dust rising rosy in the sun as well as Charlie Russell did. He just let Flo roll off his back like rain off a leaf. He was too uncomplicated to get nervous breakdowns over a woman, or so he said. Beth tried to copy her father's drawl, walk, way of sitting a horse. Vern sometimes kidded her, saying that the drawl got stronger with every generation it spent away from Dixie. Sometimes she and Vern discussed Flo as they rode around checking the irrigation ditches.

"I think Flo is awful," Beth would say.

"If she was a horse now, I'd have to take a hold of her and make her mind. But being she's human, in the generic sense of the word, I get the same results by just ignoring her. And I'd advise you do the same."

Sometimes Beth thought it over. Her mother wanted her to be a girl. Her father wanted her to be a boy, because she had no brothers and somebody had to run the ranch someday. But she knew they were both wrong, because she was neither. She was a horse. Those mares and foals had breathed her soul right out from her bones and snorted into her their own.

She knew she was a horse because she could feel the two sensitive ears swivel around on top of her head, cocking toward the least tickle of sound. And her tailbone rose high for balance as she galloped, and her tail hairs floated on the air. She was not very good at girls' basketball in high school because she ran shifting her weight and changing leads like a four-legged beast. Her face felt long and bony, and she could flare out her nostrils to suck in the wind and all its smells. Sometimes she had a decided sensation that she was four-legged, and when she looked back she could see the sturdy, hard-muscled hindquarters, with the hocks working away and the tail held high.

The children in the Cottonwood county schools teased her, calling her Beth the Horse, and that was why she sometimes wondered if other people could see the ears and tail too. The children said, "Some girls are *horse* crazy. But old Beth Stuart is horse *crazy*." She didn't study hard in school, because her mind was usually on the ranch and her 4H Club horses, and she was always doodling horses in her notebook, trying to draw like Vern.

In her little room at home, with its plain Colonial antique furniture, bearskin rugs, and old racing prints on the walls, she had a lot of shelves that her father had fixed up. Some of the shelves were crowded with figurines of horses. Big ones and little ones, cheap plastic ones and expensive ones of china and bronze, with plaster ones in between. New items for this collection were automatically added on Christmas and birthday. In a weak moment, Flo had even added what she called an antique English sterling silver horse.

The rest of the shelves were crammed with books about horses. There were children's classics like *National Velvet, Black Beauty,* and *Misty of Chincoteague,* and there were adult books as well, ranging from *The Bard of Armagh* to heavy tomes on horse breeding. Her favorite reading was about Thoroughbreds, because the Thoroughbred was the most highly developed, versatile, and beautiful of breeds, or so Beth thought. Thoroughbreds were about the only subject on which Beth and Vern disagreed. She was sorry that he didn't raise Thoroughbreds instead of punchy little Quarter Horses, and she often told him so. But his eyes would get that dawn-reflecting look and he'd say, "Bethy, I raise Quarter Horses because there's good money in them right now. The minute there's money in Thoroughbreds, I'll switch right over. Just ask your gyp friends over at the track about how broke you can go fooling with those bony bangtails."

Of course, Beth had never seen any famous Thoroughbreds race, but every May she listened to the Kentucky Derby on the radio, and a gust of chills broke over her as she heard the announcer's cry, "They're off!" and the roar from the packed stands that she would never see. She knew all about the Biscuit, War Admiral, and the champions of long gone, right back to the Godolphin Arabian and the Byerly Turk. Her favorite old-time champion was Man O'War, even though he was long dead. While other girls in her class wrote off to Hollywood for pictures of Warren Beatty, Beth wrote to this farm and that farm for photos of her favorite living horses, like Kelso. She also read a lot of racing magazines, filled scrapbooks full of magazine pictures and newspaper clippings, and mulled in her own mind which colt would be named Horse of the Year. But it all happened far away and out of reach, in the newspapers, or in the newsreels that she saw in the Cottonwood theater when she went with Vern to see John Wayne in the latest Western. It all had nothing to do with her, like the Vietnam war, presidential elections, or the distant roll of summer thunder.

Fully as much as for the great horses, she cared for the great jockeys who rode them. They were little like herself—Earl Sande, Johnny Longden, Eddie Arcaro, Willie Shoemaker, Angel Cordero. She was both the jockey crouched in the mane and the mane itself. She was the strong little hands hauling on the reins and the mouth itself, stretched back by the bit and frothing as she fought to run. She was out of her body, pure unhindered movement, speed and light, beauty spied on through a drop of water, through a flower's mouth, through a stone's eye. She was disappearing forever into another world.

"Vern," she said, "I just might run away from home with my gyp friends over there and be a jockey."

"Now, Bethy. You'll get over this jockey business and settle down and run the ranch. It's all part of growing up. You want to be a jockey like I wanted to rodeo."

But there were things she couldn't tell Vern, such as the speed of the wild blue iris changing into seed pods, as if it were galloping away into endless distance. Or the way the fields burned at dawn without destroying themselves—she marveled as she walked over them (halter in hand, to catch her horses) that they didn't smell scorched. Or the way the horses ran to fling themselves into a burning rainbow that was out of body and out of mind, and the way the cottonwood trees fell slowly against the sky. In everything she saw, an iridescent fire burned. She wondered if this was part of growing up too and if she'd forget all about it. But she didn't forget. As the years passed and she entered high school, the sensations grew sharper. Sometimes they hurt her, like a sweet headache. And the pair of ears on her head pricked toward everything, listening, listening.

Last spring, a ranch boy from up the valley had asked her to go to the Junior Prom with him. He had written her a note in study hall to that effect. Beth blinked and then wrote back to say no, thank you, she had to train horses, help her dad keep ranch books at night, and take care of her brood mares for her 4H project. The boy didn't ask again.

When Flo heard about it, she winced and struck her forehead with her hand. Ever since Beth's freshman year, Flo had been armed against the eventuality of the Junior Prom with more and more little formals from one of those stores in New York. She said, "I could swear you're not *my* child. They must have switched babies on me in that hick little hospital in Cottonwood." And she began outlining to Beth a complicated strategy for getting the boy to reissue his invitation.

"Leave the girl alone," said Vern. "She'll discover boys on her own good time, if she wants to."

She met Speedy the summer she was sixteen, after her junior year in high school. Her father was showing a stallion and several mares in the Quarter-Horse classes at the fair. Beth was showing a brood mare and colt in the 4H show. They had taken the horses over to the fairgrounds and installed them in the livestock showbarn.

After helping Vern shake up their straw and fill their water tubs, Beth set off to explore the rest of the fairgrounds alone. She was wearing filthy jeans and an even filthier T-shirt that the horses had slobbered on, and she carried a half-eaten hot dog in her hand. A decrepit straw hat was clamped down on her curls and on her feet were the old black Justin riding boots that she'd worn ever since Vern gave her her first horse. Time and again Flo had tried to throw those Justin boots out, but Beth always rescued them from the garbage can.

The fairgrounds was all pandemonium—Tom Chance had told Vern it would be the biggest fair ever. Tom was a top roper himself, so he knew how to do things right when he did a rodeo. Top rodeo hands were stopping by to compete on their way south from the Calgary Stampede—men like Dean Oliver and Shawn Davis. Cattle and horses were pouring in for the livestock show. A carnival had

camped near the fairgrounds, and as Beth strode along, eating the hot
dog, she could hear the wheezy tune of the merry-go-round and see
the ferris wheel turning through the cottonwood trees. The grounds
echoed with whinnies, bawls, and squeals. Horse vans and feed trucks
roared by, keeping dust always in the air. Horses tromped down ramps.
And as she watched, open-mouthed, a tractor chugged past her, pulling
a brand-new green electrified starting gate for the races. Last year they
had still been using the old-time tape that snapped up, probably the
same kind of tape used when Reveille beat Tammany. She stood gazing after the starting gate as they pulled it out onto the track, thinking
how the racehorses would spring from those little gates amid the far-
off roar of the crowd, "They're off!"

So she ambled up and down the shed rows, peering at the horses
in their stalls. All the stalls were taken, and the overflow camped on
the grassy flat across the creek. There Thoroughbreds were staked
right by their owners' trailers and tents, dancing this way and that,
slashing at flies, whinnying. Beth looked the horses over carefully,
noting the pathetic condition of many. Of course, she knew that even
the champions had injuries. Equipoise had a bad hoof, Seabiscuit had
popped knees. But the Biscuit, for instance, had been kept in top form
and run only when he was in shape for it. These horses ran day after
day on these rocky little tracks, with their bowed tendons and their
spavins. She saw cut legs stained with iodine, oozing galls on shoulders.
Yet the beauty was there too—the piston hindquarters, the long legs
like steel rods, the slender, deerlike neck, the fine nervous head lifting
to look about, and the little ears pricked to listen everywhere.

Then, as she strolled along the row where the best stalls were, a
certain sorrel horse thrust his head out over the rain-darkened door
and sent a train whistle of a whinny ringing across the barns. The
door shuddered as his hoof struck it, pawing. Beth stopped to stare.
This was a different kind of a horse. His coat gleamed like a new
penny with bloom and health. And he looked just like all the pictures
of Man O'War in books she had at home—the same arrogant head
with a white blaze down the forehead, the same look of eagles. She
smiled blissfully and drifted closer to peer in the stall.

At that moment, she saw herself walk up to the horse from another direction. Actually it was a slight, dark boy who looked part
Mexican or part Spanish. He was neatly dressed in red sweatshirt,
tight new jeans, and well-worn little brown boots. He was so small
that he couldn't have been more than five feet tall. As he snapped a

lead shank onto the sorrel's halter and led him out, Beth saw his face half-turned. It was a thin, dark, beautiful face, tense as a tightened cinch—a face scarcely human, with wild-looking black eyes.

The sorrel stallion danced around the boy on long, perfect legs, holding out his carefully combed auburn tail, and the boy watched him dance with such intent study that Beth had the creepy feeling he was creating the horse from nothing, out of his imagination. Not a blemish marred the horse's frame. Beth thought he must be about five years old. Never among those broken-down gyp horses had she seen such an animal.

The horse whinnied again, and the boy said softly, "Ay, caray, shut up, you pretty shit."

Beth just stood there staring, watching herself turn and hold the springing sorrel. The boy must have been aware of her stare, because without even turning those terrible black eyes at her, he said, "You like this horse, huh?" He said it unsmiling, stroking the horse's neck and looking him over.

"Yah," said Beth.

"That's one lot a horse. My mother's horse." The stallion returned the compliment by savagely nipping the boy's arm. He swung this way and that, full of devils and gusts of copper wind.

"He looks like Man O'War."

"You're warm. His grand sire is Count Fleet. Name is California Count. My mother spent all her money on him at a yearling sale, and he kept us in groceries ever since. Never once finished out of the money."

"Who's your mother?" Beth went closer, politely let the stallion sniff her hand, then stroked his nose. The nostrils sucked in her scent, the brain considered it, the ears stayed pricked, indicating the horse accepted her existence. He lipped her bare arm, and then, with a clack of his big yellow teeth, he pinched it.

"Rita Gonzalez," said the boy. "She's a trainer. Look out, he always bites like that. She's married to Walt Fromann. That's mother-fucking old Walt over there, saddling that bay mare. We've got seven in our string. All good horses. No pigs."

"What's your name?"

"Speedy Gonzalez." The boy stooped, running his hands down the horse's forelegs as if searching anxiously for the smallest swelling, and the stallion nipped him right in the middle of the back. "You know—Speedy Gonzalez is the fastest mouse in Mexico."

Beth giggled. "What's that mean?"

"Nothing. It's something from a movie. Walt says it all the time to get my goat. I'm his jockey."

"A jockey," she breathed. "Like Eddie Arcaro."

The boy grunted. "Not yet. I just got my apprentice license." She noticed that Speedy had a big bruise on one side of his face.

Just then Walt came stomping up. He was a big, heavyset man, with little blue veins in his nose and a paunch that exploded open his leather vest. He jerked the lead shank out of Speedy's hand, cuffed the boy across the face right where the bruise was, and growled, "Damn lazy greaser kid." Then he stomped back up the shed row with the Count springing along at his heels. Beth stood paralyzed at the sight of the blow. As Speedy turned away to follow Walt, Beth noticed that blood was trickling out of his nose, onto his upper lip. But the boy wiped the blood away with one sleeve as if it were just snot. Beth noticed that the sleeve had a pretty fair number of dark stains on it.

The woman holding the bay mare shouted in a thick Mexican accent, "Dom eet, Wolt, queet heeting my boy." She was a slender little dark woman with slanty black eyes and high cheekbones, like an Indian. She wore purple lipstick, gold earrings, a red silk shirt tucked into a pair of old jodhpurs, and she had the most amazing dyed orange hair that Beth had ever seen.

"He's a lazy greaser kid," Walt shouted back. "Chewing the fat with a broad while we got seven horses to blow out. He'll never make a jockey."

"Ay *chihuahua*, Wolt, he work harder then you, you beeg boolee. When you see heem talk weeth a girl las time?"

Beth felt so sorry for having gotten Speedy cuffed on the face that she went up and said, "I'll help. What can I do?"

"Beat it," growled Walt, saddling the Count. "Damn pesky horse-crazy kids always hanging around."

"My daddy raises Quarter Horses," Beth retorted, "and I bet I know just as much about horses as you."

She looked at the woman and saw Rita suddenly smile. Rita and Speedy were grinning at each other, Speedy still wiping his nose on his sleeve. They jabbered a minute in Spanish, then Rita thrust the lead shank of the bay mare at her and said, "Here, *hermanita*. You hold and I go saddle thee Count." So Beth held the bay while Speedy and his mother saddled the obstreperous stallion. Walt didn't say a word, just puffed and cursed as he cinched the boy's little saddle and checked the stirrup leathers.

"Who's your daddy?" Walt finally asked in a half-mocking voice.

"Vern Stuart."

Walt straightened up, a spark of interest in his bloodshot eyes, "Yah? I know about your dad. He raises some mighty good Quarter Horses. Some of the best in the country. I'd like to buy me some good Quarter Horses one of these days, if the Count doesn't bite me in half first. More money in Quarter Horses than in these racehorses, that's for sure."

From the other side of the Count came Speedy's voice. "She knowed this is a Man O'War when she first saw him. And that's more than you knew when you saw him."

"All right, little girl," said Walt. "You can come hold my horses anytime. You want to walk hots? I pay you a dollar an hour. We're kind a short-handed."

Both horses saddled, Beth watched Walt throw Rita up onto the bay mare. Then he gave Speedy a leg up on the Count. Speedy sat easily in the little saddle on the great red horse's back, talking soft nonsense as the Count danced this way and that, saying, "Ay, *chulo*." His black hair tossed in the breeze. She felt like she had walked right into the photographs scotch-taped into her racing scrapbooks.

As Rita and Speedy rode off toward the track, Walt followed on foot with his stopwatch. Beth might have said, "Can I watch them blow out?" But she remembered that she'd promised Vern she'd come back to the livestock barn soon. She hesitated in agony, watching Speedy's red sweatshirt disappear down the row of stalls. The boy had forgotten her existence now. His head was bowed and his back tense as the big horse fought to jog and he fought to hold him in a walk. Then Beth thought of her own horses in the show barn, so she went slowly back.

Vern was brushing the show horses down. "Daddy," she said, "I just saw the most beautiful horse. There's this guy Walt Fromann owns him."

"Yah, I know Walt. He is a mean old son of a buck, but he has good horses. Takes mighty good care of them. Don't know where he gets the money. Fancy coolers and all. He runs a real classy stable, not like some of those old birds. Maybe he's a bookie on the side, or runs marijuana up from Mexico."

"Daddy, they said I could help them sometimes. Could I, every morning?"

"Why, sure, Bethy. Don't I know how crazy you are about those skinny hat-rack horses? But you don't neglect anything at home, you hear?"

"I promise, Daddy."

The next morning around six, Beth went over the track, just as the red dawn runners went over. She was riding Flash—she had to take him over there anyway, to school him around the barrels. At the sight of Flash, Walt Fromann dropped what he was doing and walked around the little stallion. He looked at Flash's teeth and eyes, ran his hand down his legs. "That's a nice kind of a little horse," he said. "Hey, Speedy, come look at the quarters on this little Anglo horse. Bet he could have the Count charred and gutted at a quarter mile."

Speedy came out of the Count's stall, straw in his hair, a fresh bruise on his face. He didn't smile at Walt's joke. "Sure he could beat my chicano horse at a quarter mile," he said. "But not at a mile and a quarter." He solemnly scratched Flash's ears, and though his eyes never left Flash, Beth again had the eerie feeling that he was looking straight at her.

"Would you be hurting to sell him, young lady?" Walt said. "I really do have a yen to start buying Quarter Horses."

"No siree," said Beth. "I need him for barrel racing."

They let her hold horses while they saddled up. When Walt threw Speedy up on the Count, Beth was right up there in the sky with him, only not quite so high, because the Count stood sixteen hands and Flash was not quite fifteen. When they started off for the track, Beth tagged along. "Mind if I watch?"

"Hell, no, young lady," said Walt. "Long as you don't get in our way."

They rode through the gap and the racing strip curved out before them, steaming gently in the morning sun. At that moment, the place seemed more immense, silent, and mysterious than a desert. A handful of gyps walked along the backstretch picking rocks off the strip. "Looka that boulder," said one, wrathfully hefting a big rock in his palm. "Turn a horse ass over bit," and he hurled it over the rail into the weedy infield. A few old men hung along the rail, watching the horses gallop by.

While Walt leaned on the rail too, Rita and Speedy started the warm-up walk around, keeping to the outside. Beth rode with them, her heart bursting like a seed pod. She felt as if she were riding forward out of herself, leaving the mundane Beth behind and entering as another Beth into the sweet world of newspaper clippings and photographs. Rita chattered like a magpie in her Mexican accent, saying "Ay *chihuahua*!" and "Ay *caray*!" and asking Beth about her 4H project. Beth decided that she really liked this little woman with her orange hair and her vulgar golden earrings. Speedy didn't say a word, preoccupied with making the Count do just what he wanted. After a while they cantered. The Count fought to run, trying to grab the bit, and Speedy grimly held him down, guided him, made him mind. Beth was open-mouthed at his skill.

She held Flash in the gap while Rita and Speedy breezed the two Thoroughbreds, blowing them out three-eighths of a mile each. The Count skimmed along the far rail like a silent red blur, Speedy just a little dark form on his back. Then he leaned into the turn, then the backstretch, his hoofs drumming up sound now. His stride was so long that he hung in air without effort. He flashed by and was gone in an explosion of sound, like a racing car. Beth felt a knot of emotion in her throat.

Then Walt hefted his stopwatch and said, "All right, young lady, you blow the little stud out and show me what he can do."

So Beth and Flash made the same dizzy circuit of the track, leaving sound and time behind, leaving the other Beth behind forever. The rail slipped by her so fast that she could not see how its white paint was peeling in flakes. Flash's mane stung her face as she leaned over the horn of her Balanced Ride in an imitation of Speedy's crouch.

When she pulled up and brought the blowing horse back, Walt grinned and said, "Not bad, young lady. You're going to sell him to me yet."

"Not on your good life," said Beth.

After that they went back to the barns, and Beth learned how to walk hots. You walked the blanketed horse around and around the tow ring until he was dry. The tow ring was worn deep into the ground like an Indian migration route. You walked until your feet turned to fossils. "Loook at my leigs," said Rita, pulling up one leg of her Levis. Her leg was a snarl of varicose veins, like black yarn caught under the skin. "Ees from wolking hots. Ay *chihuahua*."

From then until the end of the fair, Beth hung to the Fromanns like a foxtail burr to a pants cuff. The Fromanns taught her to wind bandages, clean racing tack. The only hot they wouldn't let her walk was the Count, because of his habit of slicing playfully with his teeth. It was Speedy who walked him. Speedy had nip marks all over his arms and shoulders. When work was over at noon, Walt and Rita got in the truck and drove into town to eat. Speedy, however, wouldn't move a step away from the horses. He stayed there, sitting in the extra stall where they kept the tack, doing extra things like polishing the brass on the halters. So Beth stayed with him, and they sat on a bale of hay and talked about horses.

They talked mostly in the abstract, because Speedy spoke of himself only indirectly. Beth even had to figure out for herself what all the Spanish words he used meant, because he got impatient with explaining.

He called himself a chicano, which apparently meant he was born California Mexican-Spanish. He uttered the word with self-conscious dignity and a certain defiance. He said that Rita couldn't call herself chicano because she had emigrated up from Mexico. Beth, unfortunately, found herself called Anglo. She got the impression that Anglos and chicanos didn't get along too well. Anglos were rich, callous ranchers, fruit growers and wine makers, while chicanos were mostly poor and lived on tortillas. A few anglos were downright *gabacho*. When pressed for a translation of *gabacho*, Speedy said it meant "motherfucker."

Macho was something that Speedy had to be, on a horse or off, and it was something he praised in other men. Walt, for instance, was not *macho*. As for the horses, Speedy had a lot of words. When the Count was good, Speedy told him in a singsong voice that he was a *chulo* and a *caballito*. And when the Count reared up or pawed, Speedy said things like *huevón* and *chingada* with magnificent vehemence.

Beth was fascinated by these words, though she could scarcely pronounce them. One morning the Count nipped her and she said, "*Huevón*."

To her astonishment, Speedy snatched the Count's reins out of her hands and scowled. "If you want to stay around here," he said, "you don't say things like *huevón*. *Huevón* is a shitty bad word. If Rita thinks I taught you that, she'll hide me."

"But Rita says *huevón* too."

"Rita gets away with a lot of things," Speedy muttered turning away. "She would tell Jesus that he was a son of a *chingada*."

As they talked, the track was momentarily silent, the horses drowsing in their stalls till it was time to saddle for the first race at

1:30. Speedy didn't seem to mind her being there. Every day he asked her when she went home in the evening, "See you tomorrow?" Beth guessed that he must be lonely. She figured out that he never ever left the track, that he was there twenty-four hours a day, waking and sleeping, every day of the year.

One noontime when Beth confided that she wanted to ride like he did, Speedy said, "All right, go get that old Flash."

They wound gallop bandages on Flash's legs, put a pommel pad and a little saddle on his back, and the light bridle with snaffle bit and thick rubber reins on his head. Flash seemed to recall what this was all about, because he danced and sweated. Then Speedy gave her a leg up, and she sat there on the little saddle, crouched and feeling strange because the near stirrup was longer. Speedy untied a lead pony, vaulted on bareback, and they rode to the track. The strip was still empty, and people were just starting to trickle into the grandstand for the afternoon's events. A few rodeo cowboys were riding around in the infield. Beth ignored them, considering herself intimate with something much better.

She and Speedy rode side by side around the track, and he gave her a lesson. "Keep your heels down. Turn your heels in a little. Grip the reins a little farther forward." Now and then he reached over to touch her hand or knee, and an unfamiliar shiver gusted over her every time he did that. They trotted and he showed her how to post. Then they cantered a little, and Beth found herself balancing easily in the short stirrups, gripping the reins up short, feeling how right the shorter stirrup was when she went into the turns. Finally, they galloped. Speedy kept that fat pony right at her girth, riding it like an Indian and pounding its butt pitilessly with a little cottonwood branch he'd broken off.

When they pulled up, they were both laughing for some reason. She had never seen Speedy laugh before. In spite of the scabs on his face where Walt was always hitting him, he looked more beautiful then any boy she could think of in her high school, his hair blowing, his teeth white as cottonwood in his dark face.

"Tell you what," said Beth. "I'll run away from home with you and Rita and Walt and be a jockey too."

Speedy snorted. "Girls can't be jockeys. Against the law."

"That's not so. And even if it were, I could pretend. Daddy always tells me I look just like a boy. Flo does too."

"They'd never let you. Know why?"

"Why?"

"Because——." Speedy suddenly reached over and patted her chest. "Because your titties show through your shirt, that's why."

Beth was so startled she nearly dropped the reins. Again that strange thrill rippled her like wind over grass, and at the gentle touch her nipples rose so hard that they hurt her. She almost put her hands over them to push them back down. They had a habit of doing that on cold mornings lately, and Beth had never paid it any more attention than annoyance. Flo had insisted that she start wearing a brassiere, that she was getting too big to run around like that, that it was indecent, and so on. She bought Beth fancy little white lace brassieres, and Beth carried them out and dropped them in the garbage can when Flo wasn't looking. In school not long ago, the girls were playing a silly game. They told each other to look down their necks and spell "attic." Beth did it obediently, and then didn't understand a thing when they all shrieked with laughter. They had to explain to her why it was so funny.

Speedy must have read her mind, because he bent over the lead pony's neck, choking with laughter. Beth blushed, didn't know where to look, blinked her eyes. To her relief they went back to the barns then, and started getting the horses ready. Speedy disappeared into the tack stall, and when he came out, he was wearing Walt's cherry-red-and-white silks and his little black boots, with the cap pulled jauntily onto his head. He looked at her hard and started laughing again. Beth wanted to hit him.

After the last race at 5 P.M., the crowd stampeded out of the grandstand, and the parking lots emptied. Melancholy dust hung over the fairgrounds, and the track flooded over again with its primeval silence. Beth trudged around and around the tow ring with the bay mare, last of the Fromann horses to race that day. Then she stayed on talking with them till nearly dark, when her father came by with the truck to get her and drive home.

Rita was always hugging Beth and saying ay *chihuahua* she wished she had a daughter like that. And Beth hugged Rita back, because she was so warm and somehow soft in spite of all her riding muscles. Rita rocked her gently, while Beth let her head loll on Rita's shoulder and toyed with her gold earrings. And Speedy would sit nearby polishing the brass on halters or winding bandages neatly in rolls, singing some little song in Spanish in his tuneless voice.

Back home, in her Colonial bed, Beth lay awake for a little while, thinking how skillfully Speedy's small, lean black hands buckled the halters.

When Flo found out where Beth was spending her days, there was what Vern always called "war in the camp."

"Those trashy racetrack people! How could you possibly allow your daughter to wander around over there alone? The idea!"

"She's only with the Fromanns," said Vern, "and they're okay. She's with them whenever she's not helping me show horses. Rita Fromann looks after her, sees she eats and so on. Rita is a real fine woman. I wouldn't worry if I were you."

"And who is this Speedy Gonzalez that Beth is always talking about?"

"That's Rita's son, their jockey. Nice, hardworking boy. So wrapped up in his horses he never sets foot away from the barns."

"*My* father wouldn't have let me associate with jockeys. Not that I would have wanted to."

"He didn't mind your associating with pint-size cowboys, now, did he?" Vern did his most cheerful shrug, the sign he was about to walk out of the house.

"If anything happens to Beth, you'll never hear the end of it from me."

"Well, I haven't heard the end of anything from you yet."

When Vern and Beth had left the house, Vern winked at her. "I'd trust you with Rita like I would with your own mother. More, in fact."

"I wish Rita was my mother," said Beth.

"That's not a bad idea," said Vern. "Unfortunately, I am stuck with Flo till death do us part."

The last day of the Tri-County Fair was a day of triumphs, that hurt the eyes of her memory like a bright light. It was a Sunday morning that galloped in autumn-fresh and cool—the day that California Count was to run in the Cottonwood Derby. As Beth rode Flash over to the track, she knew the track would be fast that day. The gyps greeted her with new respect—yesterday Vern had won grand champion stallion and reserve champion filly, then proceeded to sweep the cutting-horse class on his famous bay stallion, Bobcat. And then, in the horse division of the 4H Show, Beth had won grand-champion project with her brood mare and foal.

"We'll have to catch up with you Stuarts today," Walt said to her. "We'll have to win your little old Cottonwood Derby with the Count."

When noon came and the stable work was done, Vern rode up on Bobcat, leading Flash. "Come on, y'all," he called out, "the parade's about due to start."

Walt and Rita came up, dressed in formal Western, leading borrowed saddle horses. Walt looked the great Bobcat hungrily up and down, noting that even for parades Vern stuck to plain leather. "What?" he teased. "No silver-mounted saddle for that nice kind of a horse?"

"I don't believe in gilding the lily," said Vern, grinning.

As the four of them rode away toward town, Beth looked back and saw Speedy going into the tack stall. She wondered why he imprisoned himself with the horses like that. It occurred to her that she would have thought less of him if he'd joined them for the parade.

In town, the parade formed up in front of the Rainbow Hotel, on a side street. A crowd of horsemen swelled there, rodeo greats like Dean Oliver and Shawn Davis and Cottonwood's own champion roper, Johnny Chance, rubbing stirrups with local ranch kids and trick riders in sequined shirts and pants. Beth looked Johnny Chance up and down as the famous little Indian sat his Appaloosa horse smoking a cigarette, and she decided that he wasn't as clean lined and beautiful as Speedy. All the local ranchers were there too, except old Pinter Brodie, who scorned parades and such. She listened to the rodeo people gossiping about who made what winning time where and how that old Rattler horse of Johnny's had such a killing stop. And through it all she could hear Speedy's voice telling her to keep her heels down. She wondered if he would touch her again like he did that morning.

Finally, at twelve thirty, the parade got under way. Crowds jammed the sidewalks on either side of Main Street. Even the habitual inhabitants of the bars came out to see. They clapped and hooted as the fair board chairman, Tom Chance, came along first, riding a big flashy palomino horse with a silver-mounted saddle and carrying the American flag. The horse obviously wasn't used to flag-toting, as he jigged, sweated, and rolled his eyes in terror. After Tom came the high-school band, a bizarre assortment of tall, short, skinny, and fat boys and girls in rumpled maroon band suits with tarnished gold braid, all walking out of step, their instruments pointing every which way. As they thumped out "Stars and Stripes Forever," a single majorette pranced along in front of them, her white satin costume soiled from last year's football games. Beth was sure the girl was trying to prance like a horse and her lip curled in scorn.

Next came the rodeo queen on her float, as the horsemen sat in the side street still waiting their turn. The float consisted of the big Fulton's Nursery flatbed truck, covered with red, white, and blue crepe. The queen sat on the back of the truck on a makeshift throne hung with bunting. She had long black bangs and big eyes, and she was wearing a white tulle formal her mother had sewn especially for the occasion, plus a rhinestone necklace and rhinestone crown loaned by the Flynn Jewelry Store. She carried a bouquet of wilted gladiolus. Beth's lip curled again as she looked at the rodeo queen, a town girl whose family had bought her a saddle horse and who had pretensions at being a good rider. Beth leaned over to Rita and said, "She looks real pretty now. But she's entered in the barrel race, and wait till you see Flash and me run her right into the ground."

Rita reached and squeezed Beth's hand. "*Caramba*, Bes, theey weel make you rodeo queen someday."

"I already had my chance," said Beth. The horsemen poured out onto Main Street following the float, and a thunderous clopping of iron-shod hoofs on asphalt drowned out the band music. "My 4H Club nominated me for queen last year. But I guess I didn't care much about it, because I didn't sell near enough rodeo tickets. You have to sell tickets, you know. *That* one had her whole family selling for her."

A long line of horses stretched along Main Street now, as if sweeping away the fripperies of flags, marches, queens, and bunting. Nothing remained but manes tossing, muzzles slobbering, bits shining, tails busy at flies, well-groomed hides reflecting sunlight like windows catching dawn. The crowd applauded the rodeo greats, who modestly tipped their wide Stetsons. The rodeo clown came along on his little burro, wearing suspenders and Levis twelve sizes too big, and tried hard to make the kids laugh. And the kids, who were already cynics, yelled, "Get a horse," at him. All the way up Main Street, Beth thought about Speedy sitting alone in the tack room.

The parade broke up at the other end of town, by Jensen's Chevrolet Garage, and everybody galloped back to the fairgrounds along various residential streets. Beth and Rita stopped at the diner, got down, and went in to order some hamburgers to take out for Speedy. "He like weeth lot of onions," said Rita.

Back at the track, Beth gave Speedy the hamburgers herself. He was already wearing his silks, and he said, "*Caramba*, I could eat a raw dog," and he sat down on a bale of straw and ate them one after the other.

"Don't eat too many," said Walt, "or you won't make the weights for the first race."

By the first race at one thirty, the grandstand was packed. Bucking horses were already shut, humped and nervous, into the chutes for the first rodeo event, bareback-bronc riding. From the food stalls under the stands, there drifted up the smells of greasy hamburgers frying and cotton candy being whirled onto paper cones. In the infield, one famous trick rider was readying his four matched albino geldings for an exhibition of Roman riding. Ropers were riding around shaking out practice loops. The Cottonwood County posse was forming up for their act of fancy drill riding, all on bay horses, all wearing white Western clothes. Off across the track, the merry-go-round still tootled, and Beth could see its battered wooden horses sailing up and down through the cottonwood trees.

But to Beth everything now centered around those seven stalls back in the barns. She even forgot about the barrel race she was supposed to be competing in. She led over the horse that Walt had running in the first race, a big blonde mare named Firefly Baby, and Speedy rode behind her. When the racehorses left the little paddock and paraded out onto the track, the announcer played a recording of "Boots and Saddles" over the loudspeaker system. By then Beth was sitting on Flash in the infield, shaking with nervousness and suspense. World champion bronc rider Shawn Davis was sitting a horse nearby, and she didn't even glance at him. Speedy's tiny figure sat easily on the mare's back as she plodded without theatrics toward the post.

Then the field was in the gates, and springing out in an explosion of dust. Beth shouted joyfully as Speedy, riding like a demon and pounding the mare with his whip, drove her home in second place.

When he brought the mare back and she grabbed his rein, she saw a couple of white welts rising on his neck as he slid off, there were more welts across his hands, and one emphatic one across his nose. He saw her look of horror, and snapped, "That *gabache* Greer kid lugged in on me, and I whipped the holy shit out of him." Then he added, "He whipped it out of me too."

After that race, Beth had to reenter the rodeo world to be in the Grand Entry, as the rodeo got under way. Beth thought the Grand Entry was silly business, but she knew Vern would be hurt if she didn't participate. The fair board chairman galloped his silver-mounted palomino and flag dramatically around the arena, and the crowd stood up and applauded and the band played "Stars and Stripes Forever," while all the rodeo entries galloped in after him, two by two. Beth galloped by Vern. Then they all had to line up before the stands and be introduced, and she and Vern spurred forward together and raised their hats at the people as the announcer cried, "Vern Stuart and his daughter Beth, from right here in Cottonwood." Out of the corner of her eye, she could see Speedy sitting among the cowboys along the arena fence, watching her. Up under the grandstand roof hung a blue cloud from thousands of cigarettes and frying hamburgers.

Race by race, a huge excitement grew in Beth and towered like a cottonwood tree. Speedy was more in demand than any other jockey, and for every race that he didn't ride one of Walt's horses he was loaned to another stable. His silks got dirtier and dustier, and more welts appeared on his neck and face. Suddenly, between the fifth and sixth races, the announcer broke into her world, booming, "And now, ladies and gentlemen, the girls' barrel-racing event! All girls entered in the barrel-racing event please gather at the main gate to the arena. . . ."

Beth listened to that voice echo around the fairgrounds, ricocheting along the board walls of the track, dying out across the parking lots where rows of cars dazzled in the sun. She sat Flash out in the infield, Speedy behind her clutching her belt.

"Shit on the barrel race," she said. "I'm watching it from here."

"*Caray*," said Speedy, "if Vern hears you've been learning words like that from me, he won't let you walk hots for us no more."

"I don't care about the barrel race."

"Go on now. *Caramba,* your poor daddy wants to see you win it. You've trained for it, and all." She felt his hand reach around to squeeze her arm and the warmth of his face against the back of her neck. Then he took her bat and pushed his own little whip into her right hand. "Here. Use this."

Her hand tightened around the whip handle, still warm and sweaty from his palm. She shuddered under a violent emotion, like the dirt track as forty pounding hoofs tore along it. "All right," she said, and cantered Flash gently to the arena gate. Speedy slid off onto the fence, and she joined the ten other girls who had entered.

As ring men set up the three red-and-white-striped barrels out in the arena, the girls eyed each other with a malice that the male contestants had learned to disguise. A few of them were professionals—

wives or daughters of cowboys who followed the circuit and rode expensive, streamlined little Quarter Horses like Flash. One was Pat Chance, Tom's oldest sister. Beth was vaguely aware that Pat hated her, because she always beat Pat. (Beth knew why too—Pat didn't rein her horse properly into the barrels.) The rest of the female contestants, like the rodeo queen, were local girls on cow ponies.

Beth watched Pat Chance make her run for 16.2 seconds. When her own turn came, she poised Flash at the starting line, feeling Cottonwood's eyes on her. Everyone knew that she had turned down offers of $8000 and more for that little horse. She determined to ride him like Speedy in the Cottonwood Derby.

At the gun, she hit Flash a good one on the haunch, and he jumped toward the first barrel. He had done that cloverleaf maneuver so many thousands of times that he could have done it in good time without her aboard. Dirt flying, he skidded around the first barrel, pounded for the second with Beth lying low in the saddle, shaved around the second, and lined out for the third. She could feel, rather than hear, the crowd's exclamations and applause as they saw the way Flash rounded each barrel while leaning over at an incredible forty-five degree angle.

As he dived into the third barrel, Flash gave an extra spurt, in nervous expectation of the whip's next whack on his rump, and his shoulder brushed the barrel. The barrel teetered from side to side, and the crowd groaned, "Oh!" But the barrel didn't tip—it settled back, and the crowd applauded as Flash shot back toward the gate, running flat out the way he used to in those Quarter Horse stakes down southwest. He plummeted out the gate and past the rodeo queen on her cow pony, like a bolt of light from the sun.

"Time for Beth Stuart," cried the announcer, "thirteen seconds flat. That's very close to the world's record, ladies and gentlemen. . . ."

Gloating, Beth rode over to the arena fence and Speedy slid on behind her again. "I know I won," she said. "I had the fastest time yesterday and the day before, and the three girls left are riding old cow ponies."

"Nice going," said Speedy with his usual poker face, taking the whip. "Damn shame you won't never make a jockey." But he squeezed her arm again.

"He's got a bad third barrel because he knows I'm going to hit him," she said modestly.

Finally the eighth race loomed, the Cottonwood Derby. Beth

shivered with suspense as she watched Speedy parade the Count to the post. She stood at the paddock fence with Rita and Walt and watched the big red horse curvet and dance, bowing his neck as if he knew how splendid he was and what illustrious names he had on his registration papers. The race was to be longer than the preceding ones —one and a quarter miles. So the field would start in the middle of the backstretch and run two and a half times around the little track.

"He'll win," said Walt. "He's the only horse in the race as can stay at that distance. He'll break in front and stay there. You'll see." He glanced over his shoulder at the tote board. "Looky those odds. Two to one. Not even worthwhile betting on him."

"Ay *chihuahua,* what you expect?" Rita wanted to know. "He ween heere last yeer, and see year before too."

"I'll bet on him anyway," said Beth grandly. Marching over to the weather-beaten little parimutuel windows next to the paddock, she put all she had, which was five dollars, on Speedy's horse to win. They stood watching the horses file slowly around the turn and finally go, one by one, into the starting gate.

The bell rang far off and faint, the gates popped open without a sound, and the field sprang out in a burst of dust. The crowd started to shout. Beth could see the Count out in front and increasing his lead with every giant stride. Speedy was not even using his whip—he was riding easy, like during a morning blowout. "Come on, Count!" she was yelling without thinking. The horses skidded into the far turn, streamed past them along the homestretch, and were gone. Dust blew behind them into the near turn. Beth could feel every stride thudding up her own spine. As the horses slid along the backstretch with a far-off flurry of hoofs (the starting gate had been hurriedly pulled into the infield), the Count had widened his lead to six lengths, but one black horse was making a bid, slowly moving up on the great-grandson of Big Red.

As they turned for home the second time, the black horse was hanging at Speedy's girth. The boy was still riding easy, as if he didn't even see the black challenger. They rattled by and curved into the near turn for the last time. In the backstretch the black moved up right beside the Count, as the crowd shouted louder, more frantically, for their favorite. Beth saw the red horse take fire, bulldogging the black back. Faintly she saw the two jockeys beating each other with their whips. Finally Speedy brought the whip down on the Count's pumping haunches once, just once. The big horse gathered. He towered like a tornado, like a thunderhead, hardly touching the ground. Every ounce of rage in his great frame brightened, like the flash of a lightbulb before it burns out. He pulled away, and the black faded and dropped back.

The Count led by three lengths as they leaned into the far turn, then four, then five and six as they ran down to the wire. At the finish line, Speedy was actually pulling hard on the horse's mouth.

The noise of the crowd died abruptly, bettors running toward the windows to collect. The Cottonwood fair was over for another year. It occurred to Beth that Speedy, Walt, and Rita would be leaving tomorrow morning. She jumped up and down with a knot of tears in her throat, hugged Rita, then watched possessively as Speedy fought the horse clear into the backstretch, trying to slow him to a canter. Finally Speedy just let him come the rest of the way around and hauled him into a trot coming out of the far turn.

The crowd was stampeding out of the grandstand toward the parking lots as the announcer said, "Good-bye, folks, God bless ya, and hope to see ya all again next year at the Cottonwood County Fair, the biggest little fair in the Treasure State." As the Count came up, Walt and Rita ran out onto the strip and Walt caught the blowing, lathered stallion by the reins. The Count swung wildly this way and that, his nostrils swollen wide, still wanting to run.

"Ho, Count, ho," said Speedy. His nose was bleeding.

"Speedy Gonzalez is the fastest mouse today," said Walt. Neither Walt nor Rita seemed overly excited, and Beth realized that to them, this was another little county derby, for a $500 purse. Nothing like Santa Anita or Tanforan. "He damn near pulled my arms out of joint," Speedy complained, giving her an unsmiling wink from the dizzy height of the Count's back. Drunk with joy, she gazed up at him and winked back. A moment later the Count was posing for the photographer from the Cottonwood *Post*, with a little wreath of wilting gladiolus over his neck, while the crowd paused in their rush to the parking lot to applaud one last time.

Then Speedy jumped down, and Rita, coming up on a pinto lead pony, seized the Count's reins and trotted off toward the barns, leading him. Walt, Speedy, and Beth followed on foot. It wasn't until they got to the gap on the other side that Beth remembered she'd forgotten to collect her ten dollars.

At the barns, they went through the sweet, relaxed after-race rituals. They did the Count up, pouring water over him, scraping him off with an aluminum bar, flinging his green cooler over him. The gyps hung around, commenting. "Ran 'em right into the ground, didn't he, the Count?"

"That's right," said Walt. "He'd run till his damn heart bust. He's got more bottom than a battleship, that horse."

"Bess, *hermanita*," said Rita, "go find me the hooof peek. Look like he got a rock in hees hooof."

So Beth walked down the shed row to the tack stall. She pushed the door open and was already in the dimly lit stall before she realized that Speedy was standing there naked beside a bucket of water. His silks were flung across a bale of hay, and he was sponging the afternoon's dust off himself with one of the sponges they used on the horses. "Oh," said Beth, blushing and backing off. "Rita told me to find the hoof pick."

"Hold on, I'll get it," he said. She stood looking down (she asked herself why she looked down) and saw Speedy's lean dark feet, with shiny boot calluses on the toes, move across the stall's dirt floor in search of the hoof pick. Then she felt it shoved into her hand. Speedy burst out laughing, the way he had that noon he'd made the remark about her titties. "What's a matter with you? Never see nobody without no clothes before?"

She shook her head, still looking at the floor.

"You don't know much, do you? Well, if you stick around these motherfucking barns long enough, you'll learn plenty."

She heard the water slosh again, looked up, and saw him squeezing the sponge over his head. In the dimly lit stall, the water sparkled darkly as it sluiced down his body, then formed a pool around his feet. He had the same kind of thin nervous body as the horses did, with muscles and tendons catching the light everywhere. Even his veins had the same horse's way of standing out along his arms and thighs. She noticed with some surprise that he had something between his legs like the Count did. She had seen her father's horses use this impressive apparatus. It grew till it was three feet long, and then the stallion reared gently onto the mare's hindquarters. She had watched matter-of-factly when Vern put Bobcat to her 4H brood mare, knowing that this was a necessary formality to get colts. But now that gust of unfamiliar feeling hit her again, like a wind arriving suddenly from a point of the compass that was neither north, south, east, nor west.

"Go on, look," said Speedy. "You see the horses naked every morning. Dumb Beth." He put one finger down to his apparatus and flipped it at her. Clutching the hoof pick as if it were a weapon, she fled.

Pretty soon Vern came along. He was in high spirits from all the triumphs of the weekend, and he invited the Fromanns to go into town with Beth and himself and have dinner at the Sneberger Cafe. He knew better than to invite those trashy racetrack people to his house and expect Flo to serve them a little candlelight dinner. Speedy, however, refused the invitation. "I'm staying with the horses," he said. "Anyway, I'm bushed and I'm going to sleep."

So Beth, still disturbed by what she'd seen in the tack stall, went with the rest of them in Vern's truck.

The Sneberger Cafe was the most popular restaurant in town, which wasn't saying much, since Cottonwood had only two restaurants and one diner. It was a gleaming aluminum monstrosity that stood on the main highway leading out of town, not far out from the somber machine-gun-manned towers of the penitentiary. It had a huge red-green-and-yellow flashing neon sign showing a steak being grilled, and, on this last sweet fair night, the parking lot around it was crammed with cars and pickup trucks.

As they walked in, the big jukebox, with its whirling rainbow of colored lights, was playing "The Tennessee Waltz." Every table was crowded with rodeo and race people. The air was blue with cigarette smoke, and a burning haze from the huge grill where T-bone steaks sizzled. Vern, Beth, Walt, and Rita had to stand in line to get a table, so they talked about horses. Walt went on and on to Vern about his admiration for Quarter Horses. The waitresses rushed back and forth with aluminum platters of sizzling steaks and French fries, and huge wedges of apple pie with soft ice cream. Finally they sat down and ordered, and Walt had a couple of whiskies right away, while Rita just smiled and smiled at nothing. Vern listened to Walt with one ear and looked at Rita with the other eye.

Beth didn't talk or look at anybody, just sat there thinking about Speedy's body. At the counter beside her chair, Jimmy Alderman and Dean Oliver were solemnly eating hamburgers, and she didn't pay the least attention to the two great ropers. Speedy was small but perfectly proportioned, like a little Arab stallion that barely stood fourteen hands. Not like some of the jockeys, who looked grotesque with their huge heads on withered little bodies. She listened to the jukebox playing "The Tennessee Waltz" over and over—people kept pushing in money and pressing that same button. The song had stayed popular in

Cottonwood for fifteen years, and no one could figure out why. Finally Jimmy Alderman turned his head toward the jukebox and shouted, "Hey, let's us have an Oklahoma Waltz for a change!" Everybody stopped eating a moment to laugh, and the next song that came out of the jukebox was Johnny Cash singing "Folsom Prison Blues."

Walt had a third whiskey and kept talking about Quarter Horses. Vern just nodded his head, grinning at Rita all the while. Rita sat strangely silent, her eyes sparkling. She was wearing the first dress Beth had seen her in—a full-skirted blue dress that needed ironing— and scuffed high heels. It struck Beth how feminine Rita looked, and she wished Flo could see her. Flo was always lecturing about femininity, and Beth realized that, whatever femininity was, Rita had ten times more of it than Flo. Something brushed her knee and, looking under the table, she saw Rita's and Vern's feet tangled together, and Vern's hand on Rita's knee.

Startled, she looked back up. Rita was smiling out the window, and Vern was saying, "Now you take that Driftwood horse," to Walt, who said, "You damn right."

Beth sat puzzled for a moment. Finally she said, "Rita, you look pretty."

Rita kept smiling, shaking her gold earrings, and squeezed Beth's hand with her horny little right hand that curried horses and cleaned hoofs. Her eyes went on sparkling enigmatically. Her other hand was under the table, and Beth realized that it must be doing something with Vern's hand.

"Rita, I wish you weren't going tomorrow," she said.

"We write you letters sometime, eh? Next yeer we come back, and thee Count ween thee derbee again, eh? We mees you too, Bess." Rita's ice cream was melting, untouched, on her wedge of apple pie.

After coffee, they ordered a sackful of hamburgers for Speedy, then left. Walt said he wouldn't ride back to the track with them. He said he wanted to visit Brown's Saloon and soak up a little more whiskey before they hit the road in the morning. He said Speedy went absolutely loco if he dared touch a drop of whiskey on the road. So Vern, Beth, and Rita drove back to the track.

It was nine thirty now, and just dark. Beth had never seen the track so late at night. Lights glowed in tents and trailer houses. Fires still sent up a few wisps of smoke. Through open trailer and tent doors, Beth could see people playing cards. Tethered Thoroughbreds stood with heads hanging, one hind foot cocked. Everything was silent except for the tootling of the merry-go-round off through the trees, where the bright carnival lights still winked.

"Bethy," said Vern, "you be a good girl and go take the hamburgers to Speedy and wait for me a few minutes. I have to talk to Rita."

"About what?" said Beth, astonished.

"About horses," said Vern.

So Beth climbed out with the still-warm sack and stood there open mouthed as the truck drove off in the darkness, its taillights disappearing among the cottonwoods. Then she walked slowly across the abandoned tow ring and up the shed row to where Walt's stalls were. She wondered if Speedy would still be awake. She knew that the Fromanns slept in sleeping bags on the floor of the horse van. But when she walked up the ramp and looked into the van, the sleeping bags were empty. She stood there not knowing what to do. Then she wondered if he was in the tack stall, working on something. She walked toward the stall—the door was just ajar. The stall was dark —he couldn't be there.

Then, as her hand reached out to push the door open, she heard a girl's voice say something inside there, and a rustle of straw. Then Speedy's voice answered something, hoarse and blurred. Beth's hand stopped in mid-air, and for some reason her hair stood on end. Then the girl in there said, "Oh, Speedy. Oh."

Beth backed off from the door, blinking. Then she went back down the shed row a little way and looked in the Count's stall. The horse stood drowsing, but at the sound of her step, he swung around and came to the door, always inquisitive and looking for mischief. She rubbed his nose but she could scarcely see it, because tears were rising in her eyes like water filling a bucket at the thought that Speedy was sitting in there talking about horses with another girl. The Count took her hat in his teeth and dropped it on the ground. He sniffed at the sack of hamburgers, nipped her arm tenderly, blew in her ear.

Finally Beth sat down on the dirt, leaning her back against the Count's door, and sobbed. She told herself that she would take the motherfucking hamburgers and walk home, and Speedy could go hungry. But it was two miles to the ranch, and the thought of walking it in the dark frightened her. So then she told herself that she would go over to the carnival and have a good time all by herself, and Vern, Rita, and Speedy could all go to hell. She would ride round and round on the merry-go-round, up and down on the battered wooden horses with their gilt flaking off. But when she searched her pockets for money, she found that the five dollars she'd fed into the betting window that afternoon was the last money she had.

So she just sat there, and finally the tears dried on her face. The Count nibbled her hair awhile, then pulled back into his stall and abandoned her. Soon the tack-stall door opened and the girl walked out. It was the rodeo queen. Beth had beaten her that afternoon by ten whole seconds. The rodeo queen stopped to comb straw out of her bangs, then tripped off into the dark on her high heels.

After a few more minutes, Speedy came out. His shirt was open, and he stood there buckling his belt, then stretched and yawned. He came up the shed row, whistling tunelessly, apparently wanting to look in on the Count for one last time before going to bed.

"Beth. What're you doing here?" He bent, shook her shoulder. "Beth."

"I brought your supper." Rigid with rage, Beth thrust the sack up at him without looking at him. "Vern and Rita told me to wait with you. But you were busy."

"Busy?" Speedy sat down by her, pulled out a hamburger, unwrapped it from its grease-stained paper, and bit into it. "You mean that girl?"

"That's right," said Beth. "Real busy. Talking horses." She stared straight ahead at a manure pile directly opposite them.

"Where did Vern and my mother go?"

"They said they wanted to talk about horses too. They went off in the truck somewhere. Everybody's crazy to talk about horses tonight."

Speedy started to laugh and nearly choked on a piece of hamburger. When he finally managed to swallow it, he said, "Beth, you're a funny girl. You don't know nothing. I never saw anything like it." Beth didn't answer, still glaring at the manure pile, so he finished the hamburger before he went on. "Men are like that. They have to be *macho*. I don't chase girls, but if one comes my way, I don't say no. I get lonely sitting here every day of the year. And how do you know what I did? Maybe I just sold her some marijuana. I pick up a few bucks selling Mary Jane to the kids."

"Why should you get lonely? You've got the Count. You're friends with him like in all the books I've read."

Speedy snorted. "That's not the same thing. *Caramba*. Are you ever dumb. You don't even know what's happening right now, for instance."

"What?"

Speedy bit into a second hamburger. "That your Anglo daddy and my *tijuana* mother are parked somewhere and fucking."

She looked at him for the first time. "You mean, hugging and kissing like in the movies?"

He looked at her strangely, then dropped his eyes. "Yeah. Hugging and kissing. From what I hear tell, my mother is even better at that than she is at finishing horses."

"But doesn't Walt—"

"He don't give a damn. I'll bet he's off in town drunk."

Beth considered the idea of her father hugging and kissing Rita. "Well, Rita's nice. If he wants to hug and kiss Rita, it's okay with me."

Speedy started on a third hamburger. "Nice of you to be so broadminded. Christ, I am sick of hamburgers. I'd like some tortillas and roasted chilis."

"Were you hugging and kissing that girl, then?"

"You're shitting right I was," said Speedy, biting ferociously into a pickle. "For all I was worth. Speedy Gonzalez, the fastest mouse in Mexico." When he finished the hamburgers, he crumpled the sack and tossed it over onto the manure pile. Then he lit a cigarette and smoked a few moments in silence. Beth had observed that he never smoked in the horses' stalls. He said he was afraid of starting a fire. Looking sideways at him, Beth suddenly noticed that even in the dark he looked exhausted—dark circles under his eyes, hard lines around his mouth, older looking than his eighteen years. He drew up his knees and put his head down on them as if deeply depressed.

"Tired?" she asked.

"Tired's not the word for it. My back hurts, too. I'm fed up with these lousy little tracks and with Walt. All I can think about is finishing this apprentice business and getting a contract with a big stable. And taking my mother and the Count with me."

"Maybe next year you won't be back."

"Maybe yes, maybe no." He didn't raise his head from his knees, and his voice had gone so low that she could scarcely hear. "Don't know how I'll manage without you to help me to muck stalls." Suddenly he raised his head, gave her a grin so gloomy that it frightened her. "Well, you want to be a jockey so much—why don't you leave your old Quarter Horses and come along with us?"

Beth didn't know whether he was serious or just fooling. "I couldn't do that, not really," she heard herself saying. "My daddy needs me around here."

"I was just kidding," he said, stubbing out his cigarette in the hoof-trampled dirt. "You're too young and too dumb to be bumping around these tracks. Maybe next year when I come back, you'll know a little more about hugging and kissing, and then we'll talk about it."

"Okay." She didn't know what else to say. She looked across at the manure pile and smiled.

"Still mad at me, Beth?"

"No."

Speedy slipped one arm across her shoulders and drew her against his side. Then he even took one of her hands and squeezed it. But it seemed to her that he did all this a little timidly, all the time watching her reactions, as if not sure what she would do. So she didn't do anything, just sat there and looked down in her lap. In the distance, a dog barked. Someone yelled, "Hey, Robbie, how about one more crap game before we sack out?" Over at the carnival, the merry-go-round was playing "Blue Danube" over and over. The horses moved softly in their stalls, rustling straw. Beth wondered if Speedy was going to try to hug and kiss her, and she was frankly curious to know what it was like. But he didn't, so finally she just lay her head on his shoulder, and they sat there unmoving. It seemed to her that Speedy was trembling a little. The sweet chill came and stayed on her.

"You'll forget," she said.

"You think so?"

"You'll hug and kiss rodeo queens all over California, all winter."

"Maybe so," he said.

They sat awhile longer, and finally Speedy said, "Jesus, they're taking their time, aren't they?"

Shortly the truck pulled up and Rita got out. She said a cheerful goodnight to Vern, who waved just as cheerfully. Speedy gave her hand a last squeeze, and she squeezed back, very gently, then let go and went toward the truck. As they backed around, the glare of the headlights showed Speedy and Rita climbing the ramp into the horse van.

As they drove home, Vern said, "Sorry we talked so long, Bethy."

"That's okay," said Beth. "Speedy and I just talked too."

Vern whistled the "Tennessee Waltz" all the way back to the ranch.

The next day Beth helped the Fromanns load their horses into the big green van. All around them, race owners were doing the same thing, as the exodus to the next meet began. Speedy looked gloomy, but Rita was still cheerful, singing little snatches of "Paloma" as she packed the tack trunks. Finally they were ready, Walt and Rita climbed into the cab. Speedy touched Beth's hand. *"Hasta luego,"* he said, "See you next year. Maybe."

"Bye," she said. She watched the van drive slowly off down the little lane under the cottonwoods. Sun and shade spilled along the van, as it swayed with the weight of live horses. The leaves were already turning yellow and falling into the sun-cured grass. Beth wandered around over the desolate tow ring, where the hoofs of hundreds of horses had packed the earth down two inches deep. She looked at the white ashes of fires where kettles of water had been heated for bandages. The track steamed gently in the morning sun, and the gap stood open, but no horses came and went. She went and sat in the empty tack stall. A smell of Absorbine and leather still lingered in the air. She sat down on the dirt floor and wept.

When she went back to high school after Labor Day, she found that Speedy Gonzalez hadn't escaped the notice of Cottonwood's high-school students. The girls were all screaming, "Oh, wow, that Speedy. God, those dark eyes! And those long eyelashes!" The boys made derisive remarks about Speedy's small stature. A couple were smoking the marijuana they'd bought from him in the boys' bathroom. For her part, Beth looked the boys over and decided that, with their petty interests in cars and basketball, they were not to be compared with Speedy.

The girls had also noticed that Speedy had spent a lot of time riding around behind Beth between races. They had all seen it from the grandstand. Their questions hovered between malice and envy: "Beth, is he your boyfriend?"

"Are you kidding?" Beth answered coolly. "His daddy and my daddy are friends, and we were all talking around about horses."

She wondered anxiously if a long line of girls had visited Speedy in the tack stall, and if the girls would think she had been in there too, hugging and kissing with the Cottonwood County Fair's hit jockey. But apparently the rodeo queen had been the only one, and she wasn't bragging about it. Now and then, during study hall, the rodeo queen looked pensively at Beth from under her long bangs, and Beth looked back with what she hoped was bored indifference.

That winter, as she busied herself with her senior year and her Quarter Horse project for the local 4H Club, she actually got a post-card now and then from Tijuana, Agua Caliente, Tanforan. Some-times Rita wrote flowery little messages such as: "Darling, we have sun and good weather down here. The sun helps my veins a little." And sometimes Speedy wrote. "Having a good time, wish you were here (to help me muck stalls)." Or, "The Count is fine."

Beth didn't put the postcards in her scrapbooks. Instead she kept them in the top drawer of her desk, all by themselves. The truth was that she didn't have time for the scrapbooks any more. She never failed to leaf through the racing magazines to look for their names, and sometimes saw them in the race results of the California tracks. Ashton's Polly, W. Fromann, J. Gonzalez up, carrying 106 pounds, placed third in a claiming race, with a claiming tag of $1500. Beth hoped that they would never put the Count up for claiming.

But her scrapbooks gathered dust as she spent more and more time with her own horses and her father's. In February her brood mare foaled again. Beth saw the foal born. It dived slowly out of the straining mare onto the fresh straw, shimmering with an opal mem-brane. An inexplicable warmth blew slowly over her. She fussed over the foal as much as she dared without antagonizing the mare, and got it up and started sucking. Afterwards she looked so wan and peaceful that Vern teased her, "Bethy, Ah think you birthed that baby colt yourself."

She had sent away for racing tack for Flash. Several winter after-noons a week she put the little saddle on him and rode him over to the track. Tom Chance had given her the key to the track gate, and she came and went as she pleased. The track lay silent and unmarred by a single hoofprint, and the naked cottonwoods creaked and moaned over the empty barns darkened by rains and winds of generations. She cantered Flash slowly along the rail. His thick coat ruffled in the wind, and his nostrils snorted steam into the sparkling air. She tried to re-member everything that Speedy had told her. Sometimes she rode around among the silent barns, and a nostalgia of county fair, red summer mornings, and the smell of Absorbine made her breastbone ache. She wondered how many rodeo queens Speedy had hugged and kissed down in California.

Along in April, Vern gave her a second brood mare for her project. When the mare came in heat, Vern wanted to breed her to Bobcat. But Beth very quietly, without telling him, slipped out and put Flash in to that mare in one of the corrals. She watched, unblinking, as the two horses walked around over the snow, the mare squealing and evading Flash's inquisitive sniffs. But finally the mare gave in and let the stallion mount her. Gracefully, with total dignity, Flash reared onto her, embracing her barrel with his shining knees, and the huge thing that had grown between his hind legs searched for the mare's buttocks.

Leaning on the corral gate, Beth felt a curious peace and sweetness. "Do people do it that way?" she wondered. "It looks so quiet and good." When she told Vern what she'd done, he was disappointed. But she told him, "Well, it's my project."

"Well, Ah hope," said Vern a little dryly, "that you will always consult me when you're breeding *my* mares."

Vern had not been well that winter, and the doctor had diagnosed a kidney condition. Vern worried a lot about this, checked up on his insurance, and began delegating more responsibilities to Beth, so that she would really learn the fine points of ranching. He let Beth handle a few sales, keep more books, buy some of the advertising in livestock magazines, enter a few big shows—all the time checking up on her, so that she didn't make any mistakes.

Beth burst with pride at being treated like a grown-up. She even tried to study hard in school that last year, and got A's in a couple of her courses. That was why her horse figurines never got looked at any more, except by the old housekeeper, Bertha, who had to dust them. Her scrapbooks lay on the floor in her closet, with dust on their covers. As spring came on, her parents discussed her future with more and more arguing, and Beth herself thought quietly about her own future.

"I want the girl to go to the State College at Bozeman," said Vern, "and learn some more about scientific farming."

"My daughter an Aggie?" said Flo. "Are you insane? What she needs is a good private school back East. A small school where she'll stand out. How do you expect her ever to get married if she can't learn to act like a girl?"

Vern sighed. Faced with the possibility of an operation, his thoughts turned to immortality and the need to continue the family line. Flo saw the change and pursued her attack. "She's going to graduate from high school without ever having a single date with a boy. She was just invited to the prom again, and she said no again. She can always learn about scientific farming. But there's only one time to learn a little femininity, and that's now, before she hardens into one of those leathery types that go to Cow Belle meetings in town—"

"Bethy," said Vern, "where do you want to go?"

"I don't much care," said Beth. "I don't really want to go to college. But if you say I have to go, Daddy, then send me somewhere where I can ride." She smiled a little to herself. Not having seen Speedy for eight months but having the certainty of an occasional postcard, she had gotten very philosophical about the whole thing. Some day years from now, when she was an established horse breeder and Speedy was a famous jockey, they would maybe get married. But not for a long time, and not unless she began to have a better opinion of marriage than she did now.

"All right, Bethy," said Vern heavily. "We'll send you back East." Her mother wrote to the admissions office of Frith, a small and very exclusive Connecticut college of which she had a high opinion. As a compensation for Beth, this school had a fine riding stable, an indoor ring, and an impressive string of gaited and jumping horses. Beth applied, was admitted.

The grass came up green, the meadowlarks sat high on the telephone wires and sang about how the buds of the cottonwoods were swelling. The cottonwood buds were sticky with a red sap that smelled of resin and Absorbine. Beth's new brood mare was with foal by Flash. In May she graduated—fifteenth in a class of eighty.

In June she got a card from Speedy saying, "We'll be seeing you in August." It would be very nice to see Speedy. She'd show him how grown-up and responsible she was, and how well she'd learned to ride that little saddle. In June the catkins ripened on the cottonwood trees and sent the silky cotton drifting off on the wind. She helped Vern with some of the ranch work, because his kidney was troubling him just a little and good men were hard to get. She took care of the irrigated pastures, riding Flash around to change the water and check the ditches. In July, when they started to put the hay up, Vern drove the baler, the other men mowed and stacked the bales in great green rectangles, and Beth drove the side delivery rake across the shimmering fields, turning up long windrows of hay behind her.

Flo protested. "What will the Frith people think when she turns up next fall with calluses on her hands like a man?"

"Flo," said Beth, "just leave me alone. You got your way about college, so just leave me alone."

One day when Vern was in an amiable mood and they were sitting in the shade of the baling machine, eating baloney sandwiches with lettuce and drinking coffee out of thermos bottles, Beth tested Vern on the subject of Speedy with what she thought was great delicacy. They had started talking about people and then about marriage.

"Daddy, why did you marry Flo, anyway?"

"Darn if I know," said Vern, and poured himself another cup of coffee in the lid of his thermos.

"But don't you even remember?"

"Flo roped me and hogtied me and hooeyed, and I was just a wall-eyed calf. Those were my rodeoing days. I went East to compete at Madison Square, and I wound up with Flo instead. Actually, your mother married me because she was mad. She was in love with some Eastern kid. He was rich too, but not rich enough for her family. They broke the two of them up. To get back at them, Flo ran off with the next man that came along, which happened to be a bowlegged little roper name of Vern Stuart. We met when a mutual friend, a stockbroker, invited us to supper. And so Flo has been mad ever since —mad at her parents, mad at me, mad at you, and mad at the horses. Sometimes I think she hates the horses most of all. Ain't their fault, poor things."

"Daddy, what do you think of Speedy?"

"Speedy who?"

"Speedy Gonzalez." She grinned, but she was already sorry she'd mentioned it, without knowing why. "You know. Speedy Gonzalez is the fastest mouse in Mexico."

"Oh, him." Vern leaned back against the tractor tire and chewed a spring of timothy grass. "You mean you haven't forgotten that little greaser jockey yet?"

"Lord, Daddy, he's no greaser. He's only half Mexican. The other half he's chicano!"

"Don't cuss, girl. Of course he's a greaser. Rita looked like she was three-quarters Indian. If you ever get married, Ah'd like to see you marry a white man, of course."

Beth blinked.

Vern squinted at her. "You thinking about marrying that Speedy?"

"Of course not," she lied. She searched for an excuse. "I was just thinking how different people are."

"Like should go for like," said Vern, chewing on the timothy. "You wouldn't breed a Thoroughbred to a pony, would you?"

"You're a fine one to talk about Rita," said Beth. And the minute the words were out of her mouth, she was sorry for that too.

"What do you mean?" said Vern, sitting up and taking the timothy out of his mouth.

"I have a pretty fair idea of what you did with Rita."

"One, what Ah did with Rita ain't none of your business," said Vern. "Two, what Ah did with her is different." His eyes had a hard sparkle in them that frightened Beth a little. She felt a slow color rising in her cheeks, right up to the brim of her battered straw hat.

"Well, I don't care what you did," said Beth, shrugging. "Matter of fact, I approve. They're coming back this summer. Did you know that?"

"No, Ah didn't."

"Well, they're coming back on this circuit. And I aim to spend every morning at the track, like I did before. It's probably the last time I'll ever get to do it. So if you let me go over there, I'll make a deal with you. I won't tell Flo about Rita."

Vern glared at her a moment longer, then burst out laughing and slapped the sun-bleached knee of his Levis. "You little horse trader, you." He went on chuckling and pulled his hat brim down over his eyes at a rakish angle. "All right, Bethy. You can go over to the track every morning, long as you don't neglect the ranch work. You can go over even if Ah decide Ah don't want to take no more truck rides with Rita. Know why?"

"Why?"

"Because," said Vern, "Ah know you. And Ah know you won't monkey around with any greaser jockeys. You are still five years old, and you don't know your hind hoof from a hole in the ground."

Just before the fair Beth saw Elizabeth Taylor in *National Velvet*. It was an old movie that they showed on television. Beth sat without moving all the way through it, and she cried over the beautiful horse and the beautiful girl.

When the movie ended, she went and looked at herself in the bathroom mirror for a long time. She pushed her fingers through her short, sun-bleached, curly hair. She weighed herself and found that even with her muddy old Justin boots on, she tipped the scale at just ninety-five pounds. She turned sideways, stuck out her chest, and saw that even at seventeen she did not have a nice front like Elizabeth Taylor did. Of course, she still had the horse's ears on top of her head too—she could see them clearly in the mirror, pricked with curiosity. Elizabeth Taylor did not have horse's ears.

She went into her mother's bedroom. Flo was sitting in a needle-point armchair, wearing a satin nightgown, robe, and slippers, and reading an antiques magazine. "Flo," said Beth timidly, "have you got an extra brassiere around?"

Flo looked up. "Why can't you ever call me 'mother'? What did you do with the last one I gave you?"

"I cannot tell a lie," said Beth. "I threw it in the garbage can."

With a sigh, Flo got up and searched in a bureau drawer among all kinds of lace petticoats, lace nighties, nylon stockings, and other delicate things. Peering over Flo's shoulder, Beth saw that her mother had a whole cache of little lace bras in there, just like the ones she had thrown out. Her mother took one and gave it to her, then smiled a little and patted Beth on the head. "It's about time," she said.

Beth rushed to her room, stripped off her checked cowboy shirt, and put it on. It felt funny, and it really didn't make her look any bigger. But she kept it on. She even wore it to bed. She lay there thinking about the horse's ears on her head—they had to go. After awhile she got an idea. She slipped out of bed in the dark and went to the shelf where the herd of abandoned horse figurines stood. The window was open into the back yard and a gust of spicy cottonwood smell came in. She took down her favorite figurine, an expensive porcelain Thoroughbred that Vern had given her one Christmas. She kissed it. Then she knocked off its ears and tail against the edge of the shelf and stood it carefully back in its place.

Along in August she started going over to the fairgrounds to practice Flash around the barrels that Tom Chance had benevolently set up in the arena for her. Tom was mostly amused by the rivalry between Beth and his sister Pat. The track hadn't been harrowed yet, and it was hard as rock and overgrown with chicken weed and yellow sweet clover. Beth worried about the clover, as she knew it was poisonous to horses—it gave them hemorrhages.

So she told Tom, "Say, you ought to get the harrow out on that track and start working it."

"Yeah," said Tom, "I guess we'd better," and he did. Beth watched the tractor and harrow chugging around the oval, feeling that she had done part of her duty toward preserving the Count's sound legs. About a week before the fair, a few gyps were already coming in with their sorry trucks and sorrier horses. Beth waited for Speedy to come with a peace of mind that was full and spicy as the August afternoons.

Then, exactly three days before the fair started, she was out galloping on the track in the morning when she saw Walt Fromann's big green horse van swaying slowly down the lane of cottonwood trees from the highway. She hurried off the track to meet them. The truck came jouncing through the ruts and stopped in the cottonwood shade near the creek. Walt climbed creakily out of the cab with the air of a man who has driven all night along lonely Montana two-lane high-ways. Then Speedy climbed shakily out too. He looked changed from last year. Of course, he was a year older, nineteen now, and certainly tired looking—the faint stubble on his jaw gave him the poignant look of a man just rescued from the wilderness. But a certain harshness had set his fine mouth, and a ghostly anxiety had replaced the look of eagles in those eyes that had made the high-school girls swoon last year. His face had suddenly focused to hurting clarity, or perhaps it had blurred altogether.

He stood there in faded jeans and an undershirt full of holes, hands in pockets and a cigarette smoldering at the corner of his mouth, and an animal ferocity rolled out around him like a shock wave. Beth somehow wished that he had stayed the hardworking, dutiful boy of all the story books. He dissimulated, squinted at the little racing saddle and the sheepskin noseband on Flash.

"H'lo," he said. "How's it go?"

"H'lo," she echoed, waiting for Rita to climb out of the cab. But Rita didn't get out. The cab was empty. "Where's Rita?"

"Gone," said Speedy, turning away to help Walt lower the tail-gate.

"Where?"

"Back to Mexico," said Walt, "the greaser bitch."

Speedy's lips tightened, but he didn't say anything. Beth saw him go white with effort as he and Walt eased the heavy ramp down.

Beth helped them unload and exercise the horses and set the stalls fair. Then Walt went to town to eat, stop at the racing office to enter, then visit the Corner Bar and irrigate his droughted-out mouth with a little whiskey. Speedy and Beth sat on bales of straw in the tack stall, and Speedy told her what happened. His hands, as always, were compulsively busy, mending a broken halter.

"She run off with another man." Speedy kept his eye on the awl as he pushed it in and out with the heavy thread, and not a muscle in his face twitched. "I don't know who with. I don't even know where. She's my own mother, that *malinche,* and she wouldn't even tell me who she was running off with."

"But why?" Beth tried to visualize Flo running off, and couldn't.

"Because she was a temperamental woman, and she needed a lot of blowouts." Speedy savagely sewed away at the halter. "And all the time she and Walt were married, that *gabache* never laid her once. Don't ask me if he lays other women, because he never tells me what he does when he leaves here, not even when he's drunk. You see, he and Rita got married as a business deal. Of course, they could have made a partnership without getting married. But that loco woman was actually in love with Walt, and she wanted a wedding, so he said okay. Don't ask me why. She had one good horse—the Count—and no money. Walt had money, but no good horse. Together they parleyed up this good set of horses. Walt is the business brains, and she trained the horses. She was a great trainer, and he got all he wanted out of her. By and by she'd had enough. And she couldn't do the work any-more either, her veins bothered her real bad. Got so it hurt her even to ride. One night she told me she was going, and she packed her things and went."

"What you mean he never laid her?"

"*Caray,* are you dumb. Are you still dumb as last year, dumb Beth?"

Beth shrugged. "Why didn't you and her take the Count and leave?"

"Because that loco woman loved old Walt so much that she sold him the horse when they got married. And on their wedding night she found out what a big mistake she'd made, because Walt spent the night in a bar. And then Walt wouldn't sell the horse back. That's why I can't leave him either. I've got to take care of her horse as long as he can step and go. She spotted him as a runty-looking yearling, his legs went every which way when he walked, and she bought him for a song and made him what he is."

"But when is your contract up with Walt?"

"I've got a year to go yet. That's too bad, because he gets meaner every day."

Beth sat there not knowing what to say. Finally she said, "I'm sorry, Speedy." She thought about all the postcards that said "Sun and nice weather."

"So am I," said Speedy. "I'm real good and sorry. She wouldn't even tell me where she was going. She used to tell me everything. Ever since she left—it was along about the first of June—I've been thinking about it, and I don't understand it. She must have had some good reason. I tried to think if I hurt her feelings somehow. But I couldn't think of anything."

"Walt said she went to Mexico."

"That's just his little joke. He don't know where she is either. She and her family came up *tijuanas,* wetbacks, from Mexico. They were from a ranch in Chihuahua, and she'd learned about horse handling there. The whole family worked stoop labor. They picked grapes and strawberries and stuff. Her name was Chavez then."

"And your daddy?"

Speedy went on pushing the awl in and out of the halter. Finally he said, "Well, my dad was José de la Luz Gonzalez. He was a real *californio*. His people was in the state since the Spanish came there. He was on a big ranch in the southern part of the state, the Santa Cruz, that was one of the last Spanish land grants still going. They raised beef cattle and Thoroughbreds. Dad was, like, the trainer's assistant. I was born and raised on the Santa Cruz. We weren't rich, but we were better off than most chicanos. I don't really know how my dad and Rita met. I guess her people just happened through, and José saw her and asked for her. She must have decided the Santa Cruz was better than picking grapes. That was a real nice place, the Santa Cruz. Olive orchards and big pastures on the shore. We used to leg the horses up over the dunes, along the beaches. That's the way to leg a horse up—natural like. Not the way everybody does now, with a lot of fast blowouts on the track."

"Your dad really savvied horses, huh?"

"I'll say he did. He savvied them better than the trainer. The trainer took credit for what Dad did, most of the time. I never saw anyone as gentle and knowing with horses as my dad was. He broke racehorses, polo ponies, cutting horses, everything. His horses all had a finish that you could spot anywhere. He never pushed a horse, just took him along step by step, on the horse's own time. When he walked down the stall rows, all the horses at the Santa Cruz put their heads out and whinnied for him."

"So that's where you and Rita learned everything."

"Yeah. Walt doesn't want most of what we know. He likes fast blowouts. The Santa Cruz went broke, and they sold it. A big development moved in. They bulldozed down all the olive orchards and the barns and the paddocks. Then they built little square houses all over it. We lived in the *barrio* in Los Angeles for a while. But I started getting into fights in the street. And my dad didn't like the city much. So he got the idea that he wanted to try his own hand at racing. He didn't have the money to get into it at the top, of course. So we bought a quarter interest in this snaky mare with popped knees. Dad nursed her knees along, she started winning, and pretty soon he bought the other three quarters of her. Finally we had five horses. They were all locos that nobody else could do anything with. He picked them up cheap and made money-winners out of all of them. This would have been about seven years ago, when I was twelve. Dad was already training me to be his jockey, so I could take out my license when I was sixteen."

"Where is he now?"

"Well," said Speedy, "we had a little accident on the road to Salmon, Idaho." Speedy suddenly fumbled and dropped the halter, then sat there with his head down and didn't pick it up. "It was at night. A car passed on a curve and rammed our truck. We went off the road, turned over, and caught fire. Somehow mother was thrown out the door, not hurt. I had a broken arm and a few cuts, but she pulled me out of there. There was no sense pulling Dad out, because the steering wheel had crushed his chest, and he had blood all down the front of him. The horses were burning up in the truck, banging and screaming. Two of them broke out, but they were scorched and peeling from head to tail. Rita held them by the halters, and I killed them with my knife. I had to use my left hand, because my right arm was broke, and I was pretty clumsy killing them. The rest of them burned up in the truck. That was seven years ago."

Beth saw tears dropping down on the thighs of his faded Levis. His shoulders were shaking. She reached and squeezed his hand, the one that still clenched the awl and thread. He squeezed back, so hard that all the bones in her hand crackled. Then he sniffed loudly, wiped his eyes on his sleeve, picked up the awl and halter again, and finished sewing.

"With the insurance money," he said, "Mother went out to the yearling sales and bought the Count, and we started all over. He was a two-year-old and winning when we met Walt."

They sat for a while, and the horses thumped gently in their stalls. "Now I see," said Beth, "why you never leave the horses, not even to eat."

"That's right." Speedy got up and hung the halter neatly on a rusted nail. "Sometimes I have nightmares about something happening to that horse. There are sons of *chingadas,* for instance, who sneak into a stall and make a little nick on the leg with a knife—"

"Speedy, if you ever got the Count away from Walt, I'd give you Flash. Then you'd have two good horses."

Speedy looked at her fixedly for a moment, then smiled and threw one arm across her shoulder, and tousled her hair with his free hand. "Don't make no promises. I just might hold you to them." She blushed and ducked her head, thinking he'd let go right away, but he didn't. She started to shake a little, and her breasts started hurting in her little lace brassiere, like when he had patted her shirt front last year. "Still want to run away from home and be a jockey, Beth?"

"Nope." She didn't dare look up. She could feel the heat of his arm all the way across her back. "I'm not that silly anymore. I'm going to take over the ranch soon, because my daddy has kidney trouble, and he can't rustle around like he used to. I'd like to raise some racing Quarter Horses, though. I bred Flash to both my 4H mares."

He shook her gently, then let her go. "Well, if you ever need a good jockey and I'm not riding steady for Elizabeth Arden by then, just say the word and I'll come ride for you."

"Okay." Her teeth were chattering, and she could hardly get the word out.

"I'm going to make a jockey, Beth. A big stable down in California is just waiting to contract me when I get loose of Walt. They know I'm José's son. Lot a jockeys are city boys now, who only get to horses on vacations and such. I've got the edge over them, because I've been handling horses all my life. I'll get out of the gyp circuit and into the bigtime. And when I get money, I'm going to buy land. A chicano is no good without land."

She grinned. "Someday your name will be in all the books that horse-crazy little girls read, maybe. Eddie Arcaro, Johnny Longden, Earl Sande, Willie Shoemaker, Angel Cordero, Speedy Gonzalez—"

"Maybe yes, maybe no." He smiled, looking at nothing out the tack-stall door. A breeze gusted in and raised his hair a little. She thought he looked more cheerful.

During the next few days, she scarcely budged from Speedy's side, except to take care of the show horses with Vern and to do her ranch chores. Haying was over and grain harvest wasn't on yet, so there was less work to do on the ranch. Sometimes she got to the track as Speedy was putting the coffee pot on the fire, dressed in T-shirt and Levis, not even shaved yet. And she only left him at nightfall, because of her father's rule that she had to be home by dark.

Walt went into town for lunch and dinner, then brought them sackfuls of greasy hamburgers with onions and pickles and mustard. They sat leaning against the barns eating them. Walt kidded Beth a little about being Speedy's girlfriend and only fan, but he also let her gallop his gentler Thoroughbreds in the morning blowouts. He barked instructions at her just the way he did at Speedy. The only difference was that he didn't hit her if she did something the least bit wrong.

"Speedy," Walt said one morning after Beth had blown out a bay mare named Little Witch, "now that Rita's gone and left us, I think we should kidnap this little gal and take her on the road with us. She's gotten real handy with the horses."

"I think so too," said Speedy. He was riding a gray gelding named Erin Go Bragh, and they were taking the horses back to the barns to cool them out. "Only she's going to marry me, not you." He winked at Beth, and Beth sat there a little astonished, wondering if he was kidding or what.

"How about it, young lady?" said Walt. "I won't paint a rosy picture of your future. The pay's not too good, and the hours are not too good either. But we know you just love racehorses."

Beth looked from Speedy to Walt and back, still not sure if they were kidding. "No siree," she said. "I got to stay here and raise my own horses. Speedy, when are you coming over to the livestock barns and see my mares and foals?"

"I don't move that far away," said Speedy. "Bring them over to visit me some afternoon."

So one afternoon, the day before the livestock judging started, she proudly led her horses over to see Speedy, and tied them all together in the shade so he could look at them. There was Flash, her yearling colt from last year, her first mare with the colt she'd birthed that spring, and the new mare, now heavy in foal by Flash. Five in all.

Speedy looked them over for a long time. "Shit," he said, "you've got more horses than we do. Well, I'm no judge of Quarter Horses, but they look in mighty good condition to me." He stroked the five-month-old bay foal, who was very well-mannered and sniffed Speedy up and down curiously. "What's this little feller's name?"

"I named him Speedy," she said. She found she was blushing.

Speedy hooted with laughter, but he looked pleased. "Well," he said, "you've got quite a family."

Beth found that last year's childish admiration of Speedy had turned into something different. Her need to be near him was like wanting to drink a glass of water or go pee. She figured out ways to touch him a hundred times a day, if no more than to brush his hand as she helped him saddle up. She sensed vaguely that he was no longer merely tolerating her cheerfully and letting her lighten his work burden, like last year, but that he often figured out his own ways of touching her, if no more than holding her boot as he gave her a leg up on a horse.

After the first day's racing, when they had put the horses away and Walt had gone into town to eat, Speedy was sweeping up in front of the stalls. He had put in a hard day on the track, riding all eight races and booting home four winners, and he looked pale and drained. Suddenly he winced, dropped the broom, and clutched at his back right at the waist. Beth saw his face go white with pain.

"What is it?" She leaned her own broom against the barn and went to him.

He didn't answer for a moment, finally straightened up slowly. "That *huevón* Owens horse must have popped my back in the sixth race," he said. "That's all I need is a popped back." Still a little bent over, he finished sweeping before he hobbled to the tack stall. "Beth, get the Absorbine and rub my back. If it's good for horses, it ought to be good for people." He stripped off his shirt and undershirt, sank onto a bale of hay, and sat there all bent over.

A little timidly, she sat down behind him, poured Absorbine into one palm, and started rubbing. It occurred to her that a man's back was a fine-looking thing, with all those muscles rippling and the long spine with its bones showing a little. She felt that curious, hurting joy as she rubbed her hands over it. His warm skin had the sleek metal burnish of the Count's hide, but it was different. Or was it that he had started to look like the Count, from worrying over him so much?

"Harder," said Speedy. "The way you rub a horse down. That's it. That feels good. Rub down around the waist where it hurts." He made her rub for a long time—partly, she suspected, because he just liked it. When she stopped, he said, "It still hurts—inside the spine, like. Sometimes my joints hurt, too."

"You work awful hard," said Beth. She had a little prickly pain down between the legs too, as if a thistle had gotten stuck there. The smell of Absorbine hung in the air.

"Well, it's like vacation having you around. I don't know what I'd do without you."

"You mean you like me because I muck stalls so good?"

He looked over his shoulder, grinning a little. "Yeah, I like the way you muck."

The last day of the race meet, Beth beat Pat Chance and won the barrel race again. But somehow she didn't get nearly as excited about it as last year. It was getting to be a routine. And she got blue ribbons for her 4H horses too. In the paddock, she watched Walt throw Speedy up on the Count for the Cottonwood Derby, and worried because Speedy looked so tired. His cheekbones stood up white under his dark skin, and he rode the horse out of the paddock with an air of indifference to the whole business. The Count was dancing and throwing his head up and down. Beth watched Speedy struggle to hold him —the red horse's powerful neck nearly pulled him down out of the saddle. Finally the lead pony dropped back to Speedy, and the pony boy grabbed the Count's rein and made him behave. The smoky grandstand murmured as the horses paraded around the turn to where the starting gate waited in the backstretch. A dry wind blew, and dust scudded off the track. Beth saw Speedy's red and white silks fluttering madly on his hurting back.

The horses went into the gate nicely, stood still a moment. Then the bell rang, the gates banged open, and the horses catapulted out. The crowd started yelling.

"God damn, look at that," said Walt. The Count had not broken in front this time. He was back in the pack, laying third. The horses churned around the turn in a huge cloud of white dust, closely bunched. Beth could see a lot of pushing and shoving—horses bulldogging each other, jockeys' whips flailing away.

Suddenly a great scream went up from the crowd, and the announcer, who could see everything from his tower above the rodeo arena, shouted, "Folks, a jockey's down!"

The horses turned out into the home stretch, and Beth could see the Count running riderless, reins flopping on his neck. He dropped back to fourth, then fifth place. The dust blew away, and she saw a small figure in red and white silks lying on the strip in the middle of the far turn. She and Walt clambered over the paddock fence at exactly the same instant, ran across the track through the lingering dust, and ducked under the rail. Walt's eyes were on the horse, who was running last now, stirrup irons flailing crazily at his sides. "God damn," said Walt, "he'll hurt himself."

Beth kept running, stumbling through the sun-dried chicken weed, sweet clover, and foxtail of the infield. Speedy was trying drunkenly to get up. He had lost his cap and his hair was gray with dust. Beth reached him and dragged him to safety under the rail just a few seconds before the horses went into the far turn again. They burst past in an explosion of snorts, jockeys yelling, "Yaaaah!" and dirt and rocks flying.

Speedy was gasping for breath, limping. He had an abrasion on the side of his face, with dirt ground into it, and beads of blood growing on it. "The horse," he choked.

"He's all right," said Beth. "He's running, but he ain't hurt."

Speedy stood trying to focus his eyes. The field was off in the far turn now, a gray horse leading, the pack following, and then the Count galloping crazily about nineteen lengths behind, his ears pricked forward as if he couldn't figure out what had happened to his rider.

Speedy started off toward the back stretch. "He'll run all the way around. We'll stop him there."

Walt came up, his face blue with anger. "How'd it happen?"

"I got bumped real bad," said Speedy.

"Damn no-good greaser kid. Five hundred dollars out the window, up in smoke."

"Not my fault." Speedy was limping blindly along, his eyes on the Count. "That *huevón* number three horse bumped me. Lucky we didn't go down."

"You want to claim a foul?"

"Let it go." Tears of rage were running down Speedy's dusty face.

"Goddamn greaser kid. Wants to make a jockey. Falls off horses."

They reached the backstretch rail. Behind them, the crowd's yelling died off. The gray horse had won, paying 40 to 1 to win, and a few people would make a fair amount of money on the upset. The Count, seeing the field slow down and break up, galloped on around the near turn. Then he slowed and stopped near the gap, which was now shut. He stood waiting for Speedy, nose stretched out, sides heaving and streaked with white sweat. He whinnied anxiously as the boy limped up to him.

"Ho, Count. Ho." Beth gently took the reins. Speedy inspected the horse's legs, then seemed to sag with relief. "Looks like he's all right."

Walt seized the horse's reins and led him off toward the gap. Beth looked at Speedy wordlessly. Then as he started to limp after, she put her arm around him and helped him walk off the track.

Walt was so angry that he left Beth to cool the horses and drove into town. Without even taking off his silks, Speedy collapsed on his sleeping bag in the truck and fell asleep. For the first time, Beth had to put the Count away herself. The barns hummed with a crossfire of discussion about how Speedy Gonzalez had gotten bumped and fallen off, and the jockey who had ridden number three said he couldn't recollect bumping the Count, but he wasn't sure, because there was one motherfucking melee there in the far turn, he said. Vern came by the tow ring and said, "I hear Speedy fell off today."

"Yah," said Beth. "He got bumped real bad. Nothing broken, just all bruised up."

"Well," said Vern, "I'm going to start taking our horses on home. No sense leaving them here another night. Somebody might steal them. I'll take yours too, if you want."

"All right," said Beth. "I have to finish up here. Walt's gone into town to get drunk, I guess."

When she finished with the Count, she went to see if Speedy was all right. He was lying awake in the gloom inside the horse van, on his sleeping bag. She sat down beside him a little timidly, because she had never been in there where he slept before. He rolled his head to look at her. The blood had dried on his face.

"Beth, I lied. I just plain fainted and fell off. Don't tell Walt."

"Are you sick?"

"Just run down, I guess. I felt dizzy, and the next thing I knew I was rolling in the dirt and the field running over me. That's a sight now, all those bellies and hoofs. *Caramba,* one horse clipped me in the leg as he went over."

"Maybe I should call a doctor."

"No, no doctors. Walt will just get mad all over again about extra expenses. I can take care of myself." He pulled off his dirty, torn silk shirt, and Beth saw more abrasions on his shoulder and arm. She got some cotton wadding, soap and water, the awl, and a flashlight. Speedy sterilized the awl in a match flame. By the light, she and Speedy spent a cheerful half hour picking the gravel out of his hurts, washing them, and swabbing iodine on them. Speedy kept wincing and saying ouch. He pulled off his little white jodphurs and sat there in his underwear shorts, inspecting the bruise on his thigh that would be purple, red, blue, and green tomorrow.

It suddenly occurred to Beth that tomorrow Speedy and Walt were leaving.

Twilight was coming on, and the dry wind still rushed in the cottonwood leaves outside. The great trees tossed and billowed over the rain-darkened roofs of the race barns, with their roof beams sagging and their shingles coming loose. The gyps were packing to leave first thing in the morning. Speedy put on his Levis and red sweatshirt and limped down the ramp to look at the Count. Then he sat in the tack stall with his head hanging, because he was too sore to move, he said. Beth sat there by him, wishing she didn't have to leave soon.

Finally Walt came back. His step was none too steady, and the veins in his nose stood out as distinctly as if somebody had drawn them on with red and blue ballpoint pens. He hadn't brought any hamburgers either. He stood weaving in the doorway of the tack stall and said, "Goddamn greaser kid."

Speedy, sitting on the bale of hay, looked up slowly and said, "That's right. Damn greaser kid, son of a damn greaser bitch, who was your damn greaser wife and who slept with every other damn Anglo in the world but you."

Walt made a small, strangled noise. Grabbing a lead shank that was hanging from a rusty nail in the board wall, he lashed Speedy over the shoulders with the chain end of it, then raised it to lash again. Outside, a dog barked, and a radio was playing "On Top of Old Smoky." The trees rushed and billowed by the door.

Before Walt could lash again, Beth sprang up, flung herself at him, and seized the chain as it came whistling down. "Don't you dare!" she yelled, standing there stiffly, trying to drag the lead shank out of his hands.

Walt stood there, completely astonished. He blinked at Beth, let the shank go, and said wheedlingly, "Why, young lady, this is a tricky no-good dirty Mex who eats me out of house and home and falls off my horses."

"Hamburgers," said Beth. "All you ever feed him is hamburgers, you old shyster."

Walt sat down on the tack trunk, and didn't say anything. Speedy let his head hang again, and rubbed his slashed shoulder. Beth sat too. She watched the light turning bluer and deeper outside, and knew that in a few minutes she should go climb on Flash and ride home.

Just then Vern came up to the door. "Bethy," he said, "Ah've got the last of the hosses. You ride along with me, now."

"Say, Vern," said Walt, "I've been thinking. Come in and set down a minute." Vern tied up the horses, came in, and sat down. "I am getting pretty fed up with the bangtail business. Like this afternoon. This greaser boy falls off my best horse, and loses me $500."

"I know. It's rough," said Vern, lighting a cigarette.

"Put out that cigarette, Vern," said Speedy.

"Sorry," said Vern, and meekly put the cigarette out.

"I've been thinking," said Walt. "I've had a yen to phase myself out of racehorses and into Quarter Horses for years. More money in Quarter Horses, and less hard luck. I see the prices these good colts bring at auction. I've got some money saved up down in California, and I've got my eye on a nice little ranch down south of San Diego. I think now's the time to move, before prices go any higher."

Beth saw Speedy look at Walt with a haunted, terrible look. She wondered what would happen to the Count now.

"Vern," said Walt, "I'll offer you $500 each for those two yearling fillies I looked at the other day."

"My asking price is $600," said Vern. "I told you that."

"Five fifty, then," said Walt. "I can't go no higher."

Vern drew a little sigh. "Okay," he said. "You've been babysitting Beth for two years, so I guess I owe you a hundred dollars in babysitter fees."

"That's good," said Walt, grinning. He looked a little sobered up. "Then what I'm going to do is leave this greaser boy and my horses here for a week or so, and go to a couple auctions, pick up a few more fillies. And I've got my eye on a nice little stallion down in California. A King Ranch stallion. He's been raced and rodeoed and broke down, but he's a mighty nice kind of a little horse to put to stud. I can get him real cheap. I'm going to get on the phone right tonight to that guy down there, and tell him I'll buy that stallion."

"What," asked Speedy hollowly, "are you going to do with these racehorses?"

"Oh," said Walt, "I'll put them up for claiming or sell them. Not right away, of course. We got to keep ourselves in groceries until we get this Quarter-Horse thing set up. Maybe after the winter season—next spring sometime. The Count horse I can probably sell for a nice price to some stud farm."

"What about me?" Speedy kept looking at him with that death's look.

"Well, when I quit racing, we can terminate our contract. You can go on to what's their names, that want to sign you up. So, Vern, if it's okay with you, I'll settle with you for those fillies when I come back next week or so."

"That's fine with me," said Vern.

"And one more thing. This boy here is all beat up, and he'll have his hands full exercising and taking care of seven horses all alone. Would it be all right if Beth helps him steady, for the week? I'll pay her, of course. She's mighty handy around the horses."

Vern grinned. "Beth's never had a paying job. Her mother never wanted her to work. Do you want to do it, Bethy?"

"Sure," said Beth.

"Okay," said Vern. "Ah'll give you a little vacation for a week. You worked real hard all summer, helping me with the haying and all. And you're going off to college pretty soon. Ah've just hired a man that looks pretty good. So Ah'm going to let you play around with race-horses full time. But this is the last time. Because from now on Ah'm going to expect you to be mighty serious about Quarter Horses. All right?"

"All right," said Beth. She grinned at Speedy.

She rode off with Vern, helping him lead the last of the show horses. They rode away along the dark lane, with the cottonwood trees roaring all around them in the dry wind. The leaves were already starting to fall, and a few leaves blew against them in the dark.

The next day, the fairgrounds was a pandemonium of livestock being led out of barns, loaded into trucks and trailers. Beth helped Speedy in the morning but left him in the afternoon because she had to look after her mares and colts. Walt didn't leave that day, because he couldn't get hold of the man in California who owned the King Ranch stallion. He was about half crazy, afraid he'd lost a chance at that horse. But that night he got the man, and they made a deal. By evening the fairgrounds was nearly empty. Then Walt fooled around all of the next day arranging to have money wired to him from his California bank. Late that afternoon he took the horse truck and left. By that night, the fairgrounds was deserted.

When Beth got to the fairgrounds at sunup the next day, she found the place hung in an unreal silence. The dry wind had died, and everything shimmered in the red light, still as death. The stall doors stood open on rusted hinges. The wind had blown off a lot of shingles and they lay scattered over the abandoned tow ring. It was a spooky feeling she got, riding among the deserted barns—almost as if everyone had died from some nameless epidemic, and rotted away overnight. She was sure she would find skeletons of horses in the stalls, and skeletons of men and women lying around in derelict trucks and rusted trailor houses. But everyone was gone, swept away in the great dry wind, almost as if they would never come back.

She found Speedy still curled up in his sleeping bag in the tack stall, on the dirt floor. She pushed the creaking door open and stepped in. He blinked at the light, rubbing his eyes, and smiled in a strange way, half blissful, half rueful. "My motherfucking back's been hurting me again," he said. "Hurt me half the night. Wish you'd been here to rub it." He kept smiling, looking up at her. A large, beat-up alarm clock stood on the dirt floor beside him, ticking loudly. "In fact, I wish you could stay here twenty-four hours a day."

She sat down by him. "I have to go home at night. And I have to take care of my own horses. And that's that."

He sighed. "I know, I know. But listen, let's pretend—." He grinned. "Let's pretend you spent the night here. Take off your boots, and crawl in here for a few minutes." He unzipped the sleeping bag, and she saw that he slept in his underwear shorts and shirt, which were none too clean.

She hesitated a moment, then pulled off the old black boots and got in with him. He set the alarm clock for fifteen minutes later, then zipped the sleeping bag again. They snuggled down together, and she found that her head was on his shoulder and that both of his arms were around her. Her body was hurting and trembling. She wondered why Speedy always affected her like that. She felt him draw a long, shaky sigh.

"Do people really sleep together like this?" she asked.

"Poor dumb Beth. Of course they do. All night long."

"My folks don't. They even sleep in separate rooms. Guess they can't stand to sleep in the same bed."

Speedy laughed a little. "Guess not. You like it?"

"Yah," she said. "It's nice."

He tightened his arms a little, then reached up and stroked her hair. "God, are you dumb," he said. "I never saw anything like it. But you took such good care of me when I fell off the Count. It's good when somebody takes care of you like that."

"I liked to do it."

He fell silent after that, and they lay there almost without moving. Outside, the red light of dawn turned yellow, and shadows took shape by everything, by the barns, by the rocks, by Flash standing tied. Suddenly they both jumped as the alarm clock jangled. Speedy got one arm out of the sleeping bag and turned it off. "Rise and shine," he said. He looked down at Beth. "Good morning. How'd you sleep?"

She giggled a little. "Fine," she said. "But you snore something awful."

Speedy got out of the sleeping bag, shivered. "Brrrr." Beth got out too. Speedy went out and walked barefoot up the stall row to make sure all the horses were okay. Then he seized a dingy towel, a sponge, and a big bar of yellow soap. "Time to take a bath," he said.

"I already took one," said Beth.

"Time to take a bath," Speedy repeated. "My dad and mother took one every morning, no matter what pesthole of a track they stayed in. Clean people, clean horses, my dad used to say. He never tolerated no dirt on the horses, or the tack, or us. He said being clean was being hopeful about things. There's a place in the crik out there where the trees are thick and nobody can see. The gyps always bathe there. This lousy little track hasn't got no showers or nothing."

He went out and disappeared around the corner of the barn. After a moment, Beth felt a compulsion to follow him.

Back of the barn, the creek wound under the tall cottonwoods. The horses had grazed its grassy banks smooth as a lawn. In one spot, the creek ran wide and deep around a bend, and willows and beech trees hung over it like a cool green cave. Speedy stripped off his underwear, threw it on the grass, and waded in with the bar of soap. The water reflections shimmered green, blue, and brown over his body. Paying absolutely no attention to her, he sponged water over himself, then soaped vigorously until he was sudsy from head to foot. "The water's fine," he said. "Come on in. Time's a-wasting."

Beth looked around to see if anyone was watching. The place was silent, empty. Yellow leaves sifted down in the morning sunlight. Even her father would still be asleep—he had taken to sleeping in a little, because of his kidney and the good new man he had. So she took off her clothes very slowly, shivering. For some reason she had to cover the patch of brown hair below her belly button. She tried the water with her toe. "It's cold as hell," she said. She half expected Speedy to turn around and look at her, but he didn't.

"Softie," he said, his back still turned, soap running down his long lean thighs. "Used to hot running water and all the comforts."

So she waded in. Speedy handed her the sponge and soap without directing so much as a glance at her nakedness. The water was ice cold, but she soaped herself all over. Speedy was scrubbing vigorously under his armpits, where there was a lot of black hair she'd never noticed before, and around his crotch. She darted a curious glance to see what the stallion business was doing, but it was hardly visible amid a lot of soapsuds.

"Scrub my back," he said, so she obeyed. Then they both turned around, and he scrubbed her back—not gently either, but the way he rubbed a horse down. "Ouch," she said. She couldn't get over it. He was behaving exactly as if they had taken a bath together every day for ten years. She stopped trying to cover herself.

"You're shaking like a leaf," said Speedy, his hands pausing for a moment on her shoulders.

"It's because I'm half froze, stupid," she lied.

He turned away suddenly. They lay down in the water and rinsed themselves off with great splashings, like two otters, then climbed out and rubbed themselves dry with the one towel. Iridescent beads of water stuck on Speedy's eyelashes and in his hair—the light blinded her, she fell into it. The first rays of the sun felt warm on Beth's skin. A sun of well-being rose red in her.

They pulled on their clothes in the tack room. While Beth built a fire on yesterday's white ashes, Speedy propped a piece of broken mirror on a tree branch and shaved with a straight razor and more yellow soap. Then, putting the big skillet on the coals, she expertly fried eggs and bacon. "I'm going to feed you something beside hamburgers," she said. She had gone on fishing and pack trips with Vern, and knew how to cook out. They ate out of tin plates sitting on the ground, while the horses looked impatiently out of their stalls. After they washed the dishes in the creek, they went to work.

They started a kettle of water heating for washing bandages, and hung the night blankets out to air. They curried the horses, cleaned their feet, took off the stall bandages and put on gallop bandages, sponged their eyes and nostrils. Beth looked at everything in a trance —the tumbling shed rows, the abandoned tow ring, the manure piles where flies glittered in the sun. No one came around. Not a sound marred the silence of that place, saving the sounds they themselves made. In a week it would be over, and in two weeks she would be on a train for Connecticut. When she tried not to remember that, her heart felt like it had been rolled raw in dry thistle leaves.

Two by two they took six of the horses to the track, worked them out, walked them dry. Finally only the Count and Flash were left. "All right," said Speedy, as he saddled the Count, "now we're going to do things a little different."

"How?" said Beth, as she finished saddling Flash.

"We're going to work out crosscountry, like we used to at the Santa Cruz. Any open country around here?"

"Sure," said Beth. "Up toward our ranch, and on into the hills, there's some bench country."

She threw Speedy up on the Count, then shinnied up on Flash. Together, for the first time, the two of them left the racetrack.

They rode slowly down the lane of cottonwood trees, as yellow leaves fell slowly all around them. The leaves caught in their hair and in the horses' manes, then slipped off onto the rutted road. They rode slowly, not saying anything. When they came out into the open, up on the county road near the fork, Speedy turned in the saddle. Behind them lay the track, looking bleaker than a desert, hung in its inviolable silence. There Fitz Brodie's Reveille had beaten the immortal Tammany by a nose. In the infield, tumbleweeds waited for the next wind. The white paint peeled in curls from the rail and from the board fence that ran around the oval.

"Do you know," Speedy asked softly, "how long it is since I've actually been away from a racetrack? Away and going somewhere by myself?"

"How long?" Beth asked.

"I don't remember how long."

"Want to see our ranch?"

"Sure," said Speedy, looking drowsy with happiness. The sun was high in the sky now, and the air was warm and still. So they rode into the ranch, past the brick house with its well-watered lawn and Flo's rose garden, and into the rutted backyard. Vern was in the blacksmith shop supervising the shoeing of a horse, and he came out.

He shook his head when he saw the Count stepping neatly along over the ruts on his long legs.

"And what to mah wondering eyes should appear," he teased, "but Bethy and Speedy and two skinny reindeer."

"We're working out crosscountry," said Beth, "like Speedy says they used to do down in California."

"I'm going to call your ma," said Vern. "This is too good for her to miss." He went toward the house, hollering, "Flooooo! Hey, Flooooo!" After a few minutes Flo came out. She was wearing a pink silk dress and her big necklace of real pearls, and looked like she was going into town for some ladies' get-together.

Flo looked gravely at the two burnished horses, at the little saddles, at the two riders. She looked a long time at Speedy, who sat gravely looking back. A little breeze was coming up out of the southwest, and the horses' manes and tails, and Speedy's hair, blew lightly before it. She finally spoke. "Which of these two creatures is my daughter?"

"Me," said Beth, feeling silver-mounted with pride that Speedy looked so fine. "And this is Speedy Gonzalez." Speedy saluted Flo gravely with his crop.

"So this is the famous Speedy Gonzalez that I've been hearing all about," said Flo. "I thought you never left your horses."

"It's only this one I don't leave," said Speedy, stroking the Count's neck.

"I used to do a little fox hunting," said Flo, "but I didn't care much for it. Well, children, have a nice ride." She went back into the house.

Speedy and Beth left the ranch and rode on up into the hills. The late-summer heat shimmered over everything, then stirred in the wind like long, thin curtains. On either side of them, naked ravines opened up. The bare hillsides were overgrown with silver sage and sun-cured wheat grass that bent in the wind. The horses walked gaily, the sun shining red through their thin nostrils. Their forelocks blew blissfully. They rippled and gleamed with health and cleanliness—Flash like rubbed bronze, the Count like scoured copper.

"Look how happy the Count is to get away from them barns," Speedy said.

When the road reached the top level of the hills, the open plateau of the bench rolled out before them endlessly. The wind made soft booming noises over the grass. The silver sage and wheat grass tugged at their roots, straining to float away on the wind. Here and there grew patches of prickly pear studded with red ripening fruits. Speedy looked like he was in a trance. They left the road and struck out across the bench, the horses lifting their noses into the wind. Indigo clouds were piling up in the southwest.

"Thunderstorm coming," said Beth.

They touched the horses into a soft canter. Suddenly Speedy pulled the Count up and circled back and stopped, looking down into the grass.

"What is it?" Beth circled back. Then she saw what he was looking at. Half-hidden by a clump of silver sage was a horse's skull. It was bleached and old, and silver sage grew up through the eye sockets. Beth stared down at it too, and then she felt his terror. Farther on a few bleached leg-bones and part of a pelvis were scattered, half-hidden by the blowing grass.

Speedy slid down off the Count and holding the horse's reins, he pushed at the skull with his foot. It seemed rooted to the ground. Finally it ripped loose from the grass and turned over to show the jaw and the splintered, rotted teeth. Small insects wiggled away into its cracks and openings. Beth slid down off her horse too. Speedy looked at her, and his eyes were wide open and blank. He clenched the Count's rein so hard that his knuckles went white.

"Beth," he said.

"Yah?"

"Beth, I sure like you."

He bent and hid his face against her shoulder, then put one arm around her and held her against him, trying to hold the Count with the other hand. She let Flash's reins drop altogether, because the stallion was broken to stand, and held onto Speedy with both arms. She closed her eyes half out of fright, because she was sure she wasn't in *National Velvet*. He kissed her on the mouth the way he must have done the rodeo queen, but he kept having to take his mouth away and say *"huevón"* to the Count, who was nipping him. Under Beth's heavy sweater, her little lace bra became two horseshoe nails of pain against his red sweatshirt. Their breath blew against each other's cheeks like horses blowing after a run. In the distance, thunder rumbled faint and far-off.

"Beth, do you like me?"

"Yah."

"Say it."

"I can't."

He kissed her again, and she remained sufficiently conscious to think that this was beginning to be like the books she'd read, in which, after many trials and tribulations, the hopeless girl gets kissed by the handsome boy. Finally, at a louder roll of thunder and a really vicious nip from the Count, Speedy let her go.

His eyes lit inside as if the lightning were inside his head. His face seemed to have contracted. His lips were parted as if to say something, and his hair blew wildly in the wind. The hurrying clouds had reached the meridian now, and the sunlight sank into shadow. A gust of cold wet air hit them. He turned back to the skull and, standing on it, he gave a little jump. The rotten old bone caved in under him. Behind him, the indigo sky boiled with lightning. Long curtains of rain came trailing across the bench on the other side of the valley. She watched, paralyzed, her knees shaking, while Speedy tromped the skull to splinters and scattered the splinters through the grass with his boot.

"We better get back," she said. "If we get caught up here, we might get hit by lightning."

They mounted and rode at a brisk jog back to the track. Thunder was already pealing directly overhead, and the horses were snorty and snaky, feeling the charge in the air. They got the horses unsaddled and into stalls just as the first drops of rain made little lunar craters in the dust. Then they ran for the tack room.

Speedy latched the door from inside. Laughing, they flung themselves down on the sleeping bag and started in kissing again. The rain roared on the old shingle roof, roared down through the cottonwood boughs. "I hope," said Beth, "that those old roofs aren't leaking on the horses."

"They're not," said Speedy. "Because I climbed up on the roof when we got here and fixed all the leaks."

And they just did nothing but kiss until the rain stopped. Speedy took to putting his tongue in between her lips, and she thought that was nice. Except that her body shuddered almost uncontrollably, and a knot of pain had tied itself between her legs.

"What's the matter?" Speedy whispered.

"It scares me. It's too much. Too much for one body."

Evening came on. The sky cleared, and the indigo storm was disappearing over the hills to the northeast with a last few mutterings of thunder. Many leaves had been beaten down by the rain and lay in yellow mats under the cottonwood trees. The wet barns, in the empty red light, had a clean, dark color that cut the eye like glass. The shadows engulfed the grandstand, the track, the cottonwood lane, the abandoned tow ring, the barns, and the pastures to the east of them.

Speedy started the soaked fire going again with dry wood from the tack room, and Beth shakily fried some round steak that she had brought from home, and threw onto the coals some chili peppers she'd bought Speedy at the Safeway Supermarket. She staggered about as if she were drunk. Speedy watched her with just the faintest shadow of worry in his eyes. The nighthawks were sobbing in the sky above, swooping to catch insects in the last high rays of day, and their wings vibrated on the cool air with too much life: "Kwi-kwi-kwi-kwi-kwi ———kwi———kwi." Speedy ate, silent and preoccupied. They washed the tin plates and the skillet in the creek. Dark was coming on.

"I have to go," said Beth.

"Don't leave me."

"I have to. I'll be here real early tomorrow. It's only a few hours."

"I wake up a long time before the alarm every morning and lie there wondering if you'll come. Maybe someday you won't come."

"Sure I'll come." She stood a little hurt.

"It's too good to last," said Speedy, turning away. "Something will happen."

"Lord," she said.

"Okay, go on home," he said softly. "And if you don't come in the morning, I'll go drown myself in the crik."

"No, you won't," she said, shinnying up on Flash. "You wouldn't go off and leave the Count like that."

That night, as she lay in bed remembering the kissing and unable to sleep, she heard her father arguing with her mother in Flo's bedroom. She lay looking around the dark room, at the old racing prints whose color and detail she couldn't see, at the mass stampede of horse figurines along the shelf in the gloom, at the heavy linen curtains with hunting scenes printed on them, at the books she hadn't read in a long time now, at the stacks of scrapbooks in a corner of the shelf, at the unread racing magazines.

"I want to know what's going on," said Flo. Beth could hear her distinctly. "Is she sleeping with this boy? Is she going to get pregnant, and we'll have to let her marry him, or find an abortionist? How can you just let her spend all her time over there like that?"

Beth felt her stomach plunge with fear. Could she have gotten with foal just by snuggling with Speedy in the sleeping bag that morning?

"You're making a mountain out of a molehill," said Vern. "Ah trust her absolutely. They're just a couple of kids. Leave them alone. She's always been a lonely girl, never had any friends in school—"

"But she's obviously madly in love with the little scoundrel. Don't you see the way she looks at him?"

"Ah see it," said Vern. "She looks at him the way you should have looked at me once upon a time."

"Don't bring that up."

"Bethy'll get over this when she goes away to college. You'll see."

"Well," said Flo, "I can see that I'm not needed here. I'm helpless. I can't control her. She's your daughter, not mine. My opinions aren't listened to, or even asked."

"You make it that way your own self," said Vern. Their voices were rising. Beth could see that for once, Vern was getting a little riled up.

"Very well, then," said Flo. "I'll leave."

"Go right ahead," said Vern.

"I'll do better than that. I'll divorce you."

"You just do that."

"And I would rather die than ask you for a cent of alimony. My family has more money than you'll ever see on this grubby ranch. My father is leaving me a few million. And I won't ask for custody of Beth either. It's you that's getting her into trouble, and you can deal with the consequences when they happen."

"Just tell me one thing," said Vern. "How did you ever stand it for eighteen years?"

Flo was sobbing. Beth had never heard her mother cry before. She lay listening to them argue for a long time. Finally she slipped out of bed in her blue pajamas and padded across the bearskin rugs to the shelf where the figurines stood. She knocked the ears and tails off a couple more of them.

The next morning she escaped from the house extra early, while it was still dark, so that no one could stop her. Over at the track, Speedy must have heard Flash's hoofbeats coming, because he had already opened the tack-stall door and was standing there in his underwear. She wanted to go to him and hug him, but she slid off Flash and just stood there.

"What is it?" asked Speedy.

"Flo and my daddy had an awful fight last night, and they're going to get a divorce."

"*Caray*. Come in here."

She hung back. "Did you make me pregnant?"

"*Caray*, are you dumb. You can't get pregnant from kissing." She allowed herself to be drawn into the tack stall, and he latched the door. He made her get into the sleeping bag and hugged her convulsively, kissing her neck and face all over. "Every morning I'm sure you won't come," he said.

"Flo says we've been sleeping together, and she's right."

"Well," said Speedy, "laying together in a sleeping bag is one thing, and sleeping together is something else. Didn't she ever tell you the difference, for christ's sake?"

"She never tells me things, just orders me."

"Didn't she, like, when you had your first period—"

"My first what?"

"Christ," said Speedy. "You know, every month, when you bleed."

"Oh, that. Well, she told me it was something women have to put up with. The first time it happened, when I was twelve, I was real scared. I thought I had gotten a thistle up where I pee, or something. I'd been playing in the hay. I thought I was gonna die, and I told Flo. That's how she knew. Ever since then, I get these awful cramps."

"It's so you can have babies. Wouldn't you like a baby?"

"No."

Speedy lay by her with that storm of worry in his eyes. "That's what I think about. Well, let's say it runs second to winning the Santa Anita Handicap. But I think about it. A house and a wife to go away from the track to, instead of sleeping in horse trucks all the time." He smiled a little. "When my mother slept around with men, she didn't try to hide it from me. She said if I wanted to run around with girls, she would look after the horses while I was gone. She was the one started calling me Speedy. My real name is José." He mimicked Rita's singsong Mexican accent. "Speedy Gonzalez eez the fas'es' mouse eeen Mejico. Speedy Gonzalez eez a frien' of everybody's seester."

"Well, what do people do when they sleep together?" asked Beth.

Speedy was silent for a moment. Then he said, "I'll show you, if you want."

"But I'll get pregnant."

"When did you have your last period?"

"I'm about due again."

"Then it'll be all right. Don't worry."

In the dark stall, in the warmth of the sleeping bag, he curved half over her, kissing her very hard now. His eyes were closed, and he kept saying over and over again that he liked her. He put his hand up under her heavy sweater and unfastened her little white lace bra. She started, almost shocked, to feel his hand stroking her breasts just the way he stroked the Count's neck. The caresses were a torment, as if her nipples had thorns in them. The front of his underwear shorts pressed against her hip, and the stallion thing in there felt big and hard. Her hands clenched and unclenched in his undershirt, then leaned to return his caresses along his sides and back. Through the cracks in the board wall, a faint gray light showed. Falling leaves tickled on the shingle roof. The horses rustled in their stalls. The sweet pain between her legs became a knotted cramp, like the roots of a great cottonwood sticking naked out of stony soil. She gave a wailing animal cry, but she already wanted to stop. He fumbled to unfasten her belt, unzipped her Levis and started pushing them down, his hand sliding down her bare flank toward where the pain was snarled like a ball of living string.

"Beth, what's the matter with you?"

He drew back. She was shuddering from head to foot, her limbs jerking out of control. "Beth, for christ's sake." He didn't touch her anymore, and she lay with eyes squeezed shut until her muscles had stopped twitching somewhat. Finally, with shaking hands, she pulled up her Levis again. Beside them on the floor, the alarm clock ticked loudly. Through the cracks in the boards, knives of sunlight stabbed in. She opened her eyes and saw him lying on his back with his arm over his face.

"I'm sorry," she said through chattering teeth.

"It isn't going to be easy, is it?" said Speedy past his arm. "I thought if I took you along slow—"

"I like it so much that I don't want it. I'll die."

The alarm clock went off, so they got up and went through their routine. They even took the Count and Flash up on the bench again. But Speedy kept looking at her with that ghostly, anxious look. He kept telling her that he wouldn't hurt her, that it was good, that she'd like it. In the afternoon they lay in the tack stall again, and she let him kiss her some more, but nothing more. By six, as they sat by the fire in the last warm sunlight and Beth fried the steaks, they were both saddle sore with emotion. As twilight came on, Speedy fell into another self-destroying gloom. He sat with his head on his drawn-up knees and wouldn't talk to her.

Finally it was getting dark, and there was nothing to do but say, "I have to go now."

"You won't come tomorrow, huh?" Speedy didn't raise his head.

"Sure I'll come."

"Beth, listen to me. When Walt comes back, you'll load Flash into our truck and go off with us. Along the road somewhere, we'll get a justice of the peace to marry us. We'll take good care of you. Walt's mean, but he respects you, and he won't never bother you. In a year I'll be free of him, and we can come back here. Your dad'll have to forgive you, if he wants you to run the ranch."

She stood there clutching Flash's rein. "Speedy, I don't want to marry you right now. Give me a little time. I'm still part horse."

"Part horse?" He lifted his head, and looked at her strangely.

"Yah. Don't you see the ears on my head, and my tail, and all?"

"No, I don't," he said, looking a little annoyed.

They were silent for a moment. The twilight breeze breathed softly in the yellowing cottonwood trees. Leaves were floating down the creek, catching against sticks, whirling around over the little rapids and whirlpools.

"I can't leave here without you," said Speedy. "I'll kill myself first."

"Why don't you stay, then? You could get a job here, maybe with Dad. Maybe after a year or two, I'll marry you."

"You know I can't let Walt go off with that horse alone."

"We'll buy him."

"Dumb Beth. Walt won't sell him as long as he's winning. And what are you going to buy him with? Money?"

"I can swap Walt Quarter Horses for him. My 4H project is over anyway."

Speedy sat thinking. "Well, we'll try it." He got up, walked over to her, and kissed her good-bye very tenderly, stroking the back of her neck. "You can't keep me kissing you forever. You'll drive me loco."

The week passed. Beth refused all but kisses. Speedy got gloomier and gloomier. He said his back hurt him terribly. Flo was getting ready to leave—she had moving men packing her antiques and everything she'd brought with her for shipment back to New York. Flo didn't even speak to Beth. Vern didn't question her about how she'd behaved all day, and she didn't confide anything. Riding Flash back to the ranch at night, she learned for the first time to dissimulate, smoothing her taut face, making her aching body move easily, pretending that she and Speedy were just a couple of kids having a good time.

On the eighth day, in the afternoon, Walt drove in with the horse truck. Beth and Speedy, as it happened, were not engaged in kissing in the tack stall. They were cleaning tack, sitting outside on bales of hay in the warm afternoon sunshine with saddles, rags, and tins of saddle soap.

"H'lo, kids," said Walt, getting stiffly out of the cab.

"H'lo," they echoed, and Speedy said, "How'd it go?"

"Just fine. I bought me thirteen nice fillies at the auctions. They're going to ship them down to California for me. Actually, I'd planned to buy only ten or so. Got a little carried away. I'm somewhat out of money."

Walt sat down on a bale, near a manure pile glittering with flies, and told them all about it.

Finally Beth decided it was time to speak. "Walt, would you be interested in swapping me the Count for some of my horses?"

"Well now, little girl, what do you propose to do with him?"

"I'm thinking," said Beth, "of maybe not going to college after all. My folks just decided to get a divorce, and Flo's leaving. I'd like to buy two or three Thoroughbred brood mares and put the Count to stud. It would be another 4H project, as I'd want to stay in the club if I'm here."

"Well, now, that sounds like a nice idea. What does Speedy think about you buying the Count?"

"It's okay with me," said Speedy. Beth could see Speedy's hands shaking a little.

"But that means," said Walt, "that Speedy goes with the horse, don't it?"

"That's right," said Speedy.

"Well now," said Walt, "Beth, if you said something about this before I bought all those fillies, we might of made a trade. But I got carried away and bought nearly too many for the size of that little ranch I'm buying. I don't need no more fillies right now. And anyway, I don't plan to quit racing until next spring. I want to keep this good jockey and his good horse working for me until then."

Beth looked down at the saddle she'd been polishing. The fragrance of saddle soap rose to her nostrils. "Then it's no deal?"

"Afraid so," said Walt, getting up. "Speedy and the Count leave with me tomorrow morning. He stretched and yawned cavernously. "Well, I'm starved. I'm going into town to eat. Speedy, want some hamburgers?"

That last night, when it was time for her to go home, Speedy actually walked with her a little way down the cottonwood lane. Walt was back at the barn packing things and supposedly watching the Count. Dark was coming on. Speedy and Beth walked along the rutted road, holding hands and not saying anything. Beth was leading Flash and Speedy was slightly bent over because he had been complaining about his back all day. A cold wind made a deep roar in the cottonwoods, as if welling up from lungs deeper than the universe. Everywhere among the cottonwood trunks, the yellow leaves lay matted.

About one hundred feet along the road, Speedy stopped dead and looked back at the barns as they disappeared among the trees. Beth realized that he would not walk a step farther.

"Beth." He wrapped Flash's reins around a cottonwood limb, pulled her off among the trees and started hugging her. He was shaking with cold, and his hair blew against her face. "I'm asking you one last time."

"No, Speedy. Next year."

"There's no time like that left. There isn't a year."

"What do you mean?"

"Don't tell Walt. The Count is going lame."

"Yah?"

"I could feel it during his workout this morning. There's just a little swelling in the near front ankle. Walt didn't notice. I wonder if he hurt himself when I took him out crosscountry."

"Walt will get rid of him if he breaks down?"

"Shitting right. And I'll have to go with him, right to the slaughterhouse. And *adios* my nice contract with that stable." They held each other very tightly, buffeted by the kicks of the wind. "Beth, if something happens this winter and I write you a scared loco letter, will you come to California? And if the Count is put up for sale or claiming, will you try to loan me money to buy him?"

"Well, Daddy is giving me money for a bank account at college. Maybe I'll have enough to get the Count."

"He's your horse too." Speedy kissed her and stuck his tongue in her mouth. Her legs gave way under her, so he had no trouble pushing her down on the mat of spicy yellow leaves. Above, the trees roared and swayed, paying absolutely no attention to them. Across the road, the white board fence around the track turned its back on them, and its paint went on peeling with a blind dignity. Beth's mouth sifted kisses upwards like yellow leaves disobeying the law of gravity. The earth bent and flowed under the wind. A humming came from the empty grandstand. A tree root was digging into her back, because Speedy was lying right on top of her, and his knees pried her thighs apart. Beth started biting at him and pushing him away. Yet at the same moment her legs opened, letting him press in against her where there was a terrible twitching sensation, like a dying animal writhing inside her body. It occurred to her that this was an odd position—horses did it standing on all fours, from behind.

"That's the way," Speedy gasped, and he started trying to take off her jeans again. Beth tried to push him off and get up. They struggled savagely, plastered with wet leaves. The earth slowly turned upside down, so that the cottonwood trees pointed downward into the blue canyon of twilight, so that they were wiggling against the yellow-matted ceiling as if pinned there like two insects. Beth suddenly found herself standing upside down, leaning against a cottonwood, watching another Beth tear herself loose from Speedy's grasp and hit him hard across the nose a couple of times. She observed that this other Beth's face was contracted and twitching, her eyes glittering.

They got up slowly, Beth staggering, Speedy holding his bloody nose. His eyes narrowed to black slits. With magnificent deliberation he hit her back three times across the face, with all the strength in those small arms that could hold back the horses of the sun. Beth wept.

"You don't try any of your motherfucking Anglo tricks with a *macho* like me," Speedy said softly. His body vibrated with anger.

"Speedy, don't be mad."

"You know what you are? You're an Anglo ice-ass, like all the other Anglos I ever met." He hit her again, shoved her against a tree. "My mother may be a *malinche* whore, but she's a real woman. I'll bet she was the best piece of ass your Anglo daddy ever had. I should know better than to mess with Anglo ass." He stalked back down the road toward the race barns.

"Speedy, come back."

He turned around and yelled into the wind, "I'll find me a nice chicano ass who'll give a man what he needs without making such a shitty fuss."

Beth jumped on Flash and galloped him back to the ranch, weeping the whole way. Flo was packing to leave. The hoofbeats blew off in the wind. Beth was left standing under the cottonwoods, not able to follow either or both of them. The wind blew straight through her head, and yellow leaves drifted slowly down through the dark clear liquid inside her eyeballs.

The next morning she found Speedy and Walt packing too. Speedy was silent, hunched over, unshaven, his eyes sunken in. He looked at Walt, then back at her with a deathly, unblinking look. She realized that he would not show his feelings in front of Walt, that he would not ask forgiveness because it wouldn't be *macho*, and that he had spent the night surer than ever that she wouldn't come.

When Walt led the first horse into the truck, Beth touched his hand. His hand closed around her arm so tightly that she winced. He closed his eyes and sighed. At the last moment he shoved something into her hand. "Something to remember us by," he said. It was a big glossy black-and-white photograph, corners bent from being in the tack trunk. It showed the Count standing lathered and arrogant in some winner's circle, a blanket of roses over his withers. Speedy was up, dusty and grinning. Walt and Rita, grinning too, held the Count's bridle.

The last horse was tied in the van, the tailgate raised and locked.

"*Adios*," said Speedy. He wouldn't kiss her because Walt was there.

"*Adios*. See you next year. Don't lose my college address."

"Yeah, I'll write. I'll send my address when we're somewhere permanent."

"Come on, Speedy the Mouse, let's go," Walt sang out, climbing into the cab. "Let's hit the road to Mexico." Still unsmiling, Speedy got into the cab too. He looked out at her as the truck drove slowly off down the cottonwood lane, swaying through the ruts with its precious live cargo. Yellow leaves blew past it, tree shadows flowed over its top and down its back. Then it went out of sight around the corner, behind the white board fence of the track.

Beth sat down in the empty tack stall, where the smell of Absorbine and good leather still hung in the air. She sat there on the dirt floor and cried for a long time.

The lobby of the freshman dormitory at Frith was milling with girls and parents. They chattered, they wept, they hugged all around. Parents dispensed last pieces of profound and useless advice. Beth, with her deep tan and sun-bleached curly hair, stood there alone by her trunk, clutching her old black boots in the crook of one arm and carrying a bridle hung over the other. She was wearing a plaid skirt, a knit pullover, loafers, kneesocks, and a college blazer, all bought for her by Flo before she left for Reno. But all those other people knew she didn't belong in clothes like that, because they stared at her. Beth wondered if she was turning back into a horse again. Maybe the sensitive Thoroughbred ears that had been just disappearing were now sprouting back again, swiveling this way and that to listen to everything.

As she unpacked in her room, the first thing she did was take a few of her favorite horse figurines out of her suitcase and stand them on the dresser. They were ones she hadn't broken yet, among them the antique English silver thoroughbred with a docked tail. Over the figurines, on the wall, she carefully scotch-taped the picture of Speedy and the Count. The wall had a flat blue color that made her uncomfortable, as if she couldn't walk through it no matter how hard she tried. But the window looked out into the secret world of a maple tree that was now turning orange and red. The leaves fell slowly onto the grass outside. They were the wrong color—in Montana all the trees turned yellow. The grass was wrong too—it was too green for this time of year.

Another girl came in, lugging two suitcases. She left and dragged in two more suitcases. A porter pushed in a couple of trunks. The girl was tall, with a fineboned, nervous Thoroughbred face and auburn hair like the Count's tail. She had jewel-green eyes with long black eyelashes, and perfume wafted from her as she moved. Beth noted immediately that she had a nice, soft, high bosom, like Elizabeth Taylor, and was elegantly dressed like Flo.

"I presume," said the girl, "that you're my roommate. My name is Kathleen Veille O'Byrne."

"Guess so," said Beth glumly. "I'm Beth Stuart."

Kathleen opened all the luggage at once, pulled everything out in a great heap, then sank down on the bed. "Christ," she said. Her eyes moved around the room and lit on the picture of the Count and Speedy. "Christ, who's that?"

"My boyfriend." Beth blushed a little, pushing sweaters into a drawer.

"Christ, he's handsome. How did you land him?"

Beth smiled sadly. "I helped him muck stalls."

"You engaged?"

"Not officially. He's still an apprentice, but he's going to get a contract with a big stable on the West Coast."

"I'm unofficially engaged too. He's a journalism student at Columbia." Kathleen sighed, her eyes still on the picture. "But, wow, he's not as handsome as that."

Beth felt a prickle of rodeo-queen jealousy. "You should see him race a horse," she said.

Kathleen sat on the bed amid her mound of clothes and told Beth about how her father was an air force lieutenant colonel and how she was therefore an air force brat who had lived in Europe, South America, the Far East, and just about everywhere. She hated college and was only there at Frith because her parents made her go. What she really wanted to do was go live somewhere called the East Village and write revolutionary poetry. That sounded nice. She sat there smoking a cigarette with something of Flo's refinement. Beth listened politely, putting her own things neatly away in her closet and bureau drawers.

Then, when she offered to help Kathleen put away her clothes, Kathleen pleasantly let her do most of the work, while she jabbered about Paris and Lima and Djakarta. "I'm terrible, absolutely *terrible*," said Kathleen. "I can't do anything."

During the first weeks at Frith, Beth moved in a daze, trudging with her books from classroom to classroom, wearing her plaid skirt and blazer. The lectures were about things she didn't consider necessary, like history and culture. She daydreamed through them, thinking of Speedy, her chin in her hand. Her pencil, instead of taking notes, doodled horses along the notebook margins. She thought of Speedy at night too, lying in her narrow little bed in the dorm and thinking until her body hurt.

"Thinking about him?" asked Kathleen.

"Yah," said Beth.

"I know what you mean," said Kathleen.

Beth missed the ranch and her horses so much that it was fortunate Frith had the famous riding academy that her parents had read about. She was able to take riding as a substitute for all her physical education, and spent five classes a week at the ring, as well as spare hours on Saturday afternoons. The smell of good leather and Absorbine nearly made her weep. Speedy had already taught her things like posting and changing leads, so she had no trouble at all with Eastern-style riding. Soon the instructors were putting her on the

best of the walk-trot horses, and she went round and round the big
indoor tanbark ring. A couple of the girls who were real experts and
had competed in the Madison Square Garden show made fun of her,
considering her a Montana hillbilly. But she looked down her long
horse nose at them, knowing that she would catch up soon. Outside the
ring, beside the strange red barns in the cramped little pastures with
their tumbling stone walls, the red and orange leaves fell—all the
wrong color.

Her first-quarter grades were all C or C minus, except for riding,
which was an A. About that time, a postcard from Speedy wandered
into her mailbox. It was postmarked somewhere in California and said
that both he and the Count were holding up pretty well, and that he
missed her. But it had no address on it.

Beth soon found out that Kathleen was every bit as odd as herself, and that the college had done well to make them roommates.
Kathleen wrote long mournful poems about love and revolution that
she read to Beth in the evenings, as they sat on their beds. Beth wore
her blue flannel pajamas and Kathleen wore a filmy lace nightgown
with her long red hair flowing. Sometimes Kathleen wore absolutely
nothing at all and wandered around the room with even less modesty
than Speedy had. In Beth's opinion, her body was very feminine, like
Elizabeth Taylor's must be—it had thighs the color of the mother-of-
pearl that adorned one of Vern's prized antique six-shooters, and round
breasts that looked like they didn't have a single muscle in them. Beth
didn't understand Kathleen's poems at all, but she listened because she
was beginning to regard Kathleen as a kindred case. Kathleen didn't
have horse ears, but she had other problems.

For instance, Beth found out that while Kathleen washed herself, she never washed her underwear. She wore a pair of panties or
pantihose two days, a bra a week, then threw them in the wastebasket
and bought new ones at the shops in town. The maids who cleaned the
rooms must have been pretty surprised at the parade of jettisoned
undies in Kathleen's wastebasket. At first Beth thought this was a
crazy kind of cleanliness. But then she noticed that Kathleen never
changed her bed either, even though the maids brought fresh sheets
once a week. Pretty soon the sheets were black. Speedy wouldn't
have approved. Kathleen also had lovely clothes, but as soon as they
needed washing or dry-cleaning, she gave them away to whatever
girl they fit and bought new ones. Beth was too small to wear Kathleen's
cocktail dresses or pantsuits, and besides, she looked pretty silly in

most of them. But she did acquire a lot of Kathleen's sweaters this way.

"Take this blue one, Beth," said Kathleen. "With your gray eyes, it looks ravishing."

"Gray?" said Beth. She checked in the mirror. "Well, I'll be darned. I never knew they was gray." She washed the sweater carefully and wore it.

So Beth tried to do what Speedy would have done and kept Kathleen clean. Her own half of the room was set as fair as one of Speedy's stalls, and pretty soon she was cleaning Kathleen's half too, before room inspection. Once a week she changed Kathleen's sheets when Kathleen wasn't around. Kathleen always thanked her effusively, the two of them got to be inseparable, walking to classes and meals together, sitting over coffee in the tea rooms in the evening. The other girls started calling them the Bobbsey Twins. Kathleen reviled the other girls behind their backs, saying that they lived in the past, that Frith was one of the few colleges left in the country where there was no revolution or social conscience.

The freshman house mother, realizing that Kathleen was a problem, asked Beth to help her, saying, "Dear, you're a good influence on Kathleen." Later on, Beth found out that the house mother had given the same little talk to Kathleen, saying, "Dear, you're a good influence on Beth."

Kathleen and Beth sat over coffee and laughed over that. "I'll be even more of an influence than she thinks I will," said Kathleen.

Actually, Frith, in its ponderous, myopic way, was advancing slowly toward modern liberalism—while parietal rules didn't yet allow boys to visit girls in their rooms, they did allow the girls to smoke in the dormitories. Kathleen taught Beth to smoke. At first Beth coughed, like she had heaves, but soon she could take a suave drag just the way Speedy did when he was several yards away from the horse barns. She really inhaled too, right to the bottom of her lungs. She reflected that in ten years she'd have a pretty fair case of lung cancer.

One night Kathleen produced some funny-looking long brown cigarettes. "What's that?" asked Beth. "You roll your own?"

"That's grass," said Kathleen. "Ever try it?"

Beth grinned. "Speedy and Walt were always telling me about how they smuggled a ton of that stuff in the horse van every time they came back from the races at Tijuana. They sold it for a mighty nice price in California." She puffed on a joint and found that it didn't affect her much—it just gave her a pleasant sleepy feeling.

They lay awake at night smoking marijuana and talking about their boyfriends. "Those cretins," Kathleen said, referring to the rest of the student body, "haven't discovered pot yet. They still think it's smart to drink."

It soon became plain to Beth that Kathleen knew an awful lot about boys—more than she herself would ever learn in a lifetime, probably. One confession led to another, till finally one night Kathleen told her how, when she was thirteen and her father was stationed in Santiago, Chile, she had been walking home from a girlfriend's house one evening, and a strange man dragged her into an alley and knocked her over the head. When she came to, she was bleeding between the legs. Then, sure enough, she got pregnant. Her parents were worried that everyone would find out about it and that their reputation would be ruined. So they got Kathleen an illegal abortion. The abortionist had goofed the job just a little, and now Kathleen could never have babies.

"So," said Kathleen, gazing dreamily up at the ceiling, "I have built-in contraception, and don't have to worry about the population explosion." Beth frankly didn't think it was any great tragedy not to have babies. They were curled up on Beth's bed, and Beth's head was pillowed on Kathleen's long hair. It was past lights-out, and the room was dark. Beth wondered if Kathleen would weep, and she stood ready to hug her and comfort her. But Kathleen didn't cry.

"Do you sleep with Speedy?" Kathleen asked.

Beth was about to lie and say she had. But then she thought that Kathleen had probably told the truth about that business in Chile, and so she said, "Never did."

"Christ, are you still a virgin? I thought virgins were extinct, like dinosaurs."

"What's a virgin?"

Kathleen explained.

"Then," said Beth, "I guess I'm one."

"I can see that I'll have to educate you," said Kathleen. "Why wouldn't you let him? Are your parents Victorian and repressive, or something?"

Beth knew what those words meant, because she had listened in her psych class with one lone ear cocked. "No," she said. "Well, maybe my mother was. But that isn't it. I just wasn't ready for it, or something." A lump rose in her throat at just the remembrance of some of those goings-on in the horse barns, while the yellow leaves fell outside.

"You know, the other day in history class the professor was talking about Greek mythology, and for once I listened real close. He said there were things like half man, half horse called—what was the word? Sen-tars. That's what I am, only I'm a lady sen-tar. I have to turn all the way into a girl before I can sleep with Speedy."

"That's bullshit," said Kathleen. "The centaurs were always raping young maidens of the human species. You could sleep with Speedy even if you had hoofs. Your problem is, you feel guilty."

"No, honest," insisted Beth. "I don't feel guilty at all. I'm just real sorry that I didn't. But I couldn't. I just about went loco when he tried. I even hit him."

"Slapping boys' faces," said Kathleen, "went out with the waltz."

"Next year, though, I will, when he comes back for the race meet. My ears are gone, maybe. All I have left is a broom tail, like a mustang."

"You've blown your psyche."

Beth giggled. "We all look like horses. You look like a Thoroughbred filly. Me, I'm a Quarter Horse, I'm little and punchy. I wish I had nice titties like yours."

"Let's see yours."

Beth turned on the lamp for a minute, risking demerits, and opened her pajama top.

"Hm," said Kathleen. "Nothing wrong with them. But they look awful hard." She touched one, and right away they both started hurting.

"Don't," said Beth. "He did that, and it just about drove me crazy." Kathleen giggled, and they started tussling on the bed, Kathleen trying to touch them, Beth fending her off and trying to touch Kathleen's. The bed creaked dangerously. In the room next door, a girl pounded the wall to make them shut up. They ended up all tangled together, with Kathleen's hair wound around them and Beth's face against the front of Kathleen's filmy nightgown.

"Mmm," said Beth.

"Like that?" Kathleen ran her fingers through Beth's curls. "What else did he do to you? Tell me about it."

Smiling beatifically, her eyes closed, Beth told her in a low voice while Kathleen stroked her head. Beth realized that it hurt less to remember it than to do it.

About once a month, as winter came on, a postcard or a short letter came from Speedy, postmarked from various places in Cali-

fornia. He said the Count had a bowed tendon and knee trouble that
weren't responding to treatment. He said Walt was feeding him vita-
mins and beating him less, but that didn't help much either—his back
hurt all the time now. But he also said that the big stable was still
waiting to contract him.

Whenever Beth got a postcard, she spent several days in a frenzy
of nostalgia. She could actually feel him thinking about her, and the
tail almost disappeared just from thinking. She quit going to the college dining room for meals and lived on hamburgers and boxes of milk
in her room, trying to study a little. On the rare occasions when she
went to the dining room, she and Kathleen walked over both in the
same coat, Beth in front holding the lapels together, the two walking
lockstep to keep from tripping. Beth went without breakfast, because
she and Kathleen usually talked so late that they both needed to sleep
in. Once in a while she missed a morning class, and once in a while she
cut a class too. She wanted to write to Speedy, but there was no address to write to.

Along in November she came down with mononucleosis and spent
a couple of weeks in the college infirmary. Often she was dizzy, and
once in a while she blacked out completely and walked around like an
automaton, coming back to herself hours later. Sometimes she felt a
splitting pain in her head, exactly as if somebody had pounded a
horseshoe nail right into her brain. It was like a little opening in her
skull that let in a sharp, blinding ray of light. Sometimes she had the
sensation that she was walking right out of her body.

She remembered how Speedy stood in the creek, squeezing the
sponge over his shoulders. Blinding streams of water ran along his
body, like white-hot horseshoes melted into light and water. The creek
was the hole in her head turned to a flow of light. She blinked, covered
her eyes.

Kathleen continued educating her. She took Beth on several blind
dates, locating everything from clean-cut Ivy League fraternity men
to hairy NYU boys for her. Beth found them silly and was too bored
to talk to them. None of them ever asked her out again. Kathleen also
succeeded in making Beth wear light makeup, a little pale lipstick, and
even some of her Vent Vert perfume. She took Beth on a few shopping
expeditions in New York City on Saturdays. They went to a big
department store called Bergdorf Goodman (Beth vaguely remembered
seeing this name on the labels of some of her mother's clothes). There
Kathleen bought her some dresses, a little suit, and a coat that she said

would play up Beth's little-boy look. Gazing at herself in the multiple mirrors, Beth agreed that she didn't look at all bad. She had the idea that Kathleen knew what she was talking about. She even let Kathleen draw a little eyeliner onto her eyelids. Not much, just a little.

Finally Kathleen, finding out how ignorant Beth was about basic technicalities, gave her some books. They were pretty startling, with photographs and diagrams and all. Beth devoured the books in a state of shock. She read them long after lights-out, with her desk lamp under the covers, even after Kathleen had fallen asleep. She shook so much that she could hardly turn the pages. For the first time she connected her own nameless, terrible emotions with the dignified way the stallions reared onto the mares. But what they had in common, she wasn't sure, because the horses were so calm about it.

So she found out about something called Sex, which was not exactly the same thing as when you filled in the blank on a horse's registration papers that asked for the animal's sex. Sex was, she guessed, just about the most important thing in life, or so the books said. If you couldn't fool around with Sex in a calm, cool, and collected way, she told herself, then you wouldn't amount to a row of beans, and there was no hope for you. Everything you did was Sex, said the books, even the littlest old things like sharpening pencils. Even your ears and your hair and your toenails were reeking with Sex. Men and women had Sex mainly to find if they *could* have it or not, and spent a lot of time worrying about it before and after. Those were her conclusions.

Beth studied those books the way she hadn't studied her history or philosophy books. Her report card might have read: Horsemanship, A; Sex, A; and F in everything else. After she read the books, she and Kathleen had long after-hours discussions.

"This stuff is fantastic," said Beth, "but there's something missing. How do you have Sex unless you know who you are? I mean, how do you do something with yourself unless you know what it is that you're doing something with?"

"That's existentialism," said Kathleen. "That's idiotic."

"But Sex isn't my problem," said Beth. "I got enough of it for two people."

"You're blind," said Kathleen. "You can't face the truth about yourself. You're just afraid, that's all. Your puritanical parents warped you. You really hated your mother and wanted to sleep with your father."

"No siree," said Beth. "I hated Flo, all right. But I wanted Daddy to sleep with Rita."

"Evasions, cover-ups, lies," said Kathleen.

"And now I have a new mother that I really love a lot."

"I'm just a substitute."

Beth shook her head. "Even the horses don't think about sex all the time. Most of the time they just pull grass."

"Okay, amateur philosopher, what's important then?"

"Looking a stone in the eye. Or turning into something. A drop of water, or a horse. Except that when you turn into something, you can't ever come back again."

"You," said Kathleen, combing her hair, "are a crummy mystic."

Beth shrugged. "Do you mean God?" She shrugged again. "God is a horse."

By Christmastime she was trying a little jumping. She had decided that she didn't want to have anything to do with five-gaited horses, with their mutilated tails filled out by switches and their air of phony formality. She gravitated instead, toward the handful of monster Irish Thoroughbreds that the college kept for jumping. She sailed them over the poles and daydreamed about riding in steeplechases. In her head she could feel herself part of the Grand National, with horses floating over the furze at Beecher's Brook, horses falling, stirrups and hoofs flashing, and jockeys rolling on the trampled turf. The head riding instructor had already put her on the list of girls to be in the college's little horse show in May. But her professors were concerned by her C minuses and D's, and they all talked to her about it for a long time. Beth looked them right in the eye, as if they were stones.

When Beth took the train home for the holidays, she wondered if by some miracle Speedy would come up from California to visit her. But he didn't. The house looked different without what Vern had always sarcastically called Flo's "an-tee-cues." He had filled in with rugged handmade pine furniture and bear rugs, plus deer's antlers and his paintings hung all over the walls. Vern told her that Flo had gotten her divorce case into court in Reno, and that he hadn't bothered to contest it, so he was a free man.

Beth spent Christmas moping around the ranch. She had no enthusiasm for the tree that Vern and Bertha put up, nor for the presents under it. She looked after her ex-4H horses and rode Flash. The stallion had gotten soft, with a hay belly that Vern said was beyond belief. He had winter hair two inches long and looked like an over-sized Shetland pony, especially when Beth saddled him up with the little racing pad. But Beth didn't care, and every morning she rode him over to the empty fairgrounds anyway.

The track was shrouded with snow, unmarred by a single hoof-print. Big drifts covered the grandstand seats. Beyond the sagging board fence, the naked cottonwoods clawed at the gray sky. She gal-loped Flash slowly around the track, and his breath rushed white out of his furry nostrils. In the tack stall where Speedy had slept there was a big drift of snow which had blown in through the open door. Out-side the barn, she kicked in the snow and turned up the ashes from their morning fires. Along the creek, a few holes in the fern-crystalled ice showed her the black, scary water slipping along.

Then she sat down in the tack stall, leaning her head back against the time-darkened boards and closing her eyes. She kept thinking about the arguments she'd had with Vern in the past few days. It was finally occurring to Vern that Beth might marry the little greaser jockey after all. Likewise, it was finally occurring to Beth that the reason Vern had never worried about it before was that he simply didn't think of her as a girl.

"But, Bethy, he wants to marry you for your money. A hide-poor greaser like that. His kind work for seventy-five cents a day in the fields down there in California. He just wants to get his hands on this good ranch and these solid-gold horses."

"He isn't that poor. And he doesn't give a damn about Quarter Horses."

"Don't cuss, girl. And you won't marry any spic jockeys as long as I'm around. From now on, you account to me for every penny you spend, here and at school. I don't want you sending no money to him."

The sunlight fell through the tack-stall doorway onto the snow-drift and nearly blinded her. Taking off one mitten, she slid her hand inside the front of her jacket and sweater and stroked her own breasts. They hurt, but less than before. A pinpoint of light struck into the top of her skull. "Speedy," she said out loud, "this time I'll make it up to you. Come on now." When he started kissing her again, she didn't stop him. She let him take off her clothes, and it was just like the books said, only better. She felt herself go out into everything like a flash of light: into Speedy's eyes and hair, into the snow and the light on the snow, into the weathered wood of the board wall and the sunlight on the wall, into the light within the light. He still wanted her to go off with him, and she said that she would. She said, moreover, that she would marry him.

Her hand slid out of her sweater, limp now. After a while, she opened her eyes and sat forward. With her index finger, she printed in the snow, "Speedy Gonzalez is the fastest mouse in Mexico."

Back at school, she didn't hear from Speedy all during January. Then, in February, she got a letter from San Diego. In his grade-school scrawl, Speedy wrote that things weren't going very well. Walt's deal to buy the little ranch had fallen through. Walt had gotten panicky with all those Quarter Horse fillies eating up all his oats and hay and not bringing him any groceries. He finally ended up by selling all of them. He was stuck, however, with the broken-down King Ranch stallion. The tone of Speedy's letter was brisk and cold. He also mentioned that he himself wasn't too good. He had fainted and fallen off during a race again. This time, he said, he was going to stop putting it off and see a doctor. "It ain't sifilis," he added, as if reading her mind. Beth was mournfully proud of herself for having learned what syphilis was. Once again, he had not included an address at which she could write him. But she figured that soon he'd write again and let her know what the doctor said. He probably had mononucleosis, she thought. His letter didn't say anywhere that he was thinking of her, but he must have been.

In March, he didn't write. He didn't write in April, as the Connecticut countryside got much too green again, and all kinds of strange trees came crazily into bloom. Soon she was crying about it on Kathleen's shoulder. He had probably forgotten her and married some chicano rodeo queen who knew how to have sex. But she didn't rip the photograph down off the wall.

Then one day in late April, as she was practicing for the horse show with a black hunter over a course of jumps in the indoor ring, she was surprised to see Flo sitting in the empty gallery with the head riding instructor. Flo had on a spring tweed suit, a white suede hat, kid gloves, and a little pink chiffon scarf at her throat, and she sat watching Beth jump with a small smile on her face.

At first Beth went rigid with anger in the saddle. Flo had a haystack full of nerve to show up now. She ignored Flo's little wave and went on jumping with insolent skill, right past Flo's nose. But then it occurred to her that warm and soft as Rita had been, she had ripped

Speedy out of her life the way a race trainer would rip off the little aluminum shoes after one race. Yet Flo had come back looking for her child.

So, when Beth dismounted and handed the horse to a stable boy, she went slowly to the gallery, very straight and defiant in her tweed coat, jodhpurs, brown boots, and cork hat. Flo stood up, still smiling that enigmatic smile, and bent to kiss her cheek, but Beth stood back and offered her hand, saying, "Hi, Flo."

"I've just found," said Flo, "that the only place on campus you can be located is here."

"She's done very well," said the head instructor. "Too bad we don't have a summa cum laude in horsemanship and stable management."

As they walked away from the arena to the black limousine waiting, Flo said, "I've been wanting to see how you were getting along. Will you have dinner with me, off campus somewhere?"

As Beth dressed for dinner, she had half a notion to embarrass Flo by wearing her most bagged-out skirt and most scuffed loafers. But then she decided to show Flo how feminine she had gotten without any maternal aid, so she put on the pale-blue wool suit that Kathleen had insisted she buy for spring. Kathleen helped her line her eyes just a little and sprayed a cloud of Vent Vert on her. When she went to meet Flo in the dormitory parlor, she saw Flo's eyes take in the suit's good cloth and cut with relief.

"You look lovely, my dear," Flo said, patting Beth's hand with her kid glove, as the limousine whirled them through the Connecticut countryside, past all those little pastures and stone walls that Beth always found so annoying. All those dogwood trees coming into bloom seemed so vulgarly white when you thought of the quiet way cottonwood trees came into green.

"So you came because you wanted to see if Frith made me feminine?" Beth asked. "Does Vern know you're here? Did you ask his permission?"

"One answer at a time. No, Vern doesn't know, and I didn't ask him."

The limousine stopped at a country restaurant that Flo said had exquisite French food. Inside, they sat at a window table, with headwaiter and wine waiter running back and forth, and a bowl of fresh anemones between them. Beth looked at the twenty-dollar entrees on the menu and thought how somewhere in California Speedy was waiting for Walt to bring him hamburgers.

"I moved back here last winter," Flo said, "after the divorce came through. But I couldn't make myself come see you right away. That's the way we all are, isn't it? I should have left Vern years ago, or he should have left me. You should have run away from home to your horses, or made up your mind to stay."

"Where are you living?"

"We're fixing up a lovely house on East Eighty-fifth Street. I'm going to get married again. A suitable man, this time. I'd like you to meet David."

"You sure didn't waste any time, did you?" Beth poked at the varied strange hors d'oeuvres Flo had ordered her, finally decided she could eat the French potato salad. She thought how Speedy had yearned for tortillas and roasted chilis.

"On the contrary. I already wasted too much time," said Flo bitterly. "And Vern is sorry about our mistake too. Maybe he'll marry his kind of woman this time. A vulgar, earthy type, like that Rita, for instance."

Beth's mouth opened a little. "You knew about Rita? Vern told you?"

Flo raised her eyebrows ever so slightly. "I knew about Rita without being told a word."

Beth bent her head over her plate. "You'll be happy to hear that Rita ran off somewhere, and she never did come back. It nearly killed poor Speedy."

When the wine waiter filled their glasses, Beth was about to protest that college rules didn't permit drinking, but then she saw that the label said Paul Masson, California, and she tasted the wine. It had a taste of Rita's picking grapes and Speedy's childhood on the Santa Cruz exercising Thoroughbreds over the dunes and along the shore, and the bulldozers' pushing the olive trees into piles. She shrank down in her blue suit, and the tears covered her eyes like racing goggles.

Flo gave her a clean handkerchief. "Don't let the waiters see you cry. What about Speedy? Do you hear from him these days?"

"Not lately."

"I thought so."

"I think something happened to him. He's sick or something. I know he doesn't forget."

"Was he serious about you?"

"He wanted to get married. But I couldn't make up my mind. I promised I'd give my answer this fall, when they come back to Cottonwood for the fair. I've got four months to make up my mind."

"You're smarter than I thought you were," said Flo, leaning back in her chair.

The waiters changed their plates, and the next thing Beth saw, as the tears drifted away like hoof-stirred dust, was a huge crab lying before her, sea moss still sticking in its leg joints. Its ugly dead face and steamed eyes looked straight at her.

"Christ, what's that?" she whispered.

"A crab. Try it with the sauce. I'll show you."

"But it's dead."

"Of course it's dead. The potatoes you just ate were dead too."

Beth watched her mother break it up expertly and dip it in the sauce. Finally she broke off one leg and nibbled the meat. It was sweet and delicate. So she broke up the rest of the monster with grim relish. "So you came to see me," she said between two mouthfuls, "because your conscience bothered you."

"Darling Beth, my conscience is finally at rest. David and I plan a quiet little wedding at the end of May, and we'd like you to be there. I want to show you my world. You haven't had a chance to make up your mind about it yet. Don't forget that your father's family were once silk purses, before they went West and turned back into sow's ears. You don't have to stay in my world, but it might interest you." She paused, then added, "It might even help you make up your mind about Speedy Gonzalez. If you want to marry him, marry him. Certainly he can't offer you any future. But know what you're doing and where you belong."

Beth was aware, as she finished her crab, of the shrewdness of this last remark. She smiled as she rubbed the butter off her mouth with the snowy linen napkin (Speedy would have used his sleeve), and said, "You might as well know that I didn't ever sleep with Speedy. But I intend to, when I see him again this fall."

Flo raised her eyebrows again. "Well, I'm not going to tell you what to do. I know there's no controlling you."

"All right," said Beth, "I'll come to your wedding, and throw rice at you and your old David."

When she told Vern about it, the next time she called home, Vern was skeptical and disturbed. "You be real careful with that woman," he said. "If she'd been Robert E. Lee, the South would of won the war."

"Well, I want to see her."

"Bethy, you're beginning to crowd me real hard. You even want money from me to buy that racehorse of Speedy's. Well, I don't have money to buy any bony bangtails for any greaser jockeys. My health won't stand the strain, Bethy."

"I'll sell a couple of my own horses, then."

"Not while I'm around, you won't."

So Flo started sending the black limousine for her on occasional weeknights and on every weekend. Flo met Kathleen too, and was charmed by her (that was because Kathleen acted like a sophisticated child of military brass in front of Flo). Beth wandered warily through that townhouse on East Eighty-fifth Street, sniffing the air like a mustang turned loose in the Spanish Academy's baroque riding ring. She watched new brocade drapes go up, the Chippendale highboys she remembered being carried into place, and the old racing prints going up on the walls.

Beth was ready to hate David, but instead she found it necessary to feel warm and pitying about him. David was a useless but pleasant man in his forties, tall, slender, and without a single muscle. He had earnest, empty blue eyes too close together in a long, pale, aristocratic face straight out of one of Flo's Early American portraits. His gestures were languid, with a gentle pomposity that mocked themselves. He was an automobile heir who never bothered with business (his older brother had all the brute brains needed for that). David loved Italian opera, dabbled in theater producing. Kathleen said he was one of those rich liberals who loved humanity but restricted their friendships to six or seven people.

Beth tried hard to shock David, telling him about Speedy's world and using some of Speedy's favorite English obscenities in front of him. But David lived beyond shock. He'd roll up his eyes at the brocade drapes and laugh, and say, "Beth you're an original. And I'm so bored with debutantes." Then he'd mimic her, till Beth got hysterical with laughter.

At little dinners and cocktail parties, Flo showed her off—at first cautiously, finally determinedly. Beth strode the streets of New York between Flo and David, holding their arms tightly. She couldn't stay away from them. She learned most of the right things to say and do, and realized that the few little cowgirl crudities that still escaped her only made her more interesting. Eligible young men asked her out to theater and dinner, and she pleased Flo by accepting them. She found that the boys thought her daring and enviable, but when they tried to kiss her goodnight, she held them off with a sparkle of malice in her eye. Her femininity was her revenge on them all.

And when she got back to the Frith dormitory, she'd tell Kathleen everything, and the two of them would yelp with laughter, till the girls next door pounded the wall. Then they'd lie around naked and smoke a little marijuana and Kathleen would jerk her head rhythmically as the stereo played what Kathleen called funky rock. Sometimes Beth found herself suddenly sobbing stupidly. The depressions, blackouts, and body-leavings came oftener. She studied fitfully and was just barely passing her courses. Speedy still hadn't written, but she was sure that when August came he would turn up in Cottonwood right on schedule.

"Beth, sweetie, you're so troubled," said David. "Would you like me to arrange an appointment with a psychiatrist friend of mine?"

"There's nothing the matter with me," said Beth. "I'm just tired and living on hamburgers. It's all too much for one body. I'll rest up back on the ranch."

"No, you won't. Flo tells me you work like a man out there. Flo and I are going to spend a month in Europe after the wedding. Why don't you come? Europe is something else you should know, even if just once."

When she called Vern and told him she was going to Europe instead of coming right home when school let out, Vern was angry. "I need you out here," he said. "Summer work's coming on, I'm short of help, my kidney's been bothering me."

Beth found herself getting just as angry. "Well, I'm going. It's only for a month. I'll be back in time to help with haying."

"That woman is poisoning you against me," Vern raged.

"She never even talks about you."

"Beth, I always trusted you more than I did myself. I just can't believe you'd do something like this to me."

"I'm not doing anything to you. This is for me."

"Don't you think you're overdoing this femininity business a bit? I liked you just fine the way you were."

"I have to go, and I'm going, and that's it," Beth shouted into the telephone, shaking uncontrollably, her eyes turned to cottonwoods shedding their leaves.

Afterwards she looked at herself in Flo's antique bedroom mirror with the eagle on it. She patted her eyes dry with a clean lace handkerchief, turned sideways, and pushed out her chest. She never would measure up to Elizabeth Taylor, but she was getting closer all the time. It occurred to her that she was looking like a little doll. Flo had just taken her to Mr. Nathan, a famous hairdresser, and her blonde curls fluffed out brightly against the chandelier behind her, gentling the saddle-hard line of her cheekbones and jaw. Delicate touches of pancake, lipstick, mascara, and eyeliner floated her face halfway from horse to cameo lady. She could hear Flo's and Kathleen's voices echoing, "We have to play up what you've got. Thank heaven for your small bones and good legs." They had chosen this blue silk shirtwaist minidress that was richly ruffled down the bosom and the little-girl blue shoes with grosgrain bows. David had picked her the narrow gold bracelets and the tiny earrings at a jewelry store called Tiffany's.

She smiled at herself in the mirror. Picking up one of Flo's perfume atomizers, she sprayed a little on herself. Not too much, just enough. Speedy would approve. She ignored, for a moment, the ghostly horse ears that still showed somewhere in the back of the mirror, pricked, listening, listening.

At the wedding, she wept and hugged Flo and David. She threw rice and got a little drunk on champagne. With Kathleen's help, she found the perfect wedding gift: a real antique Colonial weathervane of a galloping Thoroughbred. When Flo unwrapped it, she smiled a little sadly, her head cocked to one side. But she put it up over the fireplace in the library of the townhouse. In the horse show, as David and Flo watched from the crowded gallery, Beth jumped the black Irish horse like a fury and placed third against two girls who had competed in Madison Square.

But Flo remained remote. Despite all her smiling attentions and painstaking strategies, she was as far away as a mirage of cottonwood on a hot summer afternoon, on a hill too far to ride to. Flo knew how to squeeze Beth's hand without surrendering a single spark of that tiny fire she kept shut inside, like a diamond ring in a little velvet box. Speedy would have said that Flo didn't have any *carnalismo*.

And when the three of them sailed from New York, and spent long days in deck chairs and long evenings in the salons, Beth began to realize that this newly foaled marriage would never stand up and suck. Flo and David had separate staterooms. They smiled at one another, had exquisite conversations, and were always respectful to each other. Flo took good care of David—she was always making sure that his plaid deck-chair blanket protected him from Atlantic breezes, or that the hollandaise sauce didn't disagree with his stomach. She would make sure David would never feel any pain. David was another beautiful ornament that Flo had acquired for her house, a rare antique, like that $30,000 Massachusetts chest she had picked up at Parke-Bernet's just before the wedding.

Beth stood moping by the ship's railing, looking down at the wake rolling away from the bow, boiling cold and white. It was a long way down to the water. She thought for a while about jumping off. Instead she drew out of her pocket the last of her figurines, the little English silver Thoroughbred. She held it tenderly for a moment—the metal was warm as flesh. Then she let it go. It fell, winking in the sun, straight down into that roaring wave.

David came up and leaned beside her. He was wearing a tennis sweater, and his thinning black hair tossed in the wind. She looked up at his face, gently lined by forty-five years of profound and futile thoughts. She knew that David had seen her drop the figurine, but he didn't say anything, just studied her sorrowfully.

"I hate the sea," said Beth. "It's full of creepy crawly things. Crabs and octopuses and monsters."

"You're not used to the sea yet. You're a land-bound westerner."

"Poor David."

"Why poor David? I'm a very happy man."

"If Speedy's in trouble and needs money right away to buy the Count, would you lend him a few thousand? I'll sell my horses and pay you back."

"Of course, Beth sweetie. What's a few thousand?"

She was weeping against his tennis sweater—monstrous, strangling sobs that wrenched at every joint—and David was stroking her hair helplessly. "Where am I going to look for him? Where am I going to look?" she said.

Afterward, when David asked her about it, she didn't remember what she'd said.

In Europe, getting suntanned, wearing her drip-dry dress and leather sandals and carrying her shoulder-strapped handbag, she stared at the Eiffel Tower, the brick towers of Bologna, the tower of Pisa, the Gothic spires of Chartres, the Moorish bell tower of Sevilla cathedral. They fell dizzily against the blue sky like cottonwood trees in disguise. Speedy Gonzalez was hugging and kissing his chicano wife or having sex with her. Beth had folded the photo and carried it in her purse now—it was cracked as well as dog-eared. She carried it through the Tower of London and up the winding tower stairs of Notre Dame cathedral.

There were moments, along some noisy city street in Italy, or in a dusty Spanish village as the tourist bus roared through, that she saw a certain dark, skinny boy with curly black hair. But when she got close up, she was never sure. European men were very fresh and were always saying little things to her on the street that she didn't understand, but whose intent she divined by the beady look in their eyes. They tried to crowd up behind her in streetcars. She gleefully defended herself with a hatpin that Flo had given her, first letting them get up close and then jabbing them.

One afternoon, in Toledo, Spain, when David and Flo were taking a siesta, Beth went out alone and wandered around in the hot, narrow little streets. She gazed up at the cathedral's Gothic tower that fell slowly, like a ton of yellow leaves shoved over a cliff. Speedy came up to her. She stared and stared at him. He stared back, smiling and talking Spanish in a low voice. He had beautiful eyes, black and long-lashed, but he was dressed better than Speedy, in a dapper suit and pointy little shoes, instead of an old red sweatshirt that smelled of horse liniment.

When he took her arm, she went off with him, just like that. The sun was shining brightly through that hole in her skull. She saw herself from everywhere, around corners, down long, narrow, hot streets, walking off with him. The narrow crooked streets were filling with people again after siesta, the shops opening. As they walked in the crowd, he stroked her bare tanned arm, whispered in her ear, using the word *bonita*, which Speedy always used to the horses when they were good. He took her away to the edge of the city, where the old wall was tumbling down into the river gorge. There, with the distant sound of the creek, hidden away behind a rose trellis in the evening shadows, he started kissing her and petting her. She returned the kisses with what the books would have called total abandon, putting her tongue in his mouth and pressing against him. He got wildly excited and unbuttoned the front of her little sleeveless drip-dry dress, and she cried out softly with shut eyes, like she was supposed to do, her body driving those breasts through his hands like horseshoe nails. He started unbuttoning the front of his pants, and it looked like he was all set to do it right there, standing up like a horse.

So she fumbled in her purse for Flo's hatpin and really gave it to him, right in the thigh. He cried out with pain, then got mad and stomped off. As night fell, she sat there on the wall and had a crying fit. After a while she got up and walked away. When she looked back, she could see herself still sitting on the wall crying. A long broomtail trailed from under her dress. It was auburn-red and smoothly combed, like the Count's tail.

Back in Cottonwood, she absentmindedly helped Vern with the haying. Soon it was early August, and only a couple of weeks remained before Speedy and Walt would be coming. She and Vern both worked hard and hardly spoke to each other, partly because Vern was still angry she'd gone to Europe. The town was going into the final frenzies of preparation for the centennial pageant.

One afternoon Tom Chance drove over to see her.

"Say, Beth," Tom said, "we're needing a couple of people who know how to ride jockey-style. We're going to have the match race in the pageant—you know, when old Brodie's Reveille beat Tammany."

"Yeah," said Beth, "I know. Why don't you get a couple of real jockeys when the fair starts? Speedy Gonzalez will be back. He'd do it for sure."

"I don't want to get involved with no real jockeys," said Tom. "They want money, and we are just about out of money. I've got one little whang-leather kid from up the valley that's done a little race-riding. Would you be the other one?"

"Sure," said Beth, her mind suddenly busy with this prospect. Tammany had been a sorrel horse, like the California Count.

"That's fine," said Tom, looking pleased. "Now, the next problem is the horses. We'd like to get horses that look pretty much like Reveille and Tammany did. But we can't just up and borrow somebody's precious Thoroughbred for the scene. He might break a leg or something. So I located this sorrel horse over in Ellis, a Thoroughbred, that used to race. They're using him as a cow horse now. Damned poor cow horse too, they tell me. This little whang-leather kid says he'll ride him, so that takes care of Tammany. Now, if you'd ride your own little Quarter Horse in the race, that would be just fine, because Brodie's Reveille was a bay, and he was kind of on the little side."

Beth was disappointed that she couldn't ride Tammany, but she liked the idea of riding in a race, even if it wasn't a real race. So she said she'd ride Flash.

Vern cheered up a little when he saw Beth get involved with the centennial pageant. He made a few remarks about how it was high time that Beth got interested in local affairs. Beth participated in the dress rehearsal of the pageant with a tight feeling of suspense under her breastbone, knowing that any day now, any hour, Walt's horse van would be jouncing into the fairgrounds. But when Friday came, the first day of the fair and centennial, and Walt's van still hadn't shown up, she started getting worried. Maybe Walt and Speedy had had a breakdown on the road, or even an accident. Her heart clenched like a fist as she thought of the Count flailing in the burning truck, his tail blazing like dry pine needles, his hide blackening and splitting open, and of Speedy pinned in the wreckage with blood all down the front of him.

On Friday night, she put her racing tack on Flash, dressed in the musty, old-style racing silks that the centennial costume committee had borrowed from somewhere, and rode toward the fairgrounds blazing with floodlights. Cars streamed into the parking lots and the grandstand was filling with people. Word had circulated throughout the state that Cottonwood was doing things with its usual style, and Montanans were driving in from all over to see the first of the three nightly performances of the pageant. Flash seemed to know that he was going to race again, even if not for real, because he jigged and sweated, and his ears played back and forth nervously. Beth's head ached, and she took two aspirin.

Awaiting her scene outside the arena, Beth glared at the little whang-leather kid from up the valley, who sat his skinny sorrel horse with grim expertise. The horse looked nothing like Tammany or California Count—in fact, he looked soft and his legs were muddy. The kid, in spite of his honorably stained old silks, didn't look anything like Speedy Gonzalez. He had a pug nose, freckles, and hard little Anglo eyes. But in spite of this, Beth was tempted to lose the race that she was supposed to win, tempted to let the ghost boy and his ghost horse cross the line ahead of her. Her headache was worse, and the night seemed to shine in through that hole in the top of her head, like a dark and terrible light.

Amid a swirl of touts' cries and bettors' shouts, Beth found herself parading to the post. The announcer played the recording of "Boots and Saddles." The grandstand murmured, and the dust blew away from the two horses' dancing hoofs into the night. The floodlights blinded Beth. She felt ill, out of focus, reeking with some smell that was not her own. She wondered if she would faint and fall off, like Speedy did. There, looming before her, was the old-time starting tape that somebody had resurrected from a storage shed on the fairgrounds and put in working order again. The two sweating horses swung this way and that before the tape—as far as they were concerned, this was a real race.

The tape snapped up and Beth smacked her bat onto Flash's rump. The two horses jumped into a gallop and swept past the grandstand, which wasn't cheering because it wasn't a real race. The rush of cool air and the slash of the horse's mane against her face revived Beth, and a black clarity of thought poured into her brain. She had no business fooling around with history and thinking of losing. Moreover, Speedy wouldn't approve if she threw a race, even if it wasn't a real race. All the reverence for duty inculcated in her by both Vern and Speedy now took hold. She pounded Flash's butt with her bat, and the little stallion, all laziness forgotten, flattened his ears back and tore up the track. Behind her, the little whang-leather kid was whipping his own horse too. But the sorrel, who had been wading around in the cow manure over there in Ellis and not galloping much, couldn't keep up. As they pounded along the floodlit backstretch and into the far turn, Flash was pulling ahead. At the wire it was Reveille by six lengths instead of the historic nose.

As Beth brought the blowing stallion back to the winner's circle, and gentlemen in top hats and ladies in bustles swirled around her, she had a strange, exultant feeling that she was still moving at full speed. She and Flash were galloping off the edge of a cliff and falling, falling without end, the way the cottonwoods did when you looked at them against a sky full of moving clouds.

Beth had walked around among the race barns for an hour now, and she still didn't see Walt's big green van parked anywhere. Maybe Walt had a new truck that she didn't recognize. She paused for several moments before the stalls that Walt's horses had used last year. Strange horses thrust their heads out at her or stood haughtily inside, eyes gleaming in the gloom. Sour mares who laid their ears back.

Scarred, sleepy old geldings. A burro that must belong to the rodeo
clown. A flashy pinto that must be a trick roper's. The tack stall of
last year was empty.

Just then she ran into Tom Chance. "Hey, Tom. Is Walt Fromann here yet?"

"Walt who?" Tom lit a cigarette, looking worried about something else.

"Walt Fromann. You know. He owns California Count."

"Oh, him, nope. Haven't seem him." Tom squinted around. "A
few other people aren't showing up this year. Some stalls empty."

"What for?"

"I don't know. Lot of gyps can't make ends meet anymore. Feed,
transportation, all kind a costs going up."

Beth walked on, peering hopelessly into stalls where she'd already
looked once or twice.

Then she rounded the corner of a shed row that faced off into the
cool cottonwood shade, near the creek, and she saw the big sorrel horse
that had galloped past her on the strip earlier. He was rearing up on
his hind legs and pawing at an exercise boy, ears flat back against his
neck, mouth opened to show his big yellow teeth. A little bearded
man with a black waistcoat and watch chain was shouting and waving
a walking stick. The horse careened this way and that, right over a
fire, one hind foot upsetting a coffee pot and a kettle of bandages
with a hiss and cloud of steam. It was the Count all right, the California Count, great-grandson of Man O'War, with all his fiery
Hastings blood ablaze.

Beth stared. The Count's coat was dull and dusty, his flanks
pinched in, his ribs showing like slats. He was just a skeleton padded
out with tendons and a few strings of muscle. He had scabs and
bruises all over his head. Both his knees were swollen up as big as
softballs. Worst of all, he must have reared over backwards in the
starting gate recently, because the crest of his neck was chopped
through. The heavy scab had broken open, and pus was streaming
down the Count's neck. The stallion sliced again at the old exercise
boy, who yelled and ducked, and let go the lead shank. That force that
Speedy had controlled so well was now loose in the world, like a San
Francisco earthquake, like a new volcano heaving up out of the Pacific.

The stallion veered away from his tormentors and came trotting
clumsily down the shed row toward Beth. His head was cocked to one

side so he wouldn't trip on his dragging lead shank. Beth blocked his way and said, "Ho, Count. Ho."

The horse jolted to a stop. His ears strained forward. Eyes shining questioningly, he stretched his nose toward her and his nostrils opened wide with a rattling snort as he considered her smell and her voice. Then his bony frame shuddered and his whole muzzle quivered as he uttered a long, low "huh-huh-huh-huh-huh." The nicker came right up from his entrails, in acknowledgement of her association with someone kind from not long ago.

Beth took the lead shank, trembling with rage. "You remember I was with Speedy, huh?" she said to the horse. She ran her hand down the dusty, uncurried neck to that terrible oozing gap in the mane. Now she noticed that the near front ankle was freshly pockmarked by the firing needle. They had probably been packing the leg in ice before races, or shooting it with novocaine. The stallion renewed his acquaintance by pinching her arm painfully with his teeth and snorting slobber all over her blue shirt. Beth turned, leading the Count, to confront the little bearded man, who had just hobbled up. The man's red face told her that he was in the habit of drinking the liniment that he should have been using on his horses.

"Mister," she snapped, "how you come by this horse?"

"How d'ya do. Me name is J. P. Moriarty, Esquire, lately of Cork, Ireland, home of the world's finest Thoroughbreds," said the little man, bowing grandly. "And may I inquire to whom I have the honor and pleasure of speaking?" As he came near, the Count whipped back his ears and started looking mean as a rattlesnake again.

"I'm Beth Stuart. I'm a friend of Speedy Gonzalez and Walt Fromann, and I want to know how you got ahold of this horse."

"Would ye be caring to sit ye down?" said the Irishman, indicating a bale of hay as if it was one of Flo's brocade-upholstered antique sofas. "I'd offer ye a cup a coffee, but the horse has doused the fire with our coffee, bless his black heart. And, darlin', ye hold him for a little while and let us catch our breath. Would you be believing, darlin', that a horse a mine once placed third in the Irish Derby?"

"To look at this horse," said Beth, not sitting down, "I'd of thought you wouldn't even dare enter the Irish Derby." His brogue struck her as phoney. He wasn't from Cork at all—he was probably from Davenport, Iowa.

"Walt Fromann put this devil in a claiming race, he did, after

the horse went bad in the legs," said the little man. "I was thinking
I could keep him running a little, and I claimed him. But he's cost me
more than he's won me, may he roast in hell. If it is that horses go to
hell."

"Poor Speedy." The words escaped Beth without her thinking
them.

"Ah, yes, the boy now. A good jockey, that one. He was very
attached to the horse. Walt had to beat him before I could take the
horse away."

"Why aren't they coming this year?"

"Well, darlin', Walt was getting discouraged with horse racing.
Too expensive, he says. He got rid of his whole string and bought a
bar near the track at Santa Anita. Being a friend of Walt's, I stop by
when I can, and we drink a little good whiskey together and talk
about the few good horses we had."

"What stable is Speedy riding for now?"

The little fake Irishman took out a big old-fashioned gold watch
from his vest pocket, looked at it for several moments. Then he slowly
put it back. "Darlin'," he said, "you weren't knowing that Speedy
Gonzalez is dead?"

The stallion nipped her again and blankly she fended him off.

"When Walt let the horse go," said Moriarty, arranging the
watch chain carefully across his stomach, "the boy was already ill.
Late this winter it was. Leukemia, darlin'. The kind that starts in the
marrow. His back was always hurting him, he said. Walt took him to a
hospital and left him. Three months later—in May, I think it was—
they called him and wanted to know what to do with the body."

The stallion put his nose to Beth's ear and blew a hot blast of
impatience into it. "You mean," said Beth, clutching the lead shank,
"that he died alone in the hospital, with no one around?"

"Darlin'," said Moriarty dryly, "Walt's interest in the boy ended
when he could no longer boot home a winner. Besides, Walt couldn't
bear to look at dyin' people. Sure and I went once to see Speedy. They
had him sharing a room with a paralyzed gentleman who had a clot
on the brain. Crazy with the pain he was, and told me he was seeing no
one, and that if I came back he would tell the nurses to be throwing
me out. Ye said ye'd be Beth Stuart, did ye now?"

"That's right." Numbly Beth's hand sought the stallion's neck
and stroked it.

"Walt told me to give ye something should I come up this way.

He told me about ye and Speedy. Sure and it'll be some small possessions of the boy's."

The little man rummaged in his tack trunk, among decrepit
halters, broken curry combs, bent hoof picks, and empty whisky
bottles, and finally fished up a little wooden box. The box sounded like
it had dirt and gravel rattling around in it, and it had a grimy envelope
addressed to Beth tied on with the kind of twine used to bale straw.
Beth could see that the box had been knocking around in that trunk
for many hundreds of miles, many race meets.

Trying to hold box and stallion both, she ripped open the letter
from Walt.

"Dear Beth," it said. "By now you know that Speedy has rode to
the post for the last time. Rita never did come back, and he had no
other relatives that I know of. I didn't have any notion what to do
with him. So I had him cremated and here are his ashes for you to do
with as you see fit. I was sorry to put the Count up for claiming but I
needed the money. It is a good thing you did not marry Speedy, as
you would have been left a widow and it might have gone very hard
with you. Take my advice and don't go into the horse business. Best
way I know to go broke."

Beth clutched the box and lead shank in one hand, and with the
other shoved the letter into her hip pocket. The box was not very
heavy. Speedy was only five feet tall, weighing in at ninety-six pounds.
They wouldn't have needed a very big fire.

"Mr. Moriarty," she said in an even voice, "when all's said and
done you're a decent man. I'm much obliged to you. Now you're going
to do one last decent thing and sell me this horse. How much will you
take?"

"Darlin', would ye be crazy now? He's only got three legs. I
claimed him for $1000, and I'm not hurtin' to sell him, mind ye. But
I'll take $1500, not a penny less."

Had it been another horse, Beth might have done a little trading
and worn him down to $900 or so. But she whipped out her ranch
checkbook and wrote the check against the rain-darkened board wall
of the barn.

"And how should I be knowing if the check be good?" said
Moriarty, looking it over.

"Call the Cottonwood Bank and Trust in town," said Beth
harshly, walking off with the Count shambling behind her and trying
to nip her in the seat of the pants. Light pierced her skull like a hoof

pick. In fact, it was like the top of her head was caving in, with more and more light beating through.

She untied Flash, stepped up on him and, leading the Count, rode slowly out of the fairgrounds, down the cottonwood lane, away from the tow ring and the ancient shed rows. The track disappeared from sight behind her, its board fence peeling in the morning sunshine. Out on the strip, jockeys stood up easily in their stirrups as horses rocked along under them. The cottonwoods collapsed slowly like towers that had been dynamited. Already some leaves were showing yellow. That afternoon she would ride in the barrel race for the last time. In three weeks she would be on the train to New York. She would room with Kathleen, and they would talk about boys. She felt herself slowly ride away out of herself, as if she were a camera lens going out of focus, so that there were two Beths riding two Flashes, leading two California Counts and carrying two boxes.

"Speedy," she heard Beth say to the box, "why didn't you write me to come? I had the money all lined up. I could have caught the next plane. Didn't you believe I'd come?"

The box, of course, didn't say a word.

"Speedy, I'll take care of him as long as he can step and go. You'll see. He won't race again, but we'll work on his legs and put the bloom back on him. A good soft pasture, plenty of linseed in his feed, mares to service. He'll sire some good colts, maybe."

Then she saw how Beth looked over at Speedy, who was sitting bareback on the Count, riding easily on that bony spine, his hips moving with the horse. He was wearing Levis and an old red sweatshirt, and his black curls coiled crazily in the wind. He had on racing goggles, and instead of a nose, there was just a scorched, triangular hole in the middle of his face. His lips shone as if in a terrible heat. Then she saw Beth stretch out one hand, and Speedy reach out his own and squeeze hers hard. The tendons stood up white in the two lean little hands. Then they rode on, side by side, the Count's bony rump standing two hands higher than Flash's rump, the two horses' tails swishing peacefully. They rode out into the open, along the dirt county road. Beth followed, watching. She noticed that when they came to the fork, they didn't turn toward the Stuart ranch, but instead rode on up toward the bench. It was noon, and the distance shimmered with heat devils.

Soon they were up on top. The open plateau spread before them. Beth could hear them talking in low voices. Speedy was telling how, down on the Santa Cruz, they used to leg the horses up along the beaches. Beth watched, pressing the box in the crook of her arm, the splintery edge of it cutting her ribs and her wrist. The sun poured down through the top of her head.

Up ahead, Speedy and Beth left the road and touched the horses into a canter. A sharp smell of bruised silver sage poured up. Far away and below lay the valley—the river winding among the cotton-woods, the town, the tiny oval of the racetrack and the toy grandstand, the glint of cars on the highway. And beyond lay the Pacific, shining so brightly under a last ray of sun that it cut across her eyes like a knife blade. The shore seemed strangely near—she could actually hear the distant roar of the waves, or a single wave. Far out over the ocean, dark blue thunderheads were boiling up. Lightning stabbed at the water, and long curtains of rain came trailing. Thunder fell, and echoed and echoed over the water. The sea and the open plateau turned slowly, dizzily, against the cloudless sky. Puffs of dust sprang up under the horses' hoofs. Beth and Speedy were racing away, neck and neck, yelling shrilly at the horses. They moved away very slowly.

Beth sat on Flash, watching them go, clutching the Count's lead shank. Thunder fell, nearer this time. She felt the earth move slightly under them and noticed the horses look quickly toward the sea, their ears straining forward. Something huge was rising from the sea, the waves draining off its back, cascades of foam running down its legs. It was a giant crab. She watched it come slowly up on the shore. Behind it, lightning raked the sea, and long gray curtains of rain came trailing across the dark water. The light in her head dimmed as the rising thunderheads cut off the sun. Flash and the Count moved nervously, the Count swinging this way and that, his eyes glittering with fear. The wind gusted stronger, lifting the horses' manes, bringing a stink of fish and sea moss. Beth looked ahead to see if Beth and Speedy had noticed the monster, but they were still galloping away, growing smaller yet staying in the same place. Speedy's neck shone frighteningly.

Down in the valley, the giant crab stepped nimbly across the river and the highway, not knocking over a single cottonwood tree or speed-ing truck. It crawled slowly across her father's ranch, and she saw its shadow fall across the aluminum roofs of the barns and the brick porticoed house. Its pincer claws were held in front, open and ready to snap, as it climbed up the hills toward her. Now that it was getting close, she shuddered to look at it, because it didn't have an ordinary crab's face. Instead it looked at her with a horse's skull, and its eyes grew on stalks out of the empty sockets. She could plainly see the splintered nose-bone, the niches where the ears had been, and the rotted teeth.

The crab now stood on the plateau's edge. Lightning riddled the valley just behind it, reflected on the crab's wet carapace and armored, bristly legs. Flash and the Count were wheeling around in terror—she could hardly hold them. Looking back, she saw that Speedy and Beth hadn't seen anything. They were racing straight into the shadow of those gargantuan claws.

If only she had a gun or something. Then she remembered the chain lead shank. The Count half-reared up with a shrill whinny, nearly jerking her from the saddle. Fumbling desperately, she managed to unsnap the shank and set him free. With a whistling snort, he whirled on his hind feet and ran. Half in tears, she watched him disappear across the plateau faster than a cloud shadow, faster than light and sound, leaving himself behind, wild and free.

Then she spurred Flash toward the crab, through the racing Speedy and Beth. Flash reared and frothed at the mouth, but she spurred him ahead. The crab towered over them, the sky falling against it with a roar. Its eyes swiveled on their stalks, shifting from the galloping pair to herself. It stretched out its claws. The chain was suddenly long, heavy, and lethal. With this weapon in hand, she whipped Flash right up under the crab's splintered nose and swung the chain with all her strength. The earth turned slowly. The chain crashed across the crab's skull and split it right down the middle. Thunder roared in streams off the crab's back. The skull fell in splinters all over her and Flash.

Headless, the crab staggered backwards, its legs thrashing in all directions, its pincers opening and closing in spasms. From the black oozing socket where the head had been, a deafening racket of a thousand monsters screaming and bellowing came out, like a thousand jet planes cutting the sky in half. She could see straight into the crab's gizzard, which was packed with half-digested bones and a lot of ashy grit. Still screaming, the crab slid backwards off the plateau edge out of sight. One claw waved a last time against the indigo sky, against the drapes of rain. Then the screaming stopped.

Beth sat in the saddle, going limp. Down in the valley, the rain had already swept across the river and the highway. All around her, the silver sage and the wheat grass rippled away in the wind, running away like the Count had. Beth and Speedy were far off, rippling and blowing away. Beth watched, her eyes going dry, her hand still clenching the lead shank. The whole top of her head had fallen in now, like the shingle roof of an abandoned racehorse barn. The lightning flashed right on her naked brain. And when the rain finally reached her, it beat right down into her shattered skull, running gently down along the ravines of her brain, all across the plateau that sped away from under her.

She opened her eyes. She was lying in the grass. She must have been asleep. She felt a relaxed, swooning comfort. She shaded her eyes with her hand and smiled, rolling her head to one side. Then she sat slowly up.

Her bare legs were a little flushed with sunburn. Her jeans and boots lay in the dry grass nearby, next to a horse's skull that must have lain there for years, because grass had grown up through the eye sockets. Farther away, caught against a clump of prickly pear, lay her hat. And right by her, shaded tenderly by a bush of silver sage, sat the wooden box. She felt wet between the legs and noticed that her thighs were smudged with dried blood. She must have gotten a thistle up herself. She looked around for the horses and saw them grazing a little way off. The Count, still tied to Flash's saddle horn, was snatching hungrily at tips of grass within his reach.

Moving slowly, still smiling, she pulled on her clothes, rescued her hat, carefully picked up the box, and caught the horses. Then she rode back down to the ranch.

Crosstying the Count in front of the main barn, she went inside to fix up a box stall for him. She cut open a bale of straw and, seizing a pitchfork, she spread the straw deep and thick in the stall. Vern's foreman came along, saw the Count, and asked her, "What's this crowbait?"

Beth didn't answer. The foreman wiggled his eyebrows with puzzlement and left. Beth got a shovel and, scraping aside the straw in one corner of the stall, dug a deep hole in the clay floor. She sat by the hole for a while, pressing the box to her cheek. Finally she placed it gently in the hole, pushed the dirt over it, and tamped it down with her boot heel. Next she got some red paint and a small brush. Kneeling in the straw, she printed across the board wall the words "Speedy Gonzalez was the fastest mouse in Mexico." Finally she led the Count in and fed him. Watching as he bolted the feed, she resolved to put a bit on him next time to make him eat slower.

Work done, she walked across the barnyard to the house. She was hungry and hoped that Bertha had sandwiches as well as soup. In the living room, Vern was waiting for her, sitting on the very edge of the leather sofa. He rose slowly, looking at her in a funny way.

"Bethy, where've you been all morning?" he asked. "And wherever did you get that skinny bangtail? And whyever did you mess up your room like that?"

Beth looked him up and down. She had the curious feeling that she had never seen him before. She looked around the room; it seemed so strange, with its pine-paneled walls, its big stone fireplace, its Navajo and bearskin rugs, its rugged furniture and leather chairs, the antique guns and deer antlers ranged over the walls, the magazines in the rack, and Vern's paintings with their careening horses and dust rising rosy in the sunlight.

She had never been in her bedroom before, but strangely she knew the way there—down the hall and turn left. In the center of the floor, there was a whole pile of broken horse statues. On top of them, as if ready for a bonfire, lay a lot of books and scrapbooks. Whole chunks of pages with newspaper photos of racehorses scotch-taped onto them had been torn out of the scrapbooks and lay scattered. One glossy photograph had been ripped in half—all that was left was an arrogant horse's head with a white blaze and a winner's wreath of roses. Curious, she picked up one book. The title was *National Velvet*.

Beth shrugged, turning to look at Vern. She hadn't done it, that was for sure. She hadn't been there.

"I was over at the fairgrounds," she said. "Speedy Gonzalez is back."

Old Men, Old Horses

"Don't chase that heifer so hard!" Pinter Brodie shouted.

He sat helpless on Crowder, his old black gelding, and watched his one and only cowboy, Vin, galloping after the young cow. They had just started gathering up the cow herd to drive them from the summer range down to the home ranch on the other side of Cottonwood, and the heifer had spooked away from the bunch. Brodie so trembled with rage that under his scarred old leather vest, more fit for a museum of Western history, and the faded blue shirt he kept patching himself, his chest heaved up and down. He knew it was a bony chest with a few silvery, curled hairs on it, because he inspected it so often these days, worrying about the tightness around the heart that he felt inside it. The little leather snapper at the end of his stockyard whip made a kind of faded, angry, ornate script against the hazy August sky, like the writing in the old ledgers back at the ranch house. That stockyard whip was a concession to his sixty-eight years —it wasn't buckaroo gear, he reminded himself once again, and he shouldn't be using it to gather cattle. But he could reach farther and more comfortably with it to tap cows on the tail and make them move on.

His rage rippled out in the silence and died, as he watched Vin and the cow galloping off. He might have been all alone there on that sweep of sun-cured bench country—though had he been alone, he wouldn't have noticed it anyway. His rage died in the nearby gullies where the wild roses, long past their bloom now, displayed their red heps like exposed hearts in autumn's surgery. His rage died farther away on the dry mountain slopes, where the lupine thrust up podded spikes more silvery than his own head under its old black high-crowned hat. Finally his rage died on the peaks that ringed the

Cottonwood basin—he could scarcely see those few stubborn streaks of snow on their summits that always survived summer, because his eyes weren't so good anymore.

Nearby, he could actually hear the decaying of the dark, weathered cabins and pole corrals of his 5 Up 5 Down cow camp. It was as audible as the hoofbeats of Vin's horse. He could hear the chinking crumbling from between the logs, and the poles rotting and cracking. He didn't use the cabins anymore, because it cost too much to keep them fixed up, and kids that came into the hills to hunt always broke the windows. He rented out those cabins to the pack rats now, and he just rode Crowder up from town to count the cattle and check the water. Out of the corner of his eye, he could see the Chance cow camp a few miles away—it wasn't even a real cow camp, just an old cabin built by some honyoker who drifted into Cottonwood around 1908 to try dry-land farming there and went broke in a dry year and abandoned the place. The Chances had money (or thought they did) and kept that cabin fixed up, with a man living there to look after the cattle on their summer range.

Farther off to the side, he could see Cottonwood smoldering down in the valley. The sawmill sent up its guilty haze even though it was Sunday and everybody in town would soon be heading for the rodeo, the horse races, and the last performance of the centennial pageant. Just east of Cottonwood, the sun ricocheted off the Fulton Greenhouse, not like a bullet but like a laser (he had read all about lasers), and so brightly that it struck deep into the antique dark of his heart.

It wasn't even silent up there on the bench, though a city pilgrim might have thought so. He could hear a jet plane flying over high up. It reminded him of the SST he had read about. He wondered what kind of noise that SST would make, and if it would affect his cows, but he guessed he wouldn't have to worry about that. He could also hear a bull bawling a mile or so away—maybe one of those two mongrel bulls of Honeycut's that were forever roaming loose on the county road. Brodie was always worrying that they would breed his cows through the fence. He hoped they weren't loose today, because he and Vin had to drive the cows along that same road. He could hear the whapping of hoofs on dry sod as Vin and the heifer raced off. He could hear the sawdust crackling in the burners down in Cottonwood, could hear soil washing away from overgrazed federal ranges, turquoise-green wastes pluming their way down a clear creek, could hear a wolf gagging on strychnine bait dropped from some government plane. He even thought he could hear the drums from the Indian camp down in town. The town had invited a couple of hundred Indians from all the Montana reservations to come celebrate the centennial with them. That was ironic when you remembered that the cattlemen, who built Cottonwood, had dispossessed the Indians of the virgin grasslands where their own humpback cattle, the buffalo, had ranged. Now the cowmen themselves stood to be dispossessed by time and greed. Brodie had not so much as glanced at the Indian camp or the centennial pageant, but he sympathized a little with the Indians. He was beginning to find out what it must have felt like. Chief Joseph had been speaking for more than the Indian way of life when he said, "From where the sun now stands, I will fight no more." As Brodie sat there on Crowder, he could hear the world quietly—almost gently—coming to an end, like a blade of grass passing its seed time and its curing time and stiffening toward frost.

He shouted and cussed, watching Vin chase the cow farther and farther away. The heifer ran like a deer, tail straight up, long, pale horns high. It was just his luck that he had the most inept cowboy in Cottonwood, Brodie ranted to himself—not even a cowboy, but a twenty-seven-year-old pilgrim kid, probably the last kid in the West who wanted to punch cows. Then for a moment he forgot Vin and the heifer again and saw just a human being mounted on a fast if primitive means of transportation, busy chasing an ever faster fancy. Vin might have been a pilot in a fighter plane chasing a flying saucer, or an astronaut crunching over the glassy benchlands of the moon. Brodie couldn't help knowing that things like moon landings were going on in the world. This thought of saddles turning into satellites was the apparition of his cured-on-the-stem years, and he still didn't know whether to cherish it or chase it away. God damn, he asked himself, why did that gunsel Roosky kid chase that red-blooded American heifer so hard? She'd come back to the bunch by herself if only Vin would leave her alone. A real buckaroo could have turned that heifer neatly at a trot, before she'd gone five yards, without such a Hollywood production of a chase.

Brodie watched, the whip trembling more and his heart almost strangling in his chest, as Vin and the heifer raced farther and farther away, across the dry pasture shimmering in the late-morning heat, along the barbed wire fence. That fence was another minor concession—he'd been forced to build it a few years ago when the old jack-leg pole fences had fallen over, exposing his cows to the predations of Honeycut's two bulls. He and his irrigator Skookum Joe had dug every one of those post holes and strung every mile of that wire.

Brodie knew why Vin was in such a big hurry to get that heifer back into the bunch. Vin was hoping that they could finish the drive in time for him to get to the fairgrounds, so he could see the last few events of the rodeo. Vin had no savvy of real cowboys like Pinter Brodie, Brodie told himself, and real cow horses like Crowder. Vin wanted to see those polyethylene bronc stompers, a lot of them city kids who might make a nice show on a half-rank horse but who didn't really know animals. And supersonic ropers on their shiny aluminum Quarter Horses, like that punk Indian, Johnny Chance, who wouldn't have the faintest idea how to bust a big steer out in the open. In fact, Vin had told Brodie a tale he'd heard in the bars in town, that Johnny Chance had roped an eagle and gotten bucked off and clawed up. Served him right, thought Brodie. Vin, however, had thought it was quite an exploit.

As Brodie told himself all this, he knew full well that Vin did indeed have some use for old Pinter Brodie, or else he wouldn't be working there on the 5 Up 5 Down at all. Vin was hoping to soften the granite heart of this old bachelor cowboy and maybe inherit the historic old ranch with its fifteen thousand acres of good range land and native hay. Brodie was trying to decide whether he should let his heart be softened or not. He still hadn't drawn up a will yet, though Dr. Erickson had told him he should.

Finally, near the fence, Vin caught up with the heifer. Swinging his big roan horse into her head, he tried to turn her back. Hot and angry, the heifer tried to drive on past the roan. Vin blocked her way again, riding with reckless abandon. So the heifer charged him, her curved-up horn slightly grazing the roan's belly—Vin twisted the horse out of the way just in time. A third time he tried to head her off, crowding her unprofessionally close.

This time the frantic heifer veered away and sprang straight against the barbed wire fence, nearly flattening it. A whole quarter mile of fence thrummed like a guitar string, and Brodie could feel a couple of good cedar posts cracking as if they were his own ribs; his mind instantly calculated the labor and materials necessary to replace them. The heifer bounced back, then leaped insanely at the fence again. Brodie flinched and yelled incoherent cussings, foam in the corners of his mouth. He could feel those barbs puncturing his own face. Vin was too far away, and only the nearest cows, and the nearest clumps of wild rose, heard Brodie's shouting.

Finally, with Vin spurring and whooping behind her, the heifer came whirling back. As she galloped past Crowder and piled in among the other cows, Brodie noted her eyes white-ringed with terror, her muzzle draped with foam. Blood trickled from a couple of dozen deep tears on her face and nose.

Vin triumphantly jerked his horse down in a cloud of dust. He was a towheaded, blunt-nosed, tanned little Slav with high cheekbones and slanty, anxious brown eyes. His sideburned face was always trying to unsquint itself from uncertainty. Vin already had on his Sunday-go-to-rodeo clothes—fancy piped shirt, forty-dollar hat, and good tan britches, plus the cartridge belt and Colt .45 pistol that he had affected ever since he came home from fighting the Commies in Vietnam. Brodie was of the opinion that Vin should have stayed in Vietnam as a career soldier.

Brodie glared at Vin. He had control of his right hand now, and the long stiff stockyard whip had stopped shaking. It stood steady against the sky like a lone pine beside a dry gulch, growing where some bird dropped the seed a century ago.

"Don't run the cattle so hard," he snapped. "How many times I have to tell you? A day like today, it's hot already, and they get ringy, and you can't drive them."

Vin's face screwed up with hurt and puzzlement, just as Brodie knew it would. As usual, Vin had imagined that he was doing a good job. "I thought you was in a hurry to gather this herd," said Vin testily.

"I'm in a hurry, all right," said Brodie. "But not that much of a hurry. Look at those scratches on her. We'll have to fix her up down home. The damn horn flies will get in those scratches—"

His tirade ran out, and the whip trembled a little again. He watched the heifer find her calf and smell it. The calf got his head under, found the teat, and sucked gluttonously, butting her pink-ivory bag. The heifer whipped her head around and glared everywhere, looking for more Vins.

"That's a good little bull calf," Vin muttered, trying to change the subject. Vin didn't have the trace of an accent, because his DP family came to Cottonwood when he was four years old. Lately he had been careful to pick up from Brodie all the cowboy lingo he could (though he still sometimes talked in his native Slavic tongue with his mother at home). Of course, foreigners had built not only Cottonwood but the entire Montana cattle business, Brodie reminded himself. All those pioneer stockmen had been foreigners: Pierre Wibeaux and the Marquis de Mores were Frenchmen; Conrad Kohrs, German; and his own Grandfather Brodie, a sullen, songful Irishman; and Nelson Story, a Texan, by god. But they didn't have to worry about time and legends, because they were too busy making money. Now they were dead and as native as the grass. Their deeds would die with Brodie, the last cowman left in the state who could remember them, and their foreignness would die with Vin, who couldn't even imagine them properly.

"Yeah," said Brodie, "a good calf, and born way too late. That's what I get for turning the bulls out so late last summer. And I'm three weeks late again this year. Here it is the end of August, and we've still got one more stack of hay to put up, and now we've got to take time and monkey with these cattle."

He tried to make his voice sound more casual now. He didn't discuss the reason for his lateness. It was the way that he ran the ranch that always made him late, these days. Last year he'd been late because he still insisted on fertilizing his hayfields with a team instead of a tractor and because he already hadn't felt well then. Now he would be late because he had to move the cattle off that range early, due to Intermountain Metal and Chemical, Inc.

His mind moved off like a cloud as he thought of Intermountain. The company carried out open-air refining of high-grade copper salts and reclaimed metals and chemicals for use in water-treatment plants; Intermountain predicted a big statewide increase in water consumption. When the company decided to settle in Cottonwood County, they had first tried to buy a piece of Brodie's upper range, since he owned half the bench on the east side of the valley, and that flat open country was ideal for constructing settling ponds. Brodie told them no—even if he had wanted to sell, they wanted the land too cheaply. So Intermountain tried the Chances, who owned the other east half, and the Chances said no for the same reason. The other side of the valley was firmly in the hands of the prison farm, the Stuarts, and a phosphate plant that the conservation people and the ranchers over there had been trying to shut down because it put fluoride in the air, stunting cattle and making people sick. Finally Intermountain settled beyond Brodie's range, just below the foothills, on federal land that had always been leased to cattle grazing. The government had neglected to keep the land reseeded, and now it lay bare and eroding, invaded by thistle, and the local cattlemen had taken their leases elsewhere. After some elaborate negotiations, Intermountain acquired the right to open up an old mine ditch and bring water down from Madigan Lake to fill the settling ponds.

Then, last year, Intermountain threw up its silvery metal buildings. A company bus started taking a few dozen Cottonwood men up along the dusty county road to new jobs. Few people in Cottonwood were displeased with this provision of employment, or with the broadened local tax base that Intermountain afforded. Brodie and some others, however, watched with some worry as the bulldozers scraped out a dozen huge settling ponds. They were native Montanans across whose days the long shadow of the Anaconda Company had fallen, and they all knew a little about copper. That porous gravel bench, Brodie thought, was no place to be messing around with poisonous copper wastes. The area drained into Skillet Creek, the main water supply on Brodie's range and the Chances' range, and from there into the town water supply before it emptied into the Cottonwood River. The county health officer and the county sanitary engineer got mildly upset too, saying that geological factors and the type of waste made the plant site inadvisable. But the company officials assured everyone that they wanted to be good neighbors and that the settling ponds would be lined.

The plant had started operating that spring, and Brodie had been watching Skillet Creek all summer. Every time he rode up to look at the cattle, he peered suspiciously at the water. At times he thought the water had a turquoise tint, but he was never sure, and his eyes were getting bad anyway. From time to time he took a sample down to the sanitary engineer, and the engineer said, "Well, yeah, there's some copper in that water. But not enough to worry about. Some of those ponds are lined and some of them aren't."

Then, just yesterday morning, when he had ridden up there to check things, the first thing he noticed was that Skillet Creek had turned a pale blue-green. He rode Crowder along the banks, looking for dead fish, but he didn't see any. He didn't see any sick or dead cattle either. He followed the creek clear up to his east fence, tied Crowder there, and crawled through the wires onto Intermountain property. Duty and honor allowed him to trespass on the property of anybody who bothered his cows. He walked farther up the creek, hidden from view by the quaking aspens. Was it his imagination, or were the aspens turning yellow a little early? It hadn't been an exceptionally dry year.

Opposite the plant, hidden in a thicket of willows, he found what he'd been looking for. A thick black hose ran down the slope from those eerie silver buildings, almost hidden by the great thistles. That hose was bootlegging an oily blue-green ooze into the creek. Here, the aspens were showing curled, dead leaves.

Too numbed even to think, Brodie tramped back down the creek. Finding a discarded beer can, he took a water sample. Only when he was on Crowder again, riding back along his own stretch of the creek and watching his cows wading peacefully into it to sip that turquoise flow, their gentle pink muzzles sunk in it, did he begin to vibrate with horror. Right away he cut out his bulls and drove them to cow camp, where they could drink from a tiny clean creek that fed into Skillet farther down. When he got home to the ranch, he climbed into his ancient Model T truck with frayed canvas flaps along the sides, known to all in Cottonwood as the Jack Rabbit. He took the water sample into town to the sanitary engineer.

"Wow," said the engineer when he'd completed the analysis. "There's chloride and ammonia in there too."

"Will it kill my cows?"

"Well, it's getting close to the tolerance level. I'd take your cows out of there. We'll get the sheriff and go up there and take some pictures of the hose."

"You can't win, can you?" Brodie told the engineer in the high singsong voice he reserved for anger. "After those people up the valley went through all that grief to shut down that phosphate plant. Every time, you have to fight the same fight all over again."

"Yeah, looks like we'll have another Skillet Creek Fight," said the engineer. "Only this time, won't no Indians get shot."

Brodie told himself that it was a hard thing to understand. Back in the old days, when the government was slow about sending law and order into the territory, it had sometimes been necessary for the stockmen to form a little secret association, then ride out and hang a few cattle rustlers or horse thieves. They didn't pause to inform the culprits of their right to counsel either. Grandfather Brodie had personally hung some rustlers down on the Powder River. The cowmen brought the money into the territory, and they were only protecting their investment, so no one criticized them much. Now, though, it was business that brought in the big money, so any poor cowman who might string up a few company executives to protect his investment would get little sympathy from Washington. You had to go to court, and that cost money. Even after the Supreme Court had handed down an order for that phosphate company to stop putting fluoride into the air, the company just shut down for a year and lay low—and then they started up operations again, putting out as much fluoride as they had before. For outfits like that, Brodie told himself, the line of duty and the line of lowest costs never met.

So now Brodie had to move his cattle off that range two or three weeks earlier than usual. Ordinarily he would have left them up there into September, or as long as there was enough grass. Now they'd be grazing the hay meadows around the home ranch for two or three weeks longer, which meant he'd have to start feeding hay sooner this winter, which meant that he might not have enough hay to get through the winter. He might have to spend precious dollars to buy hay. Of course he'd have to hire a lawyer too. If Intermountain didn't have that creek cleaned up by next spring, when it would be time to turn the cows out on the range again, he didn't know what he would do.

"Over at the Chances," said Vin, breaking into Brodie's thoughts, "I hear they got a tank out on one of their dry pastures. They truck water over there and put it in the tank." Vin had never learned not to mention the Chances to Brodie, who'd thought badly of the whole family ever since Tom Chance had played a practical joke on him once. Brodie was aware that practical jokes were in the best buckaroo tradition. But he told himself that when God was making cowboys and got around to Pinter Brodie, God had already run out of buckaroo sense of humor, so he wasn't able to appreciate practical jokes.

"Yeah," said Brodie. "I hear they got a million-dollar debt over at the Chances too."

Vin shook his head. "And if it was me running this ranch," he added, "I'd get out the horn weights when that little bull's horns bud out. Them horns on your cattle is awful dangerous. That heifer just about perforated my horse back there."

Brodie disdained to answer Vin. How could he explain that it was a crime against nature to deprive a horned critter of its horns? In all his years in the cow business, he had never put horn weights on his calves to turn their horns meekly down. There was something fine and proud about a cow who could raise her sharp horns against the stars. The sight of a whole herd of cows with their horns left natural was even finer. He wondered if that feeling was a little of the old Spanish reverence for cattle horns that had somehow leaked through to him in the twentieth century. Brodie had read somewhere that in Spain they put men in jail for tampering with the horns of fighting bulls. Grandfather Brodie had come up from Texas with thousands of Spanish cattle, then lost 70 per cent of them in the blizzard of 1887 and had to restock with northern cattle of Shorthorn and Devon blood. Finally he went into Herefords. Those old longhorn steers were not much good for well-marbled New York-cut steaks—they were all horn, bone, and orneriness, Brodie thought. But Jesus Christ, they were fine to look at, with their big old horns spread against the sky. On the buffalo range over at Missoula, the state government kept a last few mottle-faced longhorns as a tourist curiosity, and Brodie sometimes dropped by there just to look at them through binoculars. But he wasn't about to explain this to Vin, of all people.

"All right," he said, "let's stop chewing the fat and gather this herd now. Jesus Christ, it's eleven o'clock in the morning already, and we're four hours late starting down. We're fifty years and four hours late."

Brodie didn't explain, either, the reason they were four hours late. The crippling chest pain had made it hard for him to get out of bed that morning. It took four cups of black coffee, and quite a bit of thinking, just to get his stringy old muscles going. If he had been in any other business, he could retire now with a gold watch and a pat on the back and go live in California and play golf. But he was in the only business where they handed you a kick in the tail instead of a gold watch. Besides, he didn't know how to play golf. Very shortly now he was going to have to listen to Dr. Erickson and decide what to do about himself.

Vin's eyes got more anxious and angry as he turned his horse away with a dashing curvet, spurring hard. Brodie turned old Crowder more slowly, out of respect for the old horse's knees, and rode after Vin, trying to calm himself down. He studied the powerful hindquarters of Vin's big six-year-old roan gelding, Curlew, and tried to think only about horses for a moment, and not about a million other things. Brodie had bred and broke that roan, as he did all his old-time-style horses. He didn't believe in buying horses, especially those muscle-bound, high-test Quarter Horses. So he kept a little bunch of cold-blooded mares and a good little mustang stallion that he'd spotted at a dog-food auction a few years ago. Brodie had named the roan colt Curlew because of his high, piping whinney; but the fact was that the colt's namesakes—those long-billed curlews that used to dart everywhere in the meadows, piping their sad cries as the saddle horses flushed them out of the grass—were now nearly gone, like so many other things. Brodie believed that the town had killed the curlews when it sprayed DDT from airplanes to kill the local mosquitos. This last Curlew was as close-coupled and cool-headed as a mule, such a good cutting horse that Brodie was sometimes sorry he'd sold the horse to Vin (except that he'd needed the $900 badly at the time).

But even thinking about horses made him remember the passing of time, for they kept bringing his mind back to his own Crowder, and to the fact that Crowder—who was foaled in 1945, the year Brodie was forty-three, some time before Quarter Horses got popular—was getting old.

Crowder was a real Montana horse, with that mix of Spanish cayuse, Steeldust, and Thoroughbred that was typical of the northern ranges. The mustang blood showed in Crowder's narrow chest, short back, and deer neck, while the functional, rangy look he had betrayed the Thoroughbred. Twenty-five summers and winters now, Crowder had swung his way through roundups with that high-striding walk of his. He was as fine lined and worn as the effigy on an old gold dollar, as black as an obsidian arrowhead you might pick up on a gravel bar along some shallow prairie river. He was as serious, humorless, and hard-working as a small-town banker. A certain fitting melancholy showed in his wide-set eyes. He had a star on his forehead, whose whiteness was now sifting out into his sunken temples and down over his muzzle. But he was still trim and hard, though his front knees were bad. Brodie scrupulously fed him up, nursed his knees, and kept his tail pulled short at hock level. Crowder's line prompted as many thoughts as Crowder himself—he was out of Uncle Charlie's favorite mare, Old Sin, who was by Brodie's father's cowhorse, Rambler. In his turn, Rambler was by Reveille, Grandfather Brodie's great working stallion. Reveille was half mustang, half Thoroughbred, and he was as good on the racetrack as he was cutting out fat cows on the open range. One time he beat copper king Marcus Daley's famous Tammany in a match race right down in Cottonwood. The Brodie family had always regarded this match race as their personal victory

over the dark forces of eminent domain, because the copper people
had once condemned a piece of the Brodies' best mountain range for
a new mining operation.

Brodie's middle age and old age had blown through Crowder's
mane, had worn a few coin-sized honorable white saddle spots into his
black back, had been polished into the seat of the old-time saddle with
its tall horn and cantle, its narrow tree, and its single center-fire cinch.
You couldn't even put a saddle like that on one of those round-bar-
reled little Quarter Horses. Vin, riding a modern factory-made saddle
with its broad tree, low horn and cantle, and double cinch, had dared
to kid Brodie about that relic of a saddle, that might better be hanging in Johnny Quigley's Frontier Town museum and educating the
tourists.

As Vin and Brodie moved on the first little bunch of cows and
calves, Crowder stumbled over a gopher hole and nearly went down.
Brodie had to pull up hard on the limp, dark old reins and the beat-up,
long-shanked, Spanish-type bit to keep the old horse on his feet. Vin's
Curlew wore stiff new red reins and a shiny, short-shanked aluminum
bit.

"Your old pony is getting on," said Vin unkindly. "I'll sell you
Curlew back for $1000."

"The damn gophers," said Brodie, not rising to the bait. "Somebody, I think it was me, got too enthusiastic about killing wolves, and
now the gophers make Swiss cheese out of my best range." He drew
out a pack of papers and some Bull Durham tobacco (the stuff was
getting hard to buy, and he figured he'd rather die an early death than
switch to Marlboros) and rolled himself a cigarette with his cracked
fingers. He cupped his hands against the hot northwest breeze to light
it, and exhaled the smoke as calmly as he could. "Yeah," he said,
"poor old Crowder can't line out after a cow like in the old days."

It wasn't going to be much of a cattle drive, as cattle drives went,
Brodie thought. Not like when they trailed thousands of steers to
Abilene or Miles City, swimming them across rivers and filling miles
of cattle cars. Not like when they talked about having a National
Cattle Trail the way they talked about building Interstate Defense
Highways today. All he and Vin had to do was drive those 628 cows
and 550 calves (quite a few cows had gone dry on him this year),
along the dirt county road across the bench. Then they would trail
them off the bench along Powderhouse Hill, where the road sloped

down into the valley, past Fulton's Greenhouse and the old brickyard, and across Interstate 10. They would push them through the Alfalfa-ville development east of Cottonwood, skirting the fairgrounds to get to the north side of town, where they could strike the old highway and follow it about ten miles north to the home ranch. The drive was some twenty miles in all. Most of the cows had traveled the road several times, some of them a couple of dozen times, so they should be easy to drive. But Brodie worried that they might not get past the fair-grounds before the rodeo ended—he could visualize that horned she-stuff milling around in the car traffic. There were Honeycut's bulls to worry about too. He hadn't seen them when they rode up that morn-ing, but he knew how often they were loose on the road.

They pushed the little bunch of heifers along toward the main herd. The cattle were scattered peacefully along the bench, grazing amid the sagebrush on the last of that year's stem-cured wheat grass and grama grass. Brodie was careful about managing and reseeding that grass. Some cows were sheltering from flies and sun farther below, in the still-green bottom along Skillet Creek. There the water curled, a sudden, ominous copper-green, among clumps of willow and tough-leaved iris. The willow leaves were already yellowing—Brodie won-dered if it was from the waste in the water. The iris seedpods were already burst and empty. His eyes again anxiously scanned the bottom for dead cows, but he didn't see any.

He looked back at the cow camp, at the maze of empty corrals, at the cabins with their roofs caving in, at the toppling sheds nearby. For some fifty years now, he had looked back like that. There was something in the Bible about Lot's wife looking back and getting turned to salt, no doubt the red kind you put out in blocks for the cattle to lick. There in those corrals, generations of purebred Brodie Herefords had been vaccinated, branded, earmarked, castrated, horn branded, tallied, tested for TB and Bangs disease. Brodie used a beautiful old hand-forged iron to stamp on their hides the 5 Up 5 Down brand that Grandfather Brodie first registered in 1871. Life was a series of small compromises, even in those corrals: he refused to use a calf table for branding, and kept his rope in practice by hind-footing the calves and dragging them to the fire for Vin and Skookum Joe to brand; but he put the cows through a modern chute to test and tally them. Since he couldn't handle the roping all alone, he grudg-ingly invited Tom and Johnny Chance to help out. They always were glad for the opportunity to practice.

Back in the 1930s and 1940s, Brodie had been in the vanguard of Montana breeders with his Blanchard and Domino bloodlines. But after World War II everybody decided they didn't like big, long-legged dark bulls anymore, because the packers were demanding an animal with more meat, smaller-size cuts, and less bones and guts. So the cowmen started experimenting with newer bloodlines, breeding selectively to get a little shortlegged yellow bull. Brodie could see the meat sense of that type of bull, but he was alarmed by the way they were bending nature around. So he kept on breeding Blanchards and Dominos when everybody else was putting Triumphants and Milky Ways into their herds. His sales dropped badly, and he had to stop going to cattle shows because the judges wouldn't look at his big dark bulls with their businesslike horns.

For a few years there, Brodie recalled, he just hung and rattled. "Hang and rattle" was a good cow-country phrase that Vin had learned, though the boy had no idea what it meant. Hang and rattle was what you did on a real rank bronc, half out of the saddle, maybe one stirrup lost, your hat gone, your brain being jolted right out of your skull. You hung and rattled, but you didn't come loose. If Grandfather Brodie hadn't left nearly a million dollars in a trust fund, he would have come loose and gone broke. He made a few extra dollars by switching half over to feeding fat commercial steers, and practicing the most dedicated kind of penny-pinching in every aspect of his life that didn't involve duty and honor.

Then in the early 1950s, nature backlashed, as the newspapers he read always liked to say. Suddenly all those fancy little yellow cows started dropping dwarf calves that grew into stunted monsters. These dwarf cattle had stubby legs, pop-eyes, grotesque big heads, short necks, practically no windpipe. After a few months, you had to get your jackknife and bore a hole in their trachea so they could breathe. Even so, they usually died before they were yearlings. The stockmen panicked as they figured out that some of the newer bloodlines had become carriers of the dwarf gene, and that when you crossed two normal looking carrier animals, you got a dwarf.

So Brodie witnessed the anguish of men who had brought in carrier blood in the form of a couple of $75,000 grand-champion bulls, then suddenly found themselves getting a 90-per-cent-dwarf calf crop. Many men dumped their purebred stock on the slaughter market and went bankrupt. A few cooler-headed ranchers figured out that the old bloodlines were still clean, and that if you crossed a carrier line with a clean line, you could breed yourself out of the bad dream. That was when they realized that old Pinter Brodie up there at Cottonwood, Montana, was good for something after all. They all came running to buy his big, dark long-legged clean heifers and bulls. In a couple of years, he made so much money that he was still coasting on it.

But the day of reckoning was going to come soon, he told himself—what with inflation, impending lawsuits, and Dr. Erickson's warning. Pretty soon, for the first time in his life, Brodie would have to sit down in a leather chair in the bank over in Butte and ask the banker for money to finance part of his annual operation. When this happened, he would be following all the other stockmen in the country deeper and deeper into the plastic immorality of deficit financing. He might even have to think about selling out his historic Herefords and restocking with those exotic crossbreds that many cowmen were messing around with now, where you ended up with an animal that was one-sixteenth Hereford, one-sixteenth Charolais, one-sixteenth Angus, and so on. Or maybe restocking with those huge meat-and-milk-producing Simmental cattle from Switzerland that many other American cowmen were switching to. Simmentals gained so fast, matured so early, and produced so much more meat per animal that they cut your overhead in half. Right there in the Cottonwood basin, the big Carson ranch down near Ellis was going into Simmentals. Brodie had no use for those colorful crossbreds—Grandfather Brodie had already tried crossbreeding long ago, and he had been fond of saying that the first cross was good, it produced a hybrid vigor that could stand those northern winters, but the second cross was no good. As for Simmentals, Brodie liked the idea of saving all that overhead, but after all, they were *dairy* cattle.

"Nature always has the last laugh," he said to Vin.

"Huh?" said Vin.

"Oh, nothing," said Brodie. "Just an old man and his old horse thinking out loud." He glanced back at cow camp again.

"How old is the old man today?" Vin asked.

"About 120, I guess," said Brodie. He sucked the last draw out of the tiny butt, leaned down to rub it out against his boot, and threw it away.

"Gee," said Vin. "Yesterday you was only eighty."

"I go up and down like the cow market."

For twenty years now he had looked back at cow camp with that lethal regret. Perhaps it was because he was burdened with the memory of the last great roundups on the open range in the early 1900s. A man couldn't be burdened with a memory like that and still be fit to live in 1970. Sometimes in the evenings, as he glanced at newspapers and magazines before falling asleep and read about atomic power plants, lasers, and space travel, it all seemed a little unreal, as if he were reading about things that hadn't happened yet.

How clearly he could remember that last roundup on the dry fork of the Missouri! He had been just a kid wrangler then. The sun-baked hills and flats rolled all around, and the cattle were scattered over them by the tens of thousands. Riders of half a dozen outfits brought them in from this circle and that circle. In the rainy evenings, the outfits pitched tents. Cook fires burned, hundreds of horses milled in the great rope corral. The cook yelled, "Grub piiiile!" when his Dutch-oven stew and biscuits were ready, plus son-of-a-bitch-in-a-sack for dessert if he was in a good mood. Brodie remembered all the men from those roundups—great riders, he told himself, with plenty of cow savvy. He could still recite every joke they had told and the names of every bronc they had ridden, and if he had been talented at drawing, he would have been able to put on paper every line on their wind-burnt faces. Those men were lucky to be dead now, safe on the other side of the Great Divide, where the creeks and grass were still sweet and free.

Sometimes, during those evening readings, he thought about how he was a walking encyclopedia of the range days. He was the last man left in the state who had lived through them. He thought about how he should write something about them. He used to write "Bunch Grass and Blue Joint" type poetry when he was young and innocent—he still had some of those poems lying around somewhere. He was sure he could write something good. The Southwest had its Frank Dobie, but the Northwest had never found anyone to tell the tales of men, cattle, and grass. Of course, Charlie Russell had written stories—Brodie had known Russell briefly as a boy, before the Montana artist's death—but those stories lacked the ring and fine style of Dobie's *Longhorns*. Brodie had been telling himself for years now that he had to sit down and start a book about those days on the Big Dry and all the things that were in his head. But there was never any time to do it. He was always late—just like today.

He looked back one last time. The cow camp stood far off now, shimmering in the heat waves. He could still, however, hear the chinking crumbling.

"What you looking at?" Vin asked. "We didn't miss any cows back there."

"Just thinking how one of these days I'm going to set those old buildings on fire and watch 'em burn. They're a disgrace."

"They'll get you for arson," said Vin.

"Euthanasia, more likely," said Brodie.

They rode clear up to the east fence bordering Intermountain land and began to work the cattle west, making sure that none were left behind, hidden in the willow thickets or in the little gullies where the wild roses bled with ripe heps. At Brodie's direction, Vin worked one side of Skillet Creek while Brodie worked the other. The cattle crashed out of the willows or rose heavily from their beds among the iris clumps where they had been chewing their cuds. They massed and drifted down the creek, cows bawling for their calves. A smell of crushed silver sage rose from their hoofs. Brodie threw a killing look across the fence at Intermountain's silvery buildings. The government's habit of leasing land without asking to what use it was being put was like giving a blank check for destruction. As he rode along Skillet Creek, he kept glaring, too, at that turquoise water, wondering if he'd see dead fish or, worse still, dead calves.

In the hot shining air he could feel the wind shifting away from the northwest into the east. An east wind meant it would rain in a few days, which usually was good. But right now it was bad. It would have been easier to drive the cattle with a west wind, because then they would have been pointed upwind most of the way and able to breathe easier when they heated up. There was always one more bad thing. Today, if just a few more bad things happened, he might stop hanging and rattling and just come loose.

From habit, as he gathered them up, he recognized each cow as an old friend. There was No. 857, a handsome young cow with one crooked horn, a tick of white on her back and the number burned on her horn still crisp. She had her first calf last year, with a lot of trouble too—he and Vin had to cut up the calf and pull it out dead. But this year she had calved normally, a good little heifer that trotted now at her flank. Over there was old 94, the matriarch and lead cow. She was the best cow that Brodie had ever had. Every year for fifteen years she had presented him with a good bull calf. Now she had a cancer in one eye. Her hoofs had grown up long and curled—he'd

have to get her in the chute and trim them. Her big horns were so
fissured with age that Brodie could hardly read her number now.
Worse, she was dry this year, and Brodie would have to make a sentimental decision about whether to cut her out and ship her.

But this morning his mind couldn't concentrate on the cow biog-
raphies filed in his memory. Grasping the stock of the long stockyard
whip and resting his rein hand on the saddle horn, he felt wasted and
cold in the heat pouring down from that sawdust-burning blue sky. He
felt as if all the suns in the universe could form a ring around him and
yet still not warm him. Even on these temperate summer nights, he
shivered with cold under several blankets. He would have to give up
sleeping outdoors in summer—his old bones, like rotted fence poles,
would soon cave to the ground.

It had taken much too long to do the fertilizing and haying this
year, sitting day after day behind the team. He drove the mower
himself because he didn't trust anyone to cut his good timothy and
alfalfa the way he wanted it done. Besides his permanent men (Vin
and the old irrigator, Skookum Joe), he managed to scrape together
a hay crew of transient drunks, traveling hippies, college kids, Indians,
and prison trustees. When they weren't fighting with one another, they
drove the teams and the rickety old machinery—the side rake that
swept the cured hay into windrows, the dump rake that pulled the
windrows up into piles, the buck rake that pushed the piles over to the
stacker, and the creaky old beaverslide stacker that slid the piles up
into heaven, then dumped them on the stack. There the stackers
spread the hay around with pitchforks. Every year Brodie got an
ulcer trying to convince the stackers that the hay had to be spread
artistically, so the stack would shed water. The machines were museum
pieces that should be put in Mr. Henry Ford's museum of Americana.
Brodie kept them going with wrenches and screwdrivers, wire and odd
hunks of timber, and repaired them more cheaply than a baling
machine too. Every year he laughed a little watching his neighbors,
the Chances, trying to keep their shiny new $10,000 baler going and
driving all over the state for new parts when it broke down. Brodie
hay was later, but it was cheaper too.

Of course, even when he did the work himself, bad things happened. For instance, a few springs ago, when he was still growing
wheat, the counter on his drill broke and he planted fifteen acres over
his government allotment without knowing it. He hated the wheat subsidies, but he did take a certain pride in the wheat he grew for his

own feeding operation—it was some of the last hard red wheat left in the U.S. So the government inspector came around to measure his wheat and make sure he was obeying Washington. The inspector said, "Your allotment is 160 acres and you planted 175. Better get out there and plow it under."

"Hell's bells," Brodie said, "I'm not going to waste time plowing up fifteen acres."

"Well, you'd better do it," the inspector kept on in a threatening tone of voice. Finally Brodie, who was not normally given to melo-drama, quietly took his Winchester .30-.30 out of its scabbard in the cab of the Jack Rabbit. He pointed it at the government inspector and said, "You vamoose now."

The inspector vamoosed. The next year, though, Brodie seeded that wheat land back into grass.

Vin had witnessed the incident. Vin wanted to be as wild and woolly and full of fleas, Brodie thought, even though he had been cur-ried below the knees—clear down to the hoofs, in fact. That incident convinced Vin all over again that firearms were a gift of God. For all Vin knew, the angels wafted through paradise carrying smoking six-guns instead of harps. Vin carried a gun, Brodie sensed, in affirmation of some dark, divinely granted right to destroy. At any rate, Vin told that story about the government inspector in every bar in Cottonwood. It made Brodie feel a little embarrassed. The gesture had been too close to things he'd seen on TV.

He knew the real history, yes. He could write something about it that would put an end to all the movies, TV shows, and pulp novels. His head was bursting like a seedpod with data on the way people had really looked, talked, dressed, acted in those days. His memory was a file of thousands of old photographs by A. E. Huffman, that admirable young Miles City photographer who lugged his glass plates and tripod around over the ranges at the turn of the century. Sometimes, shaking with cold on the summer nights, he got up out of his bedroll under the cedars and went back into the dark ranch house and made coffee to warm himself. Range-camp coffee: no cream or sugar, the kind you threw a horseshoe into to see if it was strong enough, and if the shoe sank you added more coffee.

Then he would sit there in the dark, with a blanket wrapped around him, drinking cups of that stuff, smoking endless homemade cigarettes, coughing, and thinking about the ranch and about life. He would sit there worrying about how the state power company was after him for an easement along five miles of valuable hay land, so they could build a huge high-tension powerline into Cottonwood. The power company was prepared to pay him the skinflint price of twenty dollars per pole. Brodie had been holding them off for a year now, but any day he expected the sheriff to show up at his front door with a summons to appear in court, saying the power company had exercised its divinely granted right of eminent domain. Sometimes he wondered why the cattlemen alone, of all lobbies, had never been given the right of eminent domain.

Then, there in the dark kitchen, a hundred years of Montana history would start unreeling itself before his eyes, like a documentary film, as if he had seen all of it, instead of just the tail end of it.

He could see the northern prairie rippling with buffalo grass and blue-joint, the way it had in the 1860s when the buffalo still ranged it and the cattlemen already coveted it. The Indians, of course, thought the grass was theirs—the Blackfeet, Crows, Cheyennes, ancestors of the very Indians sitting down in Cottonwood right now in the centennial camp—but the Indians didn't have the right of eminent domain either. By the 1870s he could see the prairie white with bones as the government hunters slaughtered the buffalo—that was when things began to go wrong, though no one realized it at the time. In the 1870s the Indians were already limping, beaten, onto reservations, and white men and beef cattle began trickling onto the emptied ranges—Sam Hauser, Nelson Story, Granville Stuart, Bill Chance, Conrad Kohrs, Bob Ford, Dan Flowerree, Fitz Brodie, two thousand head here, five thousand head there, like horned ships going down to the sea of grass. But by 1880 the railroad was already being built west from the Missouri, millions of tons of barbed wire were already in use, and Huffman was already out on horseback taking pictures of what he knew was the last free grass in America. In the early 1880s the ranges were filling up along the Yellowstone, Sun, Teton rivers. The sheep were already spilling in. (Here Brodie's documentary speeded up.) By 1900 the railroads and the government had abandoned the cattlemen to bring in the dry-landers and the honyokers, who plowed the grass under, planted wheat, and then abandoned the land when the rains failed. Then the ghosts of all those buffalo rose from the coulees and the rolling benchlands. They piled up in clouds of black dust, they roared across the land, and they howled and keened, blowing away that topsoil fertilized with their blood. The film ended with his own birth in one of the big walnut beds in the ranch house in 1902, his mother's death in 1907, his father's death in 1910, Grandfather Brodie's death in 1914, and the last big roundup in 1913. Too much death to take in. Even when he was a boy, you could still pick up buffalo skulls on the bench and find buffalo wallows in the bottoms along the Cottonwood River.

So down in Cottonwood right now they were celebrating the town's centennial, and they had tried to put all that history into the nightly pageant performance. The centennial committee had come around and asked Brodie if they could borrow a couple of his old buckboards for the parade. He had told them nothing doing, and they had left saying he wasn't very patriotic. What did they know about all that history? All they knew was what they'd heard or read in books. He, Pinter Brodie, was one hundred years older than anybody else in town, and he remembered it all. Those soft storekeepers, retired railroad conductors, sawmill foremen, gas-station owners, prison guards had nothing to do with all that history, and the virtues that made it work. Those were men's virtues: knowing how to do a hard job well, without being told and without calling attention to your accomplishments afterward; keeping your word and doing what you said you'd do, instead of weaseling out; and above all, knowing how to die when your time came, instead of hanging on indecently. All that history— to the town people it was a chance to taste barbecued buffalo meat and trespass on his nostalgia.

His orphaned boyhood turned over slowly in his mind, like a single Huffman photograph. Its light and shadow, and its people, were frozen in sorrowful precision. Uncle Charlie Brodie, for instance, who ran the 5 Up 5 Down after his father and grandfather died. Uncle Charlie had raised Pinter Brodie, with help from the cowboys and the old Chinese cook, Tom Wing. The cowboys saw to it that Pinter learned to ride, and Tom Wing saw to it that he got fed.

Uncle Charlie Brodie was a tall, powerful man with a red beard, full of assorted Irish rages and merriments. His great physical strength had left a quaint anecdote in Cottonwood legendry: One day he climbed up on a horse that was a head-throwing maniac. As he settled into the saddle, the horse threw back its head and hit him in the face with its poll, breaking his nose. Sitting in the saddle with blood running off his chin, Uncle Charlie simply doubled up his huge fist and hit the horse between the ears. The horse folded to the ground like an accordion, knocked cold. Uncle Charlie climbed pleasantly off, wiped his nose, and waited for the horse to come to and stand shakily up. Then he climbed on again and rode off. That horse never tossed his head again.

In those days, other cowmen—Teddy Roosevelt, Pierre Wibeaux, Conrad Kohrs—were always dropping by to visit. Brodie could still remember the long evening conversations in the parlor, with tall tales, roars of laughing, and cigar smoke mingling in the golden gaslight.

Suddenly there was World War I. A few boys didn't come back home to Cottonwood—they were killed not by Indians but by Boches at Verdun. Then came the 1920s, when faint echoes of jazz and air-plane engines floated out to Cottonwood from the frivolous East. The Depression dropped the price of a cow with calf at side to eighteen dollars a head. Then came the drought years, when the east wind never blew, and the huge tumbleweeds rolled back and forth, north and south, across the scorched ranges.

How clearly he could remember it all! Sometimes a lump rose in his throat as he sat there in the dark kitchen at 3 A.M., his cigarette burned out and his coffee cold. It occurred to him sometimes that those photographs were his emotions—that he remembered Uncle Charlie instead of crying over his mother, that he thought about the drought instead of reflecting on why he never got married. In the 1930s Uncle Charlie made a half-hearted attempt to deal with mo-dernity—he sold some of his prized Belgian draft horses and bought a couple of tractors. And then, just as World War II was beginning, Uncle Charlie Brodie had a stroke and died. Brodie didn't remember for sure if he had cried while the men lowered Uncle Charlie's coffin into the gravelly earth in the Hillcrest Cemetery. But he did remember the verse chiseled on Grandfather Brodie's tombstone, which began, "Leaves have their time to fall." After Uncle Charlie's funeral, Brodie sold the tractors and went back to draft horses. It was then that the town began to consider him a character.

Brodie took over the 5 Up 5 Down with the ease of one who had been educated to it by a Plato of the saddle. World War II took a few more Cottonwood boys and haystacked their lives on the beaches of Normandy and Guadalcanal, but it did not fold his life down onto the mower blades—his ability to supply the government with beef for the GIs exempted him from the draft. Actually, Brodie was sometimes sorry he hadn't fought in the war. Maybe if he had watched the flights of fighter planes taking off from aircraft carriers instead of the flights of wild trumpeter swans taking off from the pond south of the ranch, he would have been more fit to live in 1970.

After the war, there was a brief but delirious prosperity, when a man could sell a purebred bull calf still on the cow for $5000. Then in 1953 the cattle market crashed—it was 1929 all over again, except that this time the cattlemen had it all to themselves, and their desperation made scarcely a ripple in the American consciousness. After 1953, prices stayed crying to the Lord out of the depths, while operational costs went higher than Elijah's chariot. Fools like Vin wanted to be paid $300 a month. Automation was coming in—cattle fed by machines instead of by men, by god. There were the damn subsidies and allotments, Brodie thought, and the Soil Bank thing, and creeping socialism in government agricultural policy. Family ranches were going broke, while soft, rich corporate Easterners came into the business for tax dodges. They were absentee ranchers who could scan a balance sheet but couldn't ride through a herd once and come out on the other side with an exact count of what age and type animals were in it. If it weren't for Dr. Erickson's ultimatum, Brodie would now be wondering how many years before he too would disperse and move down to California to die of curled hoofs like old No. 94.

As Brodie thought about all this, he gently roused a heifer out of her bed in a wild-rose thicket. She stood looking at him for a moment, her dark eyes grave in her virtuous young white face. Her tail curled up at the flies shimmering above her back, and her horns looked like the wings of a wild swan taking off the top of her head. Then she turned with easy dignity and walked on before Crowder. Brodie felt a cactus prick of tenderness. His hand tightened on the stockyard whip so hard that it started shaking again. After all, the cattlemen were the last outpost of good old-fashioned independence left in America, he thought. They refused subsidies and price supports, insisted on the risks of a free market, and in general made things tough for Washington socialists. He himself was a last outpost too—though he wasn't sure anymore just what he was the last outpost of.

A gunshot shattered his reminiscing. He felt old Crowder jerk with fright and looked across the gulch to where Vin was riding. Another shot rang out. He saw Curlew half-rearing and Vin holding a smoking Colt .45, just like a scene in a Charlie Russell painting (except that Charlie would have little use for Vin). The cows that Vin had gathered were spooked and running down the gulch.

Brodie splashed Crowder through the blue-green creek and galloped over there, wondering if Vin had been useful for once and shot a trespassing Intermountain man. But when he got there, Vin had dismounted and was proudly holding up a bloody jackrabbit.

"He started up out of the sage over there," Vin explained, grinning like a small boy, "just asking to be whanged at."

Rage gusted against Brodie as he saw the spooked cows still running. "Don't you ever," he said in a choked voice, "shoot around my cattle again. I've got half a mind to fire you right now. What a damn fool Roosky kid trick, if I ever saw one—"

Vin looked down, his shoulders slumping. Then he shoved the pistol back in the holster, and went to tie the rabbit to his saddle. Curlew, smelling blood and death, backed off—Vin hadn't had him long enough to break him for hunting yet. Brodie continued to shout in his best thin, high voice, "I always say, when I hire kids, that one kid is two kids, and two kids are half a kid. Trouble with you is, you're half a kid even when you're alone."

Blushing and furious now, Vin went on trying to tie the rabbit's hind feet to the saddle strings. Curlew kept snorting, backing, dancing around. Vin started yelling, "Whoa!" and jerking on the reins—like the greenhorn he still was, Brodie thought. The more he jerked and yelled, the more Curlew jumped and danced. The horse's nostrils rattled and his eyes were white-ringed.

"And furthermore," Brodie ranted, "I'll tell you why you wear that pistol. Not just because Montana law says you can. I used to have a fella working for me, a real good man, and he used to wear a .357 Magnum everywhere, including to bed. Somebody tried to dry-gulch him once, and he was going to be all ready for the next time. There was a little bitty screw loose in his head. But you carry that Colt because you think it makes a top hand out of you. But you aren't anything but a two-bit pilgrim dude, and you always will be."

Enraged, Vin flung the dead rabbit away. It sailed out against the hazy sky, dropped slowly past the blue-green creek and the yellowing willows, and hit the earth just beyond a clump of sagebrush, making a little puff of dust. Vin managed to mount his shuddering horse and whirled to face Brodie.

"I can quit anytime I want," he flung back. "Anybody else would give me a better chance than you."

"You go right ahead," Brodie shot back. "You'll have the same trouble anywhere you work. Your own dad would fire you at this rate."

When Vin heard that, his hand dropped convulsively onto the

pistol butt. Brodie saw such a dust storm of a look loom in Vin's eyes that he wondered if Vin would draw the gun on him. But Vin didn't even say son of a bitch—he just twisted his horse around and rode off to gather the next little bunch of cows. Ahead, the cattle had stopped running and stood looking back at the two riders.

After all the cattle were gathered and counted, they pushed them gently up the last rise toward the gate onto the county road. Vin rode tight lipped and slit eyed with anger. "I'm going to write the SPCA a letter," he said, "and tell them how swolled up your old pony's knees is."

"Old men, old horses," said Brodie bitterly. He felt a creak of conscience—he had inspected the swollen knees that morning before saddling up, and he knew that, if it weren't for Dr. Erickson, he should start riding one of his better colts. But he didn't need a new horse. This old black one would do him to the end. Anyway, he just couldn't get used to another horse.

He rolled another cigarette. "Well," he said, "one last roundup for Crowder, before I put him out to pasture."

"That rabbit would of made mighty good eatin'," said Vin.

"You can't eat these wild jacks around here," said Brodie. "Didn't anybody tell you they all got tuleremia? Anyway, why kill a rabbit when you've got a freezer full of TV dinners?"

"Oh, I forgot," said Vin evenly. "You don't enjoy huntin'."

Brodie's hand tightened a little on the stockyard whip again. In recent years, he knew, the whisper had gone around Cottonwood that old Pinter Brodie had given up hunting and actually talked like a paid lobbyist for the wild animals. Everyone knew it was the proper thing to kill any and all varmints and pay no attention to snot-nosed biologists who talked about ecological balances. Come November, everyone went up into the snowy hills to prune the elk and deer population. They drove the deer into the open, down timber cuts up in the national forest above Intermountain, Inc., and had themselves a live shooting gallery, firing point-blank at the deer as they galloped down the cut.

"We ate all winter off that elk I shot," said Vin hollowly.

"You'd of eaten three winters if you'd gone after those other two you said you wounded. Any hunter who doesn't trail a wounded animal and finish it ought to get a bullet through his own little bitty head."

"Trouble with you is," said Vin, "you hate people."

"People?" said Brodie, his voice going higher and higher. "I got nothing against people." He grinned evilly. "Some of my best friends are people."

"If you paid me more," said Vin, "I wouldn't need free meat."

Brodie took a long draw on his cigarette. "I told you before, I can't afford to give you a raise right now. Anyhow, only a top hand gets more than $300 a month in this business."

"Cost of living going up. Another kid on the way. Marilyn dogging me for a new washing machine."

"If you wanted big money, you should have collected bounty on all those Viet Cong you said you shot."

"And you get mad when I kill one lousy jackrabbit."

Brodie wanted to shout, "I'm against useless deaths." Instead he said, "If you spent less money on whiskey and women, Marilyn would have her a whole laundromat full of washing machines."

Vin actually put his right hand on his pistol butt again, maybe without realizing it. "That's just because you're envious." He paused and smiled coldly. "Miss women much, Dad?"

Brodie rubbed his stubble chin noisily, then bent down to grind out his cigarette on his charred boot toe again. He was now so angry that he smiled too. "Son, a real man doesn't answer that question. And he doesn't ask it either," he said in his softest, most ominous piping voice. He gathered up Crowder and turned him away. "Ride on ahead and open that gate now. Are you sure those bulls of Honeycut's aren't out on the road?"

"I told you a hundred times already," snapped Vin, "I didn't see 'em." He dug his spurs into Curlew's speckled sides and galloped ahead.

Brodie watched him jerk Curlew dramatically to a stop, bend out of the saddle to unchain the gate, and swing it open so hard that the soft old poles nearly cracked as they hit the fence. When he'd built the barbed wire fence, he'd gotten a few more years' use out of the old gates.

Brodie thought to himself, "Before the end of the day, one of three things is going to happen. Either I fire that boy. Or I have a heart attack. Or that snot-nosed boy is going to kill me."

An inexplicable panic hit him that was not all fear of death. He turned Crowder and looked back at the vast summer range, now empty save for the hidden wild animals it supported and for the copper-blue specter that stalked the creek bottom. His eyes swept the high rises, the coulees with their patches of wild rose, the deep little ravines filled with pine trees. Soon the rose heps would split and drop their silky seeds. The sick willows and aspens would drop their leaves, maybe for good, and his own tree of bone would drop its pale leaves of flesh. What he felt was partly a panic that he had left a calf lying back there somewhere in the grass, where its mother had hidden it. He wanted to ride back and scour the whole range, foot by foot, to find that calf. Then he told himself that he was behaving like a damn fool, that they'd counted the bunch and that the total tallied with the number in the battered, dirty little book he carried in the breast pocket of his shirt.

So he turned Crowder toward the road. He noted with morose satisfaction how old 94, walking doggedly on her bad feet, had taken the lead through the gate, as usual. She knew the way down to the home ranch as well as he did. The rest massed behind her, dark backs piling together like thunderheads before a storm.

"Next year both of us will be gone," he thought. It occurred to him that this was the second time in his life he had had to go through a last roundup. That kind of thing shouldn't happen twice to any man.

They had eased the herd along the county road a mile or so when Brodie glanced back over his shoulder and saw Honeycut's two bulls following them. His mouth tightened with anger like a cinch, and the whip started to tremble again. He snapped at Vin, "I thought you told me those bulls weren't loose on the road."

"Huh?" said Vin, looking back too. "I'll be damned," he said when he saw the bulls.

"Guess you didn't look careful enough."

The two bulls were swinging along at a heavy, determined walk, their eyes fixed on the cows up ahead. They were two monsters that might have come shouldering up out of the bottom of Brodie's dreams. One of them was a polled bull with popeyes and a lot of white splashed over his bony brown frame—his naturally hornless skull was huge and strangely domed, like those critters from outer space in the TV science-fiction movies. The other bull was a coarse, low-set grade Hereford with big feet. He had somehow broken off one of his horns just recently, and the horn still hung down right by his eye. His jaw was caked with black dried-up blood.

Lloyd Honeycut, ruminated Brodie, was a no-good, nester-type rancher who let his juvenile delinquent kids roam over the hills, ping away at Brodie's cows and antelope with .22 rifles, and throw rocks through the windows of Brodie's cow-camp cabin. Even though Brodie didn't use that cabin anymore, the broken windows made him mad. Honeycut apparently didn't know how to fix fences or even keep gates closed, or else he was dreadfully short of grass, because his mongrel stock was always roaming loose on the roads, up there on the bench. Time and again Brodie had seen the bulls loose along the road. The last time, he had ridden Crowder up to Honeycut's place and sworn to Honeycut that he would castrate those bulls if he caught them breeding his cows. Honeycut had said hastily, "Yeah, yeah, I'll get that fence fixed next week." That was a month ago.

Brodie looked back at his cows. They were pushing along slowly behind old 94, already heating up, with their dust hanging over them in the tail wind. Their hindquarters were wet and green with nervous manure, and they left trails of spatters behind them on the dusty road. Already the calves were dropping back to the drag, mouths open, pink tongue tips out, flanks pumping, little tails hanging limply. Brodie saw two cows in heat too—they were bulling, rearing up on the hindquarters of their neighbors, then sliding down into the mass of brown backs again.

"We've got two cows bulling in there," Brodie said to Vin. "We don't want those bulls getting in to them. You've got the young horse, so you ride back there and drive those bulls back a ways."

"Why don't you open a gate somewheres," said Vin, "and just shove the bulls through?"

"Only other gate along here is the Chances' gate," said Brodie, "and they got heifers in there."

"Thought you didn't like the Chances."

"I wouldn't wish those devil bulls on the Chances, even. Run them on back a ways now."

"Christ, we'll be up here all day," said Vin. "I'll never get to the rodeo." He jerked Curlew around and galloped back up the road. Brodie looked on as the two bulls stopped to watch Vin approach, ugly heads high and eyes suspicious. Then the polled bull swerved heavily around and ran. But the ranker one feinted at Curlew with his one good horn, then dodged past and come trotting straight down the road toward Brodie. Brodie cursed Vin's ineptness at cutting and pulled poor old Crowder around, actually feeling the soreness in the horse's knees as if it were arthritis in his own joints. Yelling his very best cow-punching "'Yaaaaah!" he headed the bull off and chased him back up the road past Vin, leaning over to pound the bull on the butt with his stockyard whip. The whip left dusty crisscrosses on the bull's brown hide. He wondered if the exertion would start up that pain in his chest again.

When Vin came back, he knew he had performed badly, and he couldn't meet Brodie's eyes. "Even Skookum Joe," said Brodie, not looking at Vin either, "can punch cows better than you."

"Seems like there's no pleasing you," said Vin, hurt eroding at the bare slope of his voice like a heavy rain. "I just try and try."

"It ain't a question of pleasing me," said Brodie. "There's a right way of doing things and a wrong way, that's all. Punching cows is only for crazy people, anyway. All the red-blooded American kids in Cottonwood, they leave town and go to the States the first chance they get. There's nothing for a kid to do in Cottonwood anymore except make trouble, like that Kitie Chance on her motorcycle. It's an old man's town. Old men, old horses. But along comes Vinsky, now, and wants to be a cowpoke. I just don't understand it."

He looked over at Vin's profile sliding along against the wire fence and the yellow cured grass beyond. The muscles in Vin's jaws were working. He wondered how far he would be able to provoke Vin that day.

After a minute or two, Vin said, "My mother says that back in Europe people read about cowboys a lot. There was this German writer, I forget his name. He wrote books about cowboys over there."

That set Brodie to thinking about where Vin had come from. Vin's real name was Sviatoslav Vinnyk, or something like that. Brodie had seen the name written out on Vin's hunting license. But since nobody in Cottonwood could pronounce the name, people had nicknamed him Vin. He had arrived in Cottonwood as a four-year-old in 1948, about the time Brodie first started hearing of short-legged yellow bulls. His mother was a DP widow who explained in what Brodie called "green-broke English" that she was Ukrainian and got mad if anybody called her a Russian. Cottonwoodians thought that anybody from that part of the world was automatically a "Rooshin." It appeared that Ukrainians and Russians had even less use for each other than white men and Indians. "Ukrainsky, no Roosky," Vin's mother would cry at her neighbors over the peeling picket fence of the old frame house on Silver Street where she had settled. Brodie had to admit that the Cottonwood centennial was Vin's too. He was no more alien than the Irish railroad conductors, the Polack mineworkers, and the Basque sheepherders who came to live and die in Cottonwood. In fact, the only alien who ever left Cottonwood for good was old Tom Wing, who saved his money for a fancy coffin and had himself shipped back to China when he died to be buried with his own kind.

Vin was always bragging about his father, who, he said, was a guerrilla killed while fighting the Commie armies in the mountains in his country. Vin's father must have been a man's man, Brodie thought —too bad he wasn't around now to show his boy what being a man really involved. Maybe that was why Vin liked guns so much. While haying every summer on the outlying ranches during high school, Vin had learned Cottonwood's habits with firearms a little too well, even for a pilgrim. He bought a secondhand .22 rifle and massacred the local magpies, taking in strings of their heads for the fifty-cent bounty. Then he graduated to a .30-.30 and poached deer and antelope. Brodie wondered how much taste the widow Vinnyk had for all that wild meat Vin brought home; it was rumored she lived mostly on spuds. Brodie also wondered if Vin hadn't poached a little veal here and there. Rustling was the only sector of the cow business, besides bank loans, that was busier and more profitable now than seventy-five years ago. Vin also got infected with the last of Cottonwood's fever for horses. But he was always getting bucked off hopelessly at the local rodeo— he never quite got the hang of riding as if the money was in the mane. Both Vern Stuart and Tom Chance finally fired Vin from their hay-crews for being fiddlebrained. But in the meantime Vin had heard that cranky old Pint Brodie was the real thing, the way the old big-rowelled steel spurs that chimed when a man walked were the real things. So after Vin had married a fast town girl named Marilyn Rainville (with whom everybody knew Johnny Chance had once been in love), and after he went to Vietnam where he got his Ph.D. with an M-16 and collected a string of Viet Cong ears (or so he said), he drifted up to the 5 Up 5 Down determined to work there as a full-time cowboy. Since cranky old Brodie (he reflected on himself) was desperate for men and unable to keep any for very long being such a perfectionist, and since Vin hung onto him like a tick on a horse's back in spring, it looked like he and Vin were doomed to play buckaroo and pilgrim to each other for all eternity.

Sometimes Brodie could feel the crush of Vin's sullen admiration so keenly that he could almost see himself reflected in Vin's dark, brutish gaze: a little old man who still stood as straight as a gopher standing on his hill. A little old man with hair whiter than alkalai, wearing outworn black britches, a broad, high-crowned black hat, and scarred old chaps with silver conchos down the side—clothes that belonged in a Charlie Russell painting. A little old man as spiky and sharp as an antelope horn. Under shaggy silver brows, his gray eyes were as unblinking and opaque as an animal's, and their defective oblong pupils, exactly like those in a horse's eyes, had given rise to the saying in Cottonwood that his mother had been a mare with few morals. He could even see himself riding in Vin's eyes. His arms flapped up and down curiously as Crowder galloped, but he sat with a skill that had left arrogance fifty years behind. He was amused at how Vin tried to copy this flapping mannerism.

Yet Vin, he knew, had never learned the grass-blade-thin difference between Pinter Brodie and the Chances. Brodie considered the Chances almost as pilgrim as Vin because, though their grandfather did settle in Cottonwood in the early days, they had sold out those virtues bred in the heat and dust of the 1870s. They had sold out to modern vulgarities, to an easy way of getting things done and living fancy on credit, when any man knew that the only way worth doing things was the hard way, cash on the barrelhead, with no complaint but a straight-faced wisecrack. As for Vern Stuart, the third big rancher there at Cottonwood, Brodie shrugged him off with his arrogant down-easter wife, his hopped-up Quarter Horses that were like tea roses compared to sagebrush, and his tomboy daughter that anybody could see had a little bitty screw loose somewhere. Vern sometimes stopped by to discuss their common water rights on Dog Creek (the prison farm had been stealing water from them both), and little Beth usually came along. Brodie always had this ghostly feeling that the girl was someone as little and crazy as he was. He understood that Vern had no sons and that someone in the next generation had to take over the ranch someday. But Beth was not the same as one of those Western women who could do a man's job if she had to. Brodie sometimes felt that ghosts of those whang-leather women had entered Beth and were always looking out of her eyes, as if they were knotholes. When a world died, its virtues remained, living a haunted life, looking for old houses and young people to crawl into.

Jessie, now, had been the right kind of woman. Many years ago, too many to count now, Brodie had considered Jessie. But in those days, he pondered, he had not yet learned the human condition by living a little removed from it and observing it from afar, as other men learned about wild animals by spying on them with binoculars. And in those days he was already late, and so he thought about Jessie too long. For one thing, he wondered if she was too young for him—he'd been thirty-seven then, and she was only seventeen. He wondered, too, if she would survive being dug up out of town soil and transplanted onto the breaks and the buttes where the wind hit hard. It would have been like trying to make a tea rose do the work of sagebrush, he thought. And while he thought Jessie over, Jessie got impatient, for she might have been town stuff but she wasn't a minute late. She married Henry Fulton. Henry ran the greenhouse on Powderhouse Hill, right along the road where he always had to pass with the cattle. From the bench, Brodie could see the sun flash off the greenhouse. Whenever he saw it, he felt something snap taut inside of him, like a rope when a thousand-pound steer hits the end of it.

He and Vin kept pushing the cows down the county road, as it ran straight along toward the edge of the bench. On either side of the road there was a twenty-foot strip of grass and a shallow ditch. The two bulls kept coming up on them. Brodie and Vin had to keep driving them back, and they kept getting madder at each other. The herd got hotter and hotter, the cows crowding closer and slower, the calves smothering in the dust of the drag. If it weren't for old 94 rolling doggedly along on her curled-up feet, the herd might have sulled to a halt. Brodie's mind became crowded with monsters. The photo archives of memory ran wild, file drawers jerking open, yellowed prints flipping over at high speed. A. E. Huffman was riding out with his tripod on his horse to take pictures of the Cottonwood valley when it had been a lake, when the flat benchland on either side of the valley had been the bottom of the lake. Then the lake dried up, leaving only the river to cut down the middle, carrying away silt and carving a broad valley. The animals in those days were monsters trailing through the valley in huge herds—the way Brodie imagined it, Huffman took some magnificent black-and-white photos of the herds of mastodons, with their huge, domed skulls and their curly tusks that looked like the horns of Texas steers. The mastodons left their bones everywhere to wash down out of the hillsides in a hard rain, and the cottonwoods made up their minds to grow along that new river. The Indians moved in, then the white men. Finally Pinter Brodie trailed down out of those heads with 628 Hereford cows and one Rooshin cowboy. Someday soon Pinter Brodie's bones would wash down out of some hillside there, and a paleontologist from the state university would sift them out of the gravel, write little numbers on them, and paint them with preservative.

The paleontologist would notice a bullet hole in the skull, though Brodie wasn't sure yet whether it would be Vin's .45 or his own good Winchester in the scabbard in the Jack Rabbit.

Vin kept playing with his pistol butt. Brodie had seen him practicing fast draws. Back in the old days, of course, there hadn't been much of the fast-draw business. There had been Wyatt Earp, of course, but most fellas, if they wanted to kill somebody, dry-gulched him quietly somewhere, preferably in the back. The heroism of the old days had been done with the soul, not with guns. Now, for lack of anyone else to haunt, heroism had moved into Vin and tried vainly to infuse its fragrance of old wood into Vin's prefabricated walls.

"Think your dad would approve of you playing with water pistols?" Brodie asked.

"My dad was a guerrilla," said Vin. "He fought the Commies, and they killed him."

"Yeah, I know," said Brodie. He turned Crowder away to gently push along a few hot little late-summer calves that had dropped too far behind.

"The Russians took a lot of those Ukrainian guerrillas prisoner," Vin went on. "And they massacred 'em all, and sent their families to concentration camps."

Brodie decided that he wouldn't rise to this play for his sympathies. "You should have reenlisted," he said. "They don't have to ride horses in the army anymore."

"Oh," said Vin, "I was just plain tired of shooting those little yella guys in pajamas. Needed a change of scene, so to speak."

"Movin' on to old men," said Brodie.

"Maybe so could be," said Vin.

Old Dr. Erickson had said that he wouldn't try to fool Brodie. Erickson knew that Brodie lived alone, but he didn't say that out loud. "Pint," he said, "I'd advise you to get your affairs in order. Sooner or later this heart condition of yours is going to incapacitate you. You'll need to be somewhere where they can look after you proper."

"You mean a nursing home?"

"Well, not exactly," said Erickson. "But I know a good place out near Spokane, better than most. It's expensive, but it's a real cheerful place, where I'd feel I could put one of my own kin."

"What you're trying to say," asked Brodie, "is that this thing is going to make a vegetable out of me?"

So Brodie had been putting off talking to a lawyer, because he didn't believe in paying lawyers. Anyway, he didn't know what he wanted to say in a will. It would be real nice to leave the ranch to somebody, he reflected. He had the idea that Vin wanted to ingratiate himself, seeing a rank old man with no heirs or relatives. But he was damn if he would leave all that good native hay land and range land to a psycho gunsel kid who wouldn't know what to do with it. What he really should do was sell out this fall, when and if the cattle market went up. He should have a big auction and sell cattle for two, three, four days. Maybe he should advertise all the antique furniture and old wagons and buggies, and auction those too—there was a small fortune in the old buggies around the place alone. Then he would let the best offer take the land. He knew he could wind up a sale in thirty days. A sheep ranch down the valley went to a mining company for a million dollars—they had struck antimony there. If he sold out, he wouldn't have the grief of trying to fight Intermountain and the power company. Actually, he should go up there and shoot a few company men —that was the only language people like that understood. Yes, maybe that was a good idea, he thought—he would surprise Vin and will all the money from the sales to the conservation folks—for instance the Environmental Defense Fund—to help finance those long, expensive court fights over pollution.

"Look," he wanted to say to Dr. Erickson, "all my life I've been getting my own self around. When I was a kid, I could lick any man in these three counties. One time I heard about a guy in the next county who was saying he could lick me. I got on my horse and rode over there—that was before there were any cars in Cottonwood, you know—and I broke him in four, five, six, seven pieces. Look at me now. In an age when all we need is one little bitty step to get a man on the moon, I can still wear out two pair of stirrup leathers a year. I laid in a whole supply of leathers from Dan Buck, in Helena over there, before his saddlery went out of business, and I've still got a dozen pair left. In the summer I still take my bedroll outdoors and sleep in the brush like an old mosshorn steer."

Dr. Erickson had only shrugged sorrowfully, as if it wouldn't have mattered whether there were twelve pairs of stirrup leathers or only one pair. Dr. Erickson was having his own financial troubles—he was always grumbling about how practicing general medicine in a small town these days was a shortcut to the poorhouse, except, Dr. Erickson added, that they didn't call it the poorhouse anymore. He was always saying that if he had any sense, he would clear out, the way the young people did. But, he said, old cottonwood trees wouldn't transplant east of the Missouri or down to California.

As for old Crowder, Brodie thought, who might be sold for dog food by a less honorable owner, there would be a .30-30 bullet in the forehead. This would be the best and most final thanks.

So there was the Fulton greenhouse down there, shining in the Sunday sunlight at the bottom of Powderhouse Hill. And there was Jessie, too, halfway out to him from town, yet whirled away from him forever now, the way the great herds were whirled away by the northers in the winter of '87. Jessie flourished in her controlled but fertile world of sun doubled through a glass roof, her world with its gentle but definite hazards (great herds of seedlings swept away forever by an epidemic of mildew), her world that would never make it into the archives and the history books. There she was, he told himself, and all he had to do was look at her flowers to know what a damn fine ranch wife she would have made. The good range had been there inside her somewhere, and simple, bumbling Henry Fulton had known how to drive around the drill and plant the right grasses. He had seen Jessie pinch back young dahlias with as gentle but severe a hand as his own on Crowder's rein when he was cutting calves out of the herd. She moved as slowly and surely as sunlight along the mossy benches inside the greenhouse. Her pansies flowed out in flats to make funny faces in the gardens of Cottonwood. Her geraniums and lobelia told tall tales about death in the Hillcrest Cemetery. Her tea roses released their quaint but immortal fragrance on the bridge tables of Cottonwood's fussiest hostesses. With her around, Brodie thought, all Henry had to do, aside from the heavy work like trucking manure and pruning roots, was keep books and watch the calendar.

Brodie managed to see Jessie two or three times a year. After the last frost in spring, he took the excuse to drive over to the greenhouse and buy a flat of her pansies to set out by his bunkhouse. He'd return just before Memorial Day to buy a few of her geraniums to put on the Brodie plot, even though he wasn't one to worry about prettying graves.

Memorial Day in Cottonwood—now that was really a piece of Americana, Brodie thought. The Veterans of Foreign Wars marched stiffly along Main Street, loaded with braid and insignias. They were all ages—creaky old men who'd fought in World War I, middle-aged World War II pilots, and a few young Korea and Vietnam veterans.

Vin marched with them, of course. The flag slanted and snapped over their caps, and a single high-school bugler and snare-drummer stepped along with them.

The Vets would march solemnly across the railroad tracks onto the concrete bridge over the Cottonwood River. There they would halt at attention while the bugle played goodnight. With self-conscious solemnity, they would fire a volley of blanks out over the sick-orange-green river—taps for the trout as well as the boys fallen on foreign soil. Then the Vets would march on out of town for half a mile, along the dusty road between the hay fields on the west side of town. The sun would beat down on them, as they turned in at the gate of the cemetery.

Cars would be parked everywhere, and people carried trowels or stooped over green florist boxes. Jessie's flowers would be everywhere —in pots, papier-mâché vases, planters, even gallon tin cans. Her flowers would lie bound in bouquets on shiny new granite plaques set level with the grass, in the modern part of the cemetery, where the cottonwoods were scarcely a dozen feet tall. They would grace the tall sculptured marble monuments of fifty years ago, that spoke of fortunes and security under big trailing birches. Even in the oldest part of the cemetery, Jessie's flowers would glow in the gloom under the thickest trees, by the toppling marble tablets and above-ground brick graves of a century ago. Jessie's flowers honored and comforted the Cottonwood dead, who—Brodie knew, because he was one of them —didn't give a damn about honor and comfort any longer. All the dead were concerned with was the slow release of nitrogen into the soil from their composted bones. Jessie complained that there were more and more traitors in town who bought plastic flowers and wreaths. Next year, maybe, Brodie thought, Jessie would come and put some geraniums and lobelia on his grave, and she would read the inscription "Pinter Brodie 1902–1971." The inscription on Grandfather Brodie's tombstone would have made a lot more sense on his own:

> Leaves have their time to fall
> And flowers to wither at the north winds' breath,
> But thou alone of all,
> Thou hast all seasons for thine own death.

(Actually, he would prefer to be buried on a high hill somewhere on his own range, where the cows and the antelope could walk gently and unthinkingly over the top of him, with no flowers to adorn him but a few prickly pears and bitterroots. But he was aware that town sanitary regulations wouldn't allow such gestures.)

All morning, as the people fussed with flowers, the VFW would march around over the dusty gravel paths of the cemetery. Wherever a little bleached flag fluttered beside a grave, they would stop and fire a volley of blanks, and the echoes would crack out against the hills. It gave the Vets something to do besides shake their fists at Commie-inspired student riots. The cemetery would murmur with quiet socializing and reminiscing, as everybody wandered around and looked at everyone else's flowers. Brodie would be there too, cranky and silent, putting Jessie's geraniums into planters at the corner of the cemetery plot. And if it had been a warm spring and the lilacs were already in bloom, he would have brought a great bunch of lilacs broken off the hedge beside the ranch house and would arrange them in big tin cans (he couldn't see wasting money on fancy vases). When the work was done, everybody would get into their cars and go home to a big formal lunch, where they went on reminiscing. Brodie was of the opinion that Memorial Day was the real centennial celebration, not the one planned for the fairgrounds.

Once or twice Brodie had even gone to Jessie in the fall to get a few tulips to stick in the ground by the ranch house. He knew, though they exchanged only the most casual words, that Jessie saw in his look that he regretted the lateness. He also saw that she smiled, that she gave him a few cents' discount on the plants because she knew what a skinflint he was. He knew that she did not judge him, as surely as he knew her geraniums did not judge him either. He would almost have preferred a sour look from her, or a bitter word, rather than the naked sight of this steadiness that he had cut straight out of his life the way he was going to cut out old 94.

So there he was on the brow of Powderhouse Hill with the herd, as he had been for years now, and he saw the sun flash off the greenhouse, as he always did from this spot. At that moment, something unrolled and stared inside of him, like a purple pansy making its funny face of death in the unweeded flowerbed of his soul.

"I'll tell you one on myself," he said to Vin as the herd started over the edge of the bench and down along Powderhouse Hill.

"Huh?" said Vin, who was whistling the cows along and not even glancing back to see if the two bulls were following.

"Yeah. About my first go-round on the cattle market," said

Brodie. "It was in the fall of '30, thereabouts. I had ninety two-year-old steers weighing out about eight hundred pounds each, and a fella offered me ninety dollars a head for them, which was a real good price in those days. And I said no, I wanted a hundred dollars, but he wouldn't go the extra ten. So I wintered those steers over, and come spring they weighed nearly a thousand pounds. And the best I could get a buyer to give me for them was thirty dollars a head, and that was above the market price too."

"Gee. That was real dumb," said Vin coolly, turning Curlew away a little and whistling at two lagging calves.

Brodie jerked as if he had picked up by mistake the glowing red end of a hot branding iron. What had he expected Vin to say? He wasn't sure. Out of the edge of his eye he saw the two bulls coming up behind again, and at that his self-control snapped, the way a galloping horse's foreleg snaps when the horse steps in a gopher hole.

"Dumb?" Brodie shouted in a shrill voice. "And you set there and let them two bulls get past you!"

The broken-horned bull shouldered through the panting calves and piled forward among the cows, his eyes on one that was bulling. The polled bull, apparently realizing that he might have to fight his partner now, but apprehensive because of his lack of weapons, paused to drop his head, sniff the road, and paw dust up over his shoulders. Then he stretched up his muzzle and gave a deep rumbling bawl.

"Making war medicine, huh?" Brodie shouted at the polled bull. "Well, go on, make war not love." He cut the polled bull back from the herd and beat it across the rump as he hazed it up the road. When Brodie wheeled Crowder back to get the second bull, he could feel the old horse struggle to respond as he had been trained for long years, fight to keep all his knees under him. Vin, pale as cemetery marble under his suntan, was fumblingly trying to reach the broken-horned bull, who was in amid the swirling cows. He was busy sniffing the hindquarters of a cow in heat, but the cow plunged away from him irritably, not content to let him mount her yet.

"Get out of my way, you dumb little Rooshin;" Brodie said. "Dumb. I'll show you who's dumb around here."

Expertly he hazed a handful of cows to one side, creating an eddy in the herd that carried the bulling cows momentarily from reach, leaving the bull exposed and confused. Brodie drove in behind the bull, between him and the eddying cows. Reaching down, he seized the bull's manure-wet tail and twisted it into a curlicue, so hard that he heard it crack. The bull bellowed and bucked with pain, then lunged into a heavy gallop away from the herd. Brodie drove him a few hundred yards up the road, cursing the circumstance that put no gates to empty pastures along this road. Then he galloped Crowder back, arms flapping with magnificent abandon.

The cows, upset now, suffocating in the heat, wouldn't drive. They milled and jostled there, bawling, bleary eyed, shoving the dazed calves this way and that. Here in the lee of Powderhouse Hill, where there was no breeze, it was hotter than ever. The herd was a cauldron of dust and tossing horns.

Then Brodie had to assert himself, the way a roundup boss would have done in the old days to squelch mutiny among his riders or silence an overquarrelsome cook—by chancing an insult so terrible that the recipient didn't dare try to avenge it. Vin was waiting for Brodie's outburst, white and tense. He had Curlew facing uphill on the side of the road, standing in a patch of suncured foxtails, near the barbed wire fence bounding the Chances' heifer range.

"Dumb," said Brodie in his curlew-shrill voice, not even looking at Vin, as if he were talking to some third person. He drew Crowder around so that his back was turned to Vin. "Only one thing dumber than an old cowboy, and that's a Roosky kid who thinks he's a cowboy. And I mean, a Roosky kid who wears his pecker in his holster."

"Dad, don't you turn your back on me like that," shouted Vin, his voice cracking with furious tears, like rocks crack in the frost. Brodie heard Curlew backing up noisily over the gravel on the side of the road and knew that Vin's hand was unconsciously tight on the reins. Curlew still had some of the sensitive mouth that Brodie had put in him.

"And no Roosky kid calls me Dad," Brodie hollered back, still not looking at him, wondering if Vin would pull the gun on him now. That would be one way of getting it over with, without all that nervous tension of getting around to doing it himself (he'd be late even for that).

Still hauling unconsciously on the reins, Vin snatched at his pistol. Brodie saw the movement out of the corner of his eye and wondered if the kid would really kill him or just try to scare him. He wasn't sure which would disappoint him more. Just then Curlew, with head strained back and mouth open, started backing convulsively downhill again, and put both hind hoofs into a huge eroded gopher hole. He strained with his strong young forequarters to keep from falling back, but failed, and rolled over backwards onto his haunches.

Brodie saw him go slowly over, like a huge fir tree with the logging crew yelling "Timberrrr!" and running clear. Curlew was an immense dignity of sweaty, speckled belly, soaked cinches, and Vin's booted feet as he fell away from Brodie like spires of rock collapsing, like a whole side of the Grand Canyon roaring off down into the river.

Jaws open, eyes rolling in terror, Curlew rolled right back over his tail, slamming Vin into the barbed wire. Brodie heard Vin give a hoarse shriek as the big roan gelding's thousand pounds of weight scraped him down along the barbs. He could hear Vin's shirt ripping, his leather belt catching and hanging, and thought he could even hear the barbs scratching across bone. His mind seemed to stop. For some reason he thought of when the government brought the Minuteman missiles to Montana. Out on the desolate grasslands, they had built great underground silos for the missiles. Now the guards were asleep or playing poker, and the missiles had gone mad and were quietly readying themselves for a launch, the consoles flashing red warnings, shining machinery pushing the missiles' snouts up into the sunlight. Brodie also remembered—was it a month or a year ago—the night he had stood in the dark ranch-house yard, after going out to move the sprinkler, and stared at the stars. After awhile he noticed one star actually moving past the others, streaking along with mute, mindless power. Brodie's hair stood on end as he wondered if he had discovered a new comet that some public-spirited astronomer would name after him. The Brodie Comet sounded fine, he thought. But then he realized that it was a satellite. Maybe it was Echo—or had Echo burned out by then? Maybe it was a Rooshin satellite. He stood watching its vulgar, unblinking light, the reflection of distant sunlight off the dead metal hull, until it faded down toward the horizon. All during the time he watched, an anger was walking up out of him, slow and dark, like a lone, lame, monster bull coming up out of the wild-rose thickets, pawing dust up on his back and making war medicine.

Curlew rolled over onto his side. Then he scrambled up, leaving the fence half down and Vin lying in the silvery foxtail grass. Vin rose to his knees, then bent over, gasping. As Brodie rode up, he could see the blood already dripping through the tatters of Vin's shirt and soaking through his sleeves as it ran down his arms underneath.

Practical man that he was, Brodie glanced at Curlew first and saw that, though the roan gelding was hunched and shaken, he looked unhurt. He had a few deep scratches on his powerful speckled rump, and one of his hind feet was bleeding above the hoof, where it had slid down into the hole. What worried Brodie was that Curlew was standing with both hind feet between two of the sagging fence wires. If he spooked and got the wire looped around his legs, he would skin the hide off them as neatly as peeling a banana.

So, forgetting his tight chest for a moment, Brodie quickly got off Crowder and went to Curlew's head. The horse didn't move, just stared at him, trembling all over. Brodie sensed that Curlew knew his precise problem and was waiting for help. He took the reins, speaking softly, and pushed the wire to the ground with one boot. Then he slapped Curlew's shoulder to make the gelding step away from the fence. Curlew lifted his hoofs very high as he stepped clear.

"Only horse I ever saw smarter than a mule," Brodie said out loud. Then he let Curlew's reins go and went to Vin.

Vin was still bending over on hands and knees, head hanging. "Dad," he said hoarsely, "I'm hurt real bad." All around him the ripe, bleached foxtails were crushed and spotted with blood.

"Well, I guess there's a god," said Brodie, "because he paid you back for running that poor heifer into the wire."

"Dad," moaned Vin, more loudly, "I'm going to die. Don't let me die."

"Why, you no-good Roosky half-a-kid, if there was any buzzards in these parts, I'd take the herd on and leave you for them." Brodie bent over Vin to see where he was hurt. Vin grabbed hold of Brodie's arm and held on with a tearing pull, like the roots of a cottonwood clinging to the ground in a high wind.

Brodie tried to straighten up (it was hard because Vin was holding onto him so hard, climbing up him like the terrible Virginia creepers that grew up the side of the old bunkhouse) and looked around at the milling cows. A realization of his predicament yawned open in him like those missile silos. His duty unfortunately dictated that he get Vin to the hospital down in town. But if he went off and left the herd, one of those bulls would breed the cows in heat. Nor could he sit there with Vin on that empty road waiting for help, for it might be hours before anyone drove up that way, especially on Sunday, with a rodeo and a centennial going on. The sunlight shone off the roof of the Fulton greenhouse, striking through him like those lasers he read about in the magazines. He hesitated between staying with the herd and going to ask the Fultons for help. If it were his son lying there, he would let the cows go to hell, he thought.

"Look," he finally said, "you get up on Curlew there and get yourself down to Fultons, and they'll call the hospital. Henry won't be there, probably, but Jessie will. If I leave these cattle, they'll scatter from Jerusalem to breakfast, and those cows—"

"I can't," Vin moaned.

Brodie pried himself loose from Vin, his feelings going hard again, like wet clay soil drying up and cracking in the sun. He got up and brought Curlew over, looking anxiously at the horse again. Curlew was limping a little. Possibly he had corked himself with one of his shoes.

"Come on now, get up there," he said, trying to pull Vin to his feet. "Don't be a baby. You lose a little blood, it'll clear your head good."

"I can't," Vin shouted, "I just can't." One leg buckled under him and he slid back down to an awkward sitting position. It dawned on Brodie then that the leg was injured, maybe broken. Vin should have climbed for the high side when Curlew went over, but that might have been hard with all those barbs in the way. The barbs had turned Vin's back under the way the honyokers' plows did the grass. Brodie felt wetness on his hands and looking, saw that they were smeared with blood.

"You old bastard," Vin shouted, "all you care about is them cows."

"Damn right," Brodie shouted back. "Even the toughest-looking dry is worth more than you."

Brodie looked back up the road. The two bulls were walking slowly toward him, about a hundred yards up the hill. He had to make the kind of decision that neither schooling or living prepared a man for, and anyway he had never gone to college. There was one last alternative, and that was to take Vin's Colt pistol and shoot the two bulls. But a man didn't do that either, not back in the day when you thoughtfully shipped your neighbor's strays with your own, so that the state brand inspector could locate the neighbor and see to it that he got a check. Yes, it was the fences that had caused all the problems, fences between yards and between people, so that when you stopped caring for your neighbor's cattle, you stopped caring for your neighbor too. Fences between what a man did and what he ought to do, fences that invited cutting, fences that tore flesh and summoned rust.

"All right," said Brodie. "You hold on here, and I'll go get some help. I'll be back in five, ten, fifteen minutes."

"I'm bleeding. I'll bleed to death. The ambulance is at the fairgrounds. Can't you stop the bleeding?"

"Well, I ain't going clear to the fairgrounds. I'll go down to Fultons there, or maybe Alfalfaville, and find somebody home with a truck."

As he turned to step up on Crowder, it occurred to him that he could ride Curlew and at least have a fast, young horse under him. But Curlew was limping a little too much for hard using. So Brodie mounted poor old Crowder again and pushed on downhill, past the herd. It hurt him so much to feel Crowder twinging downhill that he wondered if his heart and Crowder's knees were in the same place. The cows were quieting a little—not walking anymore, a few dropping their heads to graze or looking for their calves. At least, Brodie thought, they'll cool off some and they'll drive better. He didn't want to look back and see those two mongrel bulls ambling slowly up to the unprotected herd. He would lose a whole year on each cow bred, and the only revenge he could take on Honeycut would be to make steers out of the mongrel calves (if they were born bulls) and slaughter them for his meat cooler—he had no use for those tasteless cornfed steaks they sold at the Safeway supermarket down in town. Of course, at this moment, one year lost on two cows didn't matter very much, since he might not be around when the calves were dropped. What he really should have done was take Vin's pistol for his own using.

When he was past the herd, he set Crowder into a raw, rattling canter along the empty road. The road curved down past the grassy mound of Powderhouse Hill, where the old powderhouse had caved in. He passed the mournful kilns of the abandoned brickyard, where they'd made the bricks for the big houses on Grand Street and for the chimneys on his ranch house. His son lay bleeding back there in the sun-cured foxtails, his son that he had always cut away at a high gallop, like a dark shadow from his herd. He reminded himself of the times when he'd been hurt and alone. Once, when he was seventeen and alone up at cow camp, he was foolhardy enough to step up on a green-broke bronc outside the corral. The bronc broke himself in four, five, six, seven pieces and reared over backwards, cracking

Brodie's leg. He was stranded up there for two days before Uncle
Charlie missed him and sent someone to look for him. He had gone a
little stiff-legged after that. Then there was the time, just a couple of
winters ago, when he'd gotten the flu and had lain there in the old
house scarcely able to keep himself warm and feed himself. He could
have used the phone in the ranch office to call Dr. Erickson or the
drugstore, but he didn't believe in pills. So he just lay there and shook,
with the temperature at thirty below outside. It was a good thing that
he'd had that guy with the .357 Magnum to keep the cows fed. At
times in his life, it had occurred to him that he was all alone, that even
the animals were indifferent to his fate, as they were to each other's.

The Fultons won't be home, he thought. They'll both be at the
rodeo, or Sunday visiting, or gone to Oregon on vacation. Now was a
slack season in the greenhouse.

He galloped Crowder through the Fultons' gate, up the gravel
road that ended beside the greenhouse. Crowder's hoof-clops echoed
eerily along the glass walls of the greenhouse. It stood shimmering,
palatial, strange, in the afternoon sun. "Fulton's Greenhouse and
Nursery," said a neatly lettered white wooden sign. "Perennials, An-
nuals, Shrubs and Trees." The Fultons managed to keep up appear-
ances even in these days, though Jessie complained that flowers weren't
selling the way they used to. She had sold a lot of flowers to the
centennial, though, for decorating the floats in the parade. He looked
at the forest of tall pink, blue, and white delphiniums growing in the
manure-dug bed along the greenhouse (he had given the Fultons that
manure). Jessie had the plants neatly staked so that they wouldn't
lodge in a heavy rain or wind, and he realized all over again how late
he was. The Fultons' green pickup wasn't there. He thought that he'd
have to ride clear down into Alfalfaville. But as he looked over at the
Fultons' crack-walled stucco house, with a great purple-flowered cle-
matis vine spread like a bloodstain on its south wall, he noticed that
the side screen door stood open. His heart constricted, whether with
pain or relief he didn't know, as he saw someone moving around in
the greenhouse. He climbed stiffly off Crowder—for his muscles seemed
to have aged two thousand years, another glacier age to have come
and gone and another valley been carved out, settled up, and rusted
away with barbed wire, since he started down the hill—and went into
the greenhouse.

The moist heat of the place struck him like a blow, muffling the
ringing of his darkened old steel spurs. Far off across the empty

benches and stacked-up wooden flats, far off beyond a screen of hanging plants, he saw Jessie moving. He strode awkwardly among the benches. His chaps brushed a stack of empty clay pots, knocking it over and sending the pots rolling, clattering.

At the noise, Jessie looked up. She was potting some strange kind of bulb, pressing bark chips around it in the pot. Several more bulbs lay on the table, with the opened mailing box labeled by some nursery back East. She was wearing sneakers and a faded black-and-white-checked cotton dress that he thought he remembered; it hung loose everywhere on her sturdy frame except over the bosom, where it was as tight as that potted bulb. Her long, noble, sinewy, hard face, with its pink, pored skin, was a lot like Crowder's, he thought, as it focused on her work with a contained joy that was not quite emotion. Behind her, the glass wall was forested with a climbing tender tea rose, so heavy with blooms that Brodie thought he could hear it tearing loose and falling. The panes stood ajar—Jessie had told him how you had to be careful and let air circulate around the rose or it would mildew. She, at least, had her world and her time under control. Cowboys might be obsolete, but roses weren't—at least, not yet. Brodie took off his dusty, black old hat and stood holding it tremblingly.

When Jessie looked up and saw him, she smiled slowly. The smile plowed a dimple on either side of her pink unpainted mouth. He couldn't remember what Jessie had looked like when she was seventeen, except he remembered that she had had those dimples. Under her lids, iridescent with fatigue, and her short, unglamorous eyelashes, her brown eyes refused judgment, as always. She had a large wen on her chin, and always smelled of vanilla and moss. Her hands paused, still grasping the pot caressingly.

"Well, Pint, what brings you around this time of year?" she said. "It's a little early for tulips."

He stood wordless, as if he'd come to propose instead of ask for help.

"These are orchids," she said, pointing at the bulbs. "Imagine orchids in Cottonwood. Henry lets me spent a little pin money on them." She waved a hand around at the hanging plants—draped lacy ferns, red begonias, and purple gloxinias heavy with velvet Victorian blooms. "These are my plants. I don't sell them."

"Jessie, is Henry around?" Brodie croaked. "We've had a little accident up on the road. I've got a boy up there, horse fell. We need a truck."

"What happened?" Her hands left the pot, her smile closed like a daylily at twilight, and she circled quickly around the bench, not even taking off her apron. "Henry went to the rodeo with the Deusenberries, but he left me the truck. It's around back." As they hurried out of the greenhouse, she asked, "What boy is that? The one works for you?"

"Yeah. You know, the Rooshin boy."

When she came jouncing around the greenhouse in the truck, Brodie was already up on Crowder again. He galloped back up the hill with Jessie following. He could hear the truck engine making the moaning, laboring sound that trucks always made up in those silent hills, a sound that always reminded him that he was one and no more. He found the cattle scattered all along the road now, cooling, grazing a little, calves nursing. They slowly left the road in front of Brodie and the truck. Brodie looked for the two bulls and was a little relieved to see them fighting farther on. They were pushing each other back and forth, head to head, backs humped, with the dust drifting away from them. They already looked extinct. Brodie thought to himself that maybe he'd make it back in time, that one of those bulls still had to whip the other one and chase him off before he could think about cow.

They found Vin lying half-conscious by the fence. The ground around him was soaked so black and wet with blood that it looked like crankcase oil had spilled there. "Oh my," said Jessie, eyes blinking with horror as she got out of the truck.

"Yeah," said Brodie as they bent over Vin. "Wire is poison."

"Dad, don't leave me," whispered Vin. "Don't let me die." His eyes glittered with fever like two satellites lit up by some distant sun. His hand, looking suddenly pale and shrunken, clutched at Brodie's arm. With Jessie there, Brodie had to keep thinking of the son he might have had, the wheat seed that didn't germinate, the stillborn calf, the creek slain in its cradle. Feelings had to be kept safe and cool underground, away from the drying sunlight, like tree roots, like the water table.

Muttering out loud about the day's getting later and later, Brodie yanked off Vin's spurs. He tried to remove the holster and cartridge belt to make Vin more comfortable, but Vin struggled and wouldn't let him take the gun. So he and Jessie, panting and wrestling, got Vin into the cab of the nursery truck. Vin kept moaning and yipping as they moved his leg. Maybe, Brodie thought, if these bulls kept fighting long enough, he could make it to the hospital and back before the winner started to breed cows. It shouldn't take more than five, ten, fifteen minutes, and he couldn't very well leave Jessie with the full responsibility of getting Vin down there, especially since Vin was too weak to sit up and kept slumping over the truck seat. So he tied Curlew and Crowder to the fence and got into the truck.

As they drove back down Powderhouse Hill, dust boiling up behind them, Vin sagged between Jessie and Brodie, groaning and cursing. The dusty seat behind him seemed smeared with the blood of thousands of elk and deer. Jessie's apron and Brodie's pants were smeared with it too.

"I'll be crippled up for life," Vin whispered, his head falling against Brodie's shoulder.

"No, you won't," said Brodie, half-strangled with pity, half annoyed that Vin was being so noisy about his hurts. "You're just scratched up a little bit, that's all."

He kept thinking how swiftly Jessie had moved to help him, dropping everything and going off with him like that. It would have been easier if she scorned his procrastinations and his inability to get along in the world. And Jessie's children had grown up as well-pinched and gay as her dahlias—one of them was teaching over in Shelby, another was a nurse. All four of them had left town, of course, but always came home to visit. Between him and Jessie, there could be no question of words or touches, nor were they necessary—in fact, he had forgotten what those things were. He had whored around a lot when he was young, but now he remembered all the horses he had ridden better than he remembered the feeling of riding a woman. That feeling had dried up inside his fly and inside his soul too, like an old leather strap that hung unused too long in the saddle closet. He figured that Jessie, after four kids, was beyond all that too, even though she was only forty-eight—he figured that nothing mattered to her now but that instinct of older people to link one day with the next as gently as possible. Suddenly, he was sure that one of those bulls was in among the cows now, sniffing, intent, eyes bulging and bright, and he wanted to cry.

"Dad, you've been real good to me," Vin muttered deliriously, still clutching Brodie's arm. "Leaving those cows and all. I won't forget it."

"Sure," said Brodie, and his voice, instead of skidding up in anger, had sunk mane-deep in the bog of sorrow, like a lost horse. He looked across at Jessie, who was driving skillfully fast, stamping on the gears, her eyes wide open and fixed on the road. Henry Fulton was such a stumbling, innocent kind of a guy and had always been very pleasant to Brodie, even invited him in for a cup of coffee sometimes when he showed up at the greenhouse. If Henry suspected Brodie's feelings at all, he must have decided that old Brodie wasn't worth worrying about.

They pulled up with a screech of brakes at the emergency entrance of St. Mary's Hospital, in the shadow of that old brick building covered with Virginia creeper. In a minute a couple of white-coated attendants had Vin on a stretcher and were carrying him in. Inside Brodie caught a glimpse of a long, dim, cool corridor with many doors. A nun was hurrying along it, her shadow falling into each door in turn, her black veil fluttering, rosary clattering. His nostrils caught the hospital smell, the same cutting iodine and alcohol smell as when he opened the veterinary medicine cabinet back at the ranch. Someday soon he would be in one of those rooms, and no one would come visit him except Jessie and Henry, maybe, and maybe Vin. He would have to make sure and avoid that. Tonight, maybe, if he lived to get the herd home.

One of the attendants was a young, talkative redhead, the son of a Cottonwood druggist. "Some day we've had," he said.

"Oh, yeah?" said Brodie.

"Yeah. Too much rodeo and centennial. Some cases of ptomaine poisoning from the picnic—somebody's potato salad must have went bad. A couple of kids blowed up by firecrackers. A few busted ribs and a broken leg from the rodeo. Some Indians that got into a fight and cut each other up. And a finger. Johnny Chance lost a finger roping. They even brought the finger in here hoping we could sew it back on. And a nervous breakdown or something—Vern Stuart's daughter. We got her under sedation. And an old guy who had a heart attack when he won a hundred dollars at the races. Some famous racehorse didn't show up this year, and a long shot won the Cottonwood Derby. Good thing it happens only once every hundred years—"

Brodie and Jessie went back out to the truck.

"Do you want me to drive you back to the cattle?" she asked.

"Yeah, that'll be all right."

They were silent as Jessie drove back through town. Brodie sat with his callused, dark hands spread on the knees of his dusty black corduroy britches with their hand-done foxing and meditated on the sight of all that animal blood dried on his hands. When they reached the herd again, Brodie saw that the broken-horned bull had just bred one of the cows in heat. The huge, long, inflamed pizzle was still right in there, under her tail, as the bull straddled her hindquarters with his coarse forelegs. The polled bull stood dusty and defeated a way up the road. Rage shook Brodie like a rattle. He saw Jessie avert her eyes from the sight. He shoved the truck door open.

"Is there anything else I can do?" Jessie asked, barely managing to look at him. For a second he remembered how Grandmother Brodie used to talk about "gentleman cows."

Brodie looked back at her, half out of the truck. "Yeah," he said. "When I go, keep some real nice flowers on my grave."

"If I'm still around myself," she said, smiling a little.

"Actually," he said, "when I've moved the cattle on, would you lead that roan horse down and tie him up at your place? He's gentle, won't give you no trouble. I don't want to leave him on the road. Those Indians might steal him. I'll come get him later."

"I'll do that," said Jessie.

When she'd driven off, Brodie untied Crowder and mounted. Anger swept across the open country of his brain like a stiff wind, like the big wind of the 1930s that took the dry-landers' topsoil up to heaven. Duty, hell, he thought, and anyhow he wouldn't be around for Lloyd Honeycut to complain to. He looked around to make sure nobody was coming in either direction, to see what he was going to do. And then, setting his hat firmly and gritting his teeth, he cut that broken-horned bull out of the herd.

He unlimbered his dark rawhide rope, softened with use (he couldn't abide the feel of those new manila or nylon ropes that the rodeo ropers used), and shook out a long loop. A. E. Huffman was right there on the side of the road, tripod up and plates in the camera, to put it all on film for future generations to see. Galloping after the broken-horned bull, Brodie roped him neatly around the neck, feeling a great flash of pain in his chest. Taking a quick dally of the rope around the horn, pitching the slack over on the bull's right, and swinging Crowder away to the left, he jerked that heavy bull down as neatly as he ever had a fat steer on the open range. The rope came tight around the bull's quarters, spun him around, and threw him flat on his side on the road. The crowd would have been watching some fancy roping down at the rodeo, roping as phony as plastic flowers. Too bad they couldn't see old Pinter Brodie now. He was probably the only man left in the Northwest who knew how to jerk down like that.

Crowder staggered but gamely kept going as the bull's weight hit the end of the rope. While the bull lay there stunned and windless, Brodie jumped off and hogtied him. Then, digging his jackknife out of his pocket, working in a cold, lucid frenzy with sweat dripping off the end of his nose while the pain brightened the dark inside him like lightning, he stooped over the bull and grabbed the heavy, wrinkled, pink-white scrotum. As deftly as if he were cleaning trout, he slit out the testicles and tossed them into the ditch among the dry foxtails. The bull shrieked and struggled, his bound legs jerking. Crowder held the rope taut as he was supposed to do, bracing gallantly on his sore legs, his mane sticking to his sweat-streaked neck.

After Brodie loosed the bull and took his rope off, he got on Crowder again and started after the polled bull. He swore that when he got done with them, neither of those bulls were going to feel like philandering with purebred cows. But as he went to jerk the polled bull down, the old rope's honda broke, and the loop snapped free of the bull's neck. Raging and swearing, Brodie started toward where Curlew was tied to get Vin's rope, until he recalled that Vin never packed a rope—the boy's main interest was the pistol. So he decided to get Vin's pistol and shoot a little red hole between the polled bull's eyes, but then he remembered that the pistol was down in St. Mary's Hospital.

The broken-horned bull stood bawling, blood dripping from his empty scrotum. The polled bull, ringy and mad now, was once again circling back toward the cows. There was nothing to do but cut him back, then start to gather up the cows, and cut him back again and again. As Brodie whistled and hollered, the cows stopped grazing, a little bunch here, a little bunch there. Soon the whole herd was moving again, with old 94 trundling along in the lead. Now all he had to do was get them through Cottonwood. The way the highways, fences, streets, and other properties were now laid out, there was no way to bypass the town—you had to take cattle right through. It would have been real handy, he thought, to have a dependable man to ride the point with old 94, to make sure the cattle didn't detour down the wrong street somewhere. If they had been six hundred crazy steers or scatterbrained heifers who didn't know the road, he would probably lose the whole herd. He hoped he could count on the old cows who knew the way.

Howling and sere as blown dust, he drove them down Powder-house Hill. He scarcely noticed Jessie peering anxiously out of the greenhouse to watch him pass. Old 94 swung along on her grotesque feet, cancered eye blinking, horns swaying, a glitter of flies hanging over her back. The polled bull kept following. Time after time he beat the bull back, till finally he broke the whip over the bull's spine. Had this happened in the old days, it would have been written up in the books as "the time when old Pinter Brodie moved a big herd all alone." Now, not even the Cottonwood *Post* would run a small item about it.

He drove the herd across Route 10, stopping a lot of cars leaving town. They lined up north and south, honking impatiently. Brodie was reminded of the rodeo, which was probably getting out right now—a bad time to be passing the fairgrounds. He drove the cattle on through Alfalfaville. Kids yelled, "Get a horse." One boy threw a lighted firecracker in the street. The cows exploded in every direction as it went off, and there was weeping and wailing in Alfalfaville as cows trampled lawns and flower beds. Brodie felt like riding the boy down and hitting him with the broken whip, but he was too busy.

At the fairgrounds, the rodeo was just ending, as he had feared all day. Old 94 and the point cows walked straight into the traffic jam leaving the parking lots. The hot, feisty heifer that Vin had run into a fence now took her revenge—she charged a Buick and dented its fender with her horn. Brodie rode old Crowder pitilessly, wheeling him here, wheeling him there, trying desperately to keep the cattle together. But as the herd kept pouring past the fairgrounds, the mix of cows and cars got worse. Bawls and horn toots deafened Brodie's ears. Spectators trying to flee slipped in cow manure. Women screamed. Shortly all 628 of his cows were milling wild-eyed through the fairgrounds.

A town cop who'd been directing traffic came running up to Brodie on foot. "What the hell are you doing, coming through here with these cattle at this hour?"

Brodie hauled Crowder up to answer. He was cold and patient as a river; he had left the heat of his rage up on Powderhouse Hill, where the testicles would now be crawling with flies and drying in the ditch. "I would of come by sooner," he said, "but my cowboy had an accident and I had to take him to the hospital."

"I've got half a mind to arrest you for disturbing the peace," shouted the cop.

"You just do that," said Brodie, coolly polite. "There isn't any other way for me to take these cattle through here."

"Well, get them out of here then!" The cop made a grand sweep of his arm.

A young crewcut rodeo cowboy with red chaps came riding up on a squat little Quarter Horse. "What's going on?"

"This old coot," said the cop, "is driving these cows through here all alone, and he's lost control of the whole son-of-a-bitch herd."

"Hey, Pops, you need a little help?" the rodeo cowboy asked Brodie.

Brodie glared at him from under his shaggy silver brows. "Much obliged, son, but I'm doing fine. I'll have them out of here in a little bitty minute."

"Hey, Pops, you're going to be here all day. I'll go rustle up some help." The cowboy galloped off toward the fairground horse barns, where rodeo cowboys were riding in from the arena, unsaddling horses beside trailer houses, loading them into trailers. In a minute, half a dozen contestants came galloping up to Brodie, looking like a Marlboro ad with their broad, crisp Stetsons and their punchy little horses. How strange he must have looked to them—a shy, sick old silvertip on his deer-necked cayuse. He looked around in despair at the cattle milling everywhere in the fairgrounds—they were trotting up the alleyways between the racehorse barns, disrupting the Thoroughbreds in the cooling ring; shying away from the tootling merry-go-round; even wandering into the livestock exhibition barns. Brodie didn't see that polled bull anywhere, and he wondered if the bull was breeding that second cow in heat. So he decided that he'd better accept their help.

He barked orders at them the way he would have done seventy-five years ago, as if he were a roundup boss sending them out to scour this creek and that creek, cover two hundred square miles, and bring in two thousand head. And they cheerfully did as he told them. More and more of them came riding up as word of the trouble spread. A couple of them even threw their saddles back on their horses. Vern Stuart rode up on his famous cutting horse, Bobcat, and did some fancy work getting fifteen or twenty cows out from among the carnival booths, where they had tipped over a cotton-candy stand. Brodie was surprised to see Johnny Chance join them, riding a flashy buckskin and looking pale and ferocious, with one braid undone and the long hair flying loose over his shoulder. His left hand was bandaged, but he rode with an air of pretending that nothing had happened to it. With Johnny was a huge old Indian in stockman's clothes riding a rough-looking bay that had a dozen brands on its hide. Whooping and yipping, the two of them brought up thirty-five head that had scattered out onto the racetrack.

Tom Chance fell in beside Brodie on his big sorrel roping horse and said, "These the cattle you had up on Skillet Creek?"

"Yeah," said Brodie, feeling very uncomfortable with all those Quarter Horses around. "That creek is just loaded with copper. Greener than Ireland."

"We'll move our heifers off there tomorrow. Looks like we'll have to get together and slap a little injunction on Intermountain."

"Yeah, looks like it," said Brodie, feeling as if the pain in his chest must be sticking out through his vest—he hoped they couldn't see it.

The men were bringing the cows back, a little bunch here, a little bunch there, throwing them all together on the cottonwood lane just beyond the racehorse barns, as Brodie had directed. Old 94 had already walked through onto that lane all by herself, without spooking or detouring anywhere. One contestant came driving the polled monster and called, "Here's your bull." Brodie roared that it wasn't his bull at all, and to pen him up somewhere, so they did. Two cows fell on the manure-slick asphalt and stifled a leg, forcing Brodie to leave them behind for the moment, so the contestants penned up the lame cows too. Some contestants went on ahead to ride the point and make sure that the cattle kept heading up toward the old highway. Spectators huddled along the racetrack's board fence or peered from cars and screamed or cheered or yelled, "Ride 'em cowboy!" And not A. E. Huffman but the Cottonwood *Post* photographer stood flashing pictures of it all.

Finally the herd was together and moving again. Johnny Chance came rattling up on that buckskin, looking sick and fiendishly cheerful. "You're a little late for the centennial," he sang out at Brodie.

The crowd of cowboys laughed—all but Tom Chance. Vin had told Brodie that there was bad blood between the two brothers. Even Brodie laughed a little, as much as his chest would allow. He looked at the two Indians and it occurred to him that the Indians in the centennial camp had been drinking the same turquoise water as his cows. In spite of himself, he felt an impulse of concern for their health.

The rodeo contestants helped him get the herd safely onto the old highway and point them north. Brodie kept struggling with his feelings. He had maligned the rodeo cowboys, yet they too had a few of the same ghosts looking out of their eyes. They too could hear some of the same hoofbeats carried away by the big winds. They had fallen in to help him in a way that Grandfather Brodie would have understood. As the herd started streaming up the highway, a few teams and buggies that had participated in the centennial pageant pulled over to the side to let them pass. The buggy drivers, in old swallowtail coats and beaver hats, sat waving, and the women in Gay Nineties flounces peered out and giggled. Brodie had a curious feeling that time was a winding, shallow prairie river, and he was riding straight, cutting across the bends.

The rodeo contestants said good-bye—they had to go eat, get their horses loaded, and hit the road. Brodie thanked them, and they all galloped back to the fairgrounds, raising a great grey dust. Johnny Chance and the old Indian rode off toward the Indian camp, where the Indians were already striking their lodges. Tom Chance and Vern Stuart stayed with him, because they were going home that way.

"Sorry to hear your daughter is in the hospital," he said to Vern.

"Oh . . . ," said Vern vaguely, his forehead wrinkling. "I ain't too worried. She was over in Europe, and I guess she got overtired. They gave her some pills to make her sleep. When she wakes up this evening, I'll bring her home. She's a tough little gal, Beth is." When Vern reached his own lane, he turned Bobcat down it with a so-long.

Tom Chance rode glumly beside him for another mile or two up the highway. "Too bad about Johnny's finger," said Brodie.

"He's leaving us," said Tom. "He's going back to his tribe."

"You don't say," said Brodie.

Some years ago, Tom had wired a big firecracker under the hood of the Jack Rabbit when Brodie had left it parked on Main Street to go into the bank. When Brodie came out and stepped on the starter, the firecracker blew a hole in the radiator. Brodie had just put in antifreeze. While Tom and a few others yowled with laughter, Brodie got down on his knees in front of the Jack Rabbit, trying to catch the antifreeze in his hat. He lost every drop of it, though.

"Say, Tom," he said, "I almost forgot. That crazy Vin had an accident up on Powderhouse Hill today and rolled his horse into your fence. The fence is down. I didn't have time to fix it because I had all those cows running all over."

Alone finally, he drove the cattle on up the old highway, feeling the terror of being almost home and the desire to have reached it. He passed the "See Frontier Town" sign and one remaining Burma Shave sign that announced enigmatically "Car in ditch." He knew that he would never make it home, that Crowder was going to stumble and break his chicken-wrinkled old neck, or that his heart was going to give out at last, or that the bullet that Vin had fired at the jackrabbit that morning was going to go round the world, come full circle, and hit him, as it had been meant to do.

He wanted to be home. The ranch rose in his mind like an undiscovered mountain range rising before Lewis and Clark, snow streaked and silent. Its valleys would brim with mysterious indigo shadows, because it would be that time of year when the new green growth in the timber had matured toward blue and winter. And somewhere in those mountains, in some ravine choked with down timber, he would stumble over his own bones. His rein hand felt numb, and the reins felt like two strange flat strips of dark old leather, so strange that a man from Mars might have put them in his hand as some kind of gift whose purpose he did not know.

As he whooped the herd past the abandoned dairy, with its great barn caving in and its board pens full of tall, poisonous, yellow clover, he had a moment of pity—and it was just a moment, as when a meteor streaked phosphorescent back into the black like the scratch of a match or when a firefly fired its frail greenish lamp over the swamp northeast of town (actually, there'd been no fireflies there since the town DDT'd the swamp for mosquitos)—a moment of pity for Cottonwood, hanging and rattling and about to come loose from the saddle. A moment of pity for Johnny Chance and Beth Stuart, dragging their lives patiently with fevered eyes, like a stifled cow dragging her swollen, useless leg. He wondered likewise if they had ever pitied him—the chances were good, for they must have at least thought of him a couple of times in their lives. After all, he was the most feared and misunderstood character in Cottonwood, that little old bastard up the valley who stepped out of the brush with his .30-.30 whenever any of the good citizens from town were raiding his crabapple trees or poaching his deer (he had told Ralph Applegate and his son that he would leave them for fishbait the next time he caught them fishing his creeks without asking permission). That little old bastard who had a million dollars in gold stowed away somewhere in that old ranch house (which amused him highly, as his money was all in the bank). He was just curious about whether they had ever thought of him or not—he didn't really care.

It had been a hard day in Cottonwood, the last day of the centennial, one finger cut off, one case of eating loco weed, and one old man driving his cattle all alone. A day not to remember in Cottonwood, because nobody knew all three of those events from inside, a day to be forgotten and delivered over to the oblivion of the copper-poisoned river, the boarded-up stores, and the blue haze from the sawmill. Nothing for Cottonwood to do but hang and rattle, along with the cattle-and-horse life that had built it. Twenty-five years from now, this great mountain basin, which had produced some of the finest wild hay in the world and grazed millions of cattle, would be a sink of blue haze, crisscrossed by developments like Alfalfaville, with bulldozers scraping and silvery industrial buildings shooting up everywhere.

Things were closing in, and he didn't want to be around to feel the pressure. It was one time, he told himself, that he wouldn't play functional illiterate about reading that writing on the wall. People were already discovering that Montana had just about the sparsest population in the country, with more cows than people, and they were beginning to trickle in from the big urban centers. Industries and resort developments were hunting feverishly for sites on Montana rivers and lakes. Even outside teachers were suddenly fighting for posts in Montana schools. Hippies and gray flannel suits all wanted in.

Brodie had read about something called the Public Land Law Review Commission, in which the government socialists had spent the last five years figuring out how to relieve urban population pressures by filling up the country's government-owned land with people—something like the Homestead Law that had meant the death of the open range. This new idea would mean the slow end of leased cattle range, national forest, and wilderness country in the West. He had also read about some insane scheme called the North American Water and Power Alliance, which would dam up a five-hundred-mile lake there in the Rockies, across the U.S.-Canada border, impounding rivers that flowed north through Canada to the Arctic and sending those waters to the Great Lakes, Texas and California along great canals. The plan would probably put the whole Cottonwood basin under water, but not before the great valley disappeared under developments and silvery Intermountains.

He thought about how American farm and range land was being rapidly lost to mismanagement, industry, and urbanization, and he wondered where these crazy-eyed engineers and developers thought they were going to get their meat and bread in another twenty-five

years. "Let 'em eat barbecued plastic," he thought, "and vanilla fluoride for dessert." If cattle would be bred at all in future, they would
be bred in millions of tight cages, whole skyscrapers full of cattle
cages, like those chicken factories he had read about, so that the land
could be used to feed bulldozers.

There had been poetry, and poetry would die. He wasn't sure if
"Bunch Grass and Blue Joint" was as good poetry as Shakespeare's
sonnets, but they both rose like mist from some clean river in early
morning. There had been love, and love would die too. He wasn't sure
if his way of seeing oneself was the only way, but it would fade away
into thistles like an overgrazed range. There had always been old men
and old horses, and they would always die. Johnny Chance was leaving
town, Beth Stuart had come home, and Pinter Brodie was going to
drive his cows forever in the sky, like in that song "Ghost Riders" that
Vaughan Monroe used to sing.

The herd reached the point where the old highway passed between
his fence boundaries. It was all his land now, on both sides of the road.
All those hundreds of acres of timothy, redtop, and clover that old
Skookum Joe rode around to irrigate, opening a flume on the main
ditch here, moving a canvas dam on a contour ditch there. The fields
were all cut now, dry and sleek. All Brodie had left to do was finish
one stack and pay off his crazy crew. But he wouldn't have to do that.
He wouldn't have to get over the fields with the water one more time
before frost, so that he'd have enough grass and hay to winter the
cows on those fields. The power company wouldn't have the pleasure
of serving him that summons for the easement along the highway here.

He strained up in the saddle to glimpse the ranch buildings ahead.
They were still there. The rusty corrugated roofs of the barns and
sheds showed among the cottonwood snags. The day had been so long
that he'd been afraid the 5 Up 5 Down would go to sleep while he was
gone, like some kind of bronc-stompers' Sleepy Hollow.

So Brodie kept pushing the cows gently along, dabbing his broken
stockyard whip on this cow's back and that calf's tail. The cattle were
cooler now that the sun was low in the sky. He didn't have to whip
the bull back anymore. He didn't even have to gallop Crowder ahead
and open the gate into his south eighty, because he had left the gate
open that morning, not wanting to have to depend on Vin to do it.
Old 94 knew just what to do—she turned off the highway and trundled
through the waiting gate. The rest of the herd streamed after her.

When they were all in, Brodie shut the gate. He rode slowly

around, watching them drift down into the wide bottom along Mullan Creek. The day's efforts slowly drained out of him, the way the red would bleed out of the sky when evening came, leaving the black scab of night. He felt dusty, shriveled, almost mummified, with the blood flaking off his hands like a dark buffalo dust.

He watched the cattle drift down to the creek and shoulder into it to water. They waded and shoved, burying their muzzles in the pure water. New arrivals shifted upstream to find an unmuddied spot to drink. The great cattle drive was over. Old men, old horses, old wolves, old Indians, old stones and stars. It was all over forever, the days on the Big Dry and the Little Missouri and the Mussellshell and the Sun, those rivers whose names rang like old steel spurs. The skies and the buttes were swifter than cloud shadows, speeding off into the gentle, indifferent distances. If some astronomer looked through the most powerful telescope on earth, he might see—like a dim star swimming in the dark natal dusts of the next galaxy—a young night wrangler named Pinter Brodie rolled asleep in his dewy blankets, while a thousand horses milled in the rope corral nearby, and the riders sat around on the ground with their tin plates heaped with beef and sourdough biscuits. The scene would be farther away and dimmer than those neutron stars he had read about, that had burned out long ago but whose ghostly light still wandered the void in search of some eye to see it.

The Winchester .30-.30 waited for him in its scabbard. It was time to think about that.

But first he had a few errands to do. It wouldn't be right to leave them undone. He unsaddled poor old Crowder and turned him out. Then he got into the Jack Rabbit, after a glance or two at the rifle lying there on the back of the seat, and drove back to the Fultons' to get Curlew. The roan was waiting patiently, tied by the greenhouse, his scraped ankle a little swollen. Henry and Jessie came out to chat a minute.

"I hear you had quite a day," said Henry. "Come on in for a cup of coffee."

"Much obliged," said Brodie, as he tied Curlew to the back of the Jack Rabbit, "but I've still got a few things to do before dark." He didn't think that, this last time, he could bear having a cup of coffee with them. "This horse behave himself?"

Jessie giggled. "Well," she said, "he nipped off a couple of my delphiniums there. But he paid me for them," and she indicated a magnificent pile of green horse manure that was already drying and winking with flies. Both the men laughed softly.

"Quite a rodeo today," Henry said. Henry had never been on a horse in his life, but he was a real fan, and paid five dollars for a good seat. "You should go to the rodeo, Pint. It's downright unpatriotic of you to stay away. Our local boys did real well too. Jimmy Simms made a real rank ride in the saddle event. And Johnny Chance made a great comeback. Don't know what happened to Beth Stuart in the barrel race, though. She entered but she never showed up. Pat Chance won it."

"Oh, yeah?" said Brodie.

Jessie had gone into the greenhouse for a minute, and she came back with a fistful of freshly cut tea roses wrapped in damp newspaper. "Here, Pint, take these," she said.

"Who, me?" he said, accepting them awkwardly. "You mean, take 'em to Vin?"

"No," she said. "Put them on your supper table tonight, and sniff them once in a while."

He wondered if she had divined what was on his mind. "Now, what's a smelly old cowboy going to do with roses on his supper table?" he asked. But a lump, like a knot in pine, grew in his throat as he drove slowly back to the ranch with the roses lying on the dirty, threadbare seat beside him and Curlew trotting behind the Jack Rabbit.

Then he drove to the hospital to see Vin. The sun was going down onto the western bench, and the sky was crisscrossed with whiplashes of red and pink. The air was already cooling off, with that glacier chill of creeping fall. A few firecrackers still echoed in other parts of town as he strode stiffly up the walk to St. Mary's.

They had Vin on the second floor. He was lying on his side, still pale, his eyes still ricocheting the light of fever. His back was all bandaged, and his leg was in a cast. A worn old religious medal, with writing on it that Brodie couldn't read, hung down his bare freckled chest. He smiled a little when Brodie came in. Brodie sat down in a chair by the bed.

"Dad," said Vin.

"You're fired," said Brodie.

Vin's face stiffened, as swiftly as rigor mortis hits a bird, minutes after death. All expression frost-killed in his eyes. Brodie wondered what had hurt Vin more—the death of his father or the death of his fantasies. He was sorry then, too—sorry for all the twisted innocents who landed out in this ex-grass country, sorry for those who arrived hoping to make legends when it was possible only to be devoured by legends, sorry for those who came dreaming of being giants when there was only room for ghosts, or imitations of ghosts, to be exact. Sorry, too, for himself, that he had to inflict such a haunting in order to be free of haunting. Government and big companies held eminent domain over the land, but eminent domain over the soul was held by shadows. At that moment he pitied Vin, though he was sure that Vin would never pity him.

"Dad, give me another chance," said Vin.

"You cost me a lot of money today," said Brodie. "A down fence, a couple of stifled cows, some extra gas, and whatever Honeycut is going to ask for that bull of his that I committed mayhem on. Money's tight, and you can't be depended on."

"You can't manage alone."

"I managed real well alone, all day today," said Brodie, getting up again. "So I guess I can manage from now on. You've got $300 coming, and I'll give the check to your wife." At the door he turned. "If you're so set on cowboying, there's plenty of other ranches in the state looking for help. And there's always rodeo."

Next he drove through town to Vin's house on the other side of the tracks. It was one of the last houses on the west fringe of town, an old log house with a tar-paper addition that Vin had never put clapboard on. A barn was falling over nearby. Three or four rusting auto bodies were scattered about, with yellow sweet clover growing tall around them. Rolls of rusty wire, a disemboweled mattress with the springs trailing out, rotted bushel baskets, buckets, and other garbage were lying around.

Fat Marilyn stood at the door in a wrinkled black skirt and smudged white blouse and cried as Brodie wrote the check against the doorframe. She had her hair in pincurls, and her child-high belly shook as she stood and cried, one arm folded across her stomach and the other hand over her face. Over her shoulder, tacked onto the wall, Brodie could see a Jennings Feed Company calendar bearing a reproduction of Charlie Russell's "Roping a Wolf."

"And to think," Marilyn said, looking up, her mascara smeared down her doughy cheeks, "that I could have married somebody else."

"I'm real sorry to do this," said Brodie. "I haven't deducted any of today's losses either."

"I'd like to walk away from here."

"Trouble with walking away," said Brodie, "is there's nowhere left to walk to."

His last stop was Brown's Saloon. The place was empty now that the rodeo cowboys had left town. He ordered one beer and asked Mary, "Can I use the phone?" He rarely set foot in the Cottonwood bars, but there was no harm in one last little spree, and this way he could save on the phone call. Mary was generous with that phone to patrons.

"Sure, Pint," she said.

He called up Lloyd Honeycut and told him in his best shrill voice that he could find his Hereford bull up on the county road somewhere and his polled bull locked up down at the fairgrounds, and if Lloyd had any complaints, and if Brodie's two cows settled with calf by that bull, they could discuss it at some future date. Then he sat at the long mahogany bar, polished by the elbows of generations of Cottonwood drunks, and drank that beer slowly. On the jukebox Patti Page was singing "The Tennessee Waltz," a song he had always liked—he could recall hearing it for quite a few years now. He sat slumped, staring over Mary's head at the murky mirrors and rich stained-glass bar cupboards going clear up to the ceiling. A big painting of cowboys by Vern Stuart hung there, already darkened and fly-specked. The truth was that the pain in his chest was going away a little. It occurred to him that he hadn't eaten since breakfast, but he wasn't hungry. He felt curiously lightened and freed of care by the decision he had made. Too bad he didn't have that pistol of Vin's—he would shoot his way out of town one last time, the way the boys had done seventy-five years ago.

After half an hour of sipping his beer and listening to "The Tennessee Waltz," he paid Mary and went out on the street. It was dark; the streets were nearly deserted. He did notice a couple of his hay crew stumbling out of the bar down on the corner—he wouldn't have to round them up tomorrow morning, or bail them out of jail. He wouldn't have to take a truck to the fairgrounds and get those two stifled cows either. Up over Main Street, the cloth banner saying "Welcome to Cottonwood Rodeo and Centennial August 24, 25, and

26" was blowing, forgotten, in the night breeze. Serpentine and popsicle wrappers were scattered in the gutters from the parade that noon.

Brodie got in the Jack Rabbit and drove on home.

As he parked the Jack Rabbit in the barnyard and got out, carrying the rifle and the roses, he stood for a moment listening and looking around.

Not a single light burned anywhere—all the buildings were dark and silent. A dead moonlight lay over the ranch, as if from some distant sun, as if the ranch were streaming through space, luminous, like a comet's tail. The light was dead, yet it moved and flowed like a wind. It billowed the silvery willows that sprung up around the feed pens nearer the Cottonwood River. Yet it was only the real wind moving in the flourishing cottonwoods that had been saplings only a few years ago. It was only the wind telling tall tales about nothing among the dead, ghastly gray cottonwood trees that had been alive only a few years ago. If he had not known that his horses, cows, and steers were scattered everywhere over the river bottom, he would have thought that not a single live creature was there on the ranch, not even a bacteria. Yet even the ranch was more alive than he was. There in the dark, it lived its life that had nothing to do with him.

He stood paralyzed, his scalp prickling, as he listened to the moonlight blowing, banging the doors of sheds. He could hear all the lonesome sounds of a ranch in his head—a truck laboring up a steep mountain road, a pump whining in a pumphouse on the main irrigation ditch, a horse whipping its head around to snap at a speckled deerfly, the roar of rain on a corrugated tin roof, a wolf gagging on strychnine bait, soil eroding down the overgrazed hillsides, the rustle of a thick black hose being dragged through tall thistles.

In a nearby corral, old Crowder strained his thin, sweat-streaked neck over the poles at him. First he would have to take care of Crowder. So he walked slowly over there, that pine-knot lump growing in his throat again, and let himself into the corral. Crowder came up to have his ears scratched, and even in the dark Brodie could see the swollen knees, the streaks of salt on the old horse's head, the crust of dried slobber around his lips from the bit. Crowder's mossy, agate-brown eyes were mournful with some excess of knowledge—Brodie sometimes wondered if his own thoughts overflowed into the old horse's brain.

He stood back from the horse, threw a shell into the chamber, and raised the rifle to his shoulder. Crowder, sensing something, swung nervously away a few steps and then looked back questioningly, head high. Brodie squinted along the sights at the white star on Crowder's forehead. Then he started thinking about the will he had to write that evening, about how little legal lingo he knew. There was no point in taking care of Crowder if he didn't get a will that satisfied him first.

So he lowered the rifle, leaving the shell in the chamber, scratched Crowder's ears again, and left the corral. He walked down the lane between the bunkhouse and the ranch-house yard, his feet almost tangling in the shadows of the great weeping birch that had grown halfway across the lane. A loose piece of tin banged on the bunkhouse roof. The chinking was crumbling out from between the rough-squared whitewashed timbers of the long, low bunkhouse, and its corrugated roof seemed ready to cave in under the masses of Virginia creeper that had twined up over it along the doorways. The bunkhouse had been shut up for years now; nothing was left in it but a few dusty iron beds, a pine table with a bullet hole through it, and a few dented cooking utensils and wooden spoons in the kitchen cupboards. In a narrow flowerbed along the cookhouse wall, some yellowing pansy plants still sprawled, gallantly unfolding a last few faces. In the moonlight, even the pansies' shadows said "Shhhhh!" against the log wall. In June he had bought that flat of pansies from Jessie and planted them there, to make it look like someone still lived there.

Beside the empty woodshed, he checked a couple of chipped china bowls, which held canned milk and scraps for a last few half-wild barn cats. While he wouldn't want it known in town that he had any feeling for cats, he always made sure there was something in the bowls. One striped tom crouched suspiciously at the corner of the woodshed, eyeing him. He could afford a few cents for milk for that last faithful crew of the 5 Up 5 Down. The surly old half-blind collie Bob waggled up to him slowly, his fur matted with burrs and foxtails. Brodie patted Bob's whitened muzzle, feeling as burned out and ashy as an old campfire, the beer euphoria already leaving him.

With Bob limping after him, Brodie passed the saddle-horse barn, where he had hung the battered old saddle in the saddle closet, among a dusty tangle of ancient bronc saddles, hackamores, horsehair bridles with high-curbed, Spanish-type bits, rawhide ropes, silver-studded martingales, and even a few mummified pairs of chaps. Beyond that was the old buggy shed, and he could envision the vehicles piled haphazardly in the dusty dark within, thick with cobwebs and dust—buggies, a surrey or two, buckboards, a swan-bodied sleigh, even a rare old military ambulance that had brought wounded cavalrymen in from the Skillet Creek Fight—thousands of dollars of wheeled junk that buggy collectors would have bought long ago, had he not been even more miserly with his daydreams than with his dollars.

His footsteps crunched on the dirt lane. There was no sound anywhere but the wind telling lies in the yellowing leaves of the cottonwoods. It made little creaking noises in the crumbling, weatherbrowned sheds and in the toppling pole fences. It swished like footsteps in the quack grass that had grown up in the unused corrals. In one trampled pasture, the work teams wandered in the dark or drank from the mossy old trough almost overgrown by forget-me-nots. In the barnyard, the decrepit old haying machinery stood where his crew had left it yesterday afternoon. Too bad he couldn't hold on another twenty-five years—someday that crazy old machinery might be worth as much as the buggies.

There was no sound anywhere but the wind and the footsteps of wild animals moving back onto the ranch, making one last sortie before urbanization wiped them out. The elk and antelope came boldly right into the barnyard to thieve hay from the horses' feedracks. The skunks had burrowed in under the floorboards of the barns. Even black bears raided his garbage can. Some years ago the town had twisted his arm into selling a few border acres down south for a sewage settling pond. He had consented after they convinced him that the sewage would break down naturally in the sun and air, without any smell. When the pond was complete and the bulldozers left, he had watched amazed as the wildfowl discovered it. Soon he took to riding down there on Crowder in the evening and would sit watching all the different ducks and geese. Great blue herons waded in the green shallows, crucifying frogs on their long bills. In spring, even the trumpeter swans, the last few of them, would light on that pond for a day or two on their way north. When they left, he watched their proud, snowy takeoff, heard their harsh cries dying out over the willow flats, and thought of them beating their way north into Canada, running a gauntlet of poachers' guns, high-tension power lines, and jet exhausts. That pond was the only piece of Cottonwood progress that he had ever approved of.

He had discovered in his old age that if you managed a range carefully, it would support a certain quota of wild animals and cattle together—he didn't need any radical-talking young biologist to tell him that. Anyway, in this valley the elk and antelope never got crowded and the deer never died of black tongue, due to the over-population of year-round hunters. Yet, he told himself, you couldn't talk to a lot of ranchers he knew about bighorn sheep or trumpeter swans or bald eagles. It was the one lesson that some of them had never learned, for all their wisdom about keeping the grass right side up. Yes, in his old age, he had found himself feeling a treasonous and sneaking alliance with the wild animals. He thought to himself that if he ever ran into a wolf up in the hills, he would just look the wolf in its yellow eyes and say, "Old men, old horses, old wolves." He used to see a wolf up there along the timberline, probably the last wolf left in those parts. Then one winter day, as he was cutting across the Chance range to get home quicker, he had found the wolf hunched dead in the snow, its snarling jaws frozen open. Nearby lay a joint of poisoned meat. He figured that Tom Chance had put that strychnine bait out there. He remembered getting up at Montana Stockgrower Association meetings in Miles City and saying, "It's too soon to be using all these new things before we know what they do," and hearing them laugh at him. He admitted, anyway, that you did have to dip cattle in that new malathion to kill the cattle grubs that riddled their backs. "Too soon," he had cried out in his high, cracked voice, when all the rest of them were rushing to feed stilbestrol to their steers. He had had the last laugh when they all found out that stilbestrol caused meat to shrink 10 or 15 per cent. He had been guilty of compromises, he used malathion like everybody else, but he had managed to stay out of debt by simply not having many of the fixed operating expenses that the others had, like wives who wanted dishwashers, and baling machines that broke down, and kids who went off to expensive colleges and never came back.

He walked slowly up to the ranch house, the rifle weighing his trembling arm like a handful of giant horn weights. In front of the weathered, rambling clapboard house, the cottonwoods that Grandfather Brodie had planted in 1889 were full of dead limbs. One tree was completely dead—he wouldn't have to cut it down now. A single rusty sprinkler whirled senselessly on the broad, violet-ridden lawn—he kept the sprinkler running day and night, moved it around when he remembered to, in order to keep the big lawn from burning up. He had managed to mow the lawn one evening during haying, but now it was grown up in bluegrass again, going to seed. He wouldn't have to mow it again. Nor would he have to paint the picket fence that was peeling visibly even in the dark.

He pushed slowly through the creaking picket gate, closed it, and went shakily up the walk, his boots crunching over the lichens on the granite flagstones. The peeling green shutters hung crookedly, and one of them was banging in the wind. The pillared porch was settling away from the house. Out of habit, he detoured off the walk and moved the sprinkler to another place that looked burned yellow. The lawn sloped down through a little grove of cedar where he had always spread his bedroll at night. Beyond that was the great hedge of lilacs, choked with dead wood and wilder than a jungle. At the very bottom of the slope was the semiformal garden that he had stopped having tended years ago, for lack of time or a chore boy to do it. There, quack grass had long ago covered the flagstone walks and choked out the last of Grandmother Brodie's delphinium and moss roses.

As he turned his gaze back to the house, he noted again its two stories of dark, dusty windows, with the cracked green shades pulled down inside. He started for a moment, seeing a light move slowly across two of the windows in the old office, almost as if someone were carrying a kerosene lamp inside. People in Cottonwood insisted that the old place was haunted, but he had never seen a ghost there, and if there were any, he was sure they would be happy ghosts, loathe to leave the scene of those gentler pleasures. But the light faded, and he realized that it must have been the reflection of headlights from a car on the old highway.

It occurred to him that he lived in that house. He wondered how long it would be before they found him. A few days, maybe? Vin coming around to try and get hired again, and noticing a smell? Or Honeycut coming to complain in person about his bull? Brodie felt lightheaded from drinking the beer on an empty stomach and was not inclined to dwell on the thought.

With old Bob creeping along behind him, he opened the door; its wire screen was riddled with rust holes as if from a gunfight. He unlocked the door and pushed it open (it always stuck) and the cool fragrance of the old house—outmoded fine woods and lost sachets— struck his nostrils. He would have lived here with Jessie and had grandchildren banging in and out by now and met a smell of fried potatoes.

He turned on the light in the hallway, then in the parlor. Everything was the way it had always been. The old house hadn't gone to sleep at all—it was more alive than he was. The yellow-oak rocking chairs and the ebony library table with the Oriental rug thrown over it still stood on the expanse of worn red-and-gold Brussels carpet, with the old gas chandelier hanging above. Along the walls were oak bookcases with glass doors, crammed with books—*The Last Days of the Flying U, The Trampling Herd, Bunch Grass and Blue Joint, The Longhorn, Vigilante Days and Ways, Good Medicine, Across the Wide Missouri.* On the dusky rose walls, ornate oak frames enclosed Huffman photos of 5 Up 5 Down cattle flung across the plains. There was the blue steel stove with its delicate enameling and the grandfather clock that had stopped ticking in the big earthquake ten years ago and a carved-wood Swiss barometer with a deer head on top of it that always said *Stürm* no matter what the weather was. The floor creaked as he walked across it, and he again had that feeling that he was being watched by some curious but gentle presence.

This was the house, and the ranch, that had been declared a historic site despite all his objections, and he had refused to have this status legally confirmed, because that would have meant he'd have to spend a quarter of a million to restore it and keep it up as a showplace and then let any and all tourists tramp through it. It was, he had been told, one of the last ranches left in the country that still had all its old buildings intact. It was better to have the lichens and the pack rats making visits, he thought.

Old Bob flopped down on the carpet by one of the rocking chairs, where a worn, hair-caked spot testified that it was his favorite sleeping place. Brodie laid the Winchester down on the library table, then went into the bathroom. The walls there were paneled with yellow oak; the washbasin and deep tub were tin-lined. A flowered china pitcher, furry with dust, was on the stand. Brodie turned on the water in the washbasin and scrubbed the dust and blood of the drive off his hands and face, then dried them on a filthy towel.

Through the open door lay the one bedroom he used in cold weather. Under its faded wallpaper with sprigs of roses, the plaster was coming loose. Its green Turkish rug was threadbare in places, and the huge Victorian walnut bed still had its straw mattress, covered now with army surplus blankets. In the corner was another enameled stove. He knew where all that furniture had come from and what it was worth, because he remembered slender, melancholy Grandmother Brodie talking about it in her soft lisping voice—she had had it all brought upriver and overland at great expense. In the other rooms, closed up and draped with sheets, there stood $100,000 worth of old Swiss, French, and Victorian wood, vitrines full of bric-a-brac and rare

seashells, delicate old clocks, a rosewood piano still somewhat in tune
and draped with a paisley shawl that the moths had riddled with their
gunfire, a music cabinet crammed with old sheet music, even a pump
organ with wooden cupids all over it—all too much trouble to dust or
even look at anymore.

As he hung the towel back up, Brodie found himself shaking
slightly. He started trying to think about the will that he would have
to compose beforehand. He knew something about legal language, but
maybe not enough. He unbuckled his chaps and threw them across a
Hickock chair in his bedroom, and then he went toward the kitchen.
What he really needed was not an end to it all, but a cup of coffee.

Over the great oak doors of the dining room hung a spreading
pair of Texas longhorns mounted on red velvet. In the dining room,
the yellow-oak table had none of its twenty leaves in it, and the two
dozen tall-backed chairs with cracked leather seats were lined along
the wall. No Teddy Roosevelt or Marquis de Mores or Pierre Wibeaux
for dinner tonight. The old German cook wouldn't have to keep food
hot behind the screen, painted with scenes of peacocks. No one would
have to open the ceiling-high corner cupboards and take out any of the
dust-filmed crystal goblets. No one would have run the Bissel sweeper
over the great red Persian rug (Grandmother Brodie had always said
it was Persian) afterwards and clean up the bread crumbs and cigar
ashes.

In the kitchen, he put the roses in a glass of water, then set a
pot of coffee on the electric stove. He had installed the stove in a
moment of weakness about ten years ago, because he decided that the
time wasted cutting wood and building fires could be put to more
important uses. The huge old range still stood there, though, as well
as the wooden table where the cook had kneaded bread. The cottage-
cheese strainer still hung on the wall by the window. On a chipped
plate lay half a bannack that he'd made that morning, mixing the
batter and frying it in a big iron skillet, and he really should warm it
up and go down to the cooler and cut himself a slice of round steak.
But there didn't seem to be much point in eating. Anyway, he still
wasn't very hungry, though the pain in his chest was definitely going
away.

When the coffee boiled, he poured a cup full of it. Then, carrying
the cup, he made the long trip back through dining room, parlor, and
hallway, into the old office where he'd thought he'd seen a light earlier.
Turning on the wall lamp (an old brass gas fixture converted to elec-

tricity) beside the huge yellow-oak roll-top desk, he sat down. He hunted around among the ledgers, letters, bills, and livestock magazines for a blank piece of paper. He dipped the nib pen into the ink and started writing in an angry, ornate hand, "I, Pinter Brodie, being sound and sane in mind. . . ."

Then he stopped, because he wasn't sure what to say next. In the golden light, he could make out the gilt titles of the heavy tomes on cattle breeding that crammed the yellow-oak bookcase. He knew every link in the chains of the little gold-weighing scales still on the top of the desk and every crack in the forehead of the buffalo skull that sat on a mahogany stand in a corner (he had picked it up somewhere on the summer range around 1920). On the dingy, copper-rose wall hung an oak-framed oil portrait of Crowder's great-grandsire, Reveille, its canvas cracking and fly specked. The horse was done in the old way, with a big, long body and tiny head, standing in a straw-strewn stall. He was black with a blaze down his face and three white stockings, and the anonymous painter had lovingly highlighted every vein and tendon in his frame.

Brodie studied the painting for a little while, wondering, as always, why Grandfather Brodie had the horse painted as a racer and not as a cow horse. If he didn't phrase the will exactly right, all that good money of his would get stolen by taxes and court costs, and he wouldn't be around to defend his interests.

He put down the pen, rolled himself a cigarette, and sat there drinking his coffee for a while longer. Old Bob came humping in and lay down by his chair. Then Brodie got up and went back to the parlor, so old Bob had to get up again and creep after him. The truth was that Brodie wasn't sure he wanted it to end like this: the sharp echo of a gunshot in this house where silk rustlings of ladies' bustles, tinklings of the piano, and stockmen's raucous laughter in the evening gaslight had still not petrified into echoes.

In the parlor, cigarette clamped firmly between his thin, cracked lips, Brodie turned on the TV set and hobbled over to one of the oak rocking chairs. It was time, anyway, for Walter Cronkite and the evening news.

When he'd bought that TV, they had kidded him a lot in town about being extravagant. He was glad nobody knew him well enough to suspect that it served as his binoculars, allowing him to spy on modern times. With it he could measure exactly, to the mile or the minute, how far he was falling behind. He'd had trouble installing the antenna too, because the brick chimneys were tumbling and the roof was settling in. He drank his coffee and watched the news, mesmerized by beer, caffeine, and fatigue. Cronkite showed him a riot, a helicopter banking over the Vietnam jungle, drug addicts in New York, and diplomats arguing in Paris.

Then there swam before his sun-bleared eyes a vision of the astronaut climbing slowly down the ladder of the lunar module. He wasn't sure whether the TV set really showed this scene or whether he just remembered it. The astronaut moved one step at a time, finally putting his huge boot firmly onto the crunchy desolation of the moon. Brodie and everyone in the world held their breaths. Finally both of the astronauts were out there, monstrous in their space gear and their glass-faced helmets, standing by the little American flag stiffened with a stick for want of a wind to furl it out. The harsh light and shadow of the solar terror fell across everything. The picture was so gritty and real that he was sure Huffman had taken it, had ridden his tripod-laden horse out through space to get there, with small meteorites pinging off his black-glass photo plates.

For the first time, Brodie felt neither rage nor puzzlement as he considered those two frail little men, their suits so vulnerable to the strike of some maverick meteorite. They too were already obsolete and soon would be swept away from that glassy desolation they had made when they invented God and gave themselves dominion over the universe. Brodie felt some distant and still undiscovered peace reach him, some peace of solar winds arriving to rustle the aging cottonwoods in front of the house. It was a comfort from soulless stars yet unborn, from the planets that would circle them, from the wild trumpeter swans that would rise crying from virgin ponds somewhere on those planets. If all went well, there would never be a single man to watch those swans fly up—not even himself.

The moment of the rifle would surely come, but it hadn't come yet. For one thing, it wouldn't be right to take care of Crowder but abandon all the other stock he had on the place. He had to take care of everything properly, and not in a big hurry. For the moment he'd put Crowder and old 94 out to pasture.

Now that he was free of Vin, he could obliterate his holdings as he saw fit. He would sell the cattle this fall, because he couldn't be sure he'd have a range to run them on next year. He would sell the antiques, too, down to the last old saddle and buggy, not because he was no longer sentimental but because they were worth a lot of money. He would put the land in perpetual trust as a wildlife sanctuary. No one would ever touch that land, even if they built glass skyscrapers on every other square foot of the Cottonwood Valley. The old ranch papers he would turn over to the Montana Historical Society.

With the money he got together, he would hire a good environmental lawyer, and he and the Chances would take Intermountain to court. If they won the case and Intermountain cleaned up Skillet Creek, then Brodie would have to make up his mind about restocking with Simmental cattle. Better Simmentals and financial freedom, maybe, than Herefords and a trip to the banker every year. On the other hand, Simmentals were *dairy* cattle. He should really stick with his big dark Herefords. A herd of good straightbred Herefords would be like money in the bank, one of these days, when all those exotic crossbred birds started coming home to roost, Brodie told himself. If, however, Intermountain went on bluing that creek in defiance of the law, Brodie would appoint himself a one-man stockmen's vigilante committee, and he would go hang a few rustlers. He knew those mountains better than anyone in the valley—he could fire a shot or set dynamite and then fade away among the lodgepole pines like an old wolf. If the government decided to defend Intermountain against him, then they'd just have to exterminate him, the way they did the wolves, the buffalo, the Indians. If they didn't kill him before that moment when he felt his ability to get around really failing, then there'd be time enough to think about the rifle. Time enough to lie down somewhere with the barrel in his mouth and his big toe on the trigger.

He picked up his cup and swallowed the last of the cold black coffee.

"Don't you tell me about walking on the moon," he said out loud to Walter Cronkite on the TV screen. "This old man and his old horse have ridden all over the moon."